# HANDBOOK FOR MORTALS

## BOOK ONE OF THE SERIES

# LANI SAREM

GEEKNATION PRESS, INC.
LOS ANGELES, CA

© 2017 by Lani Sarem

Published by GeekNation Press, Inc.
www.GeekNation.com
www.handbookseries.com

Cover Art by: Ryan Kincaid – RyanMKincaid.com

Colorist for Cover Art by: Milen Parvanov

First Hardcover edition: August 2017

Printed in the United States of America

ISBN-13: 9781545611456

This is dedicated to:

**The granddaughters of the witches you could not burn and for all those who believe in Magic.**

# CONTENTS

# Foreword

MAGIC. SOMETHING THAT HAS FASCINATED THE WORLD since the beginning of time. The ability to do things that the mortal mind simply cannot comprehend. It cannot be explained by science or the rational mind; therefore, it must be *supernatural...* or *magic.*

I've known Lani; that's Lani Sarem for a few years now. It is Laannee or as she would say Annie with an L, just in case you were also wondering. At first, I wasn't even sure of the pronunciation of her name... was it Lae-nee or Lan-ee?! In the subsequent years, I've learned how to pronounce her name, and throughout our friendship I've also learned she's a bit of a gypsy soul. She's always traveling around with the bands she works with while living the nomad life and getting amazing views of the dumpsters near the tour buses parked behind the venues.

Though we are very different people with different outlooks, political beliefs, and one of us is technically a Catholic who doesn't believe in or practice a lot of the hoopla associated with it (so Christian is how they're titled) and the other is Jewish, we're also very much alike.

We met in quite an unprecedented way. You see; this bestselling young adult vampire series was filming the final two of the five films in the series near my home in Baton Rouge, Louisiana. Because my friends were superfans of the series *and* one the actors in the films, I started a Facebook page for fun.

What started as a humorous moment between friends quickly became a sensation, and within a few days there were thousands of "fans" on the site. Within a week and a half, the fan count was up to the tens of thousands. Blogs, Facebook pages, and entertainment publications dedicated to this series were now following my page.

In a twist of fate, people from the film crew reached out to me. Several of the actors began following the page. Various people associated with the film began communicating with me, giving me little morsels of information and exclusive content to share with the fandom. This is how I came to know Lani.

One afternoon, I received a message on the page from Lani. She told me she represented the band that one of the actors from the film was a member of. I'd advertised some of the locations that the band was playing around town on my page. We started messaging back and forth and within a very short time I realized what a genuine person she was. Our friendship was formed.

While filming was happening the band played a concert in town to raise money for a local school in need. Lani offered me tickets and backstage passes as a "thank you" for all of the posts about the band and the film. This was the first time we actually "met".

Filming eventually wrapped in Baton Rouge and things went back to normal, or as close to normal as it ever was here at home.

I had been a freelance journalist and editor for independent authors before the craze of the fan page had taken over and I went back to that life while staying in touch with my new friend, Lani.

Soon, I decided to take the plunge from editing other author's books and decided it was time to write *the* book I'd been creating in my head for the past ten or so years. I wrote my book. A book about a rock star and the woman he left behind. Lani offered to read the book and give insight and feedback since I was not in the music business and could only write what I thought things in the music business would be like but that business *was* actually her life. That book became an International Bestseller within one week of its release. She gave me the edge I needed with her real world insight into the world of musicians.

She's since helped me on several of my other "music" novels.

One of the things I learned about Lani through our texts, phone calls, and infrequent visits as she returned to the bright lights of the West Coast (where she lived and worked when she wasn't traveling with the bands she worked with, and I settled into my life as an international bestselling adult romance author in Smalltown, Louisiana) was that she wrote screenplays.

About two years ago, she asked if she could send me this screenplay she'd been working on for years. I, of course, said "yes" and sat down to dive in and try to understand this new thing for me. That screenplay was **Handbook for Mortals**.

She asked me for my opinion on it and though it was vastly different from the novels I write and the process, layout, and depth of description are nothing alike, I devoured the plot. The story was *good*.

I gave her my thoughts on the plot, characters, and important points and that was that.

Sometime later we were talking, just catching up on life and everything in it. She told me that she was converting the screenplay into a book and that she was thinking of publishing it. She asked a few questions about the process and I shared what'd I'd learned about the "book world" while she worked on the conversion. As she traveled the country with various bands, spending most of her time either on the road, on the West Coast, her primary residence, or on the East Coast, where she found herself working she found enough time to complete the book.

Not very long ago, Lani trusted me to read her baby, the result of years of dreams, ideas, and work and provide honest feedback. I did.

The world she'd created was spectacular. A young woman from Nashville with dreams of making it big as an illusionist in Las Vegas. Two men she's drawn to, who both call to her on different levels. Secrets that come to light. Intrigue, romance, twists and turns, and above all else... *magick*. I was completely enthralled.

I told Lani that I enjoyed this book far more than other books of the genre that have exploded. That wasn't idle talk or a friend telling another friend something nice so as not to hurt their feelings. It was real and it was honest.

I could not be more excited to introduce Lani Sarem and **Handbook for Mortals** to you. As an author myself, I tend to be a bit snobbish about books. While I enjoy a good many books for their entertainment value and I absolutely respect every single author that has the gumption to take a chance and put themselves and their work out there, I rarely "love" a book. *This* is a book I loved.

**Handbook for Mortals** is a book I cannot wait for you to read. I see big things ahead. After all, who can resist succumbing to a little *magick*...

- Skye Turner

Some people are magic...While others are just the illusion of it.
– Beau Taplin

It's still magic even if you know how it's done.
– Terry Pratchett

I like the night. Without the dark we would never see
the stars.
– Stephanie Meyer

Some journeys take us far from home.
Some adventures lead us to our destiny.
– CS Lewis

# CHAPTER 0

# THE FOOL

I'VE ALWAYS ENVIED THOSE WITH NORMAL LIVES. I don't think I've ever even had a normal month, a plain week, or an average day. At best, I've had brief normal moments here and there. They tend to be few and far between. I'm sure most people would envy me, but some days I think I'd trade places in a heartbeat. To me, those moments of feeling normal or getting to do average things have always felt like a cool sparse breeze on the hottest summer day, or the first breath you take after holding it underwater for as long as you can.

Isn't it true we always want what we can't have? The grass is always greener, so to speak. Of course, if you really checked out the other side, you'd probably find out that the grass is Astroturf—fake and brittle and lifeless. It sure is pretty from your side of the fence, though.

I won't cover everything that has been crazy or unusual in my life. If I did, this would end up being a much larger book and would take entirely too long to read. Instead, I'll start on the day I left home. It marked a turning point—a fork in the road, if you will. I knew I was choosing a path, and hoped it was the right one. Either way, I knew that once I made my choice that was it. I couldn't double back and try again. It was to be how it was to be.

I personally believe some things in life are chosen by Destiny and some things are your choice. You have options in most situations, but there are certain paths that you have no choice but to go down. Ever try really hard to make something happen, but no matter what you do you can't seem to make it work? You fight and kick and scream, but you end up right where you are supposed to be—which might not be where you want to be. That's when Destiny has grabbed your hand and said, "Hey! You're coming with me!"

My advice? Don't fight it. Destiny will always win. I'm pretty sure Destiny doesn't play fair, either, but I don't think that even matters here.

People say some memories will stick with you forever. They burn brightly in your mind and each detail is as clear as the day it happened. Each color, each smell, the way things felt, the way *you* felt—it all pierces your mind each time you think about it. You can practically place yourself there at that moment, as if it were happening all over again. Close your eyes and breathe in deep and all of a sudden you are back in that time and that place.

For me, I will never forget one particular July morning; the grey clouds that hovered over the ancient trees lining the street; the wind that blew swiftly through my blonde hair. It also spun about the chunky pieces on the lower half of my long hair, which I had dyed to be a multitude of fun colors. Today they were pink, purple, blue, and a turquoise green, but I have a habit of changing the colors frequently. My perfectly cut bangs stayed mostly unaffected by the wind except for a few squirrelly pieces. The smell of rain was strong and crisp; it's a smell I love so much I wish I could bottle it up. Even though it wasn't raining yet—and you couldn't even hear the thunder—you could see the lightning. You knew the storm was coming. It was exciting; the energy from the storm that ran through my veins felt electric. The hairs on my arms stood up and goose bumps popped up all over my skin.

I've always loved thunderstorms. Most people prefer sunny days and puffy white clouds, but not me. I hope for thunder so loud it makes the ground shake, and lightning so bright it illuminates the whole sky. Those types of storms are rare and magical in my mind. They have an air of danger and mystery, and it always feels like something exciting could happen at any moment. I paused briefly to watch the streaks of bright light spiderweb across the sky. I wished I had the time to stop and just watch the storm, but this day was important and I had to keep moving. I took comfort in the fact that day storms are not nearly as magical as the nighttime ones.

I'd lived in that one-horse southern town my whole life, practically a quarter of a century. My family has owned land in this place since the early 1700s and my ancestors basically established the little town called Centertown, Tennessee. It's about an hour or so outside of Nashville and smack dab in the middle of the state, hence the over-obvious name, Centertown. Old people say that it was the capital of the state for one whole day before Andrew Jackson decided that the capital should be moved to Nashville. I guess it's true, though I've never really been able to confirm that, nor do I guess it really matters. It makes the people who live there and tell that story really proud, though.

My mother is the area tarot card reader and spell caster. People come from all over the state—and sometimes farther than that—to see her when they are heartbroken mostly. In small towns like ours a lot of people believe that folks like my mother come from the devil. It's the silliest thing I've ever heard. People who can see the future are in the Bible. All the kings of the Bible talk to soothsayers, including the most revered king of all, King David. Even so, it's hard to convince people of anything otherwise. Those judgmental, stuck-up snobs are the same people who still sneak out to us and come see my mom when things in their life get bad. That might be the worst part, knowing they actually believe in it as well but they are all just afraid to admit it. Though if they really knew what we actually were they'd probably end up reopening the old "burning people at the stake" idea. Something our family is quite familiar with.

Regardless, it's been hard for me because of it. Growing up, some kids weren't allowed to be friends with me and some wouldn't even talk to me. I've had boys like me and then be told they aren't allowed to take me on a date. It's hard to be looked at not for who you are but for what people think you are.

After one long, deep breath I pushed myself off of the top step of the huge porch that wrapped around the antique house and pounded down the wooden steps that led away from the house my family has owned for more than 150 years. My well-worn and once brightly colored (but now badly faded with dirt spackle) Converse high-top sneakers made a quick tapping noise on each step. I had just replaced the laces on them so at least they looked somewhat decent. My favorite high-waisted Levi's dark denim skinny jeans— ripped in all the right places—made the swishing noise as I lifted my legs and my perfect flowy Lucky's top that I wear far too often billowed around me. I rarely think this but I wish a photographer had taken my picture at that moment as the outfit and the background and I may have produced a cool-looking photo.

The house is big, old, and four stories high, made of wood with large framed-glass windows. Mostly the house is well kept, the white paint is slightly faded and cracking in a few places due to the hot and humid muggy weather in the summer. It's still nice, though, and the picket fence around the house lends to its antiquated Southern look. Not quite as big or grand, but reminiscent of the O'Hara's estate in *Gone with the Wind*.

I pushed my long, many-hued hair out of my way the best I could, as I threw my luggage into my car. A dark blue streak caught the light with a shimmer. I glanced at myself in the reflection of the car side mirror. People tell me I'm pretty all the time, beautiful even. I'm not sure I see what they see. I think I'm more of a cute, average-looking girl. I'm slender but I do not believe most would say skinny. Not "hot-girl skinny," at least. I have long legs that are toned but I think my thighs are too large and I do *not* have a thigh gap. My arms are kinda flabby and while I do have an hourglass figure I have always felt my butt is a little too big and my face is a bit too round. Maybe people are just being nice. In a small town where everyone looks like they fell out of Mayberry, I think I look different. Maybe just the fact I stood out was what they were seeing. I know how the neighbors described me as sweet and kind, but rough around the edges. I've just always thought I was a determined free spirit and tough only when necessary.

I turned around just in time to see my mother, Dela, coming down the steps. Even when she was in a hurry she never looked like she was rushing or running but instead floating gingerly. I am my mother's daughter, an exact replica. Pictures of her when she was my age look like they are of me. She still looks younger than her years, though. There's something about her that says "old soul." It's something that you can see in her eyes—she says you can see it in mine, too. She says it means we've lived many lives. But I haven't felt like I've been able to live much in this one. That's all I am trying to do, I guess. Just live.

My eyes darted to her dark blonde hair, which shone despite the lack of sunlight. I took a deep breath and decided to cut her off before she was able to speak. "Mom, what would you like me to do? Stay here and read cards with you for the rest of my life?" My exasperated question was sincere and sounded more like a plea than a question.

Sheepishly, my mother replied, "But, Zade, I thought you liked reading cards. I thought you liked this kind of life."

I contemplated my answer for a moment before I responded. I shoved my last bag, my favorite Dakine duffle with it's bold pattern into the car, struggling to make it fit. She was right. A big part of me loved the place and being there with her. It was *comfortable*. And, as much as I wasn't always completely accepted by everyone in the town, I still belonged. It was home. I also really loved helping people and guiding them through difficult hardships and to a new place in life where they could be happy. My mom and I had enlightened some people in town and taught them to understand that not everything we are brought up to believe in the world is true. Some were starting to see things differently and, in a few years, maybe I would even be treated like everyone else. Regardless of all these things, I knew if I stayed I would regret it for the rest of my life. I had to do more. My mother's glare and words caused me to drift for a moment into an almost daydream state of "what ifs" about staying. While those thoughts circulated through my mind, my eyes caught the part of the concrete driveway that had been repaved when I was around eight years old. I had written my name into the wet cement, mirror image backwards. Due to my dyslexia, I could write things perfectly—but I wrote them backwards. It wasn't till I was nine almost ten I could write the proper way without a lot of thought. It baffled my teachers but was something "normal" for me. It was also a cool trick at school as I learned to write fast in either direction. Not all my memories of this place were bad and all my history was here, which made it hard to leave. Flashes of raising my own children in that house floated in my head for just a few short moments. I pushed those thoughts quickly away and knew I needed to snap back into the hurried pace I was trying to keep. She's the most persuasive person on this planet—and possibly other planets—and I knew that if I stayed a minute longer I might not leave. I chewed hard on my lip, a nervous tic of mine that I did so often I had a permanent dent on my bottom lip. I looked at her and said, as matter-of-fact as I could, "Sure, it was fine when I was sixteen and wanted a job so I could buy a motorcycle, but it can't be my life. I need to go somewhere where people don't know. Where they don't whisper and stare like I have horns growing out of my head. Where I can meet new people and just be a normal person for once."

I stood in front of my mother and looked into her deep eyes. She looked back into mine. I don't think she had ever wanted normal. I think to her it was a dirty word. I probably insulted her for even mentioning it and she probably loathed that I had said it was something I wanted. She had often quoted me one of Dr. Seuss's famous sayings—so many times I had lost count. "Why try to fit in, when you were born to stand out?" I always retorted with, "Why would I want to stand out? People who stand out get things thrown at them. People who stand out get called names and shoved into lockers. If the people who don't stand out are too cowardly to do any of the previously mentioned options then they just awkwardly whisper about you—the people who do stand out—as you walk by." I waited to see if she would try and quote Dr. Seuss one more time. After a couple of moments of waiting, she asked, "What do you see yourself doing instead?" It was technically a question, but the tone in her voice led me to believe she already knew the answer.

For a moment I pondered whether I should tell her the truth, but I didn't spend a lot of energy with that thought. Long ago, I learned that I couldn't lie to my mother. She knew the instant the words came out of my mouth that whatever I was saying wasn't true, and lying always made things worse. To this day, whenever I tell a lie, my mother will purse her lips and widen her eyes and glare directly at me. She will firmly ask for another answer without missing a beat. I'm a pretty good actress, but I'm not good at telling my mother a lie—no matter how mad I am at her. I slammed the trunk of the car shut before answering her, so I had a reason to have my back to her and didn't have to be looking at her when I responded. I ran my fingertips over the edge of the trunk before muttering quietly, "I have an audition."

There was a long pause and the wind rustled through my hair while I waited on her to respond. "You're going to audition for *that show*?" she asked—another question she sounded like she already knew the answer to. I was still facing the opposite direction and couldn't see her face but I still knew she was grinding her teeth. I couldn't tell if she was asking me or just announcing it out loud. I took one deep breath and spun around to look at her when I answered.

"Yes, Mom. You know what? I don't know how you ever got away with keeping me out here for so long, anyway." My eyes narrowed as I confronted the issue we had never really talked about. I looked down again as I finished my sentence. It was a hard subject for both of us, and something we both seemed to usually avoid.

"I had my ways," she said so quietly I barely heard her. I looked up to see she wasn't even looking at me as she answered. She was looking off into the distance. I knew that she really didn't want me to hear her answer. I sighed deeply as I glared at my mom, waiting for her to look at me again before I answered. I ran my hand over my head trying to soothe the tension headache I was starting to get. I wanted her to know that I wasn't the naïve little girl I had been when I was younger. When you're five, your parents make decisions to protect you. Except the problem sometimes is, as much as their hearts are in the right place, the decisions don't always protect you. Sometimes they hurt you and mess you up and even make you angry at them—and at the world. I think she noticed I hadn't said anything and she probably felt the icy glare from me so finally she looked up, allowing her eyes met mine. My words were slow and deliberate. I was about to call my mother out, something that rarely (if ever) happened.

"Actually, I know. What do you think started this?" I said firmly.

"Uh—" she started, but her voice trailed off. My mother, the woman who always has an answer for anything, didn't know what to say to me. I wanted an explanation. I rubbed my hands together nervously. She said nothing. I edged myself closer and directed my words so closely that she could feel my breath on her face. I wanted to be harsh this time. "For the record, I can't believe you would stoop to anything so low."

"I was looking out for you! I didn't want you to ever go through—"

My anger erupted, if she hadn't been my mother I probably would have punched her. I couldn't believe she was pulling such nonsense again. It was an age-old excuse: "I want to protect you from making the mistakes I made." I started to grind my teeth. If I had been a cartoon, smoke would have come out of my ears. I began to wave my hands in exasperation, a habit I had gotten from her.

"Stop!" I shouted in anger. "I don't want to hear it. I'm not you, okay?" I inhaled deeply and tried to relax. "I have my own life, and I think you were really selfish for what you did." She winced, wounded. The truth hurts, or so she'd always told me. I walked around the car and opened the driver's side door. "I gotta go. I'm too upset to continue this conversation." I couldn't deal with it anymore. If I let my wall down I would just stay. Forever. I couldn't do that. We both stood, staring at each other. Part of me wanted to push my mom out of the way and jump in the car, but I couldn't be that mean to her. It felt like we stood there for hours.

Finally, she just said, "Please . . . ." It was all she could say. Her voice cracked and pain showed on her face.

The next words that came out of my mouth didn't sound like me at all, but before I knew what happened I had snapped back at her, "Please, what? Haven't you ruined enough of my life?" I immediately wanted to take it back. I didn't mean it. Why had I said that? I looked down, ashamed of myself. I heard my mother's voice crack again.

"Is that how you really feel?" she asked. She was on the verge of crying. My mother never cried. The anger in me was gone. My face softened and I smiled weakly. I grabbed her hands and stared at the bold veins that ran through them. I sighed deeply before I met her eyes.

I shook my head lightly. "No. You haven't ruined my life, Mom, but you also have to let me go live it now. I need to—" I choked, unable to finish.

She grabbed me tightly and hugged me. She was still holding back tears and swallowing hard; she kept her eyes closed. She whispered in my ear, "Shh. I know. I love you." She kissed me on the forehead.

I closed my eyes and hugged her back fiercely before whispering, "I love you, too." Before I could change my mind I jumped into my car, quickly fastened my seatbelt and backed out of the driveway. I turned the radio on right after I threw my car in drive and the most appropriate song came blaring through the speakers of my car. It was the opening lyrics to the Dixie Chicks's song "Wide Open Spaces." I couldn't help but laugh at how truly that was my anthem at the moment. I took it as a sign I was doing the right thing, as I drove away, I sang along to the song.

*Who doesn't know what I'm talking about*
*Who's never left home, who's never struck out*
*To find a dream and a life of their own*
*A place in the clouds, a foundation of stone*

*Many precede and many will follow*
*A young girl's dreams no longer hollow*
*It takes the shape of a place out west*
*But what it holds for her, she hasn't yet guessed*

*She needs wide open spaces*
*Room to make her big mistakes*
*She needs new faces*
*She knows the high stakes*

No truer words could be spoken as I headed for my own wide-open spaces out west. Even the "high stakes" reference was perfect, considering that I was headed toward Las Vegas. I had a long road ahead of me—and an even longer road when I got there—but it was what I knew that I needed to do, without any doubt.

# CHAPTER 1

# THE MAGICIAN

I PUSHED OPEN THE HEAVY FRONT DOOR OF THE THEATER that led back into the incredibly lavish casino. The bright red and purple carpet immediately caught my eye. I couldn't believe that after years of thinking about moving out there, I had finally done it. The cast and crew of the show must have totaled close to two hundred people and they were an overwhelming bunch—especially when they were all standing in the foyer of the theater. I quickly tried to assess this large group who had been waiting on me. Luckily, it was fairly easy to tell what they did for the show by what they wore and how they acted.

Several of them were dressed in nothing but black from head to toe. In this kind of situation, all-black attire says "I'm supposed to blend in." Creatively called "show blacks," the uniform of a stagehand or stage tech tends to be black Dickies with extra pockets. Depending on the show, techs could be wearing anything from a black t-shirt to a formal button-down. I have to admit that I've always found something handsome about a man in show blacks. Perhaps it's the artsy answer to a man in uniform, or maybe I'm just odd. Either way, I noticed that several guys in their show blacks were handsome; one in particular caught my eye for some reason. He wasn't the most traditionally handsome one out of the bunch but there was just something really striking about him. If I hadn't been so nervous I would have probably paid more attention to him. Despite my distraction, how he carried himself still registered with me. I once read an article that said you can tell someone's personality by the way they walk and carry themselves. Since then I've always paid attention to that and it's astonishing how accurate it really is— and how few people walk with a confident stride and step—but this guy did in spades, though he also seemed closely guarded, which is an odd combination. (Most of the time, super-confident people are much more open and free.)

I also noticed several people in various stages of readiness for the show. Some were already in full costume, with hair and makeup done. Others had their costumes on one half of their bodies but the other half in street clothes. A small group of them were hanging out in more normal clothing—the management, I guessed. They had all formed little clusters and some seemed to be deep in conversation, speaking of work or something else that they were passionate about. Most of the performers looked bored. No one seemed to have noticed that I had opened the door and was standing in front of them all.

I cleared my throat and softly said, "Thank you for waiting. I'm ready." I smiled nervously and pushed the door open even wider to welcome them back into their theater. The crowd hushed and seemed to part a little. A tall man with dark hair walked toward the door. That man was the infamous magician to whom the theater basically belonged, Charles Spellman. Charles was older, but still a very handsome man. I would describe him in a similar way that one might describe Harrison Ford. He was dressed in what were obviously expensive clothes, black slacks that fit him perfectly and a button down that was the exact length it needed to be to hang out un-tucked. The shirt was tailored and had wide stitching with beautiful and intricate cufflinks that complimented it perfectly and looked to be made out of pure gold. How effortless he made casual and confident look. He looked like someone who always has an air about him that says he's the most important person in the room—and he usually is.

Charles was one of the most well-respected magicians in history; he'd been famous since he was in his twenties. He'd had TV specials and won countless industry awards, and his shows consistently sold out arenas when he was on tour all over the world. A few years ago, The Wynn Casino in Las Vegas made him an offer to have a show on the strip. Steve Wynn himself called and said they'd build him his own 2,000-seat theater for his show and would build it to his specifications—anything he wanted and no expense would be spared. You have to be a pretty big deal for Steve Wynn to call you himself, so he agreed—and the rest is history. Tickets typically have to be purchased three months in advance to have any chance of getting to see the show. The theater is "in the round" as it's called, meaning the seats circle the whole stage (that is also round) and the seats closest to the stage are basically level with the stage. The rows get bigger as they go up and the farther from the stage they are the higher they are, which means the stage is at the bottom of the room. It was designed way so there would be no bad seat in the house. And, honestly, with the prices people pay to see the show, there had better not be a bad seat in the house. I knew going in that, from the time they opened, they had done two shows a night, five nights a week, with an additional matinee on Saturday. Charles was known for being a workaholic and expecting nothing less from his cast and crew.

Standing next to Charles was a much-younger woman who could easily have passed for his daughter, had she not been so tightly coiled around his arm. Granted, I knew very little about my father—and even less about father/daughter relationships— but even I knew that daughters don't stand like that next to their fathers. She was undeniably beautiful, but she also looked extremely stuck-up, and looked to be around my age. I can't stand stuck-up people. *You can't judge her yet,* I kept telling myself. She was obviously a performer as well, and I got the vibe instantly that she wasn't even one bit happy that I was there. She looked right at me and didn't even bother to fake a smile; she just gave me the look of death instead. I smiled back anyway and I pushed her out of my mind for the moment. I had more important things to worry about.

"Zade," Charles greeted me. "It is wonderful to have you here. I'm very excited to see your performance."

"Thank you," I said sheepishly, "for giving me the chance, Mr. Spellman. I'm honored to be here." I paused, flustered, before blurting out nervously, "You're one of the greatest magicians of all time. It's like you, David Copperfield, and then everyone else." I was babbling and didn't really know what to say. It's something I always do when I'm nervous and the only thing that really makes me nervous is meeting important people. And this person was *really* important—maybe the most important person I'd ever met.

To my relief, Charles chuckled. "Don't tell David that and, please, call me Charles." At this, the beautiful woman next to him cleared her throat as if to remind him she should be introduced;

I had actually forgotten she was there. Charles glanced at her. "This is Sofia Austin. She's one of our lead performers."

"Hi, nice to meet you," I said, thrusting my hand out awkwardly. She took it, but only grasped it for a moment before loosing her grip and dropping my hand, like I'd burned her.

"And his girlfriend," Sofia said coldly, and *mean* even, placing emphasis on the last word.

"Awesome," I muttered.

For a moment I wasn't sure what to do next so I basically just stood in the doorway. One of the many techs in black (whose name I would learn later to be Tad) must have noticed the awkwardness and grabbed the door from me and pulled it open as far as it could go. He let it catch on the hook that's made to hold the door open when even larger crowds are pouring in for a show. Everyone began to head back inside the theater. I stood there and watched them walk past me, each seeming to give me a once over; I'm sure most of them judging me in their own way as they made their way past me and into the theater. Suddenly I realized that while I was mentally making notes of their behavior I was doing the same exact thing, I didn't want them to do. I was judging them as well, so I couldn't really hold that against them too much. I guess it's just human nature and what we, as people, do. I made an extra mental note that it was something I should probably try to work on, since I didn't like the fact that I was guilty of it, too.

Walking closely with Charles and Sofia was the handsome tech who had caught my eye earlier. Probably in his late 20s, he was also wearing show blacks, and frowning. His sandy-blondish brown hair framed his face perfectly, and his hazel eyes seemed to sparkle. He was slender and tall, definitely six feet if not an inch or so more, with just the right amount of muscle in his arms. *You know, just enough to grab you and hold you tight—but not enough to look like he was stung by a bee and was allergic.* I overheard Charles call him Mac. I noticed that he carried a clipboard, and learned shortly after that he was the technical director for the show.

Next to Mac was another man; thin, with reddish hair, he looked to be close to the same age as Charles. He also looked unhappy to be there and gave me quite the stare when we did catch each other's glance. Another man in a headset and show blacks followed closely behind them. I saw a piece of tape stuck to his oversized radio that read "Trig." Again, I looked back to Charles, who was flanked by Sofia and Mac. I overheard my name being spoken between Charles, the red-headed man, and Mac and decided to fall into the crowd as close behind them as I could as they walked through the lobby of the theater. Everyone was so caught up in themselves that they didn't notice me staring at them. They certainly didn't realize I could hear them. I'm not sure that—if they had realized—they would have cared anyway.

Charles suddenly stopped walking and called out in just a general direction, yet somehow knowing I could hear him. "Oh, Zade," Charles called. "This is Mac Kent, my esteemed technical director. He's been with me for all eleven years of working in this theater."

I peeked out around the group of people who were directly in front of me and approached Mac. "Eleven years?" I said incredulously. "You look too young for that. How many shows is that?"

"Well, I didn't start out as the TD eleven years ago," he replied, looking me square in the eye. "I was only eighteen. But yeah, forty weeks a year, two shows a night, five days a week with an extra matinee on Saturdays. Still here 4,800-plus shows later."

"Wow, that's incredible." I was genuinely impressed by how he had worked his way up, but before I could say anything more, Mac had already turned away.

Standing behind Charles was that thin man with wide-set eyes and reddish hair. He looked at me solemnly. Charles turned back slightly and waved the man to come forward. "This is Zeb Zagan, head illusion technician—or head magi; he has been with me for over twenty years—basically for as long as anyone has called me famous."

I had done enough research before reaching Vegas to know that Zeb had designed or helped design a lot of Charles's illusions and was well known in the magic community himself. Yet everything about him was mysterious and—even in the magic community—very little seemed to be known about him.

I stuck out my hand and said, "Hello. Nice to meet you." He looked at me and stared hard directly at me till I felt uncomfortable before he finally stuck out his hand rigidly. His handshake was stiff and he didn't smile at all when he spoke.

"Hello. I do hope you can get this going soon; we all have other things we need to do."

I didn't know what to say. He didn't seem to be happy about me being there and yet at the same time there was something odd about his coldness. I half smiled and weakly said, "I'll do my best and I hope you like it. I respect your work and opinion so much." I made sure to reference that I did know who he was. Zeb made a sort of grumbling sound and sat down in one of the nearby seats and began to stare at his phone with impatience written all over his face.

After my exchanges with Sofia, Mac, and Zeb I was starting to wonder if I was ever going to fit in. I'm not sure if Charles even witnessed the awkward exchange between Zeb and me. Charles was already on to something else and had grabbed the man I had seen with the headset labeled Trig.

That man, Trig, pressed one of the large buttons on the battery pack resting on his hip and spoke into the mic on his headset. "C.S. says it's a go. Can I get all stage crew in place, and then I'll give Zade the clear." He turned to me and pushed his mic off of his face and introduced himself. "Zade, hi. I'm Pete Trigger, but some people call me Trig. I'll answer to Pete or Trig just not Mr. Trigger cause that's my dad and it sounds like a dead horse. I'm the head stage manager, and I call the show. You know what that means, right?" That particular question could have sounded very condescending but the way it came out of Pete's mouth it just sounded like he wanted to make sure I knew what that meant. I made the snap judgment that I would call him Pete, as that seemed to suit him more to me, at least for now. He was average height with short light-brown hair and looked a bit older than Mac. I guessed late 30s or early 40s. He had small wrinkles around his eyes, especially when he smiled, but he still had a very boyish round, kind face.

I nodded and confidently said, "Of course. You call the cues, keep everything happening when it's supposed to happen." The plays I did in high school also had a stage manager, who also "called the show." I'm sure Pete was much better at calling cues than they were, after all, this show was like the difference between playing pro baseball in the World Series and playing t-ball in kindergarten. Nevertheless I got the general idea, and that was all I needed at the moment.

Pete nodded. "I knew I liked you." He glanced down at a piece of paper he'd pulled from a pocket. "By the way, I am saying your name correctly?"

"Yep. Like 'aide,' but add a Z." I grinned; I appreciated it immensely when people took the time to learn how to say my name properly. I hated it when people called me "Zaad" or something like that, which sounded more like a car or a super villain than an actual person. I was instantly fond of him for the warmth. Pete gestured that I should follow him. We walked over to another group of the crew, who were already chatting.

"Are we really going to let her do this?" I heard Mac ask Charles. It sounded much more like a statement than a question especially because he didn't pause for an answer before continuing. "I haven't been able to do any safety checks on her equipment. I don't even know what's been put in!" Mac sounded frustrated and leaned in to Charles. Most people seemed a little afraid of Charles, but not Mac. I could already tell that Mac would stand toe to toe with him—or probably anyone, for that matter—if the subject mattered to him. A strong will was an admirable quality to me and I had been taught to see that as being something to appreciate about someone. Really stubborn and thickheaded, though, usually goes hand-in-hand with strong willed and is something to always keep in mind. I realized that I was supposed to be listening to Pete and the others but instead I kept paying attention to Mac and Charles.

"Zade signed a waiver," Charles replied calmly before beginning to head down the stairs to get seated. Mac followed after Charles and Sofia along with another man I hadn't met yet. Charles nodded at that man before sitting down in the third row of the theater directly in front of where Zeb sat, still looking annoyed to even be there.

Mac turned around to Zeb. "Zeb, don't you agree with me?"

Zeb glanced up from his phone to respond to Mac. "Charles is well aware of my thoughts. Mac, do you really think you are going to persuade him of anything at this point? Why are you wasting your energy?" Mac turned back around, crossed his arms in a huff, and slid farther down into the seat with his legs completely stretched out. I could tell that he knew Zeb was right and, even though he didn't like it, he took Zeb's advice and stopped "wasting energy."

Movement close to me caught my attention and I saw Pete reach his arm out toward possibly the most handsome guy I'd ever met in person. He really wasn't my type, but I was still amazed at how much he looked like a movie star. He was pretty, too pretty, *beautiful* even. I don't think I could ever date a guy that was prettier than me. That does sound selfish, but I just would rather be the "at least slightly prettier" one in any relationship—and he was just too perfect: the chiseled jaw, not a hair out of place, and a bright, white smile. I really never thought a guy could be *that* perfect looking. Pete continued, "This is Cam Carter, our head rigger. Cam is going to take you up into the grid and get you in position." I shook Cam's hand and he cracked an even larger smile. His eyes were as kind as they were beautiful. I couldn't help but gush a little—I might not want to date him but I did like him immediately.

I heard Sofia's voice as we walked away. I strained to hear her saying to Charles, "You remembered her name. You *never* remember names."

I turned my eyes toward them and caught Charles's reply, "Most people's names aren't worth remembering." I was impressed by his clear, measured answers. He never seemed to "over speak," which most people—especially me—are guilty of. It was like someone had written his dialogue for him. The man oozed charm the way most normal people sweat in the Vegas heat. I'm pretty sure James Bond would look like your average bumbling Joe in comparison.

Next to Charles, I noticed a younger, mousy woman with glasses who looked to be an assistant of some kind. She looked focused and anxious. She had a note pad and seemed to be writing down everything Charles uttered. "So," Charles said loudly to her, "we will want to work it into the show that she will start on the floor and make her way to the top. I want them to see the jump in its entirety." I liked that he had already put some thought into adding my illusion into his show. The rest of what Charles said I couldn't hear as I moved farther out of earshot. I had to try not to worry about what was being said and focus my attention on what I was about to do.

After lots of climbing, Cam and I had made it to the lower catwalk, which was forty to fifty feet above the ground. There were a few other catwalks above us, the highest, according to Cam, being a hundred feet up. Heights make some people nervous, but not me. I love the feeling of being off the ground and as high up as possible. When I was ten years old I told my mom that one day I would live in a tree house. That still sounded like a good idea to me.

I quickly realized I needed to check on where the prop I'd requested was. I had to have a bright red rose for the illusion and I had asked for it to be brought up and waiting for me. I turned toward Cam and politely asked, "Where is the rose?" hoping he knew what I was talking about.

Cam pointed to it, smiled sweetly, and commented, "You ready, girl? You nervous? Need something to keep your mind off of it?"

I shrugged and softly said, "I'm fine." The only thing that was running through my head was how any girl could ever date him, because he was prettier than all of us put together. It was a good thing he couldn't read my mind. My mind drifted about in a way where it focused on everything and nothing at the same time while I waited for the cue from Cam to drop the rose to the ground. Cam smiled again and leaned in slightly to ask me if I needed any help from him. I shook my head but couldn't help but smile at him. *Too pretty for his own good—and mine*, I thought. Trying to focus on what I was doing, I climbed onto the top bar of the catwalk and turned around on my toes. I breathed in to relax a little. I was starting to think something was wrong when Cam pressed the release button on his radio.

"Go for Cam," he said. After a moment's pause, likely listening to a voice through his headset, he responded, "Copy that." He grinned at me. "Okay, love," he said. "Ready when you are."

I nodded to show that I understood. Before doing anything else, I picked up the rose and, after examining it for a moment, glanced at Cam; then, with a devilish grin I tossed the rose over railing. It took several moments for it to strike the metal stage below. It was a long way down, and when it finally crashed to the ground a couple of petals broke off from the flower and sprung into the air. Hopefully everyone in the audience would understand that the point of the rose was to show that the stage was solid and that something else should not be able to go through the stage—that "something else" was, in fact, me.

I took a deep breath and leaned slowly back over the bar, bending backward until I had flipped myself over the edge. Once my body had inverted into mid-air, I began to "fall" toward the stage, like a high diver would. I stretched and tensed so that my body was completely vertical as I flew toward the ground. I was falling fast, and there was nothing below me to break my fall. The audience of cast and crew gasped. A regular audience might think "trapdoor" but this group knew better because they knew the theater so well.

As I plummeted toward the stage, brightly colored sparks began to shoot from my outstretched hands. The sparks fell and hit the ground ahead of me, becoming a roaring fire directly beneath me. The fire burned a brilliant red, spreading and growing below me. As the fire burned, it changed color from bright red to a vibrant blue. I could hear the audience murmuring again, but I couldn't get cocky yet. I was near the ground and still falling fast.

The ground beneath the flames seemed to pool as if it had become liquid, and the fire melted into waves that started to lap the stage, as if a pond had formed where the stage had been just a moment before. In full Olympic-diving position with my fingers and toes pointed, I dove straight into what looked somewhat like "water." It splashed as I made impact, but as the droplets of liquid came back down toward the Earth to meet the ground, the stage had become solid once again. The rose and I had disappeared within the lapping water.

About twenty feet away from the site of my impact was an open area where there was actual, real water—basically a pool, which was used in several other illusions. I popped my head out of the water and pumped my left fist victoriously in the air as I used my right arm to grab onto the edge of the pool—the rose safely clenched between my teeth. I felt a wild smile engulfing my face even as I waited for them to applaud.

The entire theater seemed in shock. It was silent for what seemed like an eternity. Did they hate it? My smile started to fade and I was beginning to panic when they all applauded thunderously, and the whole cast rose to their feet. I sighed deeply in relief. I grabbed the rose from my mouth and tossed it to Sofia, winking at her. I laughed as I said, "For the pretty lady." Sofia glared in response and smiled with the fakest smile I had ever seen. She wasn't amused—nor did she find me funny, in the least.

"That was perfect! Just as I expected," I overhead Charles say excitedly. "Beth, let's have her sign that contract. That goes into the show right away. Wait until Copperfield sees this one! We'll put out a press release immediately." Beth Ford was the assistant I hadn't recognized before. She nodded fervently at Charles and rushed off to get on the phone with the publicist for the press release.

I quickly spotted Mac again. He had found a place to stand next to two of his crew guys, also in stage blacks. One was Tad, who helped me with the door earlier. He looked to be about Mac's age, though shorter than Mac. Tad was slightly stocker with dark brown wavy hair and brown jovial eyes. I would soon learn that Tad was Mac's best friend, an all-around good guy who worked well with everyone. In theory, Mac was Tad's boss, but they had been working together for a long time and had been friends for much longer. Tad was the kind of guy to always tell it like it is. He never believed in sugarcoating anything. He'd always tell us that his motto was, "Why take anything seriously? No one gets out alive anyway." He said it often, and meant it. Very little got him worked up. He was the epitome of easy going. Tad was also one of those people who was naturally good at most of the things he tried. I often wonder if a lot of it had to do with his attitude. I've concluded that it must be that, and being born under a lucky star. I'd probably envy him if I didn't adore him so much.

Standing next to Tad was Riley, one of the youngest of the crew at the show. This was his first real job as a tech, and he'd only been working for the show about a year. "That was crazy freaking awesome!" he blurted out excitedly, practically jumping up and down when he said it.

Even Tad, who wouldn't jump up and down if he had won the lottery, still looked pretty blown away. "Jesus! That was quite the magic trick," Tad agreed. "Holy moly! No wonder C.S. gave her free rein of the theater. Mac, how in the hell did she do that?" Tad looked at Mac, who seemed to be in a daze.

It took a couple of moments before Mac finally looked up at Tad and then stared at him for another couple of moments before responding. "I don't know."

Tad scrunched up his face and cocked his head to the side with disbelief; he eyed Mac for a moment before speaking. "The man who knows more about how magic tricks are done than Houdini doesn't know?"

Mac sighed deeply and shook his head. "Tad, what do you want? I said I don't know. Why don't you ask Zeb; shouldn't he know?" It was obvious that Mac was annoyed and disturbed that he didn't know how it was done. He didn't even have an inkling. He looked over in my direction and was staring right at me pretty intensely and directly. He didn't even try to pretend that he was looking at something else. My eyes briefly caught his and he didn't even look away. I thought it best to pretend not to notice. I wondered if he thought if he stared at me long enough that it would click with him how the illusion was done. The reality is none of them could have known.

It wouldn't have made logical sense no matter how hard they tried to figure it out because it was beyond anything a mortal could do. Tarot cards weren't the only unique skill that my mom had taught me—or that ran in the family. And, for the first time, I was starting to realize it was going to be harder to keep our secret from everyone. They were going to want to know, and I was going to have to keep dodging questions. This was a problem I was going to have to work out when I had more time to think about it.

I finally couldn't take the feeling of being stared at any longer and looked over in Mac and Tad's direction just in time to see Tad grin at Mac and laugh. "Hey, don't take it out on me. I'm gonna go introduce myself to the girl who stumped you. She's definitely worth knowing," Tad retorted as he slapped Mac on the back. Tad locked eyes with me, smiled, and even winked at me before starting to walk toward where I was standing. I could tell how much he was enjoying giving Mac a hard time.

"I'm coming with you; that was so cool," Riley added as he chased behind Tad.

Tad gingerly made his way over to me and put his hand out to shake mine. I noticed his huge grin and pearly white teeth right away. Tad Fletcher, head of automation, rocked back on his heels as he talked. Calm, collected, sweet, kind and confident cascaded out of his being. I would slowly learn that was Tad all of those things through and through, which is why he was so well liked. He also introduced Riley Wates, the youngest and newest member of the rigging crew, who seemed very nervous to meet me. Riley was young and wide-eyed, and though he was also very sweet, he lacked the confidence that came effortlessly to Tad. Even so, Riley's energy was youthful and energetic and he had a big bright smile, which made me immediately like him. "Actually youngest member of the crew, *period*," Riley was quick to explain. "That was incredible. I hope we can be friends," Riley gushed.

I smiled back and responded, "Thanks. I think we should be friends, too."

He jammed his hands in his pockets, rocked back on his heels in a very "Tad" sort of way, and blushed. I was excited to meet more of the crew who all seemed really nice. More of them came up and crowded around me to talk and say hello, but I caught myself looking back toward where Mac was still standing. I watched him fume for a moment before storming off. I didn't understand why he was so angry at what seemed to be just my mere presence in his world. *I would have to look into that later*, I decided, because I didn't have time to concentrate on it in the moment.

I had so many people talking to me all at once I thought my head was going to explode. When the excitement had died down just a touch, Beth came back over and said we had a bunch of things that needed discussing. There was a lot to figure out: things like my contract, discussions on how to put my illusion into the show, and even where else to fit me into the show's running order. The list was long and dizzying as Beth went over it with me, making notes before saying she would get back to me once the issues had been addressed with the whole creative team. She also basically told me what Charles was willing to offer me with regards to the show. It was quite generous and even Beth commented that while I should retain an attorney to look my contract over she doubted an attorney would find issue with anything it said. Beth even confided in me it was the best offer she had ever seen Charles make to anyone. She said she would have the contract drawn up if I was okay with the general terms, adding that it would take a couple of days for their legal department to draw them up and that would give me time to find a good entertainment attorney to represent me. I appreciated her candor, but I also took Beth's word that it was a great offer. I mean it seemed fantastic, but what did I know?

I decided I would double check with whatever lawyer I went to, and I'd ask the cards. I wasn't really concerned with it that much. I already had what I wanted; I had made myself a new life:

A *somewhat normal* life.

# CHAPTER 2

# THE HERMIT

AFTER WHAT FELT LIKE HOURS OF SMALL TALK AND business conversations, I finally found myself sitting in the theater, off on my own for a moment. Everyone else was still there hovering around, mingling, but they had all moved on to other conversations amongst themselves. I had been told by Beth to wait for her to come back with paperwork I needed to fill out, so I had sat down in one of the theater seats.

I felt my legs relax a little and let my body sink into the cushion. I breathed in deeply as I leaned back. I had been so nervous about the audition that I had barely slept. Sitting down, I realized how tired I actually was. I thought how lovely I would feel if I had a blanket I could wrap around myself. I'd just curl up in a ball and no one would ever know I was there. I could feel myself starting to doze off but I was trying to fight it, since the last thing I wanted was to be asleep when Beth returned. That would be pretty embarrassing—and not be the best first impression to make on anyone. Even so, I'm pretty sure despite all my fighting that I had actually drifted off for a second before Cam walked up.

"Hey there, Sleeping Beauty," Cam said softly after lightly touching my shoulder and sitting down next to me. "It looked like you met everyone that works here today. The line to say hello to you after your performance resembled an autograph signing by a boy band. I don't really know what the latest one is, but Backstreet, Five Directions, One Second of Winter, 98 Celsius, O-city, NSYNC Boys or Old Kids on a Curb or something like that."

I laughed hard at his combo of wrong boy band names and his clear indication that he knew all the boy bands; he purposely had made the small wrong switches in their names. What perhaps made it funnier was the fact that he was pretty enough to be in any of those bands. "It feels like I met enough people to fill a concert for all those bands put together. It'll take a bit for me to learn everyone's names, though."

"Of course," Cam nodded. "They all just met one person. You just met *two hundred* people. No one's expecting you to know all their names yet. You just have to know the important ones, like mine." Cam smiled and flashed his full set of pearly whites.

"Uh . . . who are you?" Cam frowned and pretended to look hurt. I laughed again before proving that I did remember his name at least. "Your name I remember. How could I forget, Cam? Is it short for Cameron?"

He nodded. "Yeah, it is. Most of us get our names shortened or get nicknames around here. See? You're good, then. Well, maybe you should know Charles's name too. Then you're definitely good." Cam shrugged a little and nudged my arm.

"Yep, I'll just start calling everyone else 'darlin', like any good southern girl would."

Cam chuckled at my response. "Sounds like a plan. Are you staying tonight to watch the show?"

"Yeah, I think so. I was told I should stay and see it tonight. Right now I'm waiting on Beth to bring back some paperwork I have to fill out, and then I think my first official day is next week. Just waiting on drug tests and stuff . . ."

"Ahem." Cam and I both looked up to see Mac standing directly in front of us, holding a clipboard pressed against his stomach. He still looked angry and bothered for reasons I had yet to figure out. I looked at him with my eyes narrowed and he puckered his lips together in a manner that resembled a very fake smile. He looked down at his clipboard as if he was reading something important before looking back at me, and then Cam. "Cam, don't you have work to be doing?" Mac suggested, his tone swift and surly.

Cam grinned, unbothered. "Just checkin' on the new girl."

"She seems to be fine," Mac snapped. I wanted to ask him if it had been absolutely necessary to be so rude, but figured Cam was a big boy who could stick up for himself. As annoyed as I was, I couldn't help but notice how piercing Mac's deep hazel eyes were when he looked at me, despite the anger that was engulfing him. Cam stood up, looking a little confused. I could tell he wasn't accustomed to Mac acting that way, confirming that Mac's odd behavior was related to me.

"What's up with you?" Cam said to Mac in a hushed whisper with a glare that resembled the unspoken word, "chill." Cam then loudly said, "Right, boss," in a very sarcastic manner before turning to me, "Well, Zade, glad to have you aboard. I look forward to working with you."

"Thanks, darlin'," I smiled as I winked. "Me, too."

Cam began to walk away. After only a few steps he turned around and called back, "Feel free to come hang out on the grid with me during the show tonight. It's a cool view from up there." He pointed up towards the grid directly above us.

I smiled again and nodded. "Sounds good." Cam waved and winked at me before turning back around and disappearing through one of the stage entrances, which in this scenario was an exit.

I turned back to face Mac, who was looking at me with still visible annoyance that hadn't seemed to lighten one bit.

"Hopefully I wasn't interrupting something important," Mac said, with no attempt at feigning actual sincerity. I could tell he didn't care that he had interrupted, or that he had been rude.

"Just kindness." I responded. I don't think he expected my answer to be truthful, and he looked taken aback. He had probably expected me to say "Oh, no worries! Nothing important." He made no comment, but backed off a little. When he continued talking, he had a bit less snap in his voice.

"I'd like to schedule a crew call for you once your contract has been signed. You, me, and all of our techs, so we can go over your trick and map out how it will be safely implemented into the show." He knew that calling what I had done a "trick" instead of an illusion I would take as a slight. It's sort of like telling someone who had just won an Olympic gold medal and was proudly wearing it around their neck, that their necklace was cute. Mac kept incessantly tapping his Sharpie on the side of his clipboard and shifting his weight between his feet.

I stood up slowly and calculated, looking him square in the eye, which probably surprised him a bit, since he was at least six feet tall. I've always enjoyed the luxury of being a tall girl. I'm five foot nine inches and so while I don't usually tower above any guys I know, I can definitely look them directly in the eye. Most girls who at five feet five inches (which, I believe, is an average height for a woman) have to look up. My height was an advantage that I never took for granted and here, again, I was happy that I didn't have to look up to him—figuratively or literally. In heels I could even be as tall or taller than him and I've always loved that part about being the height I am. I half smiled and slowly spoke, "Maybe you misunderstood. I don't show anyone how it's done. That wasn't just for the audition. I handle this illusion on my own."

Mac held still for a moment, and then glanced up from his clipboard, looking irritated. He pursed his lips and flared his nostrils. The tapping stopped. He dropped the clipboard from his stomach and held it in his hand while pointing his finger directly in my face. "Listen, lady, I don't know who else you worked for, but we don't do that Lone Ranger stuff around here. I'm the technical director and in charge of everyone's safety, no matter how stupid you want to be. You do what I say, and I keep your pretty self from getting hurt. Got it?" I'm fairly certain he growled at me as he spoke.

Myriad thoughts ran through my head and I'm pretty sure several seconds passed in silence as we stared each other down. I could feel my hands tightening into fists. I really did want to punch him. I could see it happening. I'm not strong by any means but I'm also not a wimp. I wouldn't have broken anything, but he would have been bruised and sore. I quickly ran through the possible outcomes of punching the technical director on my first day of work. It didn't really seem to be the best idea.

I leaned into him so closely that it might have looked like to an outsider that I was about to kiss him. I huffed a little and my words were slow and deliberate. "I understand this is your job and all, but I don't think you're listening to me," I hissed. I tapped his chest with my finger and he jolted a bit at my touch. He looked at me like I was speaking some kind of foreign language.

"*I'm* not listening? Lady, you need your ears cleaned," he snarled back. He turned around to walk away, as if that was the end of our conversation. If he was trying to piss me off more, it was working.

I grabbed him by the shoulder, stopping him in his tracks and swinging him around to face me. My face had flushed and I'd raised my voice to a full yell. "And you need to get some manners. I'm not showing you how it's done, okay? If we have a problem I can go to another show where the technical director doesn't have a God complex. I'm not a girl who needs a knight in shining armor." I was practically snarling at him.

Mac gritted his teeth and looked like he might hit me, but I knew that wasn't really an option for him. Guys like him didn't hit women, no matter how mad we made them. He laughed loudly. "Ha! Good luck finding a Technical Director who will treat you like the princess you clearly think you are. If I found you locked in a tower, I promise I'd leave you there." Mac whipped around again and this time saw Riley, who had been standing just a few feet away from us the whole time. Riley was pretending not to be paying too much attention, but you could tell that was all he had been doing. I couldn't blame him. Mac glowered at Riley and barked, "Where's C.S.? Riley, go find Charles. Now!"

"On the move," Riley replied with a nervous, almost panicked look on his face as he ran off to the side and disappeared.

Everyone standing within earshot suddenly seemed to be looking at the floor, but I could tell that they had been listening to every word. It was almost comical how they all tried to look like they were doing other things. One petite, pixie-like girl who I knew was in the cast, though I didn't know her name, was standing the nearest to me. She had really bright red hair that was short and framed her face. I glanced her way and she immediately looked down at her arm and pretended to scratch it over and over with her bright-colored nails that were a beautiful shade of teal. She continued to stare at her arm as if there was something wrong with her perfectly tan skin. She squinted and narrowed her eyes never looking up or meeting my gaze, but I am pretty sure she felt me looking at her the whole time. I could feel my face reddening, and I started breathing hard. I was angry and embarrassed to be so shaken up in front of everyone. *Mac could have at least tried to talk to me in private; not in front of people I didn't even know yet.*

I was back in his face, stern and loud. "Look. It was part of my deal, end of story. I didn't know Joffrey Baratheon worked here now." I wondered if Mac even watched *Game of Thrones*, but hoped he would get my reference to the child king from the first two seasons who acted like, well, a child given power he didn't deserve or know how to handle.

I didn't know if Mac was really a spoiled brat, and I knew I might have been overreacting, but I had to protect certain things—and my secrets were definitely among them. I turned around and began to storm off. I'm not even sure where I was going to go. I just wanted to leave as fast as I could. I couldn't bear talking to him for one more moment. The anger inside of me was bubbling and I could feel my blood pressure rising to unhealthy levels.

I had only taken four or five pounding steps when Charles appeared from behind one of the black curtains that hung down and around every stage entrance. I didn't even really see him walk out but I felt his presence—he is definitely that kind of man. He had quite possibly been standing behind the curtain this whole time we had been arguing, just listening. Charles called out in a calm, direct, and somehow soothing voice, "Zade, come back here, please." I instantly stopped.

My body felt like it was on fire. I swallowed, took a deep breath, and nodded my head slowly before turning around. I walked slowly over to Charles with my head down. I felt horrible for causing a huge scene. I had wanted to look professional and put together and I instead ended up looking like a five-year-old child throwing a temper tantrum. *It's not even technically my first day yet and I've already made this huge fool of myself,* I thought as I edged my way towards Charles. I was more than mortified and I couldn't even look him in the eye so I looked down at the floor as I shuffled my feet. What was he going to say? I wouldn't blame him if he changed his mind right there and just had me leave his theater. My heart was pounding so hard it felt as if it was going to beat out of my chest and my hands fidgeted, nervously.

Everyone in the entire theater had stopped to focus solely on Charles, Mac, and me. They now weren't even pretending to be doing anything else. Even those who had previously not cared about the spat Mac and I were having, were now also watching all of us. Charles looked angry, but his voice was firm and calm. He slowly leaned down and forced his eyes to mine. He reached his hand out and pulled up my chin. *I hate it when people do that. My mother does that to me, too.* I finally allowed

46

my eyes to look up and straight into his eyes. He gazed directly at me for what felt like ten years.

Once he secured my attention he dropped his hand that had been holding my chin and glared at Mac. His words were spoken slowly and as a matter of fact. "When I auditioned Zade, I guaranteed her the privacy to set up her own act."

Mac calmly answered him, "Charles, that isn't up to O.S.H.A. requirements. I can't run a show like this. People on this crew have to know how it's done. We have to be involved in the production of it. She needs help with it, I'm sure. How will we even know if something is wrong? This is crazy. We would *never* do things that way. You've got to agree with me."

Zeb, who had been talking to the show's lighting director, was just a few feet from us and shot Charles a look. I got the feeling that Zeb was the only person who could have just joined the conversation at will, and, in fact, he decided to pipe in. "Charles you know how seldom I agree with Mac, but in this case I would have to say that he *is* right."

Charles nodded at Zeb and looked as if he was giving serious thought to what Mac had just said. I can only imagine the look on my face as I began to panic about what Charles's response would be. *My mother was right. What was I thinking?* Charles looked directly at Mac before speaking again. "Mac, you raise very good points, and you are correct." I had no idea what I was going to say. What could I say to turn this back around? I was still searching for words when Charles continued, "So Zade will tell me, and *only* me. Right, Zade?" He didn't look at me until he finished his sentence.

I think it took me a couple of moments to process what he was saying. I didn't really love his idea either, but I could deal with it. I knew that he would never push to know the way it was truly done. I could give him just enough information to comply. I could make it work. The discussion definitely could have gone a whole lot worse.

I finally nodded my agreement. The entire theater was watching me. I could hear whispering. I was used to some of that from where I grew up, but even so I wanted to melt into the floor. Finally, I mustered the words, "Sure. I'll tell you anything you want to know. But only you." My words were soft, but I looked directly at Charles when I said the "only you" part.

Charles began to look around the room. "See, children? We can all play in the sandbox at the same time." It felt more like a command than a comment. What he really meant was, "Show's over, folks. Get back to work now." Charles looked back at me. "Come into my office and we can talk about this more."

I nodded and was about to walk offstage, but I realized he wasn't done talking. I froze in place. It felt like one of the longest moments in my life. Charles looked at Mac, who seemed to want to be done with this display as much as I did. "Mac, please talk to Zeb and Beth about how we are integrating Zade's act into the show." He started to turn, but paused mid-motion. "Oh, and we are cutting the Dance Illusion."

Sofia, who had been standing off to the side with another performer, looked indignantly at Charles. I watched her redden, as her eyes got wide. She looked as if she was going to kill someone. I wondered if that someone was Charles or me—or maybe both of us. She gave me one terrible death stare, so I'm guessing it was me, before storming up to Charles.

"You're cutting my main illusion?" she huffed angrily. Charles met her gaze and raised his eyebrow just slightly. I could tell that she didn't intimidate him. Everything was always on his terms, including his relationships. I doubt the word "compromise" was in his vocabulary. Charles walked closely to her, stroked her face, and took her hand in his. I'm guessing it was meant to be loving, but looked more like he was brushing her off.

"This will give us a chance to develop a new illusion for you to be in, my dear. I've been doing that silly illusion for way too long, anyway." Charles smiled briefly before dropping her hand rather abruptly and walking off. He shouted back toward me. "Come, Zade. I'd like to get this ironed out before the first show tonight. Back to work, people. The show must go on, if you hadn't heard."

Charles was walking fairly quickly so I began to follow behind. I had to pick up the pace to almost run to catch up with him. I was very grateful that I was able to get away from everyone that had been staring at me for the past few minutes. It truly had felt like an eternity. Though at the same time I was dreading what was going to happen. Was I going to be able to handle this? Nervous waves crashed over me and rippled through my entire body.

A million thoughts rushed through my head and I felt dizzy and sick to my stomach. I could feel everyone watching us as we walked toward his office offstage. As we approached his office door no one said anything until they heard the door thud to a close. It was a big heavy door that made a hard pounding noise when it shut, and then I was alone with him. Charles told me to sit down. I did so, slowly feeling my heart pound again and my chest tighten. I swallowed hard. He was facing the wall, but he spoke deliberately. "Well, my dear. Tell me everything."

# CHAPTER 3

# THE HIEROPHANT

IT TOOK ABOUT A WEEK FOR HUMAN RESOURCES TO process my paperwork and get me set up as an employee. Even though we all work for the show we are technically employees of the casino, so they had to do things like background checks. It worked out well for me, though, since I had to find an apartment (luckily, the first week I was allowed to stay at the hotel, courtesy of Mr. Wynn and Mr. Spellman). I also got some furniture and did all the other really adult things I'd never had to do before. It was starting to sink in that I really was out on my own.

Finally my first official day as part of the show rolled around. I was so excited that I could feel the energy pumping through my body. I was told to start with wardrobe. We all have a dressing room area that's inside a really big room. They are sectioned off smaller rooms—kinda like in a changing room at a clothing store—but the show also has a large wardrobe room where we go for fittings, costumer fixes, etc. They also keep certain costumes there (like the ones with intricate beading that constantly has to be repaired) and lots of the performers get dressed there because they need assistance with their complex and much more elaborate costumes, which would be impossible to put on by yourself.

I glanced about the room admiring how all the costumes were kept so neat and tidy on the racks and shelves. The wardrobe department made and maintained the costumes—a huge undertaking for the small group of women who worked in the department. All expert seamstresses, they seemed to be able to make anything and I found out that they often made side money during Halloween making killer original costumes. I definitely wanted to have them do something cool for me when Halloween rolled around. Though I never know what to be, I always want a completely recognizable costume that is something so unique that no one else has it. It dawned on me they could make incredible costumes for the Renaissance faires that I loved going to, which made my new job and life that much more awesome, since I had heard Las Vegas had a pretty decent faire that happened yearly in town. Yes, having your very own costume designer is a must for any girl.

I found myself nearly naked standing in front of the wardrobe girl, Lil, who was trying to fit me for my costumes for the show. Her full name was Lillianne, but she had told me in her first breath to call her Lil, and that only her mom and great aunt Anne called her by her full name. She talked a lot, and fast, while smacking her gum. She continued on about how she only thought her great aunt called her by her full name because her name was Anne and thought that somehow she was kind of named after her. I quickly learned more about Lil than I know about most people I've known for my half my life. She looked like the stereotypical Goth: black hair, black nails, and more than her fair share of tattoos. I'm pretty sure that if you saw her on the street the last thing you would think is that she made clothes for a living. There was something instantly like-able about her, though, which was well enough since I'd had to strip down to my underwear within five minutes of meeting her. I'm sure she'd seen the entire cast in their underwear more than once, but it was an odd thing for me to be naked in front of a complete stranger.

Lil stood in front of me, measuring each part of my body so she could make costumes as needed. She explained that the department kept detailed records of everyone's measurements so that when something new needed to be made for a performer, it could be done without a consultation. She continued to ramble on in her fast, chatty way, and pretty soon I had tuned out the random gossip and focused on my reflection in the mirror. The fluorescent lights showed off every angle of me as I stood there staring at myself, and all I could think was how white I looked, and I wished some parts of my body were different. Finally, Lil's voice cut through my distraction when she mentioned something about Mac. Unfortunately I only caught the tail end of what she had said. Not wanting to admit that I had not heard her at all, I quickly changed the subject even though I genuinely wanted to know the gossip she had spilled about the brooding technical director and the question I did ask came only from minor curiosity.

"Lil, am I assigned directly to you for wardrobe or will I have a different person every time?"

"You're assigned to me, so you'll come straight to me for any of your costumes." She paused. "I mean . . . There are other women working here, but I'm your girl."

I nodded and smiled at her. "Okay, Lil. Thanks." I liked that I had someone assigned to me. It made me feel important somehow.

"I love your hair by the way! All the colors look super fab! Do you go to a salon?" Lil grabbed chunks of my hair, looking at the different colors before I had a chance to respond.

"Oh no, I just go to Sally Beauty Supply and get the colors and do it myself. In the little town I'm from we have one hair salon, and they aren't exactly willing to do anything—in their words—'crazy.' So I had to start coloring it myself plus it's so much cheaper." I put up air quotes as I stressed "crazy."

"Wow, it's so fun; I'll have to have you do my hair some time!" Lil tossed her hair around playfully.

"I'd be happy to do your hair anytime. Sometime we should go to Sally and pick out some colors for you." Lil nodded in agreement before leaning over me. She paused for a moment. She seemed to be deciding if she was going to say something or not. I'm pretty sure it was the first time she had stopped talking and taken any sort of a breath since I walked in. When she finally did speak again she spoke slowly and her words seemed much more calculated.

"So, are you excited?"

"Super excited," I agreed.

"That was a pretty awesome illusion," she said, tentatively. "I can see why C.S. had, like, a special audition just for you. I've never seen them do that for anyone, but you sure brought it."

I'm not good with compliments. Some girls are. I've always admired those who know what to say and accept them graciously. I normally stammer over the words "thank you." It always comes off awkwardly, so I usually end up trying to say something nice in return, which is hard when you don't know the person. Since I hadn't really seen much of Lil's work, I couldn't tell her I thought she was an amazing seamstress. I began to turn red and mustered out the word, "thanks," and then we just stared at each other in awkward silence. *What do I say?* "You measured me well?" That's not exactly something you compliment someone on. I could say "You talk faster than anyone I've ever met." That also seemed like a less-than-stellar compliment.

Just when the silence had become unbearable, at least for me, she added, "How did you come up with that illusion?"

"Family secret," I responded, relieved that the silence was broken, but worried that she was beginning to pry. I had learned early on that questions lead to vague answers and vague answers get people suspicious. I wanted to get her talking about herself again as fast as I could. I scanned the room; there were a few mannequins scattered about sporting costumes in various stages of being made. Some were very bright, colorful and beautiful. "You make any of these?" I asked, gesturing around the room. She looked around and then nodded, pointing at a couple of the costumes. They seemed to be almost finished. The one closest to us was a beautiful black dress, decked out in ruffled tulle underskirts of different colors and varying lengths. The top had an incredible angular collar that stood up and away from the body. I'd never seen anything like it. It was amazing, but probably difficult to wear—and almost definitely uncomfortable.

I smiled and began to rave about how lovely it was. As nervous as I was, I probably would have raved about a dishcloth if that had been my only option, but I really did love the dress. It got us off the subject of me, but not for long enough. Once she thanked me for the kind words she went straight back to asking me questions. "So, where are you from? No one's ever heard of you before. Most performers come from other shows and so usually we don't meet completely *new* people. You just came out of nowhere."

I laughed a little before answering. "Not nowhere, just Tennessee."

*Mac slowly walked up to the door of the fitting room. He could hear Lil chattering away—mostly gossip, as usual. He raised his hand to knock on the door, but as he clutched his fingers together and balled up his hand to make a fist the door opened just a crack. It hadn't been closed all the way. Mac could see Zade standing in nothing but her lace underwear and bra as Lil pulled a measuring tape around her narrow waist. Both pieces were black and nude with lace trim and the panties, which were a high-waisted cut, framed Zade's body nicely and showed off her curves and small*

waist. Lil made a note in her pad of the measurement and moved down to Zade's hips. Under the bright lights, Zade's skin looked porcelain white. She was beautiful. She wasn't supermodel hot but there was something about her that just made her stand out. Mac couldn't quite put his finger on it but there was something there.

He tried to push the thoughts out of his head; he didn't want to like her. He couldn't like her. Zade was the enemy. He tried to repeat that to himself. He took a deep breath and kept telling himself he should just turn and walk away. He had forgotten why he was even standing in front of the wardrobe door. It had something to do with Zade and her first day, but he couldn't remember anything beyond that now. Mac was not the kind of guy to just forget things and it made him frustrated that looking at her seemed to do that to him. Despite his frustration with himself he still stood there staring for quite a while, the whole time thinking he should just look away, but he couldn't seem to actually take his eyes off of her.

Tad walked up and stopped right behind Mac. Mac was so distracted by Zade and his own internal dialogue that he didn't even notice Tad approaching. Tad looked through the crack in the door, looked at Mac, cracked a wide grin, and crossed his arms. Tad waited for a few moments to see if Mac was going to notice him or even just stop staring at the mostly naked girl on the other side of the door. Finally Tad decided that they might be there all *night if he just waited for Mac to turn around so finally he poked at Mac's shoulder.*

*Startled, Mac whipped around and quickly looked to see who had just caught him. He didn't say anything or show it but, secretly, he was relieved that it was his best friend and not someone else that had caught him watching. Tad raised an eyebrow as if asking Mac what he was doing. He knew that if he said anything out loud the girls would hear him—and he would never purposely embarrass Mac. Mac stood there, speechless for a moment, contemplating his best next move. Quickly he decided to just turn and start walking down the hallway. He knew Tad wanted to say something, and knew that Tad would follow behind till they got out of earshot. Mac picked up the pace, his heavy black work boots pounding the floor with each step. Tad—right behind him with a wide grin— chuckled quietly to himself. The moment they were far enough down the hall that their conversation wouldn't be heard, the quiet laughter erupted into actual loud laughter.*

*Mac stopped in his tracks and whirled to face Tad, glaring at him with a look that said:* Be careful. I'm not in the mood.

*"You turning into a peeping Tom?" Tad asked brazenly as he leaned comfortably against the wall.*

*"Shut it, Tad!" Mac said, cheeks reddening in embarrassment.*

Tad grinned even wider. "Why were you staring at Zade?" Tad asked rhetorically while still chuckling to himself, as he obviously knew exactly why.

Mac looked Tad dead in the eye and moved his tongue around his gums. He ground his teeth before responding, anger mounting in his words. "Contemplating how to kill her and dispose of the body without getting caught. Keep it up, and I'll be disposing of two bodies. Any other questions?" The sharp stare that followed was enough to shut Tad up. It wasn't time to push the situation, so Tad finally wiped the smile from his face and eventually stopped laughing. Mac huffed one last time before he turned and stormed off down the hall.

Tad chose not to continue to follow him. Instead, he watched Mac round the bend until he drifted completely out of sight. Tad stood there for a few moments longer, thinking, until Riley emerged from the direction in which Mac had just disappeared.

"What's up with Mac?" Riley stopped in front of Tad and asked with genuine concern. "He just plowed right into me—and then told me I needed to watch it."

Tad shrugged and rolled his eyes. "He's just having a difficult time dealing with his feelings. Don't worry about it, kid. It doesn't have anything to do with you."

I had finally finished up in wardrobe. I'm pretty sure every inch of me had been measured—and I knew Lil's entire life story. I could practically tell you anything about her, including what she had eaten for breakfast—and, no, I'm not even joking about that one. (She had had scrambled eggs with cheese, turkey bacon, whole-grain toast, and some homemade mango jelly. She had gotten all the ingredients fresh from a local farmer's market—which she recommended I go and try.)

With my mind on other things and still excited about my first day, I waltzed out of wardrobe not paying any attention to where I was walking. I still had my head turned, saying goodbye to Lil, when I collided into what one would most certainly call tall, dark, and handsome. He was exactly my type, if I ever had one. I had crashed into him so hard that I started to tumble to the ground. Luckily, he apparently had catlike reflexes and caught me in his arms. He held me there for a moment, just long enough for me to look into his deep, sparkling eyes. I'm pretty sure I turned every shade of red imaginable, as I was already embarrassed by my clumsiness—and then just in awe of his handsome radiance. He pulled me up slowly and gingerly even slightly tighter into him before he placed me upright and back on solid ground.

"Hello," he said, smiling. I just stared up at him. I didn't move. His arms were still around me and our bodies were pressed closely together. He laughed a little. "Are you okay?" I suddenly realized that I hadn't moved or spoken, as I felt him cautiously release me from his grip as if I might still tumble to the ground.

"Oh gosh. Yeah. Sorry! Uh . . . I'm uhh. Yes, I'm . . . I'm . . . I am fine. I am Zade. I'm new around here." I was babbling and stumbling over every word that came out of my mouth. *What was wrong with me?* I had just turned into a silly four-teen-year-old girl. He laughed again, and I noticed he had a guitar strap that ran around his torso. The electric guitar on his back peeked over his shoulder.

"I know who you are. I actually came up and talked to you right after your audition. I was one of the many fawning over you. I'm Jackson Milsap," he said, smiling broadly. His grin revealed two rows of perfect, white teeth. All I processed was "Jackson."

"Yes, you are. I mean—" *Oh, my God. Why can't I form sentences that actually make any sense right now? That answer was ridiculous, and even worse, he says we met before. I can't remember that! How would I have possibly forgotten someone so gorgeous?*

"I'm so sorry. I met so many people that day. It was over-whelming." *Geez, I sound as ditzy as they come. What the hell is wrong with me?*

Jackson smiled again and his cheeks dimpled. He ran his fingers through his perfectly tousled dark chestnut hair, and I realized that I was going weak in the knees whenever he smiled. I wanted to keep talking to him, but the only lame question I could think of to ask him was what he did for the show. I wished I could think of more clever banter than, "So what do you do around here?" Hopefully I would come up with something better while he was answering me. Even worse, I had a pretty good idea what he did, considering he had an electric guitar strapped to his back. I was fairly certain he was in the house band, which played live during the show. I bit my lower lip and waited for him to respond as if he was about to tell me the meaning of life. "I'm the bandleader, singer, and guitar player for the house band," he responded.

"Kinda what I thought." I smiled knowingly, at the same time frustrated at myself that I didn't just ask if he was in the house band. I pointed to the neck of the guitar protruding out over his right shoulder as I continued, "The guitar sorta gives you away. That's pretty cool, though. I play guitar as well." I blushed and fidgeted as I shifted my feet and played with strands of my hair.

"Sweet. A girl that can play, that's hot for sure. I think you get bonus points for that." The comment could have come off jerkish, but the way he said it sounded kind of sweet.

I blushed again. "Well maybe we can jam together some-time," I offered, even though I felt silly using the word "jam," especially since I really do not know even how to jam, as much as I just know how to strum a few songs. I still hadn't thought of anything better to ask when he interjected, "I have my own band, too, where I sing, and also play guitar and keyboards. Sometimes I'll even bang on the drums here or there."

"That's awesome. Actually, if it's not too forward—would you mind if I borrowed a guitar sometime?" I asked sweetly. I could have probably said something more profound about how cool it was, him being able to play multiple instruments, and my head started to flood with all the other questions I could have asked about his original band. *What kind of music is it? Who else is in the band? Where do they play?* The list went on and on, but if I was going to jam with him I should probably try to hone my skills. Plus, my guitar wasn't very nice, not even a little bit. I would be embarrassed to even bring it into the theater.

Jackson smiled and nodded. "I keep a spare acoustic in my dressing room. Nothing fancy but it'll play. Feel free to borrow it anytime." I'm pretty sure I would have been happy to stand there talking to him all day but I figured he had actual work things to do and though I wasn't quite sure what I was supposed to be doing next, I was fairly certain there was something I was probably already late for. I started to thank him in advance for letting me borrow the guitar and promised to take good care of it when I did. I was getting around to the goodbye part of the conversation when he suddenly jumped to explain that he had come looking for me.

"The reason I'm here is . . . well, you don't know where anything is, do you?" Jackson raised his eyebrow with a smirk on his face. He knew my answer as well as I did.

"No, actually I don't. Today's my first official day, and so far, I've just been measured and fitted in wardrobe. I was told to come here but now that I think about it I wasn't told what I should do after this," I explained, though not defensively.

He laughed a little. "Yeah, I was sent here to grab you. I volunteered to give the pretty new girl the nickel tour and introduce you to everyone."

I was doing somersaults in my head. He thought I was pretty. I tried to remain calm and collected on the outside though. *Must pretend to be cool*, I kept repeating in my head. "Oh, that's really kind of you. Thank you."

He put out his arm like guys do on dates sometimes when they want to be sweet. It's a weakness for me when a guy does it; it makes me feel special somehow. Maybe because it's always done to princesses and debutantes in old movies, and it just feels so romantic. "Shall we?" he cooed.

I was just about to link my arm with his when I realized that I had forgotten my phone in the wardrobe room. I was about to ruin what was a perfect moment. "Oh, hang on. I need to run back into wardrobe. I left my phone. Let me grab it and then we can start the magical tour." I was embarrassed that I had forgotten it and I tried to sound cute by calling what we were about to do "the magical tour." I wasn't sure if I came off cute or silly for it.

He didn't seem annoyed at all and shrugged as he responded, "Sure. I'll be right here . . . waiting for you." He emphasized the words "right here" and "waiting for you." I giggled like a schoolgirl. At least I got his reference and joke. Gotta be cool points for that.

I made sure to say, "Thanks, Richard Marx," before darting back into wardrobe. Unfortunately, that meant that I had that song stuck in my head and it made me wonder if that comment meant he was actually a fan of Richard Marx. I grabbed my cell phone off the counter. Luckily, Lil was preoccupied with someone else, talking their ear off. I picked it up and waved, showing her I had just come back to retrieve my left cell phone. She nodded before apologizing that she hadn't even realized it was there.

"No worries, I'll see you soon," I responded, before quickly bee-lining it back out into the hallway, where Jackson and his tour were both—as he promised—right there waiting for me. I had been so scared about my decision to leave home and move to Las Vegas, up until that very moment. A calm energy settled over me and I knew I had made the right choice. I was supposed to be there, not back home. It was a great feeling; I was surrounded by new possibilities, and that's always the best part of any change:

Knowing you have possibilities—and getting to see where those possibilities take you.

# CHAPTER 4

# THE EMPRESS

CONSIDERING HOW MUCH I WANTED TO KEEP MY SECRETS, well, *secret*, a few days later I probably brought a little too much attention to myself. I didn't really know what to do and felt like I had no choice. I had seen something. I knew someone was going to get hurt. Maybe I should have just kept my mouth shut, but I couldn't really just stand by and not say anything, could I? I knew by saying something I was opening myself up for people to start asking too many questions. What sort of reaction had I expected? I sounded crazy to any normal person.

I didn't have long to decide what I was going to do. When I get premonitions and "see things" as you might say, they come in flashes. I don't ask for them. Sometimes I'm shown things way ahead of time and other times—like this one—only a few minutes before something happens. I think it has to do with when someone actually makes the decision that affects the situation. You know, like Destiny is saying to me "ten minutes ago this tragedy wasn't set to happen and then something changed to set the events in motion." At least, that is my theory. I have no proof, but I've learned enough information after the fact, when this has happened before, that I'm fairly certain that my thoughts on the subject are correct.

I always took it at face value that, if I was getting one of these visions or premonitions; it meant I was supposed to help change the situation. After all, my choices always seemed to be able to make a positive change to something that could have been tragic, which is why I thought that they were for the good, whatever that meant really.

Before I had even thought through completely what I was going to say or how I was going to get him to listen to me without me sounding crazy, I saw Mac walking across the stage. In my effort to try not to bring too much attention to the situation I thought it best to catch up with him instead of shouting his name across the theater. I darted after him still trying to wrap my head around what I was going to say. I could feel my face scrunch up in nervousness, and my brows twitch. Mac was walking pretty fast, like a man on a mission. Each step was precise and pushed him quickly along. I soon found myself picking up my pace to get near him. I have long legs, but his are longer, so I was practically running when I was finally close enough to say his name. "Mac. Mac ...." He either couldn't hear me or was just trying to ignore me completely.

I sprinted to get just close enough to reach out and grab the hem of the three-quarter-length sleeve on his black shirt, while shouting, "Hey," which finally made him stop. I heard a slight ripping sound from his sleeve, which freaked me out, but since there was no visible damage I'm guessing I had only weakened the seams. He turned around, looking pretty perturbed. Perhaps because he, too, had heard his shirt rip, or because I had forced him to stop going wherever it was he was in such a hurry to get to—or maybe simply because I was the one trying to talk to him. Whatever the reason, I already was sure that trying to talk to him and get his help was a bad idea.

"Damn it, Zade! What?" Mac snarled loudly. The thought of this being a terrible plan swirled around in my head and I panicked. *Could I ask him something different?* I couldn't think of anything else that would have made me grab him and stop his sprint across the stage. I had to commit to what I had started out doing. "Uh. Did anyone find anything ... strange ... in the safety checks today?" I asked him as my chest pounded from having to chase after him and my breathing was slightly elevated. He thought for a moment, then he tilted his head a little. A puzzled expression appeared across his face.

"No. Why?" He softened just a bit, looking genuinely concerned. I took a deep breath. I wasn't sure how I was going to explain it. Usually I would claim I'd just "had a feeling." People generally believed it enough to just let it go. I was almost certain he wasn't the superstitious type, though, and "I had a feeling" wasn't going to get me anywhere with him, but what the hell. *Here goes nothing.*

I bit my lip. "You, um . . . Do you ever get weird feelings? You know, like a premonition?"

He nodded his head slightly before answering me. "Sure. Everyone does. Usually they're unfounded. People listen too much to their feelings instead of facts."

Yep. I could tell he was not going to go along with the "I have a feeling something wrong" scenario, but I couldn't explain why I really knew what I knew. I figured I didn't have any other options for explanations. I narrowed my eyes. "Well, I get them, and mine are never unfounded, okay?" I huffed a little. Mac looked beyond irritated. I could practically hear what he must have been saying to himself in his head. I'm sure it had something to do with how I had done nothing but complicate his job, how difficult everything had been since the moment I arrived, and how now I was coming to him with some story about a feeling I was having and how I "knew" something was wrong. It was hard for me not to admit to myself that I may have hated me too, if I were him. He rolled his eyes at me and practically growled.

"Look, I don't have time for this," he said. "You aren't satisfied with keeping me from being able to know what's going on in my own theater. Now you're going to tell me I'm not doing my job?" His voice was stern, but his eyes looked sad. I softened and spoke more gently.

"That's not what I'm trying to do. I think today something checked out okay that probably shouldn't have. It happens. You know it does."

Both of his hands reached toward his head and he started rubbing his forehead, which he had scrunched up. His eyes were closed and he had the look of someone who had been suddenly hit with a headache. He took a deep breath in and out as if to try to calm himself. His hands moved from his forehead to his mouth and he looked directly at me as if he was deciding whether he should yell at me some more or push me into the pool. He pulled his hands away from his mouth and pressed his lips together tightly. His hands folded together, close to his face. It almost made him look like he was about to pray. He finally brought himself around enough to speak again. His words came out calmly and clearly since he was standing very close in front of my face. It was even, in a soft tone, the way some people sound when they are on the edge of losing it all together.

"Whatever this is, stop it. Go get into your place for top of show. We have a rehearsal to do and neither of us has time for this. Do I make myself abundantly clear?"

I stood there for a moment looking back at him, motionless, with the exception of my eyelids blinking. In my head I had started to come up with what else I could say, but I realized that it didn't matter what I said. Even if I told him the entire truth he wouldn't do anything or believe me. I was fighting a losing battle and just giving him more reasons to loathe my mere existence.

"Crystal," I responded with no emotion as I turned around and started to walk to my spot. My only other option was to try to fix the situation without involving him. The images I had seen hadn't been as strong and were fuzzier than they usually were. Normally I got a bit more info from my visions, but this time I really felt like I didn't know enough to even come up with a good plan. I felt nervous as I started to climb the ladder towards my starting point for the show. I walked down the catwalk and put my harness on. I clipped in, hooking my harness to a metal wire, before walking out past the guard wall. I closed my eyes so I could try to get a clearer vision of what was about to happen.

Usually my hints of the future come in random flashes. So, when I try to focus, it gets tricky—like focusing a nice camera for a picture. As you make adjustments, the image gets clearer, but if you try too hard then it gets even fuzzier. I couldn't see how exactly it was going to occur . . . at least not well enough to stop it. I just saw enough to know that some part of the equipment was going to malfunction and someone was going to fall. But *what* was going to malfunction? I could hear something about "hitting the E stop" but could only tell it was a male voice yelling it. I had the feeling that if I could only see *who* fell, I could do something.

What I did know for certain was that it was going to happen soon, and I was starting to panic.

I frantically started to look around to see if anything looked out of place. Riley and Sofia were standing behind me on the catwalk. I was so preoccupied scanning the equipment and other performers in different areas of the grid, that I didn't notice that Sofia wasn't wearing her harness. Riley was our rigger for the rehearsal. I could hear him arguing with Sofia, but it was all background noise. If I had only stopped to listen to what they were arguing about, I may have figured everything out before it happened. But, since Sofia was always arguing about something with someone, I wasn't even paying them any attention.

"Sofie, you gotta put your harness on. You know the rules. You tryin' to get me into trouble?" Riley was almost begging her.

She batted her eyes and ran her finger over his chest and his own harness. "Riley. It's *really* uncomfortable," she whined.

"So are broken necks," he said curtly. *Broken necks*, wait, I heard that. *Why would Riley say that?* I asked myself. I turned around and saw that Sofia didn't have her harness on. It was too late though, at that same exact moment, Pete's voice blared over Riley's radio. "Places, everyone. Curtain up in two."

The platform we were all standing on had already started to move while Pete was talking. *That's not supposed to happen, yet,* I thought as it began to start swinging out and spinning very quickly at the same time. My legs twisted as I tried to regain my footing. Riley grabbed his radio, panicked.

"Riley to Automation. Why is the main platform moving? Really fast! Someone hit the damn E stop!" Riley was also trying to regain his footing, but the set was moving too quickly. Riley grabbed at Sofia, but couldn't hold on to her. As soon as he reached for her arm, she spun off the platform, falling toward the ground. I knew instantly that I wasn't going to be able to grab her either, and I realized that she was bound to hit the stage if I didn't do something.

I was still harnessed in and, from where I was, I was able to push her body as she was flying past me. She screamed as she accelerated toward the floor from fifty or so feet in the air. Because of my shove, she hit the pool and not the ground. But she slammed into the water on her back—there was a *smack* and then she sank.

I wanted to scream. I realized that in my vision I must have been seeing what had happened from Sofia's point of view—that's why it was all so blurry and unclear. I should have tried to refocus from a different angle. I didn't have time to beat myself up about it, though—I would have to figure out the how I could do better the next time, later.

I pulled off my harness and dove from the platform, which was still moving, and somehow aimed myself at the pool. I could feel the water, which was always a warm ninety degrees, soak into my clothes. I usually loved the sensation of swimming, but this was hardly a fun time. I grabbed Sofia's body from the depths and pulled her back to the surface and over to the side of the pool as fast as I could. She had been knocked completely unconscious.

I pushed her limp body back onto the stage and quickly pulled myself out after her—my summers as a lifeguard finally paying off. I straightened her out on the ground. She had taken in water and wasn't breathing so I needed to begin CPR. My heart was pounding. She may not have been my favorite person, but I certainly didn't want her to die. The adrenaline kicked in and I began chest compressions. As I worked, I was vaguely aware of Pete screaming behind me, "Someone call the paramedics! We have an unconscious performer!"

A visibly upset Riley had finally reached the ground. Tad and Mac, among others, ran to him and immediately started asking questions. Mac spoke first; I knew he needed to find out the details of what just occurred while they were still fresh in Riley's mind.

"Riley, what happened?" Mac asked, doing his best to remain calm.

Riley was panicked, trembling and shaking. His eyes kept darting over to Sofia. "She . . . she wasn't wearing her harness."

Mac grabbed Riley and pulled him closer, shielding Riley's view of Sofia. When I glanced up, I could see Riley was wide-eyed and scared. "Riley, why wasn't she wearing her safety harness?" Mac asked, but Riley didn't answer. "Riley, *why* wasn't she wearing her safety harness?" Mac asked again, but Riley was still distracted and not paying attention to Mac. Mac finally grabbed Riley by the arms and shook him, "Why the hell was she not wearing it?" Mac asked, looking him directly in the eyes. This time Riley responded as if he just had been woken up from a dream, but couldn't look Mac in the eyes.

"I was telling her to put her damn harness on when the platform started to move!" The panic had begun to subside into some kind of shock, and Riley sounded like he was angry.

Mac glanced up, perplexed, into the grid above the stage. "The platform shouldn't have been moving at all," he said, more to himself than to Riley. "The system must have glitched out with just the worse timing."

Tad had been standing nearby listening and realized that he needed to step in. Mac sometimes could be too matter-of-fact. Even from my distance, I could tell that Riley needed compassion at that exact moment. "Riley. It's okay. Calm down. It wasn't your fault. She knows she's not supposed to be up there without being tied off, and the platform moving wasn't your fault either." Tad smiled and nodded as he put his hand on Riley's shoulder.

Mac looked up. "Yeah, Tad's right. Go take a smoke break; stop freaking out. I'll be out there in a bit. I'm sure she'll be fine."

Sofia began to cough and spit up water. I turned her over on her side. "Sofia, you're going to be okay. Just keep breathing." I held her as she coughed. I know when someone is close to death it helps them to feel comfort from another person—even someone they may not really like. I could already feel that everything was going to be okay.

When the paramedics showed up with stretchers and took over, I was happy to be able to step out of the way. My nerves were shot. I sat down off to the side, well out of the way of what was happening.

I think Riley finally decided that Mac was right when he said Sofia would be okay, and he finally began to calm down. You could still see the guilt he was feeling, and as he walked away his head was down. I'm sure he was running the situation over and over again in his mind wondering what he could have done differently. I was doing the same thing. But, of course, the answer for both of us was "nothing."

Mac walked over to where I was sitting. He just stood there next to me. I finally decided he was waiting for me to stand up, though he didn't say anything. I rose to my feet. Tad walked up and helped me. I turned to Mac and looked right at him; I was exhausted and didn't even know what to say. A production assistant whose name I hadn't learned yet ran over and handed me a towel, which I wrapped around myself. The temperature in the building was always kept a bit warmer than normal room temperature, so even though I was wet, I wasn't freezing. Even so, the towel and being able to dry off felt nice. "That was quick thinking, Zade," Tad said. "Is there anything you don't do?" I smiled a little. There's a calming and relaxing energy that surrounds Tad like a bubble. Just like how some people have sporadic energy that makes them hard to be around. Tad is the exact opposite and whenever I am around him or talking to him I instantly feel it effect me in a good way. It's a rare but delightful quality few people possess. I decided to try to keep things light.

"Windows," I said, laughing a little.

"How'd you react so fast? You were almost in the water before Sofia was, and Riley said you even pushed her as she was falling and kept her from hitting the stage. You saved her life. If she would have hit the metal stage or anything other than the water . . . well . . . ." Tad raised his eyebrow.

I thought for a moment, wrung out some of the water from my wet hair, and said, "I just . . . I had a feeling something might happen, so I guess I was looking for it. I'm gonna go check on Riley. He looked pretty shaken up." I turned and walked away. I didn't get very far, though, before I heard Tad and Mac begin to talk about me.

*"Wonder what that meant?" Tad asked Mac.*

*"She came up to me a few minutes before all this happened telling me she had a 'premonition' that something was wrong and asking if everything tested out okay," Mac said, trying to sound dismissive.*

*There was a momentary pause before Tad replied, "Hmm. Well, next time she says that, maybe you should listen."*

"Yeah, I'll get right on that," Mac said, sarcasm dripping from his voice. I wondered if he was angry at me—or just angry that I had been right.

"Can I tell Sofie that the 'scene stealer' just saved her life?" Tad joked.

"Save it 'til she's feeling better. It'll have more impact," Mac joked back.

"Maybe you should go apologize to her," Tad said tentatively.

"Apologize to who? Sofie?" Mac sounded baffled.

"To Zade. You said—"

Mac quickly cut him off, "Maybe she should apologize! Just 'cause she had a weird feeling and something just happens to happen—"

"Don't get your panties all in a twist!" This time Tad's words sounded like an order.

"This whole damn thing is stupid!"

Tad started laughing. "Why're you letting her get to you like this? You never get worked up so much over anyone. You're always tell me nothing's worth the stress."

"She frustrates the living daylights out of me," Mac said more softly.

Tad laughed again. "Oh. I get it. You *like* her. Uh-oh. You're in trouble."

"Hell, no! You know I don't date performers!" Mac spat out.

"That's why you're so mad, I think."

"What is there to like about her, anyway?" Mac grumbled.

"Lots of things, and I don't need to tell you that. If I wasn't happily married, I might give you a run for your money on that one."

"You'd be running against yourself," Mac muttered.

"Who are you trying to convince: me or you?" Tad asked, laughing even harder this time.

"I need a cigarette," Mac said gruffly. "Go start running checks, see where the glitch is, and try to keep your opinions to yourself." He stormed off.

After checking on Riley and making sure that he seemed okay, I found myself sitting out on the loading dock. I had gone and grabbed the acoustic guitar that Jackson had so kindly said I could borrow whenever I wanted. I needed to clear my head and process the things that had just happened. I began to strum the strings. At first it was just random chords and then I was humming along. Before I knew it, it had turned into a song that I knew all too well. Somehow my mind had wandered into thinking about the lyrics to "That's Just What You Are," my favorite Aimee Mann song. Something about the words and what they meant seemed to be really appropriate for what had been going on, recently.

I was singing softly to myself when I heard the back door open. Mac walked out onto the dock and fumed as he lit a cigarette. He took a long drag and leaned against the wall. I could only just see him out of the corner of my eye but I pretended that I didn't hear him or notice he was out there. I just continued to sing.

> *Acting steady*
> *Always ready to defend your fears*
> *What's the matter with the truth,*
> *Did I offend your ears*
> *By suggesting that a change might*
> *Be a thing to try*
> *Like it would kill you just to try*
> *And be a nicer guy*
> *It's not like you would lose some*
> *Critical piece*
> *If somehow you moved Point A to*
> *Point B*
> *Maintaining there is no point*
> *Changing 'cause*
> *That's just what you are*

*That's just what you . . . are . . .*

I kept humming and strumming the guitar softly to the melody of the song. I knew Mac was listening but I wasn't really in the mood to talk to anyone, and most certainly not him. I realized that he had put his cigarette out and was still just hanging out on the dock staring at me. I figured he was basically waiting for me to look up. He must have lost his patience, because eventually he loudly cleared his throat. I stopped playing and looked up, pretending that I had only just noticed his presence.

"Hey there. Didn't know they started booking entertainment for smoke breaks," Mac commented. I thought about all the smart aleck things I could say, but decided that I didn't want to start anything with him again.

"Oh. Hey. I didn't hear you come out." All the clever things I thought about saying, and yet I ended up saying something completely lame. "I just needed to clear my head."

"Sounded like that song was about me," Mac said, sitting down next to me on the edge of the dock and nudging me slightly with his shoulder.

"Well if it is, then someone else must think that about you, 'cause I didn't write that song." I laughed a little.

"Yeah, I know." Mac nodded and pursed his lips together. "Aimee Mann did."

I smiled and I felt my eyes widen, I cocked my head to the side and looked at him in mild shock. *He knew the song and even who wrote it*. I was impressed. "Yeah, she's one of my favorites. It's basically her and Ryan Adams. I can't believe you even know who she is. Wait, do you actually *like* her?" I guess I figured that even if he knew the song and who Aimee Mann was, he wasn't really capable of actually liking her. That would have meant we agreed on something.

"I'm full of surprises. I know who she is because *Magnolia* is one of my favorite films—and you never answered my question."

*Magnolia* was one of my favorite films, too. It was also why *I* knew who Aimee Mann was.

"I don't believe you asked a question," I said. "I believe you made a statement. But yes, I may have been loosely thinking about you—just the tiniest bit." I held up my thumb and pointer finger to show how tiny the "bit" was, while grinning as large as I could. I made sure to only show the tiniest gap between my two fingers. If I hadn't known any better I would have thought he was almost being nice to me, flirting even.

Mac took a deep breath of the evening desert air. "I might deserve it—just the tiniest bit." He mimicked what I had just done and held up his thumb and pointer finger with a similar amount of space between them while curling his lip. He looked away and stared out into the darkness before continuing. "Look, maybe I have been overreacting a little, but it's my job to make sure that everything in the show goes right and that everyone stays safe. Even the thick-headed." He looked back at me when he said the last three words, but his comment didn't upset me. I wondered if this was the start of a real, honest conversation. I decided to take a chance and see if it could be.

"Well, I was trying to help you do that."

He exhaled audibly and uttered words that I definitely wasn't expecting to ever hear a few hours earlier: "I know, and I'm sorry. I was exceedingly rude about it, but usually when people try to tell me about my job, they just end up messing something up. I'm just trying to keep things going around here. You're very passionate, though, and I'll try to respect that, okay?"

I looked at him closely. I wasn't even sure what happened that caused him to break down his wall and come around. Don't get me wrong: I was grateful it was happening; I was just still shocked. His words seemed sincere and even genuine. He touched my hand softly and I knew I should try to meet him halfway. "I'll try not to tell you how to do your job. I see that you do it well. This can't be an easy place to keep going."

I was being honest. Despite how badly we had gotten along up to that point, I *had* noticed how good he really was at his job.

At first I was probably trying to catch him being terrible at it. I wanted him to be an awful T.D. so my feelings could become more justified, but instead I had quickly noticed how good he was at being in charge of the crew. He was a good boss and treated people fairly. He explained things when people didn't understand, and he never asked anyone to do anything he wasn't willing to do himself. He always offered to help when it was something that was especially hard—or the kind of thing that sucked to do. He worked hard, was good under pressure, and never jumped to conclusions. He also took the time to understand all the different facets of pretty much each job that the crew had to do, since he was over everyone. The head rigger only had to understand rigging, but Mac had to understand how to be over all the department heads and had to understand completely what every job entailed—sound, lights, rigging, automation, carpentry, and the list went on and on. The whole thing was pretty impressive, especially considering he had started out in the same theater as a teenager and had just picked up his knowledge as he went along. I understood what a difficult position he was in—and that I wasn't making it any easier on him.

"I like challenges, apparently." He had started playing with his lighter as he spoke—a Zippo lighter with a top that he kept flicking open and closed. It was silver and seemed to have some kind of engraving on the front that I couldn't quite make out.

"Look, as far as my illusion goes . . ." I felt compelled to bring up the issue that started our problems, but before I could even finish my sentence he cut me off.

"It's okay," he said. "As much as it goes against my better judgment, and how I personally feel, I was overruled. I just don't want anything like what just happened to Sofia to happen to you, too. I don't know how to help you if I don't know what's going on. I don't know what the signs of 'going wrong' even are." He spoke with care and concern, instead of with ego and haughtiness. I bit my lip and struggled with how I should respond.

"I understand. It's just a, um . . . closely guarded tradition. I mean . . . uh . . . family secret. Something I shouldn't . . . I mean *can't*—" I was babbling. I don't even think I was making any sense and was getting visibly flustered.

He noticed my panic and cut me off abruptly—though not rudely. "It's fine. We'll work something out that makes you and me both comfortable, okay? Smoke signals or something. I'm not going to pretend to understand why it's such a big deal, but it obviously is to you. Penn & Teller have an illusion that's called the bullet trick. There is hardly anyone, including their crew, who knows how that one is done either, so I'm just going to learn to deal with it."

I smiled and nodded. He wasn't nearly as insufferable as I had originally thought. *Did we actually agree on something?*

*No, wait. We agreed on* two *things and we had just had our first normal conversation, and it wasn't bad. It was nice, even—and he was almost charming.* I was so blown away by what had just happened that I couldn't think of anything clever to say, so I just smiled and said, "Thanks." We were both silent for a moment and I found myself swinging my legs off the dock. When I'm nervous I get fidgety. I looked up and tried to see the stars. The buildings on the strip are so large and bright that it actually makes it harder to see the stars in the night sky. I guess it's true what they say: the darkness helps everyone see the light.

The stars in Tennessee are bright and beautiful and, at dusk, the lightning bugs come out and make everything seem magical. That was one of the things I missed about home, the majestic evenings. There isn't even one lightning bug in the whole state of Nevada. I sighed and noticed that while I had been thinking about southern nights and home, we had both been sitting silently for a few minutes—and it had begun to feel awkward. He must have felt it too, so he changed the subject.

"I play guitar, too. That's usually what I do on my days off. Play my guitar, see movies, or ride my motorcycle through the desert." I stared at him. It was like he was describing me. How could two people who had butted heads from the moment they met, be so alike and have so much in common?

"Sounds like what I do. What kind of bike do you have?" I asked.

He tilted his head. "Triumph Daytona." He said it, but it sounded like he wasn't sure I would understand. I knew exactly what it was. I nodded.

"Nice, I love those. Super fast. Have you ever hit its top speed? They can go, like, one-sixty, right?" I bubbled with excitement when I mentioned the top speed. I love going fast. I like riding my own bike but I shocked even myself when I started to think how it might be fun to be on the back of his bike while going that fast.

"That's what they say—and I may have come pretty close to that," he said with a twinkle in his eye and with an impressed tone to his voice. *I knew the last thing he thought I would know was the top speed of his crotch rocket.* "What about you, do you have a bike?" He leaned in a little and cracked a big smile.

"I have two. One's back home in Tennessee. It's just a classic cafe racer. It's also a Triumph, a 1969 Triumph Trophy 250. It's really fun to ride but not super fast. When I got the job out here I bought myself a present. The Triumph Dakota is too heavy for me so I got myself a Ducati Streetfighter. It's not too shabby but it only has a top speed of 143. So far I've probably only topped out at around a hundred." I shrugged and hoped I didn't sound too nerdy.

"Impressive, Magi Girl." He chuckled. I'd never noticed that he had such a great smile—probably because this was the first conversation we had ever had where I had seen him smile—*actually* smile. His laugh was ever better, though. At the same time, I didn't like being called "Magi Girl" even if it did make him laugh. It has such a stigma, the term Magi actually means something like "wise," but in the magic world Magi more or less means a magician's assistant. Mac added his own twist by adding girl on the end. I guess it wasn't really an insult, but I still made a face that showed my dislike for it.

"Really? You gonna start calling me that?" I whined.

"I don't know. Nicknames are funny; time will tell if it sticks. What is 'Zade,' anyway? Is that a nickname?" He pulled out another cigarette and lit it before shoving the lighter back into his pocket. He pulled up one of his legs and wrapped his right arm around it while holding the cigarette in his left. He took a puff while I began to talk.

"Zade is short for my full name—Scheherazade Holder. It comes from a story my mom used to read to me as a kid. It's about a princess who marries this king who executes his bride each night so he can get a new one the next day. Well, Scheherazade ends up his bride. To stay alive, she tells him a story every night, always stopping at dawn with a cliffhanger, so he will leave her alive for another day. After 1,001 nights he was madly in love with her and decided to keep her. And they lived happily ever after." I looked over at him. He was still listening intently. "Do you know it?"

"It's from *Arabian Nights*. That's a great story. But isn't that kind of harsh for a kid's story though? My mom read me *Green Eggs and Ham*." I wasn't sure if he was making fun of me or not with his last comment. I didn't think it was a harsh story. I thought it was romantic and sweet. Maybe he was right; maybe that wasn't the most appropriate story for a normal eight-year-old. Then again, I was never normal—and neither was my family.

"It was my parents' favorite story. Apparently it was one of the few things they agreed on." I defended their choice of bed-time story. I wasn't so sure that Dr. Seuss wasn't dark at times as well, but I couldn't think of a good example in the moment. I do remember reading all the original versions of Aesop's *Fables* and those stories in their original forms make *Arabian Nights* seem pretty pale in comparison, come to think about it.

"I'm afraid to ask but now I have to. What's your middle name?" He grinned again. I realized it was harder to stay mad at him when he smiled at me. He should have led with that when we first met, not that I was ever going to admit that to him.

"Esther. She was another queen. She only saved her entire race," I said matter-of-factly.

"Quite the namesakes to live up to," Mac said seriously.

I had never actually thought of it that way. I wondered if my parents realized that they had given me that burden. It was something I might have to ask my mom about later. "Well, I'm not trying to live up to anything. What about you; why do they call you Mac?" I had actually been wondering that since I met him. I was pretty sure his parents hadn't actually named him Mac, unless they owned Apple or something

"It's a nickname. They started calling me 'MacGyver' and then it got shortened to Mac. I'm great at fixing things with whatever is lying around."

"So what's your real name?"

He laughed. "I don't just tell people that. You have to earn the right to know."

"I told you *my* real name," I explained, hoping that even though it was a flimsy reason it was good enough to earn his secret.

I was just about to try to come up with another reason he needed to tell me when he blurted out: "It's Clark." He looked directly at me.

It took me a moment to put two and two together on why that might be an interesting name. Clark on its own was common, and his last name Kent on its own was common as well, but "Clark Kent" was a whole different story.

I gushed. "Wait. Your parents named you 'Clark Kent'? As in Superman, Clark Kent?" I was a little surprised. No wonder that's not how he usually introduces himself.

"Yeah, they too have a favorite story. My dad always said that as a kid he knew if he had a son that's what he would name him. My dad has a sense of humor. Not sure how he talked my mom into it."

I laughed a little. "Superman and MacGyver. Those are quite the namesakes to live up to, as well." I nodded in agreement to my own statement.

"*Tad to Mac*," came over the handset that rested clipped to his shoulder. He grabbed it and pressed the button before talking into it. "Go for Mac."

Tad's voice came back over the handset. "*Dude, you better get yourself on deck, A.S.A.P. I found the glitch, but the board is going haywire now.*"

"Copy that. On the move." Mac looked at me, smiling again before saying, "Gotta run, Ms Scheherazade Esther Holder."

"Go save the day, MacGyver . . . Superman . . . whoever you are." I suddenly realized I had been enjoying the conversation and didn't actually want him to leave. Mac jumped up and started to bolt back inside. He had just reached the door when he quickly turned around.

"By the way, 'Red Vines'!" he said quickly.

"Huh?"

"That's my favorite Aimee Mann song—and candy." I laughed. I was starting to feel a little freaked out by everything we had in common. I wondered if we were friends now. I mean . . . I'm not saying that we were going to hang out and braid each other's hair or anything, but at least I was getting the feeling that he didn't hate me, anymore. I decided to take that as a win.

"Good to know. 'Going Through the Motions'—and cotton candy," I said, smiling. He turned around, grabbed the handle to the door, pulled it open, and left.

I grabbed my guitar and started strumming "Red Vines." I couldn't have been out on the dock alone for more than a few seconds when Jackson came out to the dock as well.

"Found you. I came looking for you to see how you were. By the way that was incredible. You never cease to amaze me."

I blushed at the generous compliment. "Thanks." *I will never be good at accepting compliments but I need to learn how to say something better than* thanks. *That's always such a lame answer.*

Jackson seemed to notice that I had taken him up on the offer of borrowing his acoustic guitar and pointed at it before commenting, "Glad to see the guitar is getting some use. Mind if I sit down?" I nodded my head and blushed again. He sat next to me on the dock but much closer than Mac had sat. Jackson's leg was pressed against mine.

"Have you heard anything? She okay?" I heard myself asking.

Mac's conversation had temporarily made me forget what had happened with Sofia. Jackson's compliment while very kind, also jarred me back into the reality of what had happened earlier—and why I was even sitting outside.

Jackson hung his head. "She'll never recover. Permanently damaged."

I nearly dropped the guitar. "What?"

Jackson grinned. "Her ego." I stared blankly. "Oh, you meant *physically*? A small concussion, the need for a few stitches, and a bruised backside, but she's fine."

I nodded. My heart slowed to its normal pace. I was relieved she was fine, even if she was god-awful to me. "For Riley's sake, I'm glad." I pursed my lips as I mulled over my comment. I hoped it hadn't come out the wrong way.

Jackson interjected, "Oh, her backside will heal—but, as I mentioned, her ego is now permanently bruised from you saving her life." He laughed. I guess he didn't take my comment about it being for Riley in the wrong way.

I started thinking about how Sofia had freaked out and pushed me away as I was saving her life—and her instant blame for it even being my fault. Even though there was no way for it to have been my fault. I could feel my face scrunch up as I huffed, "I think somehow she would have preferred I let her drown."

Jackson put his hand on my back and soothingly said, "Relax. I'm sure she'll get over it."

I sighed. Without any sort of sincerity, I wondered out loud, "Here's hoping."

Jackson stood up and ran his fingers through his thick, wavy hair. "We should probably get back inside, I'm sure there's some work to get done."

"Yeah, you're probably right," I remarked.

"Shall we?" he asked, offering me his hand to help me up. I grabbed his hand and pulled myself up. Once we were both standing he looked me directly in the eyes and softly smiled. I smiled back at him. I wondered what he was thinking, but he decided to share the thoughts behind the smile. "You're pretty amazing, you know that?" I chuckled nervously and blushed. I started biting my lower lip and shifted my feet.

Jackson grinned before adding, "You really are."

# CHAPTER 5

# THE EMPEROR

SEVERAL OF THE CAST AND CREW GATHERED AT *McMullan's bar for a birthday celebration for Drew, one of the audio guys. It was the spot frequented by everyone if there was any kind of hint of going out after work. This usually happened if there was a birthday or any other celebratory event—as well as on the show's "Friday" (which for the show has always actually been Tuesday night, since the show is "dark" on Wednesday and Thursday). I had learned that most shows don't take their days off on the weekend because that's when they sell the most tickets to shows and when Las Vegas, itself, is the busiest. So each shows "dark days" are not usually Saturday and Sunday, and each show in town takes a different "weekend," so no tourist will ever come to Vegas and find no one is doing a show.*

*McMullan's is really where most of the cast and crew for all the major shows on the Strip go after work, because although it's not on the Strip it's easy to get to. They give drink specials after midnight just for those of us awesome enough to work in this so- called "entertainment business."*

*Drew from the audio department for the show is a pretty good audio tech. He's nice and sometimes awkward but still generally liked, so most everyone showed up to hang out. Mac was sitting at a small table by himself with an almost-empty beer. He looked particularly tired and worn out from the long day. The conversation he had had the night before with Zade was still tossing around in his head. Had he made peace with the enemy? His hand was wrapped around the handle of his beer mug and he was swirling around the little bit of beer and foam left in the bottom. Sofia walked up with two glasses and slid one of the new beers in front of Mac right as he finished the last of the beer he had. She then placed her beer on the table directly in front of the empty chair next to Mac and, without asking if he minded, sat down next to him.*

*"Looked like you could use another one," Sofia purred as she smiled sweetly and leaned in to him.*

*Mac looked down at the new frosty beer sitting right in front of him before looking back up at Sofia, who was staring directly into his eyes. "Uh . . . thanks. I really was only going to have the* one." Mac claimed, looking somewhat confused as to why she even bought him one.

"The bartender said it's your favorite. One more won't hurt, will it?" She batted her long eyelashes and puckered her lips.

"Guess not? Glad to see you are better already. That was quite the spill you took last night. Hope you learned your lesson about not wearing a harness," Mac quipped. He took a sip of the beer and tried to edge away from sitting quite so close to Sofia without being obvious that was what he was doing. He truly wanted to give her a really hard time about not wearing the harness—and how dangerous it was and how she truly almost died—but he knew she wouldn't listen anyway, so why bother?

"I'm a quick healer and I have good genes . . . and, yes, I did," Sofia proclaimed, obviously wanting to gloss over the part where she had to admit she had done something wrong. The "yes, I did" part might have been in regards to him talking about her learning the lesson about the harness, but her answer was awkward. She stared at Mac like she was waiting for him to say something else. Mac figured she wanted something—which was why she had bought him a beer and come over—so he waited for her to ask her question. After several moments, Mac realized that either he was wrong and she didn't have anything to ask him about or she was still working up the nerve to ask about whatever it was. He decided it must be the latter; she'd never just been nice to him. Mac *figured it must be something big or else something that she knew he would hate if she was trying to work up the nerve to ask him. He had already begun to dread it, whatever it was, and figured his only hope was that it wouldn't be as bad to him as she thought.*

*Sitting in awkward silence until she worked up her liquid courage enough to ask also seemed like a terrible plan, so just to end the awkwardness Mac pondered out loud why she was out at the bar without her other half.*

*"Where's C.S.? I thought you didn't go places by yourself?" Mac questioned.*

*"Who said that?" Sofia scoffed with an over-exaggerated look of shock on her face.*

*Mac laughed just a bit, shook his head slightly, and dryly answered. "You did."*

*"Oh. Well. I don't like to, but you know he doesn't like local bar gatherings." Sofia rolled her eyes as she clarified in a rather snobbish tone. Mac seemed to digest the words and analyze what she was saying. He quickly realized what she had commented was probably truer than even she realized.*

*"He feels awkward in social settings that are genuine. I get it," Mac observed assuredly.*

*"What do you mean?" Sofia asked, confused as to how Mac had come to that conclusion based off of what she had just mentioned.*

"*Premieres, press events—those are fake social settings. Everyone's pretending, and that's what he knows how to do. Real friends celebrating someone's birthday? That's genuine. He doesn't know how to do that,*" *Mac explained, and then stared at the table. His mind had drifted off to his own issues about genuine interaction with people and how much he couldn't stop thinking about his conversation with Zade. He couldn't remember the last time he had enjoyed being around anyone (male or female) in such a long time and that was scary to him. He had woken up yesterday morning basically hating her, so the jump from hate to not hate . . . well, it took some processing.*

"*Wow. Look how observant you are,*" *Sofia complimented Mac, even though it was clear what he was saying about Charles had mostly gone over her head. She then placed her hand over his hand lightly and began to rub it. The physical contact from Sofia jolted Mac out of his mental contemplation about Zade. He started to think that perhaps he was wrong; she didn't seem to want a favor. She seemed to be hitting on him and—if that were the case—well, he'd rather she had needed a favor. He decided he would still hold out hope that maybe she was trying to butter him up for whatever favor she needed. The other option was that she was hitting on him—and he felt very uneasy about that being a possibility. Either way, he knew he should try hard not to upset her too much. He knew how difficult she could make his life if he was mean to her.*

*He figured he'd let the conversation go just a bit longer and see if she did have some kind of request.*

*He eyed her uncomfortably. "Eh. I just understand how he feels."*

*Sofia scooted her chair closer to Mac's and looked longingly into his eyes. She started to play with his collar. "I bet you understand a lot of things," she offered, breathing in deeply in the way a girl does to purposely draw attention to her cleavage.*

*Mac was finally sure that Sofia was hitting on him, and there appeared to be no favor she was trying to ask. He turned himself around enough to face her directly and pulled himself up so he was no longer leaning in to the table. This also put more space between them.*

*"Sofie, what are you doing?" he asked in a harsh tone.*

*Sofia looked surprised that he had pulled away from her. She sat back up, so she was no longer leaning in either. "I'm not doing anything." She huffed, trying to act insulted.*

*"Sofie, don't hit on me. I don't know if you are just flirting, or if you're being serious—or a little bit of both—but it makes me uncomfortable," he scolded.*

*Sofia pouted. "I was just trying to be friends."*

*Mac licked his lips and retorted, "I've been friends with Tad since junior high, and he's never tried to sit next to me like that." He sighed, trying to remain calm with her, despite quickly losing* his patience. "Look, Sofia. You're beautiful and all, but we work together, and you're my boss's girlfriend . . . . We're also at a company function. I know that nothing is going to happen, but people talk around here and rumors get started. I don't want anyone to get the wrong idea. I don't think you do either." His words were flat and toneless.

"Would it make a difference if I was single?" she coaxed.

Mac stared at her for a moment—almost as if he was either considering her question or thinking of how best to word his response, or maybe a little bit of both. He took a deep breath and looked her square in the eye.

"No, it wouldn't. It would only make a difference in how long I would allow you to flirt. And before you ask whether it would make a difference if we didn't work together—again, you're beautiful, and many guys would kill to be with you, but we lead very different lives. You wouldn't be happy with a guy like me, and deep down you know that." Mac paused, stood up, and drank the last of the beer that she had brought him before placing his glass back on the table. He smiled. "Thanks for the beer. I'll make sure to buy you one at the next get together. Okay?"

It almost seemed like it had been planned that, at that exact moment, Mel, another girl Mel, who worked for the show, walked around the corner with a large cake lit with candles. The chocolate fondant cake looked heavy and even though she had both *arms underneath the bottom of it she seemed wobbly. There was a microphone sitting on top with the words "Happy Birthday Drew" written in thick silver icing. Cam, who had been sitting at a table behind Mac and Sofia took an empty glass and a fork and began to tap it so that everyone stopped talking. Mac started to follow Mel towards the center of the room where Drew was standing, then found himself a spot right next to Zeb and struck up a light conversation. Once Cam got everyone's attention he shouted, "Hey, MOCS Cast and Crew! Let's all gather around and sing 'Happy Birthday' to Drew!"*

I had been rehearsing my spot in the show where I get to show off that I can dive from sixty feet in the air into a small area of water. I had just hurled myself off the platform and used my hands to break the water before allowing my body to fall into the pool. The liquid rushed all around me and, for a moment, I was floating, feeling calm and free. That moment is the most relaxed I know how to feel. I always wait until I am completely out of air before swimming back to the surface. The dive is actually my favorite part in the show for several reasons but mostly because I love diving and the water in general—especially in a theater where it is always a warm ninety degrees. A part of me wanted to stay in the soothing water all day but I knew that I needed to get out and dry myself off, since it was almost time to get ready for the show. I pulled myself out of the pool and onto the stage.

As I stood up and shook my hair lightly and watched the water droplets from my hair fall to the ground, I realized that Mac was standing there, like always, with his clipboard. He looked up at me, smiling. Ever since the Sofia incident he had stopped being mean to me. It went even beyond that: not only was he not mean, he had started being *nice*. It hadn't been an overnight thing but over the past few weeks he seemed to have slowly become sweeter to me—it was almost as if we were friends. He didn't seem to dread to see or talk to me anymore, and wasn't always bolting in the opposite direction when I was headed his way. I wasn't trying to avoid him, either, and was getting to the point where I just about looked forward to seeing him.

One day, I brought in a package of red vines and left them on his desk. Sure, they had been two-for-one at the store, but I sorta even surprised myself when I ended up giving him one of the packages. He seemed really happy about it and—if I'm being honest—I liked that it made him happy. Along the way, he had stopped bringing up the need to know about my illusion, which was great too, because he just couldn't know. I had actually started to wish slightly that I could tell him, but I knew that that just wasn't possible—and I had to remind myself that I should stop even thinking about it. I smiled back at him, staring into those hazel eyes that seemed to sparkle when the stage lights hit them. I felt my grin get larger, which made me blush.

"You like the water?" he asked.

"Huh?" I wasn't exactly sure what he meant by that and, in the midst of getting lost in his hazel eyes, maybe I'd missed some of his words.

"You seem to like to swim and all," Mac remarked, still smiling at me.

"Oh. Yeah, I love it," I agreed as I continued to dry my hair with the towel I kept on the side of the pool.

"Ever been scuba diving?" I could tell that he had tried to ask nonchalantly, but the question seemed to have a motive behind it.

"Yeah. I like anything that puts me in the water—and the longer I can stay the better." I wasn't really sure why he was asking me about scuba diving in Las Vegas, but he still seemed pensive, like he had a purpose.

Tad walked up and took the clipboard from Mac's hands. He began to look over it, not paying much attention to our conversation—or us. Whatever was on the clipboard must have been important and Tad was examining it pretty carefully. Mac glanced at me and back at Tad as if he were trying to work up the nerve to ask me something. I stared back at him with the best "Go ahead,

I'm nice. Ask me." look I had. Finally he worked up the nerve and blurted out, "Sometimes the crew goes camping, and we take our scuba gear and go diving out in Lake Mead on dark days. It's fun. You'll have to come out with us sometime . . . eh . . . if you want." Mac smiled again and ran his left hand through his thick hair. Every time I heard the term "dark days" it made me slightly excited. I loved the term loved the term dark days as the way to talk about days off for shows. It just made me think about how I was now a part of the show world and terms like that were now in my everyday vocabulary. I had to wonder, though: had Mac just asked me out or not? It seemed more like a "come out on this group outing" sort of ask, but at the same time it also seemed a little like a more personal invitation from him. I realized he was standing there waiting on me to respond—and even Tad had looked up, realizing that I hadn't responded.

With both of them basically staring at me, I said the first thing I could think of. "Sure. Sounds like fun. What's the depth of the lake like?" In retrospect, it was kind of a dumb question but I had been scrambling to say anything at that point. I had also never been out to the lake and truly was curious how good the diving was.

"A hundred feet, at least. Some places are even more than that."

"Wow, I didn't know it was that deep."

"'Course, I'm always willing to go deeper," Mac said innocently. I blushed right away.

"Oh! Really?" I giggled and tried to hide my face, pretending to go back to drying my hair. I didn't think he meant it the way it could have been taken but, either way, it's where my mind immediately went and what I thought when he said it. I couldn't help but turn bright red.

I think Mac realized the other way his words could have been taken as well and must have noticed how red I turned. He too now looked embarrassed and started to blush, too.

"Oh. Yeah," he said as he laughed and tried not to look me in the eye.

"Mac, just go ahead and insert your foot into your mouth." Tad laughed at him, entering our conversation for the first time and definitely helping to break the uncomfortable situation that had been created.

"Copy that," Mac said as he raised his eyebrows and nodded his head lightly. The look on his face was "Okay, let's all just ignore whatever I said." I felt bad that he looked like he wanted to melt into the floor, so I decided to help him out. I needed to go get ready, anyway.

"Well, let me know the next time you guys are going; I'd love to go," I said as I smiled and walked away.

Tad started shaking his head. "I'm surprised you didn't ask her if she likes being wet!"

"Dude, I wasn't even thinking like that. I should not be allowed to talk to women, apparently," Mac said, embarrassed.

"I thought you didn't like her?" Tad teased.

"I don't. Just tryin' to keep the peace."

"I don't know if you're just lying to me or if you're lying to yourself, too," Tad commented.

"Look. She's okay, I guess. I'll give it to you that she's very attractive, but I don't date performers, and she and I wouldn't happen—even if she wasn't a performer."

"Rules are made to be broken," Tad replied. "And why wouldn't you date her if she wasn't a performer?"

"Cause she's—"

"Just as stubborn as you are?" Tad finished.

"She's not my type."

"What is your type? 'Cause if she ain't it, then I don't know what is." Tad's lighthearted jabs had turned to confusion.

"Even if I did like her—which I don't—what makes you think she likes me—or that she doesn't already have someone?"

"I can tell she doesn't have anyone," Tad said confidently. Mac gave him a look. He didn't buy that Tad could just "tell." You learn things about people when you've been best friends most of your lives. That's one of the many reasons Tad and Mac were so close: they instantly *could call each other on their bullshit. Mac tilted his head, waiting for Tad to tell the truth. Tad made a face and then added, "Okay. Maybe I've asked her and maybe she told me she's single. Also she gets just as worked up as you do about everything and anything to do with you. You aren't that passionate about anything unless it runs deep. It's just a matter of time."*

*"Don't hold your breath."*

*Tad looked at Mac and scoffed, "I'll bet you $100 you end up making out with her before the end of the year." Tad put his hand out to shake Mac's.*

*Mac made a face. "Oh, really?" he retorted. He reached for Tad's hand, but before Mac could shake it, Tad rethought what he just said and pulled his hand away.*

*"Actually, no. I take that back. If we bet, you would* not *do it just to win and spite your own happiness. So no, I won't bet you, but I still say it happens." Tad frowned and furrowed his eyebrows. He couldn't understand why Mac wouldn't just admit it to himself.*

# CHAPTER 6

# THE MOON

A FEW DAYS LATER, I JOINED THE CAST AND CREW ON one of the camping trips Mac had mentioned. I have always loved the outdoors, but I've never been particularly good at basic survival skills.

I should have probably put my tent up right when we got there, but instead went swimming and messed about till it was after dark. I'd been trying to put up my tent for nearly forty-five minutes in the blackness of night, and I was getting frustrated. I knew I could have asked someone for help, but it had gone on too long. My pride wouldn't allow it. I restrung a rod through the holes in the tent and stabbed it into the ground, dashing up to run around to the other side. The rod hung in place for a moment, then collapsed again.

"Damn!"

On the other side of the tent, I tried again, successfully grounding two corners. As I stood again to raise the first side I'd been working on, the tent fell back to the ground.

"Hell's bells," I muttered.

"Need a hand?" A friendly voice came from the dark behind me. I jumped.

"Riley! Oh God, you scared me." I clutched my chest. "No, thanks. I've got it." I grinned at him.

"Suit yourself," he said, and shrugged as he looked at my pile of tent materials. I grinned again and he walked off, rejoining the others.

The campfire glowed warm and orange in the dark night, and the stars were shining brightly against the night sky. I'd begun to get used to being in Las Vegas, where it's actually hard to see the stars because of the bright lights that are everywhere. Apparently, moonlight and large glittery casino lights drown out all but the brightest stars. At least out here by the lake they could shine brightly and sparkled with such beauty. I think no matter how old I get I will always be amazed how stars take my breath away. It reminds me of a quote that I've always loved: "[A] star is a huge flaming ball of gas. . . . [T]hat is not what a star is, but only what it is made of." What we are made of and what we are, are not there same.

People also think that Vegas is hot all the time, but it is a desert, so at night it cools down pretty quickly and the air at our camp site almost had a brisk chill to it. I was happy to be out here feeling like I belonged even just a little bit, though I was nervous. A group of the crew and some of the cast were sitting around the campfire. Most of them were drinking beer and a few were cooking.

At that exact moment, I wished I had a guy. If I had been dating someone, anyone, then he would have also been sleeping in the tent with me—and therefore helping me put it together. Not that I couldn't do it by myself, but I liked the idea of having someone to do things with. Things like this and other things. I was fiercely independent but that doesn't mean I always want to do things alone. I looked around, making sure no one else was right around me. I looked down at the tent that was not remotely a tent at the moment—just a pile of plastic and tarp on the ground. I rarely, if ever, used my magick for mundane things, but thought maybe it wouldn't hurt to use it just once.

I looked around one more time to make sure I wasn't in sight of anyone. I rubbed my hands together and thought hard about the tent rising and assembling itself. I waved my hands in elliptical motions, replaying that image in my mind. In a few seconds, my tent had risen by itself and was sitting securely on its own. I looked at it contently. *Not too shabby*, I thought, pretty pleased with myself.

With my tent up and put together with the sleeping bag inside (figured I might as well throw that in, too), I was good to go on the "place to sleep" front. I headed toward the campfire to join everyone else. When I reached the campfire I noticed Jackson and Zeb sitting next to each other talking. They were sitting close enough to the fire that the warm glow reflected off of Jackson's face making him look almost angelic. For a split second, though, the glow off of Zeb's face somehow made him look just a tad . . . evil.

Jackson looked up at me before scooting over to allow space for me to sit down and offered me a beer. Zeb instantly looked annoyed that their conversation had been interrupted and he stood up. Without acknowledging me, he said, "I think I'm going to go stretch my legs for a bit. I'll talk to you later, Jackson." As he stomped away, he barely looked at me and grumbled "Zade" as a sort of half hello.

"Uhh. Bye, Zeb," I said sadly before I took the beer and smiled softly. "Why does Zeb not like me?" I asked as I sat down. The moment I was seated Jackson slid back toward me, taking away any extra space that had between us. The sides of our thighs were now touching. He leaned in. His eyes flashed.

"It's not that he doesn't like you. He's just used to cast and crew kind of coming and going, so he waits to warm up to people. He'll come around eventually. And, in my experience, when he does, he's awesome. He's brilliant and will become your favorite person. It just takes time with him." Jackson nodded.

"I hope so," I said glancing off in the direction Zeb had gone.

I guess Jackson wanted to change the subject and quickly changed gears to ask the mundane question. "Do you *like* camping? Are you an outdoorsy kind of girl? I mean . . . I kinda thought your tent was gonna take you down in the fourth round."

I thought about his question for a moment. I wouldn't ever have labeled myself as such but I guess to a certain extent, yes, I was an "outdoorsy type" girl. After all, witches tend to have to spend a lot of time outside. I nodded. "Yeah. I've spent a decent amount of time in the woods—and it's nice to see something other than the inside of the theater."

"Are you sick of the theater already?" Jackson wondered aloud.

I laughed. That wasn't what I had meant, but I could see why he would jump to that conclusion. I quickly clarified, "Oh, God, no. I love it. I just like being outdoors, too. Feels like home."

Jackson nodded, "Where's home, for you?"

My mind danced to a place where the weather was far more humid, every restaurant served sweet tea and more fried things that you could shake a stick at, biscuits and gravy were a breakfast staple, and people talked with a slow drawl. I guess as much as I loved it here and my new life, there were things I missed. "Tennessee," I replied.

Jackson seemed to be reading my mind, his next comment and question were exactly in line with what I had been thinking. "That's a ways away. You miss it?"

I could have gone on and on about the things I did miss and the things that existed that caused me to leave—though I couldn't tell him a lot of it, either. Instead I figured I'd simplify the answer. I responded with: "Sometimes I do, but it's kind of one of those things where I knew that if I didn't get out soon, I'd never leave. You know?"

Jackson nodded. "Copy that." I'd learned that that was an expression a lot of the crew said a lot in place of "okay." It's radio lingo that had made its way into regular conversation. It was funny to hear at first but I had gotten used to it. I even kind of liked it.

"I miss my mom a lot though. Even though she drives me crazy," I added. I did miss her. We hadn't really talked since I had left. I knew she didn't like that I was in Vegas—and I was sure she didn't really want to hear any stories about the show that she wasn't happy I was out here working for, so I didn't have much to say. I sighed a little.

Jackson replied rhetorically, "Isn't that what families are for?" I laughed and Jackson and I clinked our bottles together in agreement. At that moment, I noticed Mac getting up from where he had been sitting nearby and saunter off to lean on a tree away from the glow of the fire—and from the rest of us crowded around it. He looked a little upset as he crossed on the other side of the fire and walked away. I couldn't help but wonder why. He stayed close enough to where he could see us and therefore we could see him, which was also curious. I thought about getting up and going over to him when I saw Tad join him. They were too far away for me to hear them to know what they were talking about, so I stayed put, talking to Jackson.

Tad wasn't with Mac for very long, so whatever they talked about only lasted a couple of minutes before Tad made his way back to the group of us by the fire. Tom, one of the other members of the show's band had come over to where Jackson and I were sitting and seemed eager to speak to Jackson about something. I took my cue and, after glancing back over at Mac—who made eye contact with me and half smiled—I decided it was a good time to get up and go join him.

As the night had progressed, the desert air had gotten chillier and more crisp. Mac had on a slightly puffy jacket with the collar turned up, and he looked rather "Abercrombie and Fitch" leaned up against the tree. I realized this was also the first time I had seen him out of his work attire: his standard black Dickies and a black button down, his "show blacks," or his occasional Carhartts if he was doing something more mechanical that day. Instead, he was wearing fitted Levi jeans with the bottoms of the legs slightly rolled up and a long-sleeve red, blue, and yellow linen plaid shirt. Earlier in the day I had noticed that he had the plaid shirt unbuttoned, showing a white ribbed fitted sleeveless shirt underneath. In the south those types of white undershirts are often called "wife beaters." It's a horrible name for anything really but especially a shirt. Though, in every movie I've ever seen the redneck wife beater wears one, and without a doubt you call it that and people instantly know what kind of shirt you are speaking about. In the cool night air the long sleeves that had been rolled up had come down and he had buttoned up the shirt, covering up the undershirt. The black boots he always wore at work had been replaced with much more rugged-looking brown ones that went higher up the ankle, and he had wrapped his laces around the top. It occurred to me in that moment that I liked his style a lot. He looked somewhat like a hipster, but a hipster that could *actually* hunt and do other manly things most hipsters don't know how to do. A manly hipster without a beard though, thankfully. I was not a fan of beards, and I had come to realize that I liked it most when Mac had just shaved—though in the light from the fire he appeared to have a five o'clock shadow, and that was also nice.

Mac's eyes followed me as I approached him, but he waited for me to get right up to him before he spoke. "Magi Girl," he said as he grinned. It had become a playful nickname that I was starting to not even mind anymore.

"Hey, Superman," I said playfully. I leaned up against the tree facing him; due to the cold I crossed my arms and pinned them against my chest. Mac had one hand jammed into his pocket, while his other was holding a beer close to his face. He chuckled slightly at my response.

"Are you glad you came out?" Mac asked me, staring at the ground while his right boot pushed a small rock across the dirt. Technically, he had been the one to invite me and yet I still wasn't sure with what intention. So far he had made a point of keeping his distance to a certain extent all day—or at least that was how it had seemed. I was getting the feeling that he had just invited me to be nice, not for anything more, as I at one point had thought.

"Yeah. It's nice to hang out with people and pretend as if I have friends." I fidgeted. I paused for a moment before adding, "Are *you* glad I came?" I immediately regretted the question, and it seemed like a pretty silly thing to ask once I actually uttered it out loud.

"Yeah. I am. You're not so bad to be around, when we aren't at work." He shoved me just a little bit with his shoulder and bit his lower lip.

"Oh. Am I really the worst one at work to be around?" I grinned and asked teasingly. I was, at the very least, sure I wasn't his biggest aggravation at work as of late.

Riley walked up and, without seeming to notice that we were in a conversation, interrupted. "Mac, you gotta come check this out." Riley apparently assumed that Mac was going to be right behind him because he immediately turned around and headed back in the other direction before Mac had actually agreed to follow him.

"Nope. There are worse ones for sure . . . and here come some now." He pointed at Sofia and another performer, Mel, who were walking toward the tree Mac and I had been posted up on. Mac quickly shouted after Riley, "On the move, kid." He called out over his shoulder to me. "I'll be back." He winked at me when he turned around, which surprised me, and I was still caught up in that feeling of surprise when Sofia reached me and put her arm around me. Mel, who was probably Sofia's closest friend, flanked me on the other side. I had no idea why they had cornered me, but Sofia's grip on my shoulder told me she wasn't going to let go of me easily. It was awkward right away and for a few moments no one said anything, perhaps they were waiting for Mac and Riley to be out of earshot.

"You're wasting your time, honey," Sofia said with some sort of weird empathy in her tone that was similar to how you break the news to a twelve-year-old that her dog had just died.

"What are you talking about?" I asked. I had no idea what she was even referring to as far as what I might be "wasting my time" about, not to mention the strange new behavior from Sofia who had, so far, ignored or snubbed me when we were at the theater. Maybe she was trying to be nicer since I had saved her life. Somehow I doubted that, considering she still hadn't even thanked me—or even apologized for being mean and pushing me away when I was in the middle of saving her life.

"Mel and I see you flirting with Mac," Sofia said softly as she batted her eyes and me.

Mel interjected flippantly, "Not dating performers is a rule of his. I'm sure you've heard about them by now. The man *lives by* his rules. Don't take it personally." While Mel spoke, her head shook from side to side. It made me wonder if she had anything inside of it, or if it just kind of bobbled around with empty space.

I was more than uncomfortable already and decided that I was going to end the intervention quick. I didn't have the patience tonight to placate them, so I wiggled my way out from under Sofia's grip and turned to face them both. I was already on the defensive from the second they walked up, and I realized I had been fidgeting somewhat as I stood there. "I'm not trying to date Mac, or anyone else for that matter. I'm just trying to get along with everyone."

"Sure," said Mel, "if that's what you tell yourself to sleep at night. You can't fool us though. You're totally into him."

"Look. We get it," Sofia said as she smiled. "We both tried to tame that rugged exterior at one point, and if *we* couldn't break him, then don't think you'll change him either."

I was starting to get pissed. I'm not sure why they thought that they were so above me, or why if they never were able to have him that meant I couldn't either. I really wasn't trying to date him, I was just happy to be getting along with him now. Maybe I did think he was cute and fun. We did have quite a bit in common—but that didn't matter either. I wanted to spit in their faces for their backhanded insults.

"Well, as we say in the South, bless your heart ... and ... uhh ... thanks for the advice, or whatever you're calling it, but we are just friends. If I was after him, as you've stated, then I promise you I would have better luck than either of you." After the words came out of my mouth I was actually surprised that I had been so bold to both of them. I was proud of myself though. I stood and stared back at them waiting for their response. Zade: one; stupid girls: zero.

Mel seemed offended as she snapped back: "You actually think you're hotter than either one of us?" Mel licked her lips and narrowed her eyes as she crossed her arms and tilted her head. I contemplated my options for a moment to make sure my answer was truly a good answer—not just something spiteful.

"Physically?" I replied. "No, not a chance. You're both far more beautiful than I am, if we're talking about the outside. But have you ever bothered to see what you look like on the inside? There's a song called 'Ugly Girl' that I swear is about both of you. I'll play it for you sometime." Sometimes I wished I could be the star in my own movie so at moments like that the song I was thinking of (in this case by the band 100 Monkeys) could start playing. I looked at each of them and then turned sharply and walked away in the same direction that Mac had gone. I didn't want to be there anymore talking to them so I decided that I was going somewhere—anywhere that wasn't with them.

*Mel asked, "Why do you care anyway, Sof? So he wouldn't go out with you. He's a tech. He's the king of the techs, I guess, but*

I *only tried to sleep with him, 'cause I'll sleep with anyone that's cute."* Sofia knew that Mel had just gone along with the gang-up on Zade because she had asked her to; Mel didn't really care if Zade went after Mac or not. Mac could marry Zade for all Mel really cared—and she really didn't know why Sofia cared either.

"I don't like her, and if they start dating she'll end up more privileged than she already is," Sofia replied, resentful of being upstaged in the theater she had claimed as her own. She was bitter and angry and it showed even in the falling darkness.

"So . . . Wait . . . Do you mean that this is 'if I can't have him no one can?' You wouldn't rather be with Mac than Charles, would you? You'd be crazy if that's the case. Sure, he's cute and all, but C.S. . . . . Well . . . You want to give up the red carpet for stage blacks?" Mel had lost all interest in the whole thing and really wanted to go back to flirting with the newly single performer, Parker, who she had her eye on this week.

"No. Of course not," Sofia snapped as she glared off into the distance. Looking to her left she suddenly noticed Jackson. He was holding a beer and leaning against a tree a few feet away. Sofia and Mel hadn't even noticed that he had been there listening to the whole thing, as they had been too intent on harassing Zade. He walked over to where they were standing and looked directly at them.

"If it matters, I don't agree with her. I think she's much hotter on the outside, as well as the inside." Jackson tipped his beer bottle at them and walked away.

Mel scrunched up her face in anger at his comment and Sofia muttered under her breath, "Jerk."

# Chapter 7

# Strength

We rehearsed all the time: it's a huge show that has constant changes, so full rehearsals have always been held weekly. We typically rehearse on weekdays, and usually have to be at the theater by three or four in the afternoon so we can rehearse for a couple of hours before needing to get ready, at six, for the first of the night's two shows, which start at seven. On Saturdays, because we have a matinee at three, there's never a scheduled full rehearsal.

Everyone also needs to have a backup in case they get hurt or need to go to a wedding or gets sick or something, so we rehearse not only our own parts but also each of us has to know several other roles so we can shift around and cover for almost anyone—or a combination of anyones.

Riley and I were up in the catwalk, waiting for our next cue. Riley had duties other than being my rigger—including at the top of the show, when Sofia was up there with us—but he was mainly assigned to me; every scene I had, we were paired together. I realized, as I learned the ropes, that he'd probably asked for me when I got hired, since he was relatively new himself and hadn't been assigned to a main performer yet.

A lot of the time, it was just him and me, which I always liked. Riley and I had grown very close, very quickly; already I loved him like a little brother. I often found myself wishing that he *was* my little brother. I had never wanted to be an only child, but it's not like that's something you got to decide. There was just something about him that made me want to protect him, even though it was actually his job to protect me.

Riley spoke into his headset. "Copy that." He turned to me and made a slight face from the news he'd just heard.

"They are doing a reset of the next scene, so we're up here for a bit."

"I don't mind being stuck up here with you," I said, poking at his shoulder.

"Same here," Riley responded before starting to play with one of his rigging clips.

"Mind if I ask you something though?" I said, hesitantly. I wasn't sure if asking him about this was a good idea, but I had already spoken, so I decided I had better just ask.

"Of course I'll marry you!" Riley laughed, hugging me. I laughed along with him and returned the hug before shoving him away playfully.

"Great," I said as I rolled my eyes, since I knew he was just playing around. "Now that we have that out of the way. Why is Mac so anti dating performers?"

"Ohhh. You have a crush?" Riley teased lightly. I already regretted asking him or even bringing up the subject. I wasn't sure if he would tell Mac or Tad that I had asked, which was the last thing I wanted. I blushed and bit my lip.

"No—just curious. It seems to be such a big deal that everyone seems to knows about it; I figured there must be an interesting story behind it. Just being curious." I shrugged and leaned on the railing and looked over the side. I wondered if I was convincing him at all—or maybe I was trying to convince myself. I pulled at my bangs, searching for split ends, and waited for him to say something. He leaned on the rail beside me, smiling.

"Ah. Well I am sure you know what happened to the cat?" Riley laughed before continuing. "That curiosity could get you in trouble," he teased, and then paused for a moment like he was considering whether he should answer my question. I guess he decided he would, and slowly the expression on his face went from playful to much more serious. He swallowed and got the kind of look that indicated he was even trying to remember exactly what the story was—or at least trying to remember some part of the details.

"So this was before my time, of course, but Tad told me the story one day. I was the cat back then, I guess." He smirked. "The short version is that there was a performer here, Clara Faust. Mac was young and new, and he fell completely in love with her." I waited for Riley to continue, but he seemed to think he had explained everything, so I realized I needed to push for more information.

"So what happened?" I asked.

"I guess one night she ended up sleeping with him, and he thought they were going to be together, and she just thought that it wasn't a big deal. She strung him along and really put him through the ringer by the end of it. I've heard Clara's a terrible person—she makes Sofie look like Mother Teresa." I wondered if Riley was giving me a paraphrased version because that's all he knew, or because he only wanted me to know part of the story.

"Sounds like the reverse of what normally happens." I couldn't imagine a young and naïve Mac madly in love with some girl that was probably a lot like Sofia and Mel. I also couldn't help but wonder what Mac madly in love looked like. He definitely was a passionate person and I was pretty sure "madly in love," for him, was intense. I had never been in love with anyone. I had never gotten close enough to anyone to be in love. *Like*, yes. *Crushes*, plenty. *Love*, no.

"Yeah," Riley nodded. That seemed to be as much as he knew, or at least as much as he was going to tell me. Though my curiosity raged on I chose not to ask any further questions and changed the subject.

Rehearsal came to an end, and for some reason both of the day's shows seemed to fly by quickly. Usually I ended up having some sort of interaction with Mac, but I hadn't seen him all day. It was odd. I had heard he'd come in earlier than usual to help out with some maintenance issues, which I guessed had kept him busy. Maintenance was mostly done by the day crew, which was an entirely separate group that left by three in the afternoon, Monday through Friday. The show crew made up jokes saying that once you had kids that's where you went. Though, actually, since day jobs are rare in the entertainment business the fact you could go there at all was pretty lucky—but sadly that meant we would basically rarely see them again. I didn't even know the names of most of the guys on that shift unless they'd filled in for the show crew, which happened occasionally at some point when someone took a vacation or whenever we were shorthanded.

I didn't even see Mac during the break between shows. Sometimes we used that time to get food together, but I made out okay, since I ended up eating with Jackson.

I had pretty much given up on seeing Mac at all when he and Tad showed up behind me as I was clocking out. I simply turned around and there they were. I waited for the two of them to clock out as well before we headed toward the parking garage. I pulled on the straps of my backpack nervously as I listened to the sound of my jeans making a swishing noise. I couldn't put my finger on why all of a sudden I was nervous, but I was. I wonder if I was sensing something was going to happen.

Mac and Tad were walking with me, but were mainly talking to themselves. I heard Jackson walk up behind us with Tom and Mike, who were both also in the show band. I didn't know them very well, though they seemed nice enough. I thought the band was super talented from what I had seen—and heard, obviously—from them playing at our show. I knew Tom wrote songs and, from what I knew, was really good at it. Mike could play literally any instrument even though, in the band, he was mainly the bass player. Jackson broke away from Mike and Tom and threw his arm around me right as we had reached the parking garage. He squeezed my shoulder.

"So, Zade, you still gonna come see our band play tomorrow?" Jackson asked. He had asked me this earlier when we were eating together in the Employee Dining Room, which we cleverly refer to as the "EDR." He had told me more about the original band that they had, that played their own songs and what they called themselves.

"Oh, yeah, Plain White T's, right?" I hoped I had gotten the name of the band right.

"They are an awesome rock band, really good. Don't let how boring the show music is fool you. They have to play that. Their original stuff is great, but I've heard them play the show music 'til my ears bleed," Tad chimed in, laughing at his own joke.

Jackson joked back, "Well, until you convince Charles to let us play our own stuff instead of the tired show music, you and Leona Lewis's ears will just keep bleedin'." Tad laughed and then went back to talking to me. "A lot of the cast and crew usually go and support them. Riley, Mac, Cam, and I are going for sure."

I had realized that joking around and giving people a hard time in jest was how to fit in around here, and it was my turn. "Oh, Jackson, I'm sorry. I can't go if *they're* going," I teased. I caught Mac's eye and smiled.

Jackson piped in. "Sorry guys, you're officially un-invited. Pretty girl always wins." Jackson shrugged and gave them one of those "pity" looks. Mike made a face and over-exaggerated his voice as he said sarcastically, "Great, that's probably half our audience."

I shook my head and laughed a little. "Okay, Mike, for the good of the band they can be there, too." I winked at Mike, who smiled back.

"So you are coming?" Jackson asked me again. I wondered if this was because he liked me or because he really wanted to promote his band.

"Yeah, I'll come." *Why not? I didn't have anything else to do, anyway.* Jackson seemed pretty happy that I had agreed.

"Sweet," he said happily.

"So what do you guys play?" I asked, not really directing the question at any one of them specifically. I wondered if it was alternative or Americana or—hopefully not—metal, which wasn't really something I liked listening to. Mike, always trying to be the funny guy, responded again with another sarcastic answer: "Instruments. Duh."

Tom shook his head and decided to actually answer my question. "Ignore him. Fun Rock 'n' Roll," Tom replied, playfully punching Mike in the arm.

"The house band moonlighting as rock stars. I'm excited now."

Tom smiled at my comment. "Well, you know, we are all men of many talents. We'll see you all tomorrow, then? We gotta go rehearse. 'Night." Tom and Mike hopped into a bright blue jeep; the top was off it so they just slid into the seats without opening the doors.

Jackson turned to me. "'Night, Zade. See you tomorrow." He cracked a huge smile. "I'll buy you a drink." His eyes sparkled again, and I was beginning to think he could do that on cue.

"Okay. Deal." I nodded. Jackson kissed me on the check before jumping into the driver's seat and quickly pulled out of the parking lot. They were gone so quickly you would have thought the parking garage was the Indy 500. I laughed and wondered if that was meant to impress me somehow.

Mac, Tad, and I walked until we reached the row where I'd parked my bike. I started to unhook my helmet. "Ooh, I think someone just asked you out," Tad teased. I turned bright red and shook my head.

"I think they want people to come see their band," I suggested.

Tad nodded before he reasoned, "Probably both—but he's yet to kiss *me* on the check for agreeing to come to a show, I feel gypped now." He feigned acting sad for a moment and then he glanced at my bike. "Nice crotch rocket. I think you get more awesome every time I see you. You might be the coolest chick I know, next to my wife."

"Thanks, Tad. You have a band you want me to come see too?" I cocked my right eyebrow and glared at him. He smirked.

"Funny, too." Tad nodded his head and looked back at Mac and me. "Alright, kids. I'll catch you both tomorrow night at the show."

"'Night, buddy," Mac said, giving Tad a one-armed "guy hug."

"'Night, Tad," I said as I gave him a real hug.

Tad walked over to his black truck and jumped into the front seat. Mac and I watched as he started the truck, backed out, and pulled away with far less dramatic flare than Jackson had done. That left just the two of us.

Mac asked nonchalantly, "So, what are your big plans for the rest of the evening?"

"Going home, I guess." I shrugged and scrunched my lips.

Mac pointed to another bike in the row. It was the Triumph Dakota he had mentioned before, white with black and grey accents. "Well, I brought my bike tonight. I was thinking about riding for bit. You're welcome to tag along and show me your skills, Magi Girl."

I paused for a moment and thought about it before agreeing.

"I've been looking for an excuse to take the new bike out more, so sure, . . . Superman."

Mac and I pulled on our helmets. It had been such an odd day. I felt like I was being fought over, and I had *never* been fought over before. Maybe I was thinking about it too hard, though. I couldn't figure out if Mac really liked me or not, and I couldn't decide if I really liked him. Either way, the ride sounded fun.

I swung my leg over the seat of my Ducati. I had been riding for years, but the motion of throwing my leg over my bike was still exciting. I rested my right leg on the foot pedal and grabbed the handles. We started our bikes and Mac backed up before gunning for the exit of the garage. I guessed I was expected to just follow behind him. He had never said where we were going, but I guess I didn't really care.

We briefly pulled onto the Strip, making a left onto Las Vegas Boulevard. The buildings were lit and bright and it has always been a sight that never really stops being impressive for me. Crowds of tourists were walking up and down the sidewalks that lined each side of the road. We turned left again onto Sands and flew through a few residential streets and even jumped onto the highway before we found ourselves in a more remote area on a two-lane road. It's funny how, in Vegas, you can be in a city one moment and a desert wasteland the next.

We had been riding for at least a half an hour before the wind had started to pick up some; all of a sudden it started to rain. First it was just sprinkles, which weren't a big deal, but it was quickly picking up. Sprinkles turned into full-on rain in just a few moments. We were getting drenched and we had to slow way down as the wet pavement became dangerous. I noticed a little further up the road there was an old convenience store that was closed—but it seemed to have some kind of overhang in front of the doors. I was trying to think how I could motion to Mac to pull up there but he must have seen it—or already known about it—because before I even tried to get his attention he had pulled into the parking lot and up under the overhang.

We both tried to get the bikes up and under as much of the overhang as we could. We turned off the engines on both our bikes and huddled together in the one dry spot we could find.

"Wow. That thunderstorm came outta nowhere, didn't it?" I asked. I was soaked and shivering in the cold, dark night. When we had left the garage it hadn't looked at all like it was going to rain, so I had been caught completely off guard.

"We get freak storms in the desert. They never last long, though. If we wait a few minutes, more than likely it'll stop raining," Mac said reassuringly. He pulled a pack of cigarettes out of his jacket and lit one. He leaned against the door of the store, which looked like it had been closed for a few years at least. He inhaled deeply and exhaled the smoke carefully away from my face.

"Thanks for inviting me riding," I said, staring at him. He kind of looked like a modern-day James Dean in his black leather jacket.

"Sure, no problem. Figured it would be nice to have a little company for a change. I usually ride alone," he admitted with a shrug.

"Yeah." I was suddenly aware that we were standing very close together and that I was at a loss for anything better to say. My breath grew deeper and I could feel myself inching closer toward Mac as I looked up into his face. I wasn't sure what I expected to find, but I found myself looking deep into his eyes. It was funny that a few months earlier we couldn't stand being in the same room standing twenty feet away from each other and yet there we were, huddling together only inches apart, in the rain. I was standing so close to him I could almost feel his heartbeat. I wasn't sure I was ready for this. *Maybe I should have gone home instead.* I was nervous and uncomfortable. A part of me wanted to jump on my bike and drive as far away as possible, but the other part of me wanted to inch just a little closer to him.

Mac turned his stare out into the night; I wondered what he was thinking. He pulled another long drag off his cigarette before tossing it to the ground and putting it out with the toe of his boot. I shivered a little from the cold. The rain had gotten worse and was still peppering the ground around us. The wind had picked up, blowing some of the rain sideways to the point that it was still hitting us even under the awning. Mac must have noticed that I was shivering, because he took both his hands and started to rub my shoulders to warm me up. He seemed to thrive in the crisp air; I could tell that he wasn't cold at all.

"You're freezing," he commented.

"Yeah, a little." I was actually completely frozen. He unzipped his jacket and opened it so I could huddle inside. He wrapped his arms around me, and I felt safe and warm—or at least warmer—being so close to him wrapped in his jacket and arms. It was oddly comforting. Until he started chuckling.

"What's so funny?" I asked, staring up at his face.

"Just this," he said, laughing. "I would have never guessed after meeting you that first day that I would end up shielding you from the wind, rain, and cold." He chuckled some more.

"Life's funny sometimes." I shrugged.

All of a sudden he pulled me in even closer, I hadn't realized there was any space left between us but there was just a small amount and with that eliminated, he kissed me. I don't think I knew what was happening at first. I almost tried to fight it but the fight went out of me rather quickly as he pushed his tongue past my lips. He was an incredibly good kisser and, for a moment, I got lost in just that—but then thoughts started running through my head. *What about his rule? What was he doing?* Then I realized that if he didn't care about his rule, then why should I?

Mac pulled just far enough from my face to speak. "I knew you were trouble the moment I saw you." His speech was breathy and what he said came out sweet, not mean.

"Me? Trouble? How so?" I asked coyly. I wondered if he was already regretting kissing me.

"I have a rule. I never get involved with performers. That is one rule I have kept up until this moment." He lingered on the last three words. "Until. This. Moment." His voice was soft and it didn't quite sound like regret, or at least I didn't think so.

"I've heard about your rules. Why do you have rules anyway, and why is that one of them?" I asked earnestly. I was surprised at my boldness. *Where had that courage come from?*

"Rules keep you from doing things you'll usually regret later. And that's one of them, 'cause of what I've seen happen when it goes bad."

"Wow, I thought *I* was bitter. Why does it have to go bad?" I asked hesitantly. I was unsure if I wanted to hear the answer. I found myself biting my lip.

He shrugged. "Usually does. You know what they say: people that play with fire usually get burned."

I started to pull away, though it was hard since his arms were wrapped completely around me and I was tucked inside his jacket. I didn't understand what he was doing. I didn't want things to become awkward, or for us to backtrack to when he didn't even want to be in the same room as me. This whole thing was a bad idea wasn't it? Why did I even come riding with him?

"Well, I don't want to force you int—"

He must have felt me pulling away and tightened his grip; he cut me off before I could even get a whole sentence out. "Hey, you're not forcing me into anything. I've been fighting this for a while. I'm tired of fighting it; I have listened to REO Speedwagon. Maybe I like trouble. I've already broken my rule by being here with you," he said seriously. Then he smiled mischievously. "I figure that if you're gonna break something, you better make it count."

He smiled and looked deep into my eyes, I could feel my face flush. He kissed me again, this time more passionately. A part of me wanted to stop it. Maybe it wasn't a good idea. But before I could really think about it, I was wrapped up in being kissed and forgot about everything else. I am pretty sure I forgot where I was—and even that I was cold and it was raining. I didn't know a kiss could feel so perfect. I could probably have stood there kissing him for the rest of the night but the rain had lightened up some and it was probably a good time to try to get somewhere dry before it picked back up.

"We should head back to town while Mother Nature has slowed down," Mac suggested. I agreed.

"So, REO Speedwagon, you like playing with fire now?" I asked. He laughed, looked me straight in the eyes, grabbed my hips, and kissed me hard once more.

When he pulled away he asked one more question: "Got any matches?"

The next day I found myself at Fashion Show Mall, picking out some new clothes at a very "girlie" kind of dress shop. I normally hate shopping, but all of a sudden after last night under that rainy awning it felt even more important that I look really hot for the band's show. Mac and Jackson would both be there and as much as my ride in the rain had confused me, I knew at the least I needed to show up looking as desirable as possible.

A week earlier I had had no prospects as far as dates went and suddenly I sort of had two. The worst thing was that I did like them both—and that meant that at the moment there was no clear answer for me. I wasn't even sure who I was leaning towards. A few days earlier, I would have said Jackson, for sure, but that kiss in the rain . . . that kiss had, well, electric chemistry that I'd never felt before. Who knows? I knew that it was possible that I might kiss Jackson and feel like I was kissing my brother.

I decided that I would stick to the first decision I needed to make: what to wear. I searched through the racks and, after talking to a friendly sales associate named Maggie, who helped me locate some dresses in my style, I found a few options. Maggie was pretty with blonde hair—and seemed unnaturally cheery. Since I was by myself she stayed in the dressing room area and gave me her thoughts as I tried on several options. Even though she was sugary sweet she did seem to give me her honest opinions about how I looked in each of the dresses I tried on. The first two she didn't like, and the next two I tried on didn't feel comfortable once I was in them. The material on one of them was scratchy and then the fifth one just didn't sit right. I kept trying to smooth out the sides of the dress but it just kept pulling—and it also showed a *lot* of cleavage. I kept staring at myself trying to decide if it was too much cleavage while Maggie ran and grabbed two more that she said I would look drop-dead gorgeous in, saying that she had finally figured out what type of dress I would look the best in based on my body type.

I didn't want to look like I was trying too hard, but I knew I wanted to look hot, not cute. I settled on the second of the final two dresses she brought me, a tight-fitting dark blue option that hugged me in all the right places. She was right about it being made for my kind of shape. I had a fun brown leather jacket and heeled low-cut leather boots that would offset the black dress nicely and make it look slightly more casual, though the dress on its own with some nice heels would have looked pretty dressed up. I had to remember I was still going to the kind of venue described to me as "a step up from a dive bar kind of place so cocktail attire would be slightly overdressed." Part of looking

Strength

cool, as we all know, means looking like you haven't tried too hard. On the flip side, I've always heard you're supposed to dress like you have somewhere better to go later. Taking both of these things into account, I think I had found a nice compromise.

Maggie got chatty as she rang up my purchase, obviously feeling we had bonded. "This looked great on you," she said as she scanned the tag. "Got a hot date, or something?"

"Kinda," I said. "I've sorta had . . . ," I hesitated, not sure how much to tell her. "For the first time in my life, I have two guys interested in me, and they're both going to be at this work thing I'm going to tonight."

"Ooh, that's fun." She paused. "You work with them *both*? That could be messy."

I nodded. *It's funny the things we will admit to complete strangers who we don't know. Yet, I probably wouldn't have told anyone I considered a friend any of that.* "Yeah, it's definitely a little strange. But they both know of the other and seem to be okay with it, at least for now, so . . . ." I shrugged. "I honestly like them both." I realized how crazy that sounded when I actually said it out loud, though, and realized I should start figuring my relationships out.

"Well, I guess there could be worse problems to be had," she observed. I figured she probably didn't want to come off "judgy"

145

to a customer after her last comment, but she was right that the whole thing could get messy fast.

"I should probably figure out who I like more pretty soon."

Maggie grinned and handed me the plastic garment bag containing the dress. "Probably, or be like a guy and have fun with it for a bit! Either way, you're sure knock 'em both dead in that outfit. Here is your receipt. Have a great day!"

"You too," I said, turning to leave.

"Be sure to come back and let me know what happens!" she called from behind the register.

I chuckled. "Okay, I will." I wasn't sure how much she really was into my life drama but I probably would come back in the store—at the very least to buy something else—and so if she remembered me maybe then I would tell her what happened.

I figured I might as well shop for a few other things while I was at the mall. After all, my closets were pretty bare, since I hadn't brought very much from home. I wandered around and ended up buying a few other key items. A couple of pairs of nice Levi's denim jeans and the matching denim jacket. A cute new top, a fun, new pair of Converse shoes, and a cute bralette to wear with my sheer shirts.

As I was made my way up through the main section of the mall, I saw two vaguely familiar-looking figures walking towards me. I squinted as they approached. When they were nearly in front of me, I laughed aloud; of course they were familiar. Carrot Top and Wayne Newton grinned when they saw me, and I couldn't help but let a smile spread across my own face as I stopped to greet them.

"Hey, guys," I said, still chuckling. "I have to say you two are the last people I would think I'd see walking through a mall together."

"We had to do a charity event here today," Wayne said, shrugging. "We just finished."

"We just had someone come up to Wayne and ask him when he started dating Reba McEntire," Carrot Top said, pointing at himself. I laughed.

"You guys coming to the premiere in a few weeks?" I asked, brushing a strand of hair from my forehead.

"Wouldn't miss it," Wayne said, and I detected the genuineness in his voice. "Besides, you know Scott will show up anywhere with a red carpet." He rolled his eyes. "Including the opening of an envelope."

My brow furrowed slightly in confusion. "Scott?"

"My mom didn't name me 'Carrot Top,' you know," he quipped, just as Wayne was gesturing with a thumb to point at him.

"Got it. *Scott*. Real name. Okay," I said, trying not to blush. "So, Scott," I continued, rushing to change the subject, "congrats on winning comedian of the decade. That's a big deal."

"Thanks," he said. "Come by the Luxor and see me anytime."

"I will," I said gratefully. "Well, it was great seeing you both! Later." I gave each of them a quick hug before walking away.

I can only stand the mall for so long, before I'm shopped out. I hit my wall and decided it was time to head home and start getting ready for my night out.

I exited the building and realized it was later than I'd thought; it was still light outside, but the sun was setting. I set my bags down for a second to try to remember where I had parked my car. My mind can drift quickly and all of a sudden I had forgotten about my car and had started worrying again about Jackson and Mac. I was so engrossed in my thoughts that I didn't see a very odd-looking girl walking directly up to me until she had stopped in front of me, blocking my light.

"I know what you are," she said in a low but confident tone.

I frowned at her, confused. "Excuse me?"

"I know *what* you are. Do you?"

I studied her carefully. She had striking features: sharp cheekbones, bright eyes, wild hair—she was attractive, but was also odd in a way that had nothing to do with her looks. Something about her radiated strangeness. I frowned more deeply, still confused. "Do you mean you've seen me in the show?"

The girl laughed, a nasty-sounding cackle. "No," she said, her voice dripping with sarcasm. "Not what you *do*. I know what you *are*."

"I really don't know what you mean," I said, starting to back away from the very strange girl with her even more strange behavior.

"You know why guys fawn over you, and some girls can't stand you?" she continued as I gathered up my bags. "Even mortals can sense power."

At that, I stopped and set my bags down again. I stared at her. She grinned, but not kindly. "They don't know what it is, but I do. You should shield yourself better . . . but then again, it's so strong." She raised her eyebrows with a look of amazement on her face. "Do you even know how powerful you are?"

I pulled myself up to my full height and glared, hoping my voice didn't reflect how shaken I was. "Who are you?"

"That's not for you to know, yet. You will know when it's time. Until then, though, I'd love to test your power." With that, she marched to the other side of the parking garage and put about thirty feet of distance between us. She turned around and nodded her head at me.

"What do you mean?" I asked, feeling my muscles clench.

"This." She raised her hands to her head and closed her eyes. She was silent for a moment, and then she thrust her hands toward me. Suddenly, I was slammed back against the wall of the building with what felt like enough force to ground a plane. I grimaced in pain. I could feel bruises already rippling on the back of my head, spine, and arms.

"Come on, girl! Show me what you can do!" she yelled—something like a mix of anger and glee in her voice.

"Stop it!" I winced. It hurt even to get the words out.

"Make me!"

My body was still pressed against the wall. It felt like I was being held in place by hurricane-force winds. I screwed my eyes shut, fighting against the excruciating pain to bring my arms together in front of me. My back was still locked to the wall, but at least I was now able to bring my hands together. I cupped them into a sphere and shoved them in the direction of the girl, who stood watching with an egocentric smirk.

Colored sparks of light shot forward from between my palms, sending the girl flying backward and slamming her into the garage wall. Strips of tinted fire marked the ground, showing the path the sparks had taken to hit her. Released from her hold, I fell to the ground. I gingerly pushed myself up onto my hands and knees before standing. The girl stood, too, dusting herself off. She laughed again.

"You did that and you barely even know what you're doing," she said shaking her head. "Amazing! Well, Zade, I'll see you around."

She turned her back toward me. A bright orange Lamborghini, gleaming in the dying sunlight, pulled up to the side of the garage where she was standing. The girl stepped in through the passenger side door. The windows were tinted so I couldn't see the driver, and they sped off before I could get a better look at the plate. I felt completely out of breath—as if I had been running for miles.

I brought my hand to my forehead, as if checking for a fever. "What the . . . ?" I whispered to no one in particular.

"Hey, Zade!" came a chirpy little voice, and I jumped. A familiar person was walking up to me, smiling widely. I was still so in shock over what had happened that it didn't really click who it was until I felt Lil wrap herself around me in a warm, gentle hug. I hugged her back but was pretty sure I still looked shaken up from the past few minutes. "Funny running into you at the mall," she said happily, but as she pulled away from the hug her brow furrowed when she got a good look at my face. "You okay? You look like you've seen a ghost."

I dropped my hand to my side and collected the bags I had dropped. I still felt sweaty and sick. "Huh?" I heard myself say, meeting Lil's concerned gaze. "Oh, yeah. I'm . . . I'm fine."

Lil didn't look convinced. I forced a smile that I was pretty sure came out as more of a grimace. "Hey, uh . . . Did you see anything—unusual—when you walked up?"

Lil's concern gave way to confusion. "No . . . Should I have?"

I waved a hand as if batting a fly. "No. Never mind. Sorry, I'm just . . . out of it—malls do that to me. I gotta run. I gotta . . . get to . . . uh . . . need to get to . . . Sally Beauty Supply . . . and get some colors for my hair before they close! See you later!" I nearly ran back to my car. I could hear Lil call goodbye faintly behind me, but I didn't stop to wave. I couldn't stop thinking about the girl in the not-so-subtle Lambo. *Who was she? How did she know my name? Why did she attack me?*

*And, most importantly, how did she know about my magick?*

# CHAPTER 8

# THE STAR

I STOOD OUTSIDE THE BAR. NERVOUS. I HAD SO MANY things to think about that my head was starting to hurt. I probably should have worried more about the girl in the parking garage but I just wasn't ready to deal with her yet.

I grabbed my iPhone and turned the camera on me, using it as a makeshift mirror. I just wanted to make sure one last time that I looked good. Maggie was right, I had chosen the right dress. I was just the right amount of dressed up. I breathed in to calm my nerves. I knew Mac was already inside.

The night before, after we had made it safely back to town, Mac had invited me back to his place—but I told him I thought it would be best to save that for another night. And, honestly, I had just really wanted to get out of my wet clothes and needed time to process what had happened. Spending time with Mac under that awning was probably the most romantic thing that had happened to me in my small amount of dating experience, and I decided that perfect rain kisses were a great place to leave the "to be continued." I had bolted home so quickly we didn't talk about what was going to happen tonight when we saw each other.

Since I hadn't talked to him all day, I made up my mind that I wouldn't act like anything had happened—unless he did. Truth be told, I was kind of hoping he wouldn't either. After all, Mac was fully aware that Jackson had invited me in a somewhat "date-like" manner. I sorta wondered to myself how I got into such messes like this. I took another deep breath before grabbing the large metal handle and pulling back the heavy over-sized door.

Once I was inside, a bouncer checked my ID. He eyed me up and down and gave my ID a long hard glance before handing it back to me and stamping my hand. My baby face always made them double check and usually bouncers would look at me the way he did—they never looked like they believed I was actually old enough to be in a bar.

I had made sure to show up right before the show started so I would get a little time with Mac while Jackson was on stage. From the corner of my eye I saw Tad, Mac, and Riley standing at the bar talking. I made a calculated walk just to the right of where they were standing and approached the bar. I pretended not to have noticed them and looked towards the bartender as if my focus was on getting him to come over. I waited patiently while he poured someone else a drink.

I didn't have a lot of experience being in a bar, but I tried to be patient and act like I was relaxed and comfortable. I finally couldn't help but look toward where Mac was standing and, just as he had caught my eye, I felt a hand brush my back. It was Tim, Jackson's bandmate in our show—and in the Plain White T's as well; he gave me a quick hug and sweetly remarked, "Good to see you, Zade." I hugged him back before making eye contact with Jackson, who was standing right next to him. Jackson looked extremely excited to see me, with his bright smile and sparkling eyes.

"Hey! You came," Jackson said as he grabbed me and hugged me tightly. The hug was nice. He startled me just a little bit when, as he started to release me from his hug, he kissed me lightly on the lips. It was one of those kisses that a friend might give you and it would not mean anything—or I could have taken it in a much more romantic way. I wasn't sure how to take it and, of course, I wondered what Mac thought since I was sure he had seen Jackson kiss me.

Standing next to Jackson was another guy who looked familiar enough to me that I knew he must work at the show in some regards. I noticed that he was looking at me like he was waiting to meet me. Jackson noticed as well and quickly introduced us. "Oh, sorry, I don't think you've officially met. Zade, this is one of our other guitarists, Dave. Dave this is Zade."

"Nice to meet you, Zade."

"Nice to meet you too, Dave."

"We're just about to go on, but I hope after the show we can hang out? You promised to let me buy you a drink." Jackson was so enthusiastic about it, it would have been impossible to say no.

"Sure, sounds great. I'll be . . . right here waiting for you."

Jackson laughed as he caught my reference to his own joke from the day he gave me my tour. He then turned and headed back to the stage; Tim and Dave had already started back there as well. I stood and watched him pick up his guitar and adjust the strap before Mac, Tad, Cam, and Riley walked up to me. I smiled and felt my face flush. Mac made it to me first and hugged me tightly. He purposely made sure he could whisper in my ear.

"Looks like Tad was right, again. Jackson definitely is hitting on you."

I started to pull away and just as our faces were directly in front of each other I softly and quietly said—so only he could hear: "Jealous?" I asked, and I raised my eyebrow.

Before Mac could say anything else Tad, Cam, and Riley were now in front of me and I quickly hugged each of them.

"Hey, Sweets," Tad greeted me.

"Hi," Riley added with a smile.

"Hey there, pretty girl," Cam cooed, always the constant flirt.

The band finished setting up all their equipment and they all walked off to the side of the stage, where it looked like they were having a quick pre-performance talk. Jackson, Tom, Tim, Mike, Dave, and their drummer who's name I didn't know, were stretching and fidgeting as they talked. You could tell they were all riled up and ready to play.

"This place is packed," I commented to the guys around me, just to have something to say—though it really was true. There were wall-to-wall people and it was pretty obvious that everyone was all waiting for the band to start. Riley nodded in agreement at my comment.

"They are pretty popular in town and rumor has it they may get a record deal soon. They really are amazing." He seemed to be genuinely proud of his friends.

I noticed an older man walk on to the side of the stage. He was tall and only slightly overweight. He sauntered across the stage like someone who had done it more than a thousand times. The crowd noticed him as he approached the mic and began to scream and pack up close to the edge of the stage. Most of the crowd pushing and shoving at the front were female and by the way they reacted you would have thought they had just found out Justin Beiber was coming on to the stage. The energy in the room was frantic.

I contemplated trying to push my way to the front as well; it did look like it might be fun to be towards the front in the middle of the excitement. I got why they all pushed and shoved their way up, but I chose to hang back. It wasn't because that's what Mac, Riley, Cam and Tad were doing—though had they gone up front I would have joined them. It also wasn't because I didn't want to upset Mac by looking like an instant groupie for Jackson and his band. Mainly I liked observing not just the band but also all the fans that were at the front. They were so enthralled by the band that they didn't notice how uncomfortable they were jammed next to each other against the stage. Some of the girls were looking over at the guys with googly eyes and bemused expressions on their faces. Some looked like they were giving the guys their smoldering "come hither" stares. Lastly, there were the girls who were pretending to ignore them as if they weren't there; when it was even more obvious they were trying hardest to get the boys' attention. I laughed at how funny the whole thing was. People-watching was one of my favorite pastimes, and I'm pretty sure I was witnessing people-watching at its finest.

The man who had walked across the stage motioned for the sound guy to turn on the mic at the front of the stage. Once the mic was hot he spoke quickly and loudly.

"Hey, everyone. Thanks for coming out tonight. I know I'm not the one you're here to see, so without further ado—Plain White T's!"

The crowd screamed loudly and the high pitch of some of the girls was enough to make my ears hurt; I'm fairly positive that I lost a few decibels from my hearing range. Even though there seemed to be no space left to push any closer together against the stage, I watched as they did, somehow, try harder to cram even more toward the front. The band broke into their first song: a fast-paced, upbeat number with lots of bass and a rad guitar riff.

I had to yell over the crowd pretty loudly to be heard at all. "Wow, it's like they're *NSYNC and they got the band back together or something!" I shouted—to Riley, mainly, though I'm sure Mac, Cam, and Tad heard me too. I knew for sure Mac had heard, since I saw that he chuckled at my comment.

I continued, "Dave and that other guy work at our show, right? I know I've seen them at work; there's just so many people to keep straight."

Riley nodded in agreement and pointed toward the stage. "Tim, Tom, Mike, and—of course—Jackson. You know them, right?"

"Yep," I responded confidently.

Riley then went on to explain, "Dave is actually in the audio department, but is also back-up guitar player for our show. De'mar is the drummer for us, and—as you can see—also for the T's. They've been around a few years now and I heard they just got offered a record deal."

I gathered from Riley's comment that "the T's" must be a shortened version of the band's name. I wondered why they called themselves the "Plain White T's," but figured I'd save that question for later when Jackson and I could chat. I was impressed to hear they were getting offered a record deal. "Wow," I said. "That's great. They must be pretty good then. This place is packed." As I surveyed the crowd, I noticed that Pete (who I still had trouble calling "Trig") had finally arrived sometime after the first song. I now had proof of what I'd been told earlier: Pete is never late to work, but he couldn't get to a social event on time to save his life.

The first few songs were loud—fun and all upbeat. As they progressed, every song they played sounded like a hit that you would hear playing on the radio. I instantly saw why there was so much excitement over the band.

I think when Jackson invited me I had imagined the crowd would be thirty or forty people max who were all there to support their friends—especially after Mike's joke about the guys being half their audience. I knew that it had been a joke but I didn't realize how much of one. By my best guess, there actually were close to four hundred people—if not more—who all seemed to know all the words to the band's original songs and would sing along, scream, and dance. They were true fans of this band. This was a real concert and the band was really good. They were actual rock stars, maybe they weren't famous yet, but they were rock stars all the same.

After a number of up-tempo songs, they shifted to a vocally driven slow-tempo ballad with resonant harmonies, called "Stay." The beat was just a little bit, well, *sassy*. I found myself tapping my foot and drifting to the music. I felt Mac lean into me and I could feel his breath on my neck and ear. I could tell he was about to say something and he made sure to be so close to me that I would be the only one who could hear him.

"You know, Jackson is a great guy, but he's so focused on the band. With someone like that, romance always comes third, after the band—and then work."

"Noted; and I'm proud of you. You didn't just start bashing him," I explained. I really wasn't sure what else to say. I still was taking in what had happened the previous night—and I wasn't even sure what that had been. Had it been just a one-time thing? Did Mac think we were dating? Mac edged me a little farther away from the other guys, who had been joined by Zeb, so he didn't have to speak quite so softly.

"Do you think you like him?" Mac inquired, trying to be heard over the band while still keeping his voice down. He was obviously trying to sound nonchalant, but there was a crack in his voice when he asked, and his whole demeanor had gotten more serious. I thought about my answer for a moment. I quickly decided I needed to be as honest as I could be without becoming mean. I thought for a moment about making a joke and acting confused—maybe pretending that I thought he was asking about Pete—but figured it might not be the times for jokes.

"I don't know. I don't really know him. But I always keep my word, so I'm going to have a drink with him. I don't plan to do anything further." I paused and looked Mac directly in the eye before adding, "He did technically ask me out before anything happened with us, though." I felt my right eyebrow rise as I looked into his eyes and my eyelashes bat unconsciously.

"That's very true." Mac nodded, rubbing his hand across his chin. "I waited a long time to make a move. Honestly, knowing Jackson had sort of asked may have had something to do with what got me to do it last night. I knew he was about to beat me to the punch." He shrugged.

I had come to enjoy the fact that Mac and I always seemed to have frank and honest conversations. Maybe our conversations were so open because our first interactions had started with both of us being very bold and straightforward and telling each other what was on our minds—typically with as much passion as we could muster. *You can't really be afraid to offend each other too much after all that, now can you? Maybe all relationships should start off that way.*

"Are you saying that last night only happened 'cause *Jackson* hit on me?" My head tilted to the side as I looked him up and down, waiting for the answer.

"Honestly, I don't know. It would have been very hard to resist kissing you in the rain either way. I'm not sure I would have asked you to go riding, though, if he hadn't hit on you."

"I like that you answer honestly."

"Thanks. I've always found it's easier that way," Mac said sincerely.

I already felt anxious about being in the middle between Jackson and Mac. I had never been in that kind of position, and I could tell that it was going to make my life much more complicated. All I could think at the time was that I needed to do some card readings on all of it, but that wasn't going to happen in the bar. I was going to have to go home and start looking at the possibilities before I took anything too much further. For the moment I just had to wonder what to do like everyone else. Maybe I didn't like this "normal" thing so much, after all.

Mac and I didn't talk about the situation any more for the remainder of the night. I think Mac could feel that he was going to just have to chill and see what happened. He moved away from me and started a conversation with Tad, Pete, Zeb, and Cam about work. Riley had walked away, and was apparently pounding back drinks like they were water. I let myself have some alone time to focus on everything going on in my head.

Towards the end of their set the band launched into another ballad. A slow-grooved rock song with a pretty sparkly pop hook called "Someday You're Gonna Love Me." I couldn't be quite sure, but it almost felt like this song was directed at me. The lyrics said something about allowing the girl time to go have fun cause the guy was going to just wait around because, well, "someday you're gonna love me." It was a super sweet, romantic thought. The chorus felt like it was being sung just for me, and Jackson's eyes were definitely looking directly at mine while he sang. At least it sure *felt* like he was, or maybe I'm just that girl who thinks she's being sung to at a concert and really isn't. Maybe from the stage, with the lights in his eyes, Jackson couldn't even see me and was just looking at the random faces in the crowd.

I glanced over toward where Mac was standing, hoping to find him still engulfed in a conversation. I found myself wishing he hadn't even noticed what I thought had just happened. Instead he was staring right at me and he had clearly witnessed the possible profession from Jackson. I only allowed myself to catch his gaze for a second before looking away and pretending that I hadn't even seen him staring. I suddenly felt overwhelmed at the possibility of something that may not have even actually happened. Luckily Jackson and the band broke back into three upbeat songs to finish their set and a couple of the dancers from our show ran over and grabbed me to dance with them. I was able to let my thoughts and anxiety go and just allow myself to have fun.

After the concert ended, the guys sold and signed several CDs while they took pictures with their fans. Jackson caught my attention and asked me to hang out till they were done and— as promised—once most of the crowd had left he joined me by the bar. I hadn't realized it earlier in the evening, but the bar also served food and Jackson said he was starving, so he ordered something to eat—for both of us. We chatted as we ate. I was quickly learning that he was very easy to talk to and was actually very funny. Although I hadn't planned it, I found myself flirting with him. His smile was hard to resist and the more time I spent with him, the more I could swear his eyes would sparkle on cue. We talked a lot about music. He suggested that I should come up sometime and play a song with them during a show. I joked that I wasn't sure he could afford me, but agreed that it would be fun and said I would—sometime.

I noticed that Mac was still hanging out while drinking a beer with a bunch of the guys from work. There was one point that I glanced over at Mac and caught him looking right at us. Our eyes met and we shared a smile. I'm pretty sure Jackson noticed it, too, even though he didn't miss a beat while continuing the story he'd been telling me. I had no idea what time it had gotten to, but I was pretty sure Jackson and I had been talking for a while. I hadn't really been able to hear most of what Mac and the rest of the guys at the other end of the bar had been talking about—which was fine by me—but all of a sudden Tad got a little louder and I could hear him pretty clearly, so I listened to their conversation without looking over.

"Mac, you about ready to call it a night? I should probably get home to the little woman—and it looks like we need to take this boozer home," Tad said. "He's had a little too much to drink."

I remembered Mac mentioning that he and Tad lived only a few blocks from each other and had ridden over to the show together. My curiosity got the better of me, and I glanced over to see which guy he was talking about and instantly could tell that Riley was wasted. It looked like he was barely standing, and his eyes looked bloodshot and heavy.

"I'm okay," Riley slurred, a clear indication of how *not* okay he was.

"I'd rather not test that tonight, buddy," Tad said, laughing and patting Riley on the back.

"Yeah, me neither, kid," Mac added. "If you're gonna drink like that you gotta learn to hold your liquor better. You're drunker than a skunk."

"Mac, don't be hard on him. You were worse than him when you were his age," Tad said.

"Is that me being hard?" Mac wondered aloud, looking confused. "Tad, I'll follow you in Riley's car and that way we can drop him and his car both off before going home," he concluded before turning to the remaining members of the band. "Alright, guys, awesome show. Have a good night."

Mac wrapped his arm around Riley's neck in some kind of "buddy lock" and began to walk to the door. Riley didn't really resist. I'm pretty sure that even in his state he knew that it was better for him to just go with Mac. Of course, that's if he was even sober enough to know who Mac was, which was questionable.

Riley did his best to say goodnight to everyone, though the sentence he formed was barely English: "Looks li' I gots to say night, too."

"'Night, guys," Tim offered.

"Thanks so much for coming," Tom added.

Tad gave them all hugs as he's just really sweet like that, then came over and hugged me as well and shot me an "I told you he was hitting on you" look. Mac just waved and nodded as he walked out, since a hug would have been difficult without dropping Riley. He gave me one last, lingering glance. I smiled briefly and waved at them, and then they were out the door.

Zeb remarked, "You know, when I was his age, if I had gotten that drunk someone would have definitely messed with me."

Cam laughed as he waved and hollered out, "You guys should mess with him while he's so drunk. Night, guys."

Zeb looked at Cam and said, "Am I still giving you a ride?"

Cam nodded and turned to us. "I think I'm going to call it a night, too. Bye, guys."

Zeb waved and told us all to be careful getting home before both he and Cam walked out, leaving us with just Pete, who was still hanging out with Tom and Tim rambling on about something that sounded geeky that they were all really into, most likely speakers or amps or something very audiophile.

It was nearly four in the morning when I finally made it home. I'd stayed at the bar with Jackson for a while after everyone else had left, and found that it was much easier to relax around him once Mac was gone.

I walked through my tiny apartment and into my bedroom. I sat down on my bed and took my shoes off, then leaned back and stared up at the ceiling, thinking about everything that had happened in the past twenty-four hours.

I really liked Mac and something kept drawing me to him, but I also really liked Jackson—and there was something about him, too, something beyond the killer smile and sparkly eyes. I guess I liked them both, and that had never happened before. I might have simply let things go along for a while if the situation wasn't so complicated. And if we didn't all work together and know each other. *And* if Mac and Jackson weren't friends. Maybe they weren't best friends, but they were friends, for sure. I knew I needed to figure it all out before things got messy. One of my favorite poets, Christopher Poindexter, came to mind:

> *"is it possible to love more*
> *than one person at a time?"*
> *i asked, staring grievously at*
> *the bottom of my glass.*

*"of course," she replied,*
*"just not with the same intensity.*
*they don't tell you that because*
*it scares them shitless.*

*love is an energy thing."*

Not that I'm saying that I *loved* either of them, yet, but it was becoming evident to me that I could. The truth was, I wasn't looking for a boyfriend or even a date, so I'm not sure how I ended up with two. Regardless, I was where I was. I just needed to figure out what I was actually doing.

I rolled over and reached for the bedside light, flicking the knob to turn it on. I made sure when I bought my bedside table that it was pretty oversized and large enough to lay my cards out. I pulled open the large drawer, which held several different sets of my cards—each meant for different situations—contained in several different-colored velvet pouches. I ran my hand over each of them before choosing my favorite set. I pulled it out of its heavy velvet bag and placed it on the bed. The cards were worn with use. I ran my fingers over the edges to help pour my energy into them. I breathed in deeply and tried to clear my mind of everything before I began to shuffle the cards and cut them into three piles just like my mother would always do.

To get a proper reading you must make sure your mind is clear and focused only on what you are trying to read about. If anything else creeps into your mind it will throw off the answers, or the answers won't make sense, or you will even get wrong answers. For a split second another issue flashed through my mind: It dawned on me I should really be worried much more about the strange girl who I encountered at the mall and what that was about. As much as I knew I should be trying to figure out who she was and what she wanted—and why that whole encounter had occurred in the first place—I just wasn't as concerned with her at the moment as I was with my love life. I promised myself to do a reading on her when I was done with this. (For what it's worth, I did—and I came up with nothing. The cards made no sense, which told me that someone had gone to great lengths for me to not get a reading on the situation at all. Short of calling my mom and telling her what was going on— which I wasn't going to do because she'd insist I come straight home—there wasn't anything I could do about it. So I pushed the whole incident—and the girl—out of my mind and decided not to worry about it till it came up again.)

My mother taught me that everyone has guides—spirit guides who are incorporeal beings and are assigned to us before we are born. They help nudge and guide us through life. Some guides will stay with you throughout your entire life, and others will pop in every now and again to help you with specific areas of your life or goals you are trying to achieve. We all have guides, not just people like me (though mine are probably just more like me). You've probably noticed yours before and just not known who they were. Your guides are the little voices that tell you to "slow down" or "buy bread" or "take notice of the cute guy in line in front of you"—all of those are direct communication from your guides or higher self. This is why a lot of people think of their guides as guardian angels, cause they are in a way, guardians angels with great advice.

Many people dismiss their voices—also called "intuition"—because what they hear is not always pleasant or what they want to hear. Do not mistake your ego for your intuition, however. Following your gut instinct is also a manner in which guides try to direct you. They sometimes send you signs as well, but the best way for me to talk to my guides is through tarot cards. After all, a person's guides can field the cards to send direct messages; I have always found it is best to talk to my guides out loud so that the messages are as direct as possible.

"I'm looking for who would be best overall for my highest and best good and for his highest and best good as well. Jackson should come up in the form of the King of Wands and Mac as the King of Cups." I breathed deeply again and start to gently flip over my cards onto my bedside table. As I laid down each card, I continued to talk aloud. "The High Priestess." That card usually talks of supernatural, secret knowledge; information she may or may not reveal to you. *Must be my mom.* I sighed and thought about my mom and the lack of communication I had with her. We had always been very close and I hated that things seemed so distant now with her. It made me sad, but I didn't really know how to deal with it. I examined the woman on the card and thought that it did somehow actually resemble my mom. There are literally thousands of options for designs on tarot decks. Some decks have a very dark feel to them and some feel warm and bright. They all look different and some people, like me, use different decks for different situation. It felt a little weird to suddenly notice how much this particular High Priestess card looked like my mom, especially since I had used that particular deck thousands of times but had never noticed till now—when I really missed her—how much that card looked like my mom.

I flipped over another card.

"The Chariot." *That card usually means a journey.* I wasn't sure if it meant *my* journey or someone else's. I laid out a third card in line with the first two. "The Fool." The fool doesn't mean you're stupid or even silly, but rather it is the card of infinite possibilities. The most traditional version of this card has a young person starting out on a journey. The bag he is carrying on his staff indicates that he has all he needs so that he can do or be anything he wants, he has only to stop and unpack. He is on his way to a brand new beginning.

But the Fool carries a little "bark" of warning, as well. He's depicted as being so busy being happy and excited that he doesn't notice that there is a huge cliff coming up and his dog is barking at him trying to get his attention. In other words, while it's wonderful to be enthralled with all around you and excited by all life has to offer, you still need to watch your step, lest you fall and end up looking the fool. I looked at what I had in front of me on the table. Those cards were definitely about me moving to Vegas and were, in essence, in my past now.

I laid down three more cards, all directly underneath the first three, which represented my present. The Magician, the Devil, and the Lovers. The Magician can mean different things but I'm pretty sure—in my case—I needed to assume it had a literal meaning in this one. I knew that the Devil card doesn't usually mean the Devil literally, but it also wasn't clear to me what he was representing, so I decided not to worry about it for the time being. Sometimes when you aren't sure what a card means you just have to let it go until something more about why a card showed up reveals itself to you. The Lovers, however, had an obvious meaning: it meant I could have a relationship. *Okay*.

Finally, it was time for the good stuff: the future, and the two possibilities . . .

I told the guides I was going to lay down two piles to represent each relationship and once again asked that the King of Wands show up to represent Jackson and the King of Cups to represent Mac. I would know by those cards which pile was about whom. I laid down seven cards together. The Eight of Wands, which is meant to represent Cupid's arrows, meant he likes me. *No surprise there.* The Three of Pentacles (a relationship), the Three of Cups, the Sun, and the Five of Pentacles meant it would be great—but it wouldn't be perfect. I kept reading and found the Nine of Cups, which meant all would be content—and the King of Wands. So that indicated for me that this was my future path with Jackson. *Sounds pretty good.* My intuition was telling me that the entire combo had an extra meaning to it, but I couldn't put my finger on what it was.

I laid ten cards down this time. The Ace of Cups meant that he'd love me. The Two of Cups, the Ten of Pentacles, and the Four of Wands could refer to marriage. The Ten of Cups (predicting a happy family) was followed by the Wheel of Fortune, which meant that those all could happen—but I also got the Eight of Swords, which meant that it could all go wrong. And after the Queen of Cups I ended with the King of Cups: Mac. I stared at all the cards lying on the table.

*Looks like it could work with either of them, either of them could be "the one."* There was something weird surrounding both of them though. It looked like Mac could also be the cause of all hell breaking loose. *Weird.* I'm not sure what to think. I closed my eyes and breathed deeply for a couple of moments.

"Okay, and for the future . . . ." I picked up the last card hesitantly and laid it down.

*The Tower.*

*Dela, far away—and hopeful—laid down the same card her daughter did. She exhaled audibly, fearful for Zade's path. She laid down the rest of the final three.*

*Dela's voice trembled as she spoke. "The Tower, the Death Card, and then the World. How is that?" She glanced at a picture on the table sitting by the candle at her side. It was a photo of Zade and she directed her outspoken words directly to the photo.*

*"Oh, Zade. You have a very difficult journey ahead. I don't know how, but after everything falls apart, it will all be okay again." Dela had been watching over her daughter in the best way she knew how—and the best way she knew how to find out what was going on in her life without actually talking to her. She'd been*

*doing readings every day on Zade and looking in. She still missed Zade's voice and actual interaction with her, but she knew she needed to let Zade be—for now. It wouldn't be like that forever, but Dela needed to be patient till it was time for them to reconnect.*

*The door in front of Dela opened, and a young woman in her early twenties entered. She was dressed modestly in jeans and a loosely fitted blouse. Her stringy brunette hair was brushed but not styled and she didn't seem to have on any make-up. She was skinny, almost too skinny, and looked sad—and slightly scared. She fidgeted, her gaze darting around the room, and stood just inside the door as if she might bolt back out if she saw something that scared her.*

*"Hello, my dear," Dela said, welcoming her in a soothing voice. Dela had noticed that the young woman wasn't very comfortable being there and beckoned her sweetly, "Come in. How can I help you?"*

*"Hello, my name is April. I was interested in getting a . . . um . . . well, a reading." Her eyes continue to dart around instead of looking at Dela and she unconsciously picked at a hangnail nervously, while not moving from her spot by the door.*

*"Of course. Have you ever had one before?"*

*"No. No, I haven't."*

*"Ah. Someone broke your heart, though, and that's why you are here."*

*Surprised that Dela knew this small bit of obvious info, April clutched her purse and slid into the chair across from her. The reality was that more than half of the people who came to see Dela came because of some matter of the heart. It wasn't too terribly hard to guess that was probably the reason why anyone, including April, would darken Dela's doorstep. Dela, however, wasn't guessing. April responded as if Dela had asked her a question, "Yes, that's correct."*

*Dela had a general speech for anyone who came in to see her for the first time. She had said the same words thousands of times. She had tweaked what she would say here or there but it was basically the same thing and she always said it with just the right amount of dramatic flare. She caught April's gaze as she explained: "So, before we begin, I need to explain to you a little of how this works. I will tell you what I see, good or bad. I do not sugarcoat. What I tell you is based on the path you are now on—and the path that those you ask about will take. I can look and see what they will do, but because this is your reading, and you are gaining the knowledge, you will have the chance to change the path, if you so desire, to get the outcome you wish. I can tell you what you will need to do to get your most desired outcome. If you follow what I say, you will see happen what you wish."*

*April listened intently to every word Dela spoke, barely moving.*

*"Now, with that said, there are things that are set in stone. Our paths are not destined, but Destiny is within everything we do. Some things you cannot change—and if this is the case I will tell you so. Perhaps you have heard the saying 'You can't fight fate.' Well, if it is fate's desire then—regardless of the path you take—you will end up in the same place. Do you understand?"*

It wasn't but a few days later when I found myself back in the mall. I may not be super keen on shopping but I had finally realized how few "going out" clothes I really owned. I didn't have much need for them back home and I didn't even bring out everything I owed with me when I moved. I guess I forgot to factor in the fact that having more of a life meant going out a lot more—and that going out meant needing something to wear. Because malls quickly make me tired and cranky quickly, I figured I deserved some lemonade for the suffering I was enduring.

"Hi. Could I get a small lemonade, please?" I asked the male cashier at the Hot Dog on a Stick stand. He was like most teenagers and some parts of his body were more manly—like his filled-out arms—while other parts like his scrawny legs sticking out of his shorts still looked more like those of a boy. He couldn't have been older than about nineteen or twenty years old.

The cashier grinned widely. "Sure. Can I get anything else for you?"

"No, that's all."

"$2.09, please," he said, smiling even wider.

As I dug through my purse for the exact change, I could feel his gaze on me. I hadn't really been paying him any attention but once I looked up I noticed he was just staring at me with the biggest puppy-dog eyes. "I'm sorry," he said. "I'm not trying to be weird. You just have really great hair."

I smiled back mostly as a reaction to the compliment. He was not at all my type even though when you looked past the braces and acne he was actually decently cute. *Talk to me in ten years.* "Oh," I said. "Thank you. That's very kind." I smiled again and nodded as I handed him the nine cents and two one-dollar bills, to go with it.

Our hands touched briefly as I gave him the cash. He smiled again. "You have really striking eyes, too. . . . I'm Alan, by the way."

I sighed quietly. "Thanks, Alan. You're sweet."

Alan handed me my receipt and I stepped out of the way to make room for the next customer in line. I pretended to fiddle with my phone as I waited for my lemonade. I checked to see if I had any text messages but I had none. I was really hoping someone would text me right then—anyone really—but nothing came in. I glanced up to see if Alan was still staring at me and he was, so he caught me looking at him. He obviously took it as me eyeing him, considering the way he was eyeing me while was barely paying any attention to the next customer or their order. I started to check my hair for split ends, and just hoped my lemonade would be done soon so I could leave.

A short, stocky girl with mousey brown hair was behind the booth preparing orders. She had obviously noticed the attention I was getting from Alan, and she didn't seem too happy about it either. She looked at Alan, then back at me, and her face darkened. "Hey!" she yelled, and even though I was already looking at her through my hair she startled me with her sharp voice. "He's taken."

I frowned in confusion and raised my right eyebrow. "What?"

The girl stormed out from behind the stand, coming in front of it to get closer to me. She tried to raise herself to my face, but I towered over her. She couldn't have been more than 5'2", perhaps not even that tall, and was struggling to look tough or mean. She glowered. "I said, he's taken. So you can cut it with that cute routine you've got going."

*Oh,* I thought, realization slowly dawning on me, *she's his girlfriend.* I felt color rising to my cheeks. "I'm just waiting for my drink," I said frostily. I squared my jaw and looked her directly in the eye. I was not afraid of much, and I was definitely not afraid of an eighteen-year-old girl with a jealousy issue.

"Don't give me that, you little skank," the girl spat as her voice got louder. You could visibly see her blood pressure rising. "I saw you batting your eyes."

I felt my own anger rise slowly and I drew in a deep breath before responding to her. "Listen," I said, in a much lower and more matter-of-fact tone than her high-pitched bark. I even leaned toward her some before speaking to try to keep the altercation just between us. "You don't want to start anything with me. I suggest you back down now." I formed my hands into fists. My body began to shake with rage. As I did so, the vat of lemonade on the counter began to rattle. It was probably unnoticeable to most people—just a slight tremor—but it was definitely rattling.

The girl stepped back, but only a small bit, and folded her arms. "I'll back off when I want to back off, you miserable bitch." I'm not really sure why I had allowed some lemonade girl to bother me—or why I did what I did next. Sometimes I guess someone just pushes you over the edge. I wanted to teach her a lesson. Sadly, though I doubt I actually taught her anything, I'm sure she will never forget our encounter.

As soon as the last word left her mouth, I snapped inside. I squeezed my eyes shut tight and shook my clenched fists once more. The vat of lemonade exploded, sending yellow liquid and shards of glass in every direction. I opened my eyes to see what I had done. When the vat broke and the lemonade went everywhere it had bowled her over and knocked her to the ground. She was drenched in sticky, sugary lemonade. I had made sure that the other customers and any passersby had all "miraculously" been spared being hit. After all, there was no need for anyone else to suffer because of her. She was soaked—dripping from her hair to her fingertips and as she struggled to get back up, lemonade started pooling around her shoes.

I shrugged and declared, "When life hands you lemons . . . ," then turned and left her on the ground.

# CHAPTER 9

# TEMPERANCE

*TAD. MAC. CAM. AND RILEY. ALONG WITH JACKSON and the whole band (Tom, Tim, Mike, Dave, and De'Mar)—and an audio tech named Drew—were all standing around the stage dealing with some work issues. Drew had always gotten along with everyone and all in all was a decent guy. He was about as vanilla looking as someone can get, with brown hair and brown eyes. He led a pretty average existence overall, and no one ever had any problems with him.*

*The other guys tended to pick on Drew, though, because he was an easy target in a theater full of more-talented, more-experienced, and better-looking people, who all led far more exciting lives. Even so, Drew always seemed to be pretty content and—compared to anyone from the small town in Iowa he was from—he was leading the best life by far.*

"Drew, we need to have a rehearsal before the show rehearsal tomorrow," Tom demanded. He had a way though of not sounding demanding, even when he was being that way. "We've gotta work this new song into part of the show," he added, explaining why he was asking.

"I also got in my new drum kit today and would like to get it set up tomorrow. DW finally came through," De'Mar chimed in.

Drew turned toward Mac. "Mac, do you have any reason that can't happen?" He turned back toward Jackson. "What do you guys need, an hour?"

Jackson nodded. "Yeah, an hour ought to do it. A rehearsal before the rehearsal." Jackson smiled, showing his whole set of pearly whites.

Mac shrugged. "Yeah, I don't know of any reason why you guys can't come in early tomorrow. Just watch the overtime this week after the show." The band muttered their agreement and continued getting their equipment ready. Mac turned to Drew. "Drew, Sofie was saying something about getting shocked by her handheld. You know anything about that?"

Drew's face flushed and he frowned. "Man, there ain't nothing wrong with her mic. I'm sure she just wants some more attention . . . or another new mic."

*Mac grimaced. "Probably both, but you mind if I take a look at it anyway?"*

*"Knock yourself out," Drew said, pointing to where the mic case was and angling his finger in the direction of Sofie's. "It's in the mic case with her name on it."*

*Mac walked toward where the mic case was sitting and located the one labeled, "Sofia"..*

*Zade walked by on her way to the main stage, moving too quickly to notice the group of men who had all stopped to stare at her. Drew had walked over to where Mac was standing fiddling with Sofia's mic by turning it off and on and shaking it trying to get any sort of reaction from it.*

*"God, that girl is beautiful! It's beyond that, there is something unique and special about her." Drew said, nudging Mac with his elbow. "Wonder what my chances are. Is she dating anyone?"*

*The question was innocent enough, but it made Mac uncomfortable. He and Zade had been hanging out a lot lately but they hadn't defined what they were. Mac just knew that he had really enjoyed all the time they had spent together and he was figuring out how much he liked spending time with her. No matter how much he saw her at work (and out of work) he never seemed to tire of her at all. He even missed her when she wasn't around. He wasn't used to the feeling of missing someone like that. The one thing Mac and Zade were sure of was that they had an unspoken rule that they really didn't talk about all the time they were spending together with anyone at the show. It was a secret—and on some level that even made it more fun. The stolen glances and the sneaking around made everything just a little more exciting.*

*To Drew, the question had been completely random but it didn't feel that way at the moment to Mac. You know that bible verse: "The wicked flee when no man pursueth." In other words when you are guilty you think other people know—even when they don't. Mac was definitely getting defensive for no actual reason.*

*"Why're you asking me?" Mac responded abrasively.*

*"I wasn't, really. Just asking in general," Drew responded, slightly puzzled at the way Mac was reacting to what really was him trying to make small talk.*

*"Maybe. How should I know?" Mac huffed.*

*"Well, I don't think she is. She never talks about anyone like that," Drew speculated out loud.*

*"Maybe she just keeps her personal life personal," Mac grumbled, frustrated at the conversation and wishing he could think of a way to change the subject.*

*"Nah," Drew said confidently. "When a girl's into a guy she gushes about him."*

*"Wow, Drew, I didn't know you were an expert on females," Mac said sarcastically. But then he checked himself, adding in a softer, calmer tone, "I don't think you're her type, friend".*

*No one was really paying attention to the awkward conversation except for Jackson, and maybe Tad, who kept looking up from time to time at Mac and Drew. Jackson, on the other hand, had actually been watching the whole exchange with his arms crossed and his mouth quirked up with amusement.*

*Drew was confused by Mac's last statement. "Why? What's wrong with me?"*

*Tad joined in: "Nothing. But what makes you think you* are *her type?"*

*Tad knew that Mac liked Zade, but didn't know that anything had actually happened yet. He did realize that Mac was starting to sound defensive, though, and he was trying to diffuse the situation before Mac took it out on Drew.*

*"I—I think I could use my charms on her," Drew stammered, his voice starting to carry a hurt—as well as confused—tone.*

*Cam chimed in, having had his attention piqued by Tad's comments. "You have charm? I'd like to see this charm," he said, smiling and nudging Drew.*

*"Not everyone has game like you, Cam." Riley felt bad that everyone was ganging up on Drew and tried to come to the rescue.*

*"It's not game just 'cause women actually like me," Cam replied, in a very haughty tone.*

*"That was harsh," Jackson said.*

"*Actually, Sir Jack, here, asked her out, didn't you?*" *Mac had realized during the banter that he could redirect the attention to Jackson and find out how far things had gone with Zade and him without having to actually ask himself. That was another thing Zade and Mac didn't discuss: how much time Zade spent—and what Zade did—with Jackson. Mac knew if he gave her a hard time about it, she'd probably demand to define their relationship, which was something he wasn't ready to do. Despite how much he knew he liked her.*

"*Yeah, I've been testing the waters a little. I'd definitely go swimming in that ocean.*" *Jackson grinned wide and nodded, making his position very clear.*

"*Did you?*" *Mac wondered, trying to sound nonchalant, even as worry spread nearly imperceptibly across his face.*

"*Nah. She is quite a catch, but we're keeping it light. She's the kind you want to marry, not just use to get laid. Not sure if I'm ready to give up my freedom just yet, but she'd be the girl to do it for, that's for sure,*" *Jackson surmised.*

"*Yeah,*" *Mac affirmed, in a daze. He was processing what Jackson had said just as much as Jackson was: Zade was the kind of girl you marry.*

*Jackson noticed the faraway look and the wheels turning in Mac's head, and he raised his brow as something clicked. "Five* years from now, wild horses wouldn't keep me away. Maybe sooner," he added, in part to see what reaction he might get.

The last statement annoyed Mac, he had learned all he was going to from Jackson and he wanted the conversation over with. "Umf. Guys, it's getting late. Everyone go finish your set-ups. Doors are in twenty minutes."

Tom commented: "You know I always feel like there is some joke there."

Mac responded, "What do you mean"?

"You know that doors being a saying about opening the doors to let patrons come in to see the show, and the fact the theater also gets called 'the house' and there is a band called the Doors, and . . ."

Mac shook his head, "And you live in a van down by the river? Kid, I have no idea what you are talking about."

"Yeah, I know. Like I said, I haven't figured it out, yet. But there is a joke there".

"Hmm. Okay. Well, let us know if you ever find it." Tad chuckled and walked away. Everyone nodded and began to disperse to get ready, except Jackson, who appeared to be pondering something. Mac began to walk away, but Jackson followed him.

"Hey, Mac."

Mac stopped and turned to him slightly, exhibiting signs of really not wanting to be bothered.

"*You gonna ask her out? She's still fair game, and I like a challenge. All's fair in love and war, you know,*" *Jackson added, hinting at what he now felt was all too obvious.*

"*Sounded like Drew wants to give you a run for your money,*" *Mac replied, avoiding the question because he didn't know how to answer it without either lying or admitting he was already hanging out with her.*

"*I said I like a* challenge, *not a massacre,*" *Jackson laughed.*

*Mac was silent and only slightly smirked at Jackson's joke. Noticing the lack of a reply, Jackson raised a questioning eyebrow.*

*Mac pretended he was confused.* "*You know I don't date perform—*"

"*Don't date performers. Right. Your rules. I thought that's just what you said to all the ones that you really didn't want to date.*"

*Mac was frustrated and realized that Jackson could see through him. But he still kept trying to insist publicly that there was nothing going on.* "*She's not my type,*" *he said firmly. It was the only thing he could think of to say.*

"*Now I* know *you're full of it! I may be pretty, but it doesn't mean I'm stupid,*" *Jackson said as he began to walk away. Then he changed his mind, turned around, and started walking backwards to face Mac.* "*Just remember what I said: all's fair in love and war.*"

"*I will as long as you do.*" *Mac nodded and smiled.*

"They're the words I live by," Jackson affirmed as he turned back around. He laughed as he walked away, leaving Mac with his own thoughts.

Later that night, Mac and Tad went on break between the shows and into the Employee Dining Room for some food. The "EDR" was basically like a buffet of free food for anyone who worked in the hotel and casino. It was the kind of place that sounded like a great perk when you started your job but, after a while, it got pretty repetitive and eventually everyone got tired of basically eating the same food over and over. Nevertheless, it was free food—and you can't really beat free.

Mac and Tad had already been through the line and piled everything that looked edible on their plates as they made their way to a table in the corner, away from prying ears. Tad had picked the table on purpose as he knew it was the only way to get real answers from Mac. They were both slightly hunched over the table eating, their hands wrapped around the forks and treating them more like shovels than utensils, when Tad wasted no time asking Mac why he had gotten so weird and defensive with Drew. Mac knew he couldn't lie to Tad, and figured it might be good for him to get it off his chest to someone. He quickly spilled about what had happened so far between him and Zade—from the moment Tad had left them in the parking garage that night till now.

"No, way! I knew you were acting weird, even for you. Everything makes so much sense now. No wonder—"

"Don't say anything to anyone. We aren't telling anyone for now—or at least we don't seem to be telling anyone for now—got it?" Mac was stressed out about the whole thing and had gradually realized that he also didn't know whether Zade had told anyone or not.

"Yeah, but if you're going to keep this a secret for a bit, you better do a better job of handling stuff like what happened with Drew," Tad warned him, shaking his head.

"He . . . just caught me off guard, that's all," Mac mumbled.

Tad started laughing as a thought hit him. "Ha! I called it! Don't forget that. But I'm glad. After all, it's about time you spent some time with someone pretty, besides me. You've been alone too long, man. It's made you bitter."

"Yeah. I didn't mean for this to happen. I mean, I knew there was attraction, but I didn't think she'd make me feel this way. I was just inviting her to ride bikes to keep the peace."

Tad was smiling. "Yeah, you definitely made peace with her. Dammit! I should've bet you; would've made myself a hundred bucks!"

Tad laughed again, and Mac punched his shoulder.

"Well, I can understand you wanting to wait about saying anything," Tad said. "This place is a big enough rumor mill as it is. There's already a couple going on about Zade."

"What rumors?" Mac asked, worried he'd missed something.

Tad rolled his eyes. "Just friggin' Sofie. She's basically pissed Zade knocked her off her high horse—and sleeping with C.S. isn't getting her the part back or her star spot on the billboard."

"Well, that's not a surprise. Most people in this place have nothing better to do than to worry about everyone else, especially Sofia," Mac said, disgruntled.

"Yeah. Definitely. One thing's for sure—she really hates Zade."

Tad rolled his eyes and frowned, he didn't understand why Sofia couldn't just be a better person. It wouldn't really be that hard, *he thought to himself.*

"You think she could be nicer to the girl that saved her life," Mac asserted, annoyed by Sofia's lack of ability to care about anything but herself.

"You're saying that like Sofie could act like a regular human being," Tad interjected with a smirk.

Mac nodded and remarked, "Yeah, well. One can always hope."

# CHAPTER 10

# THE HANGED MAN

A FEW WEEKS LATER. I DECIDED TO GO ALONG WHEN most of the cast and crew went to McMullan's after work. I was still figuring out the whole "Mac and Jackson" situation, which each of them seemed to dance around while I hung out with the other. Neither seemed to want to push the issue; maybe each was afraid that if he was the one who forced me into a decision I would go in the other direction. That said, I could tell they were both starting to get antsy and I knew that sooner rather than later they would want some kind of answers.

The whole situation was something that we didn't really display at work, although it was obvious that a few people from work had an idea (I knew Tad knew something), but we had kept it away from *most* people at work and I liked it that way. Overall, keeping it to ourselves kept our work environment drama free. At work, Mac and Jackson were just colleagues to me, and they both seemed fine together at work as well. I think they had always been friends and didn't really want to let a little friendly rivalry get in the way. It was either that or they were abiding by the "keep your friends close and your enemies closer" rule.

Although I didn't know exactly what to do, I knew that I really liked them both—and for different reasons. Jackson and I agreed on almost anything that came up and everything seemed easy with him. If I had written on a piece of paper all the things I wanted in a guy, well, he would have fit it to a T, except my ideal guy would also have powers." I had learned from my mom that it's easier when you are both magick— it's actually deeply frowned upon for someone like me to end up with a mortal. It's practically a law for us to not be with our own kind. My mom instantly became an outcast for having me with a mortal. She never cared, though, because she had always been a rebel, and I guess I didn't really care either.

It took a long time before someone explained to me the big deal. I guess the issue is when you "mix" you don't know if your children will be mortal or "gifted." Since I could do magick, mom's "excommunication" was lifted and eventually people in our world forgot and stopped caring. The worry is that if too many of us pair up with mortals, and have mortal children, then we will stop existing. I cared about this on some level but that kind of problem was something I could fret about later. For the moment, I wasn't marrying anyone so I let those worries be.

Jackson was close to perfect minus the whole "just a mortal situation" but there was just something about him that I just wasn't sure of just yet, something I hadn't quite place my finger on. It could just be fear and my lack of ability to want to make a decision. Mac, was also a mortal and we clearly had our differences—but so much passion had sparked between us. I even missed him whenever I wasn't with him. There was something addictive about his presence that I couldn't even explain to myself. I had never really missed anyone besides my mom. I have always hated making tough decisions, but usually the tarot was far more helpful than it had been so far, considering that it hadn't given me a clear-cut winner no matter how I asked it. Its "freewill clause" must have been behind some kind of weird lesson I was supposed to learn.

My mom's favorite band from the 1960s was the Monkees— who also had their own TV show, which she also loved. She always said her favorite band member was Peter Tork. Many times my mom quoted Peter from his lines from the show and real life. "You know what Peter Tork says of decisions," she would tell me. "To allow the unknown to occur, and to occur requires clarity. For where there is clarity, there is no choice. And where there is choice, there is misery." In other words, he probably had to decide between two girls. I laughed at the thought of "WWPTD—What would Peter Tork Do?"

I had to change clothes after the show and I decided to take my time and get ready slowly. Jackson sweetly waited for me and, since I had brought my bike to work, he followed me over to McMullen's after the show in his Jeep. He had asked if I wanted to ride with him but I had decided that it was probably best for me to take my bike.

When Jackson and I walked through the door the place was already pretty packed. The bar was filled with lots of people from the show, some regulars of the bar, and a few tourists, everyone yelling to be heard. The atmosphere was relaxed and jovial and everyone seemed to be having a good time. I wasn't sure how it would look for us to show up at the same time, but Jackson actually didn't seem to care who knew about whatever was going on between us and the little cool he did play, was only because he knew it was what I wanted. We were two of the last people from our group to get there and we weren't there for more than eight seconds when Jackson's bandmates had pulled him away to talk about a gig they had coming up, and merch ideas, and some other thing that De'mar was talking about that I really didn't understand.

Mac and I made eye contact and he winked at me but he also seemed to be trying to make a point of mingling and not being too close to me in front of everyone. I wanted to go over and talk to him but figured I would stay away for a bit, though I noticed he was looking my way—a lot.

I had been casually talking to people and making my way around the room but found myself standing alone at one point. That's when a guy I didn't know came up and started to talk to me. He was probably in his thirties but I couldn't really be sure, and to be honest, he was pretty good looking. He was obviously hitting on me, even though I was not even remotely interested—not just because I already had one too many prospects, but also because I am not the "get picked up at a bar" kind of girl. He was funny and it was kind of fun to have him fawning all over me and, honestly, it was better talking to him than standing by myself awkwardly.

I looked up from my conversation just for a moment and noticed Mac walking over toward us. He looked upset, and yet when he approached us he adjusted his expression to being more relaxed and stuck his hand out to shake the other guy's hand.

"Mac." He introduced himself with a quick smile and a firm handshake.

The guy shook Mac's hand, but cocked his head to the side and gave him a brazen look.

"Justin," he replied while looking at me. "Is this your boyfriend?"

I could tell this was about to get interesting. I looked up at Mac but I didn't say anything. I guess the idea of competing against more than Jackson did not interest Mac one bit. Mac looked at me for a second as if to ask me what he should say. I stayed silent. He was gonna have to figure this one out on his own. He looked back at Justin. It was a long, uncomfortable silence before Mac finally responded, "Co-worker."

"Oh, well. That's great then, but we were talking," Justin said as he motioned at the two of us and then looked back at me. "Now what was I saying?"

Mac wedged himself between Justin and me before looking directly at me and remarked, "We were about to do shots. We wanted you to join us." Mac pointed towards several of the techs on his crew who were all milling around in one area of the bar, but they didn't really look like they were waiting on me to do anything. The look he gave me said he wanted me to come with him. I normally would have wanted to be stubborn in a situation like that and would have said no just to spite him. This time there was something in his face, though, and the look in his eye said I shouldn't be stubborn. I did give him a look that said I wasn't thrilled before answering him, "Oh. Um, sure. Shots. Cool." I nodded. I was already thinking about the speech I would be giving Mac later, about the way he was acting. I started to say goodbye, but Justin—who obviously thought he had some chance he really didn't have—tried to get me to stay with him.

"Hey, babe, you aren't gonna leave now, are ya? We were hittin' it off." He sounded desperate, and if I had actually been taking his flirtation seriously that would have killed it.

"It was nice talking to you, but I came to hang out with the group, so I should get back to them," I explained, trying very hard to sound polite. I had started to walk away when Justin grabbed my arm and started to pull me back roughly. Mac instantly grabbed Justin's arm and forced him to let go. It would have been obvious to anyone who cared to look that Justin had been drinking a little too much.

"Owww! You jerk face! What's your problem, man?" Justin shouted as he released the grip he had on my arm. Because the interaction had gotten loud, some of the crew had walked closer to us. Half looked like they wanted to see what was going on, and half were ready to jump in if they needed to. At the same time, a couple of guys who seemed to be Justin's friends had walked over to back him up.

"Besides you? Nothing," Mac said sourly. Mac had officially positioned himself between Justin and me. He wasn't going to let Justin come close to touching me again.

"I'm not the problem. You are," Justin said as he swayed a little and glared deep into Mac's eyes. As he stepped closer, I started to get nervous. The whole situation had gotten way more serious than it had started out being. I didn't like it at all and just wanted it over.

"Zade said goodbye. I suggest you do the same," Mac warned.

"What are you going to do about it?" Justin said belligerently. He staggered closer to Mac and got right in his face. I tried to grab Mac and walk away but I knew he wasn't going to back down. It was too late for that. Instead Mac looked like he had reached the end of his patience and was about to hit Justin. Tad made his way over and stepped between them.

I was wide-eyed and gave Tad a grateful look.

"Look, man," Tad said, "I think you have had a little too much to drink, and I am sure that in this state you are positive that you can bend steel, but let me assure you that the sober version of you would think differently. And while I'm sure your friends are very tough, there are about twenty or so guys in here that work for this guy." He gestured toward Mac, then continued, "He's our boss and we like him—and we will make sure you never touch him. So, how about you re-think what you're about to do?"

All of the crew who were in the bar had gravitated towards the commotion and when Tad mentioned them, they all stepped forward in a way that instantly conveyed agreement with Tad's comment about them being willing to fight for Mac.

Chris, one of the show's electrician's, went straight up to the front to show that there really were several of them. At 6'3" and with plenty of muscle, Chris looked like he was made out of steel and was obviously not someone to mess with on his own—not to mention the room full of show crew. The two friends of Justin's noticed that Tad was not bluffing and they began to look nervous. "He's not exaggerating," Chris added.

Justin turned white when Chris looked his way, and you could tell even he knew in his drunken state that he couldn't take Chris.

"Justin, let's go. You're drunk and she's not interested," one of his buddies insisted.

"What do *you* know?" Justin asked his friend, still angry and not backing down.

"I know that I don't want to get into a fight for you over a girl who's obviously interested in someone else. Let's go. *Now.*" Justin's friend nodded towards Mac when he said the part about me being interested in someone else.

This time it was another of Justin's friends who insisted and seemed a little more of the ringleader of the group. His friends grabbed each of his arms and tried to lead Justin out the door, one on each side of him. He started to go with them, but suddenly tore out of the grip of his friends and charged toward Mac.

Considering how intoxicated he appeared, it was impressive how quickly Justin managed to get loose from his friends and reach Mac. Luckily Mac saw Justin charge at him from out of the corner of his eye and, while he didn't have time to do much, he did have just enough time to get out of the way. I'm pretty sure Mac would have probably preferred to fight, rather than watch Justin basically fight himself.

I just stood there wide-eyed and watched as Justin crashed into a metal beam that spanned from floor to ceiling in the main part of the bar. Mac had just happened to be standing in front of the beam so it worked out in Mac's favor when he sidestepped his would-be attacker. It was pretty impressive how hard Justin hit the metal pole, head on, like a freight train that hit the side of a mountain. His head and body went flying backwards—hard—as he crashed and then hit the ground.

We all stood there for a few moments, basically wondering if he had knocked himself out. He finally opened his eyes and slowly sat up. Mac could be very cocky when he wanted to be and leaned down towards Justin before he urged, "Friend, I think you should leave now."

One of Justin's friends piped up, in agreement, "Yeah, Justin. Now!" His friends helped pull him up and pushed him out the door.

I thought about the big knot he was going to have on his head the next day.

"Damn, I was hoping they wanted to fight," Riley said, sounding disappointed, but he cracked a smile as he said it.

"Well, that would have been fun," Tad said sarcastically. "Okay, kids, back to what you were doing. Turns out there will be no fight at recess after all." He laughed.

It was silent for a couple more moments before everyone began to resume their conversations and the laughter picked back up. Mac and I just kind of stood there looking at each other for what felt like hours but was in reality was only about ten seconds or so. He looked like he was trying to read me, and how I was reacting to what happened. I stood there for a moment looking back at him with a blank stare, mainly considering the knot Justin would have on his head in the morning, before walking away to where a couple of the girls had returned to talking.

Mac hung back with Tad and I purposely stayed within earshot so I could still hear what they were saying over the bar noise. The girls were talking about a new store in the Forum Shops that they all were "super into," but that's all I could tell you about their discussion, because I had completely tuned them out so I could hear Mac and Tad's conversation.

Tad, not being big into drama, launched into Mac right away. "That guy looked crazy and was pretty big. The only reason he didn't crush you was because he was too drunk. Are you and Zade even actually dating?" Though one of the other girls could have heard if they weren't so engulfed in their conversation about the mall, I was pretty sure I was the only one who actually overheard their conversation and I perked my ears to hear Mac's response.

Mac responded in lower tones that were much harder for me to hear, "Shh! Uh, I don't know. I've told you we hang out all the time. That could have happened—"

Tad was still trying to whisper, but I could tell he wanted to yell. He was much louder than Mac and easier for me to hear. He cut Mac off before he even finished his sentence. "You're not about to say that could have happened to anyone, are you? Because, no, it couldn't have. If you're not serious enough to say you're dating, then Zade can talk to whomever she wants. We're not fifteen. That's high school bullshit."

With that, Tad stormed off to the other side of the bar and passed right by where I was sitting. I had never really seen Tad mad like that. I wondered why he was taking Mac's actions so personally—more personally than I was, even. I couldn't really see him from where I was sitting but after a moment I heard

Jackson's voice and my attention turned back to listening to what Jackson was going to say to Mac.

"Hey, Mac. You alright, man?" Jackson sounded genuinely concerned.

"Fine," Mac said gruffly, though knowing Mac he was probably upset by Tad's conversation and not actually upset at Jackson. Mac was a "wear his heart on his sleeve" kind of guy and didn't know how to shift feelings off when dealing with someone else.

"That was pretty crazy," Jackson continued; he didn't get the first hint that Mac didn't want to talk or didn't care, so Mac was far more direct this time.

"Look, Jackson, I don't really feel like talk—"

"I'm sure Zade appreciated you defending her honor," Jackson interrupted, it was obvious Jackson wanted to say whatever it was he had to say and didn't care if Mac wanted to hear him or not.

Mac decided to finish his sentence that Jackson had interrupted. "I said I don't really feel like talking." He kept his voice measured and low.

Jackson ignored Mac's statement and continued to talk, "I just think that Zade's a big girl and she can handle herself."

There was a long pause and I presumed Mac was thinking about his response options; I had almost thought he had left and somehow I didn't hear that when he finally did answer: "You're probably right." was his delayed response, which he only said halfheartedly before I heard him walk away. I wasn't sure why Jackson made such a huge point to come say what he had to Mac, and was not sure what he had accomplished. Must have had something to do with me and the fact I was basically seeing both of them, but I didn't get what Jackson gained out of saying that to him.

Aside from the girls I was standing with, I no longer had conversations to listen to. I think Mac had even left the bar all together, though I wasn't really 100% sure on that. Instead of paying attention again to the girls I had zoned out in my own thoughts about everything and still wasn't paying any mind to them or the conversation. I finally heard someone saying my name over and over, and snapped out of my daze to realize that all the other girls at the table were just staring at me. Pearla, a tall, dark-haired girl with perfect lips who was one of the acrobats in the show, had been saying my name.

"Zade . . . Zade . . . *Zade!* Are you okay?

"Oh! Sorry, I must have zoned out. What was it?"

"What's your favorite clothing store?" she asked slowly and purposely, putting emphasis on the word store. I pursed my lips together as I tried to think of any store, but I just wasn't good at this girl-bonding thing.

"I don't know. There's so many to choose from," I had a plethora of options of stores I could have named but, at that exact moment, I couldn't think of a single one for some reason. It was a stupid response but it at least bought me a few moments to think of a store, any store. I looked down and noticed a tag on the dress I was wearing, it said "BJ" and somehow I managed to remember that stood for the name on the tag inside the dress, Betsey Johnson. "Betsey Johnson, maybe."

"I love her, but she doesn't have stores anymore, you can only buy her stuff online now, which I hate cause I like to try things on first," Nora, a tall, skinny, blonde who was a dancer in the show said very passionately, as if we were talking about world peace or something.

"That's right, such a shame. I wonder why that is." I tried to sound convincing as I shook my head like I really had known that information previously. Nora then continued to talk about her favorite stores and mentioned something called "Free People." I thought about asking if that was a store or a cause but figured I could just google it later and not sound so uncool. I was relieved that the girls had gone back to talking and had stopped focusing on me.

I needed to get out of the bar and clear my head; I really needed to figure out who and what I wanted. I'm not great at small talk and even worse when my mind is somewhere else.

Making excuses of an oncoming migraine, I excused myself from the girls' conversation so that I could leave before I started banging my head against the table.

# CHAPTER 11

# THE DEVIL

SEVERAL WEEKS FLEW BY AND I WAS IN MY DRESSING room getting ready for the show. I still hadn't quite made a decision in regards to my personal life. Every time I would start to lean in one direction something would pull me in the opposite. The cards had become quite infuriating because they refused to give me an answer, which was something I'd never experienced before. Usually, after so much time had passed, an answer would have gradually become clear. The only thing I could think was that this was the cards' way of insisting that I needed to learn a lesson about making my own decisions. I had learned over the years that sometimes the cards insist you learn lessons, that is what each of our lives is about, learning lessons to become a better being—your soul can't evolve until you've learned whatever life lesson it is you need to learn.

I sank into the director's chair in front of my mirror and played with my hair and make-up a little, more futzing than actually doing anything. The show had supplied me with any and all of the make-up, skin, and hair products I wanted, and so for the very first time I had a plethora to choose from. I was even given every color of OPI gel nail polish that I wanted. Now every week my nails can be a different color instead of the normal black I used to always do. I had asked for every kind of Benefit brand make-up that existed and then extra fun eye-shadow from Too Faced in every color they make, and lip-stick as well. It was more make-up than I could ever use, but I loved having it around. I was enjoying mixing the color palettes together to see what worked and what didn't. I also alternated between the four different kinds of Sedu curlers, because I had fun playing with the different-size curls it produced and then randomly put different moisturizers on from my Kiehl's skin products, just to see what felt nice. All of it was just a place to put my nervous energy to use. I finally stopped and sat back away from my vanity. I sat like that for a long time, anxiety washing over me, and decided I would try to just focus on my breathing—a kind of meditation, if you will. I'd heard people say that it helped them, so although it had never helped me much I figured I'd give it another shot. I had put my head down, really trying to calm my nerves, when a noise jolted me out of focused breathing and back into the room.

"Knock, knock," Jackson said, standing in the doorway of my room. I jumped and turned around. I'd left the door wide open.

"Oh!" I said, clutching my chest. "It's you."

"Sorry," Jackson said, walking toward me. "I didn't mean to scare you. The door was open."

"Right," I said, nodding. I turned back to face the mirror. "It's fine."

Jackson took a seat on the small couch next to my mirror. He had been wearing his sunglasses, which he took off and set down on the cushion next to him. I'm not used to people surprising me, so I was startled—just a little.

"So, what's up?" I asked him, trying to sound natural and calm back down.

Jackson shrugged. "Nothing important," he said. "My band's playing a late show tonight after work. I just wanted to see if you were interested in coming by."

"Oh, I can't tonight," I said, genuinely apologetic. "I'd love to, really, but I've got that new illusion to work on with Charles." It was the truth, but I still felt a little guilty as I said it. Jackson looked crestfallen.

"Break my heart, why don't you?" he said, giving a half-hearted smile. He was trying to joke, but I knew he was legitimately bummed out.

"I'm really sorry," I said again.

"Don't be," Jackson said. He hesitated. "How about a movie next week?"

I smiled. "You know what?" I said. "I'd love to."

Jackson beamed. He rose to leave, but he bent down to run a thumb from the back of my jaw to my chin and kiss me on the forehead. I could feel myself blushing beneath his touch. He knew how to be so charming when he wanted to be, that expression about leaving someone weak in the knees, he knew how to do that in spades. He just oozed charm and charisma like no one I had ever met.

"See you around," he said, and left, closing the door on the way out.

I looked at my reflection again. I was still blushing. It took me a moment to notice the sunglasses that Jackson had been wearing were still sitting on the couch where he had left them. I grabbed them, jumped up, and bounded toward the door to return them. When I reached the hall Jackson was nowhere in sight, but Charles and Zeb were in the hall and they seemed to be having a heated discussion. I couldn't help but stare and try to hear what it was about. I always jump to the conclusion that something is about me and so that's where my mind went first.

"It's not good, that much I can tell you. I just don't know how bad and what it all means". I heard Zeb say, sounding worried.

Charles responded in an equally grievous tone, "You know we have to let some things take their own course, you must let it go for now." *Was it something I'd done? Was I going to be fired?*

"Yes, I am aware of that—but I don't think you understand the gravity of the situation," Zeb replied, and then looked up and noticed me staring at him. Charles noticed the direction of Zeb's attention and also looked my way.

"Hello, Zade. Is everything okay, dear?"

"Yes, fine. Is everything okay with you?" I knew the answer, I just didn't know what wasn't fine.

Charles smiled and nodded. "Oh yes, everything is fine. Just silly magician troubles. Zeb, let's go back to my office, shall we? See you later, Zade."

Zeb nodded, and Charles turned to begin to walk towards his office. Zeb waved at me with a half smile—which I guess was better than nothing—before turning to follow after Charles. I didn't know what "silly magician troubles" meant, but I had a feeling that wasn't the real answer. I had another thing I should look into.

A few days later, Tad, Mac, and I were standing backstage by the time clock getting ready to clock out. While I was waiting on my turn, I started to feel a weird stiffness in my back and a pain that was shooting down my leg. Stretching usually helped when that happened, and I needed to deal with the pain right away. I wasn't really thinking about how I would look with my toes pointed and my leg pulled up and pressed against the wall. But the next thing I knew Cam was standing right in front of me, bent down so he was eye to eye with me, and giving me a look of pain.

"Geez, Zade. You sure are stretchy."

Cam laughed a little as he popped back up and faced the guys as I shook my head at him before bending it down to my knee.

Cam continued, "I am sure glad it's our Friday. I am so ready to get the hell out of here and go camping!"

"Yep. This has been one messed-up week," Mac chimed in. I sat up and pulled myself to my feet. Mac walked over to me and smiled. I bit my lip as worry spread across my face. I still hadn't told him I couldn't go camping. I knew he had had a rough week—among other things, equipment had broken down, causing issues during shows. I frowned slightly and pulled Mac off to the side.

"Uh . . . ," I stammered for a moment and fidgeted with my hands as I talked, a nervous habit I've always had. "I forgot to tell you earlier today, but I can't go." I said it with disappointment in my voice, because I really was disappointed that I couldn't go, but I had a good reason at least.

"Why? Everyone going camping this weekend was *your* idea." Mac sounded a touch mad, as I thought he would. He was right: I had gotten everyone on board with going camping in the first place.

"Yeah, I know, but we have to have the new illusion ready by the show's anniversary and—"

"So, you're going to spend your only two days off rehearsing with Charles while everyone else is camping?" Mac asked in a grumpy tone.

"Mac, you know we both have times when work gets in the way. Times where you have had to stay really late because something was broken. It's not that I don't want to go. I do want to. I just can't this time. I was hoping you would be a bit more understanding. I know you know where I am coming from and how this happens."

"I do. I know. I'm sorry. I was just really looking forward to this. I've been dealing with a lot around here, and getting outta town sounded so nice, but I wanted to spend time with you, too. I guess I could stay here with you."

"I think you should go. It sounds like you could use the camping trip with your friends and I'll just be working the whole time. We can hang out when you get back. I'll make dinner Thursday night." Mac nodded in agreement.

The time went by quickly and before I knew it the two days off were over and everyone was back from the camping trip. They had left in the morning on Wednesday and I knew they planned to drive back in the late afternoon on Thursday. Even so, I didn't really know exactly what time Mac would be coming over, so I was listening to music and attempting to cook us dinner when the doorbell rang. The smell of beef stew was permeating throughout my apartment.

"Coming!" I shouted.

I was about to walk over to the door and answer it when I had a thought. Things seemed . . . *normal*. Mac, whom I really liked, had just come back from camping, and there I was at home, listening to music and making dinner for the two of us. Wow. Normal. *Weird*. I glided across the room feeling happy about the normal little life I had made for myself.

I knew it was Mac, but looked out the peephole to see, anyway. Habit I guess. I answered the door and smiled at Mac, who looked just a little bit dressed up in his dark denim Levi's jeans and a nice maroon and brown patterned button-up shirt with his coordinating brown suit jacket. His sterling silver cufflinks peeking out just past the end of the jacket sleeves. He looked handsome and I immediately felt underdressed in black leggings, a grey see-through shirt, and black boots. Mac grabbed me right away and gave me a huge hug.

"Gosh, I missed you," he said before letting me go just enough to walk into the apartment and shut the door.

"I missed you, too. You look really nice tonight; I feel very underdressed."

"Thanks, I wanted to look nice, just for you." He pulled me close, hugged me again, and kissed me this time. We were standing right by the door by a small wooden table where I lay things down when I get home, so things like my keys, mail, and other random things end up there before I put them away. I saw Mac eye what was on the table currently: show tickets from David Copperfield's show—Charles had taken me there the night before—and a picture of Charles and me at dinner at Table 10, the four-star restaurant where we had eaten after the show. The picture was the kind they take at dinner as the photographer—often called a "camera girl"— walks around and before you have a chance to say anything has semi-forced you to take the photo and then she tries to sell it to you. Mac's eyes fixated on them for a moment before he released me from my hug and picked up the tickets to examine them further.

"You went to dinner and a show? I thought you were going to be working the whole time," he said, sounding brash and accusatory.

"A girl's gotta eat, doesn't she?" I shrugged, not sure what he was getting at and why he looked so upset. I smiled and batted my eyes as I said it to try to lighten the mood.

"And the show?"

"He offered to take me, I think just to be nice because I spent my off days here working. Plus it was research to see some of their effects."

"And the photo?" His voice was still monotone as he asked his questions.

"Oh. Um, the camera girl who came around to our table was really cute. I think he was trying to hit on her, so he bought photos from her."

"I see," Mac replied suspiciously. He looked like he was deciding if he liked my answers.

"What are you trying to imply?" I finally retorted. If he was getting at something, then I wanted him to just tell me. I didn't like the odd vibe he was giving off.

"Nothing. Just asking." Mac, who still had the tickets in his hand, glanced at them one more time before putting them down. He grabbed my hand and pulled me close again.

"Now, for the important question. Something smells amazing. What's for dinner?"

# CHAPTER 12

# THE SUN

I HAD JUST GOTTEN TO WORK AND WAS WALKING DOWN
the hall toward the wardrobe room. Zeb caught me in the hall
and put his hand up against the wall, creating an obstruction
and keeping me from passing. He just stood there, staring into
my eyes like I had lasers coming out of them or something.
Finally, I decided to break the silence.

"Hi, Zeb. What's up?" I asked.

"You aren't ready for this; you should have been more
prepared."

I didn't know what he meant and wasn't sure how to respond,
but had been really frustrated with how little he seemed to like
me and how cold he was. I ignored his comments and went
straight to the heart of what I had wanted to ask him ever since
I had met him. "Why don't you like me?"

Zeb looked confused. "I never said I didn't."

"Some things don't have to be said. You certainly act like you don't."

Zeb looked frustrated. "I just don't think you take our craft seriously. I take it very seriously. You need to try harder. Really important things are at stake."

Zeb really did take his job seriously, I guess. I nodded and tried to sound serious with my response. "Okay. Will you help me?" I had learned that when someone has an issue with the way you do something, asking them to help teach you what you're missing is the fastest way to get them to feel better about it.

Zeb contemplated my question before he replied, "Maybe. I'll think about it. If I see real effort from you, I'll consider it."

I nodded, unsure what else to say but feeling like I needed to add something to the silence. "Okay, thank you. I'll try to show you I'm serious." I tried to sound sincere, even though I was mainly confused.

Zeb nodded, "Fine, then. I have a meeting with Charles. I have to go right now." With that, Zeb turned and left.

"Okay. Bye." I was actually glad he had ended the conversation because I had nothing else to say really. He was such a strange guy, but Charles trusted him with everything so I wanted to win him over. I remembered what Jackson had said about having to give him time and hoped he was right. Maybe this was my first step towards that.

I was tired and in thought over my odd interaction with Zeb, which caused me to walk very slowly—so slowly in fact that had I been walking any slower I'd just not have been moving at all. I finally got near the door to the wardrobe department, when I heard the vague sounds of someone singing—a voice which got stronger and more beautiful as I got closer. I couldn't quite recognize the voice, but knew it sounded familiar. It sounded like she was singing along to the radio and she sounded better than the artist actually singing it. I stopped short of entering the room and snuck just enough of a glance to see who had the amazing pipes.

Sofia was the only one in the room. She was half dressed, with her back to the door, and was singing her heart out, apparently while waiting on one of the wardrobe girls to return with her costume. I waited for her to finish the song; she sounded so good that I really just wanted to hear her sing. My first thought was to turn around and walk away, but after my confrontation with Zeb, something stronger in me just wanted to talk to her. I took a deep breath and walked into the room. As I set my stuff down and looked at Sofia, she seemed intent on not looking back at me, instead only looking at herself in the mirror.

"Wow, Sofie. I didn't know you could sing." I made sure my comment sounded as sincere as I could; I didn't want her to think for even a second that I was being sarcastic.

"I can do a lot of things you don't know about." She was snarky when she responded, but at the very least she had apparently taken my comment the way I had intended it. I thought about snapping back at her, and a few really great replies popped into my head. I quickly pushed out those clever-but-mean thoughts and chose to be the bigger person.

"I don't doubt that at all. I can tell how talented you are." I smiled. I decided that I was not stooping to her level, no matter what she said to me.

"Uh, well. Thanks." She stumbled over her words, surprised by my honest response. I could tell she had been expecting a harsh answer from me and instead was disarmed by kindness. She stared down at the ground and shifted her feet.

I stared at her for a few moments waiting for her to look up, but it didn't seem she was ever going to. As a result, I just decided to say what I was feeling: "I'm sorry you hate me." There was a long pause and more feet shifting before she glanced up at me from the corner of her eye.

"I don't hate you. I just believe that people should pay their dues. I had to, yet you walked in and were treated like you owned the place." She had finally glanced up completely towards the end of the sentence and looked me directly in the eyes.

"Sofie, believe it or not, I *have* paid my dues. Truly I have." I spoke calmly and never broke eye contact with her, pleading for her to understand.

"Maybe somewhere else, but not around here. Doesn't count if it was in Tennessee." She shook her head as she spoke and pressed her lips together in discontent. "Playing some backwoods jester for Dolly Parton doesn't count."

I nodded and fidgeted with my hands as I apologized to her. "I'm sorry you feel that way, and I'm sorry if you feel like I've been given anything at all that should have gone to you." We stood in silence for a few moments. I wondered if I should just leave it at that, but it just felt too awkward. I didn't want it to be awkward. I bit my lip and tried again to soften her, "If you don't mind me asking—have you ever asked to sing in the show?"

She had gone back to looking at herself in the mirror. "I've mentioned it," she said while pulling at strands of her hair and making sure it was all in place.

"So you would like to?" I did say it in the form of a question and I was asking, but it really was more of a statement. I already knew the answer.

"Yes, of course," she answered quickly. Then she paused for a moment, and her eyes wandered briefly before she turned to me and voiced just one word: "Why?" I had realized in the brief moments of our conversation that I truly wanted things to be okay between us. I understood where she was coming from and—even though she had never been fair to me— in a lot of ways, I still saw that she just didn't want to be replaced. She wanted to still be treated like she was important and I finally got that, maybe just because I was actually listening to her for the first time. The mean and nasty actions came out of her hurt.

"Would you mind if I asked for you to sing something during the finale? The new illusion that Charlie and I are building, I would love to have—"

"Did you just call Charles, 'Charlie'?"

I watched Sofia's eyes bulge and her jaw drop. Her chin jutted forward and her perfect flowing hair with big curls fell ever so slightly towards her face.

"Yeah," I paused for a moment to think about exactly what I had said, unsure of why I'd gotten such a strong reaction. "Why?"

"I did that once and he bit my head off." She shrugged and the right side of her lip pulled up slightly as she raised her eyebrows. "And I was *on top of him* at the time."

"Oh," I said. While I had heard the words that came out of her mouth, I didn't register her meaning right away. I nodded my head slowly as I processed what she had said and its full meaning. It was almost like in a cartoon where a light bulb goes off over the head of someone. My own eyes bulged and it felt like they had popped out of my head. "Oh!" I blurted out again much more loudly before starting to laugh nervously. I'm sure I turned every shade of red as Sofia grinned at me, obviously amused by how uncomfortable her comment had made me. I was really unsure what to say and started to stammer words that weren't making any sense. "Well . . . I . . . I don't know, I . . ."

Sofia must have started to feel a little bit sorry for me as she finally stepped in and offered up some kind of idea as to why it might be okay for me to call him Charlie and not her.

"Maybe he didn't want me to because of what we were in the middle of; it's not as manly." Sofia pressed her lips together and smiled in an apparent attempt to be friendly.

I could still feel the heat of my cheeks being red and my eyes darted all around the room for something to look at—anywhere but directly making eye contact with her. Her comment had caught me off guard, not to mention I just wasn't used to talking about intimate moments with anyone, theirs or mine. In the south, women are still taught not to talk about such things.

"Yeah. That's probably it." I wanted to change the subject as soon as possible. "Well, so . . . about the song, would you mind? I would love to have you sing something during the illusion. I love your voice." I finally looked back up at her and smiled.

My question was sincere and I really did love her voice.

She paused for a moment and adjusted her back before seeming to really contemplate my question. She stared directly at me, reading my expression.

"Well, I wouldn't be opposed to it." It was a calm answer. She spoke slowly and hesitantly as if she was thinking it through completely. I think she was concerned it was some kind of trick.

"Cool. I'll bring it up then." I smiled at her and I was feeling pretty accomplished. I think we had *almost* had a normal conversation. As if she'd been listening outside the door, one of the wardrobe girls whose name I never can remember came in at that moment and helped Sofia into the last piece of her costume. She looked beautiful and I couldn't help but stare. Sofia turned directly to a mirror and pulled her fingers through her hair on the right side. She altered the way her curls lay across the side of her face just ever so slightly, nodding to herself as if she was giving her own approval of how she looked. She smoothed down the material that hugged her hips and gave herself one last look before turning back to me.

"Zade? You should probably get dressed don't you think? You need to be at top of show in five minutes."

I instantly looked up at the clock on the wall and realized the clock said five till seven on it. This whole time we had been talking I should have been getting dressed but I was so caught up in the conversation that I had completely lost track of the time. Here I was, not dressed at all. I frantically started pulling off my socks and shoes as the anxiety set in. "Oh! Jesus!" I exclaimed in panic.

"I'll see you in a bit. And thanks." Sofia said before she laughed and walked out.

After that evening's show, Mac and I decided to take a walk. We ended up at a park close to my house, one that *technically* closed at dusk but was always teeming with people. No one ever really seemed to care. Even though it was after midnight, we were far from alone. Shortly after we arrived, a man shuffling a stack of playing cards approached us. He looked to be in his early thirties, wearing a striped shirt and a beanie. He was smiling at us.

"Can I do a magic trick for you?" he asked, already cutting the deck.

"Oh, sorry," Mac said, without missing a beat. "She's not allowed to do magic. Thanks, though."

"Oh, uh, okay," the guy said weakly as Mac and I continued to walk.

We found an empty set of swings where, after we spent some time reliving our childhood on them, Mac paused.

"Wanna sit over there?" he asked. We lay down side by side in the grass. Mac was still in his show blacks. I'm not sure if he wore them out of ease, or whether he knew that I felt for show blacks the way most women feel about men in firefighting uniforms. I had at least changed into jeans and one of my most comfortable t-shirts, though I still had on all my stage makeup. Mac ran his fingers through my hair.

"How do you know I'm not allowed to do magic?" I said, jokingly. "You don't know that. There are a lot of things you don't know about me."

"Tell me, then," he cooed. I looked at him. He was staring at me lovingly.

"Tell you what?" I questioned, cuddling closer to him and smiling at him. I was feeling very content at the moment. That was a new feeling for me. It was a nice feeling, though.

"Anything. Everything. I want to know your past. I want to know everything you're willing to tell me," he explained in a passionate way that felt very romantic. I wanted to tell him all my deep dark secrets but I couldn't. It made me sad that I couldn't open up and show him my world. I tried to think of something I could tell him but nothing was really coming to mind. There had to be some interesting stories that didn't involve magick but in that exact moment those were the only stories I could think of.

I hesitated. "There isn't much to tell, really. I grew up in a little town in Tennessee called Centertown, with my mom. My mom's parents were actual Gypsies. My parents aren't together . . ." I trailed off. I realized that the innocent things I was saying could lead to dangerous questions. Questions like "So what do your parents do?" Talking about my mom or my dad would be bad for obvious reasons. I played with the family necklace that hung around my neck. The ball and the stone inside were very important but I couldn't even explain about that either. I guess I had a panicked look on my face with the thoughts that had taken over me.

As I hesitated, Mac put his hand on my shoulder and inquired, "Is this making you uncomfortable?"

I shook my head. "Look, I don't mind telling you anything. Really. Maybe I just feel put on the spot. You usually get to know someone well over time, because things happen and they tell you things and eventually you just know it all." I stopped. I was rambling and I was pretty sure I had made my point; at least his question wasn't about my parents.

"Sure," Mac said, but I could see in his face he wasn't about to give the topic up yet.

I tried again. "Like, say we go swimming. We're in the water and then that sparks a story about one time when I was swimming and . . . whatever. So I tell you that story. Does that make sense?"

Mac smirked and placed his head on my chest before he stared at me. "One time you were swimming and . . . ?"

I laughed and pinched him playfully. "And I tried to drown this guy who was being a smart ass."

We both laughed and he made some sort of comment about how I was about to get it as he started to tickle me. I'm extremely ticklish—which he knew—and I squirmed about while begging him to stop in between my giggles. I tried to move out of his grip but the more I tried the more he pinned me down. Finally he had to stop because he was holding my arms down and had somehow pinned my legs with his feet while his legs were straddling mine and he was hovered above me. He moved the hair that was lying across my face and said, "I'll stop if you let me do this."

And then he kissed me.

The next day, I had to go into the theater early to work on the new illusion. I had been there already for a few hours before I was able to take a lunch break. I had decided to walk across to the Fashion Show Mall and eat there since I had extra time compared to my usual break between shows. Since it was closer, I decided to go out through the front of the theater instead of going out the back into the hallway, as I would have done if I had been going to the EDR. I was leaving the theater, completely engrossed in the music coming from my headphones, at the exact moment Jackson was entering with his head down, focused on his phone. We collided, and for the second time I found myself having fallen on top of him. He caught me, again, and all of a sudden he was holding me in his arms.

"We have got to stop meeting like this," Jackson joked, smiling his movie star smile and laughing while he slowly and gently placed me back on my feet.

I blushed heavily. "Oh my God, I'm so sorry," I stammered. I was so embarrassed that I had yet again crashed into him. He was going to start thinking I was doing it on purpose.

Jackson looked mildly perplexed. "For what?" he wondered.

I straightened myself and look around to see if I had dropped anything while I replied. "I'm not usually this clumsy, I swear." I assured him with my syrupy southern drawl, which has varying degrees of prominence in my speech. Sometimes it's barely there but others—especially when I'm angry or embarrassed—it's far stronger. "You'll probably want to start calling me 'The Hurricane.'"

Jackson's eyes twinkled. "Don't threaten with a good time," he declared. "You can plow into me any time. You are my favorite hurricane." I blushed and smiled stupidly. There I went again, feeling weak in the knees.

I giggled nervously and backed up half a step. Jackson moved in just a bit closer to me. I was now almost pushed up against the wall. Jackson pressed his left hand against the wall. He had me almost pinned and was looking right at me.

Suddenly, a little girl who couldn't have been older than seven or eight ran up to me, trailed by someone whom I assumed was her mother.

"You're the girl from the show we saw last night?" the girl's mom asked incredulously.

"Yeah," I said sheepishly, from under Jackson's arm. "That's me."

"You were incredible," the woman gushed excitedly. "You're all my little girl, Sarah, can talk about. We are staying here at the hotel. Would you mind if I got a picture of her with you?" Jackson backed away to give the little girl room near me.

I smiled warmly. "Sure. Hi, Sarah, I'm Zade," I beamed down at the girl, and then bent down beside her for the photo. Sarah was adorable with cute ringlets in her hair and a smile that could melt your heart.

She threw her arms around my neck. "I want to be you when I grow up."

We smiled as Sarah's mom took the picture. "Well, you certainly can be," I explained to her, and then I hugged her tightly before rising back to my feet. "Nice meeting you both. Bye, Sarah!" I waved as they walked away.

When they were out of sight, Jackson edged closer to me again. "So, what has you here so early?" he asked with a gleam in his eye.

"Charles asked me to come in to work on a new illusion with him. I've been here all day. Just going over to the mall to eat."

"I'm sorry," Jackson apologized, with genuine pity, as if he had something to do with me working all day.

I chuckled. "I don't mind, really," I clarified. "I like being here early. Keeps me focused."

Jackson studied me. "You take your work really seriously. I like that about you." He nodded.

I blushed again. "You know what they say? Surround yourself with people that take their work seriously, but not themselves." I loved quotes and sayings. I had one for almost every situation and I could rattle them off all day. I guess it made me feel like I could always comment on something without sounding dumb. Though I was starting to wonder if I used them too much and if it made me sound cheesy.

"Well, you should stop taking yourself so seriously then," Jackson commented in a very serious tone, which I knew was him being extremely sarcastic, before he broke into a smile and poked me in the arm.

"I'll get right on that." I smirked. Although I was enjoying our banter, I was getting hungry and I wasn't going to have enough time to go and come back if I didn't leave right away. I would have invited him to come but I knew he was about to start band rehearsal. That's why he was there. "Sorry again for crashing into you."

"Like I said you can do that anytime," he remarked, eyes glinting as he raised one eyebrow and shrugged.

Charm just flowed out of him the way most people sweat in the sun on a hot August day in Tennessee. It got hot in Vegas, like 124 degrees hot, but it was a dry heat and let me tell you it was not as sweltering as a humid ninety degrees in Tennessee. You will sweat buckets without even lifting a finger the moment you step outside. "See you in a few?" I asked, even though I knew the answer; I just was having trouble with exactly what else to say before I left.

"You can count on it," he affirmed.

I began to walk through the open corridor that led into the casino. I wouldn't say the place was "bustling" but it was busy for 2pm on a Tuesday. I caught myself turning around right before the door of the theater would be out of sight. Somehow I just knew that Jackson would still be standing there watching me walk away. I locked eyes with him. Most people probably would have been embarrassed to be caught like that but if he was he didn't show it. He simply smiled and waved at me. I laughed a little to myself, smiled, and waved back. I then turned around and disappeared out of sight.

# CHAPTER 13

# THE HIGH PRIESTESS

MORE WEEKS FLEW BY. MY LIFE HAD BECOME PRETTY comfortable and happy. I should have known that things had been almost "too normal" for too long. Something was bound to break. I just didn't expect what was coming, that's for sure.

Mac and I were in the middle of rehearsals. The theater always had a damp feeling due to all the water inside. It was a muggy, humid feeling, but I loved it—it reminded me a little of home. We were standing very close together and pretty much alone in that part of the theater—or at least that's what we thought. Most of the cast was on the main stage during the part of the show we were rehearsing, and I was set to come down from the ceiling so I was the only performer up on the catwalks. I had my safety harness on, but it didn't feel quite right so I was playing with the straps, adjusting it slightly. Twisting back and forth, I was eventually bent all the way over trying to make sure that the harness felt right regardless of what position I was in.

"You know how hot you look in that harness?" Mac asked. I stood up and turned around so I was facing him directly.

"Oh, yeah, I'm sure," I said sarcastically.

"No, seriously!" Mac retorted and as he grabbed part of my harness and pulled me closer to him. Due to the humidity and temperature in the theater we both instantly felt sweaty as his skin touched mine.

"You'd say I looked hot in a burlap sack." I shook my head at him but I had a pretty big smile on my face.

"You'd look amazing in anything," he said with a mischievous twinkle in his eye. "And even better in nothing," he added as he rubbed his hand over the small of my back. It felt good, but his hand pushed one of the metal buckles into my skin just enough to snap me back to reality.

"Okay, help me up. We're holding up rehearsals," I reminded him. Mac sighed, but grabbed the clip from the side of the rail and hooked it into my harness before lifting me on top of the rail. He pulled me in for a kiss. I kissed him back quickly before grabbing the bar hanging by my head and pulling myself on top of the set piece where I was suppose to start.

At that exact moment I noticed Charles standing farther down the catwalk. I wasn't sure if he had seen Mac kiss me, but I guessed he had. And, if he had, it was too late to do anything about it. I pretended to not even notice him, thinking that maybe even if he had seen us together maybe he hadn't really seen what happened—or maybe he'd pretend he didn't see it, if I pretended I didn't see him. That was a lot of pretending, even for a magic show. Either way, I had to push the worry out of my mind and concentrate on my next cue.

Even so, I wondered what Charles was doing there. He rarely rehearsed the show with the rest of the cast unless we were adding a new element. A lot of times he would prefer to actually watch the show from the audience to make sure he was happy with how it looked. When he did that, he would use a stand-in, which is something else Zeb would do. Zeb could, technically, do the show if he needed to but Charles never has missed a show—and the masses don't come to see Zeb. So, mainly, Zeb's job was to simply stand in for Charles at rehearsal. Zeb, as a Magi, also had his own spots, though, and Rene (another Magi) filled in for Zeb's parts during the rehearsals. It works out 'cause Rene can do both his and Zeb's parts without too much hassle.

Once I was safely on the set piece, which looked like a tiny bed, and it had begun its descent into the theater, Mac turned to head towards one of the automation boards to check on his team.

*Mac hadn't seen Charles standing right behind him. When he turned to head toward the board on the lower grid, he plowed right into his boss.*

*"Oh! Hey. Sorry—didn't see you standing there," Mac said apologetically.*

*"I bet. Your mind seems to be somewhere else," Charles commented.*

*"Just having a good day," Mac replied, unsure what else to really say. He felt uncomfortable just standing there and wasn't sure what to do. Before he could excuse himself, Charles interjected.*

*"I thought I might find you up here."*

*"Oh, you were looking for me?"*

*Charles made most people nervous, but not Mac; it might have had something to do with the fact that Mac had worked with him for so long and that Mac just wasn't the kind of person that a guy like Charles could make nervous. Mac didn't get worked up because someone was famous or powerful. It doesn't hurt that Mac is a perfectionist when it comes to his job and he is also a hard worker, always on time and never calls out. He is also really good at his job and knows how to fix anything, make anything, and solve any problem, faster and quicker than anyone else. Charles also knew how valuable and rare a guy like Mac was and how much of a big deal he was to the show. Mac knew that Charles was well aware of all this and knew he didn't have much to fear*

240

when it came to work or the one person in the theater who was really considered Mac's boss, Charles. "Mind following me to my office? I would like to speak to you about something in private. It won't take but a few minutes of your time," Charles asked politely.

"Sure, you're the boss," Mac replied, curious as to what this was about. They made the long trip to Charles's office in silence. Charles slipped his key out of his pocket and waved it in front of the door. It was a magnetic lock—like on a hotel door—and you could hear the grinding of the door unlocking. He pushed down on the door handle and pushed the door open enough for them to walk through. Mac put his hand up to hold the door open as he followed Charles inside, then allowed the door to close on its own. Once inside, Charles allowed Mac to pass, and leaned against the door.

"Mac, have a seat. I want to have a man-to-man talk with you." He motioned toward one of the two heavy-looking chairs sitting on the guest side of the desk.

Normally, in all of their other meetings, Charles had immediately sat down on his side of the desk, gotten out his glasses, and opened the notebook that kept all his show notes. He would begin to read his notes and ask questions without even looking up at Mac to make sure he was ready. With Charles still standing behind him, Mac realized this wasn't a normal meeting about the show and started to wonder what it was actually about. Mac sat down before simply replying, "Okay." He was thinking back on all of their meetings, and was pretty sure Charles had never asked to have a "man-to-man talk" with him before.

Mac wondered if Charles was going to ask him to fire someone. Charles had once asked Mac to fire a lighting tech, because he simply didn't like his attitude. The guy wasn't a bad lighting guy and actually did an alright job, but Charles just hadn't liked him. Mac technically gets the say in that matter of any crew, but he wasn't too attached to the lighting guy at the time so it wasn't a big deal. He hoped this time it wasn't someone that he really liked and was attached to, like Riley, who happened to be out sick today which is why Mac was even in the grid with Zade. He would fight for Riley, but hoped he didn't have to, he really couldn't think of anyone newish that Charles might really have had an issue with.

Finally, Charles walked around to his desk. Placing his elbows on the table, he inhaled deeply. He interlocked his hands, his index fingers pressed together and against his lips, beginning to tap them together. With a sigh, he looked up at Mac.

"May I be frank with you, Mac?"

Mac, who loved being the smart-ass and typically would try to make light of things if he could, jovially responded with a laugh. "Sure. You are the boss. You can be Bob or Bill, too, if you want."

Charles looked puzzled before responding with a deadpan, "Oh. Humor."

"Yeah, sorry, it was a joke. Seriously, be as frank as you want."

"Thank you. It's been brought to my attention that you and Zade have developed . . . a more personal relationship."

"We're friends, if that's what you mean." Mac realized he was wrong about this being about firing someone and now had no idea where he was going with this.

Charles smiled, finding it funny that Mac had tried to say they were just friends. "Maybe a little more, at least from what I've seen. If you don't mind me prying, what are your intentions with her? Are you just having fun, or could this be something . . . serious?"

"If you don't mind me asking—why do you care? Lots of people in our show date, you and Sofia, even."

"Yes, of course. It's what happens in this business. Well—you both are very important to me. Professionally. I know my show would struggle without you. And she—well, you see how special and important she has become to us. She brings something extremely unique. Wouldn't want anything to cause issues."

Mac paused, trying to gather his thoughts. It certainly seemed reasonable enough for Charles to be concerned. Mac had seen the show lose someone here or there when a romance had soured. In the past, if a person had left, it never seemed to be anyone that valuable to the show, since most performers are easily replaced. On the other hand, he knew his value to the show—and had to agree with Charles that Zade was special. Charles was very right about that. "Well, I have grown to care for her. We are friends. We haven't labeled it, beyond that, though." Mac paused but Charles sat, not reacting, Mac realized he needed to say something more than that. "Whatever happens, I'm sure we will both be professional and not let anything personal interfere with our jobs." Mac seemed to have surprised himself, feeling pretty confident in his answer, and finished his statement with a nod.

"Do you love her?" Charles's eyes narrowed as he looked directly at Mac.

Mac sighed, feeling very put on the spot with such a loaded question. He and Zade hadn't even said what they were doing was dating—much less something way beyond that involving something as strong as love. "Well, I . . . I think she's amazing. I . . ." Mac stumbled over his words, unsure what to say. As he sat in the office, he had to admit to himself that he also didn't know the full extent of what was going on with Zade and Jackson, which was something else they didn't talk about. It was dawning on him that for two pretty open and honest people—who were especially open and honest with each other—they sure had a decent amount of things they just didn't talk about.

Charles broke into Mac's reverie and reminded him, "That's not what I asked. I asked if you loved her."

Again, Mac wasn't sure how to respond; he wasn't ready to admit something to Charles that he also wasn't ready to admit to himself. He thought about all the reasons that he shouldn't be in *love with Zade. Then he thought about what else he knew. He had learned that the funny thing about love is that love doesn't care if you've labeled it or not—and it also doesn't care if there might be someone else vying for the person you love. Jealousy might, but not love. You can love someone who doesn't even know you really exist. Love really knows no boundaries and sometimes it doesn't seem to make a lot of sense. You can wish it away all you want but just like Cupid's arrow, once you've been hit, you've been hit. Mac realized that was not the response to give Charles. He decided to give him the most open and honest answer he could: "Well it has possibility."*

*Charles nodded as if he was contemplating Mac's answer before speaking again. "If you believe you can both be professional regardless of emotions and the state of your personal relationship, then I will no longer concern myself with your personal affairs. Thank you for taking the time to speak with me on this, and for being honest and direct." Charles stood up and extended his hand out.*

*Mac took the hint that the conversation was over and that Charles had gotten the answers he wanted. He stood up as well and shook Charles's hand with a perplexed look on his face. He felt like he had just agreed to buy land, instead of having had a very personal conversation. He knew that Charles had never really lived a normal life; after all, he had been famous since his early twenties and Mac knew he had toured as a magician with a circus or something since he was a teenager. Charles had manners, but* sometimes lacked finesse in the way normal people treated other normal people. Mac had mostly gotten used to it a long time ago but, in some situations, like this, it still threw him off some when Charles acted strange.

"One last thing," Charles added, "if you don't mind, please keep our conversation confidential. I would prefer Zade not even be privy to it. I don't want her to think I am trying to meddle in her life. She hasn't known me for as long as you have and I'm not sure she understands the business completely yet—or the complications of a personal life; so perhaps you could even keep the fact we had a conversation to yourself. It would be appreciated."

"Sure. Yeah. No problem, boss," Mac agreed, though it made him wonder whether Charles understood more about inter-personal relationships than he let on and just chose not to con-form. Instead he used that as an excuse for just being weird. Mac always thought it was funny that if you were rich you were "eccen-tric" and if you weren't rich or famous you were just "weird." He refused to call anyone eccentric just because they happened to have money or fame.

"Thank you," Charles said in his dignified way.

Mac waved just slightly as he left, shutting the door behind him. Before diving back into work, he stood on the other side of the door for a minute in thought trying to process all that had just happened.

It was a long time before I knew about the conversation that took place that day, but I could feel the weird nervous energy that Mac was projecting the next time I saw him. He seemed "off" for the rest of the night, and I couldn't quite place my finger on why.

The next day, Mac and I found ourselves walking through a park, talking about nothing in particular. I was still trying to figure out what was going on in Mac's head when a bicyclist clipped me, causing me to drop my purse. It wasn't a big deal, but something felt weird about the collision. The cyclist was on a thin, fast racing bike with drop-down handlebars, and was wearing bright yellow and pink cycle spandex. All of that meant, to me, that he was an avid biker who knew what he was doing—not a clumsy teenager who had simply misjudged the crowds on the park paths. I wasn't too worried about the contents of my purse, except that I usually carry a deck of my tarot cards in my purse among other "normal" things like my wallet and Chapstick. The velvet bag that held them must not have been closed all the way because when my purse flew all the contents of my bagged spilled out and the cards went everywhere. I quickly bent down to collect everything.

Mac yelled at the biker loudly, "Jerk!" and kicked some dirt in the biker's direction before also bending down to help me. He started picking up some of the cards and examined them closely.

While Mac's back was to me, I let my anger get the best of me for a moment and was looking at the biker more than picking up my cards and the other contents of my purse. My pulse was racing and all I could think was that the biker. He needed to learn to be nicer and more courteous around other people, and not knock people out of the way like that. I wondered if I had been a little kid or an older person, what would have happened. He hadn't stopped to check on me—or even yelled back, "Sorry," or anything. Before I had even thought about what I was doing, I balled my fists quickly and squeezed.

The biker flipped upside down as if he'd hit a massive pothole that came out of nowhere, or at least to anyone else it probably looked like that. He landed pretty hard on his back, and made a few loud sounds of shrieking pain as the bike crashed into a bench, sending a few pieces going in different places. I was fairly certain he wasn't permanently injured, but he also wasn't going to be riding anymore today; that was for sure. Mac's back was to the biker, so he didn't even see what happened, and was too pre-occupied with examining the cards to even notice what

I'd done. I hoped what I'd done to the biker might teach him a karma-related lesson.

"What are these?" Mac inquired as he helped me pick up some more of my cards. When I looked up at him, he had a look of disdain on his face; he was holding up a few of them in his hands, the Devil card sitting out and most prominent. I looked at him and smiled, collecting the last of my cards and grabbing the ones in his hands before quickly putting them back into the velvet bag. I pulled the string tightly this time before throwing them into my purse.

"Oh, nothing really. Just cards." I stood up, ready to continue our walk.

Mac looked deeply perturbed. "You don't really believe in that stuff, do you?"

I could hear the disapproval in his voice. I thought for a moment about what I should say back. I studied his face, and then realized that if I lied to him it would just become more complicated later. This was very much a part of my life and who I was—and it would always be that way. If Mac was going to also be a part of my life then he was going to have to accept this as well. Sooner or later we were going to have to have this conversation. I would not have picked that day for it, but I might as well get it out of the way and see how it takes it. I swallowed and nodded my head a little. *Here goes nothing.*

"Yeah. I do. I mean, my mom does readings for a living. I kind of grew up around it; my family are Gypsies and practice it. It's fun. It's not a big deal." I downplayed it, thinking that if he accepted it at all he could slowly work up to getting used to it. I didn't have to shove it down his throat all at once.

At first he said nothing. Then he looked somewhat confused again, and asked, "I thought you were Jewish?"

I smiled softly, trying to ease Mac into the conversation. I almost found this a funny question for him to ask and smirked a little before clarifying. "I am. We, my family and I, are. One is not exclusive of the other." I could see that Mac was thinking about what he was going to say, and was beginning to think that I wasn't going to like his next comment as he grimaced. I could see I had pushed some kind of button with him.

"That stuff is hogwash," he growled. "You're too smart to believe in stuff like that. You shouldn't believe something just because your parents do—or your family does." He shook his head at me as if I was a child who had broken a jar in the kitchen and was getting reprimanded.

I sighed. I didn't like his reaction, but it wasn't like it was the first time I'd heard words like his—or far worse—once someone found out that my mom does readings. I'd been called things I won't repeat here but I'm sure you know what I am talking about. I knew some people thought reading Tarot cards were pure evil and that anyone who would have anything to do with them came straight from the devil.

As I stood there, I hoped I didn't have to convince Mac otherwise, but his reaction to the cards was still something I wanted to diffuse before it turned into an all-out fight. "I don't just believe in it because of my mom and my family. I believe it, because . . . well . . . because I believe it." I decided to try to appeal to his sense of curiosity. "Have you ever taken the time to learn anything about the tarot?"

"No. You know I base what I know off of logic. What's logical about telling someone's future based off of a fancy deck of playing cards? All that voodoo stuff is bullshit." Mac turned away from me for a moment. I knew him well enough to know that sometimes he had a gut reaction that didn't always stick once he had calmed down. I had learned that sometimes I just had to let him breathe for a moment and process. He kicked a rock or two down the path before turning back around looking concerned and confused. I figured I would cut him some slack and let him digest what I had told him.

"Is it okay that I feel that way? Or did I just insult your way of life—and your mother?" he asked. I was relieved that his voice sounded confused, but not angry.

"No. You didn't insult anything. I'm used to that reaction." I shrugged as I answered him and followed it with another sigh.

As much as I wanted him to be different from all the rest who had learned about my tarot cards—which were a small part of a much bigger portion of my life—the disappointment of him not understanding was starting to get to me.

I could tell he was trying to backpedal, but I wasn't sure how far apart my revelation had pushed us. "I'm sorry. I don't mean to be a jerk. I guess I just feel very strongly about this kind of stuff. You know I didn't mean to hurt your feelings. I just don't believe in that stuff."

I managed to give him a small smile. "It's fine. You don't have to believe in them." *At least he doesn't think I'm the devil now, I guess.* I wasn't sure I could count that as a win. I hung my head. I could feel the beginnings of tears springing to my eyes.

Mac cupped my chin with his hand. "Chin up, princess, or the crown slips," he said.

I laughed in spite of myself and raised my eyes to meet his, but I could still feel the tears just beneath the surface. Mac appeared to be appeased, though, and I had a feeling this wasn't the end of our discussion about our disparate beliefs but, for the time being, it seemed to be the end of the conversation. I could only hope that he would slowly come around. Mac hugged me and kissed my cheek. He kept his arm around me and I clutched my purse closer to my body as we continued our walk.

Several days later, I took Jackson up on another offer he made to take me to the movies. It had been a few weeks since the last film we had made it out to see. The last time he had let me pick the film so I figured it was only fair to let him pick this time. Of course he chose the latest action superhero flick starring Ryan Reynolds. The film was actually pretty good and even though I had had really no desire to see it prior to going I actually ended up really enjoying it. Ryan Reynolds is just really good at being clever and funny in almost any role and he made the film exciting and fun. I had also enjoyed eating too much kettle corn, because it's my absolute favorite theater snack and not all movie theaters carry it so when it's around I always stuff myself.

Back outside the theater, Jackson offered me his arm before leading me up the street. I still get giddy every time he does that; it makes me feel treasured and special.

"Not in a rush to get home, are you?" he asked, grinning.

"Not at all."

"Good," he said.

We walked silently up the sidewalk, arm in arm. After a few moments, he broke the silence again.

"Thanks for humoring me and not making me take you to a chick flick. I mean . . . it's not that there is anything wrong with them, I've just really been wanting to see that movie since I saw the first preview months ago."

I looked him in the eyes and smiled. "I actually really enjoyed the movie—and the company. It's all been really fun."

"And here I was beginning to think my love spell wasn't working." For a split second I felt my heart race, then I realized he was joking and giggled. I still found his joke interesting, though, to say the least—all things considered. Jackson apparently didn't notice my confusion as he continued. "Hey, there's a great little instrument shop two blocks up the street. Interested?"

"God, yes," I said, louder than I'd meant to. "I've been dying to get a nicer acoustic and you could help me pick one out."

"Let's do it, then."

He switched his grip from my arm to my hand, and we increased our pace. I laughed, feeling giddy. Suddenly, Jackson slowed. We were approaching a dimly lit shop with a pink and green neon sign proclaiming that palm and tarot readings were offered within.

"Hey," Jackson said, tugging my hand to get me to stop walking. "Wanna do something crazy?"

I looked at him warily. "Like what?"

"Skinny dip?" He raised his eyebrow and laughed before continuing. "But, seriously, let's get our cards read." As he said it, he pointed to the neon sign.

I blinked at him. "Really?"

"Really."

I shuffled my feet awkwardly. "From here?"

Jackson pulled me closer to him. "Why not?" I saw mild concern in his eyes.

Internally, I was kicking myself. Why was I being so difficult? Could it be so hard to believe that he meant what he said? "You don't think it's stupid?" I asked, biting my lip.

"Hell no. It sounds fun," he said enthusiastically, flashing his gorgeous teeth. He paused his excitement for a moment. "You don't believe in it, huh?"

I let out a deep breath. "I actually believe more than most people. My mom reads cards for a living." I paused. "I'm just used to everyone saying it's stupid." I looked away, thinking about how seldom my beliefs and lifestyle had been met with real acceptance—and how much it continued to hurt for people to be cruel just because they didn't understand. Even more so, it hurt how little anyone tried to understand or learn more about it before passing judgment.

Jackson gently lifted my chin with his hand, bringing his eyes to meet mine. "I'm not everyone," he said quietly.

I smiled a little. "You're right," I said. "You're so different from anyone I've ever met." His reaction was so different than

Mac's—or that of any other guy I had ever known. There went my weak-in-the-knees feeling again.

"I'll take that as a compliment," he replied, cupping my face in both hands. "And I'll take this, too."

With that he kissed me passionately while bending me back like they do in the movies until my knee popped, which anyone who's ever seen any romantic movie would know, is a very good thing.

# Chapter 14

# Wheel Of Fortune

We had just finished our final rehearsal of the newly revamped show, including the new illusion we had kept under tight wraps. Any of the cast and crew who weren't involved in it hadn't even seen it, and out of those people who had seen it not one of them (aside from Charles and I) actually knew how it worked. Everyone had had to sign agreements stating that they wouldn't share what they knew and that meant that they couldn't even talk about it with any of the other cast and crew. The less people talked about it—or speculated about how it was done—the less chance anyone had of picking up on how ... well ... *impossible* it actually was. That clause also kept me from having to answer questions that I really couldn't answer, because no one was allowed to ask me.

We had a couple of days off before the actual premiere, which had been scheduled so that everyone could have a little bit of rest after keeping such a grueling schedule lately and so that—if worse came to worse—it would give us a couple of days "buffer" to work on or fix anything that needed fixing. Charles offered to take everyone out to eat after the last rehearsal and, since you don't say no to the boss, we all went.

He took everyone to the Peppermill, a Vegas staple. It has been around since the 1970s, and still housed velvet-covered booths in very bright colors and waitresses in *very* short skirts. Since it was open twenty-four hours with both breakfast served all the time *and* a fully stocked bar, it had long been a popular haunt for show people. It was pretty late by the time we finished rehearsals and got over there, and all of us were fairly exhausted, but starving. The crew showed up all in show blacks, while the cast was mostly still in full hair and makeup above our street clothes, as we all had come straight from the theater to here. A cheery hostess greeted us as we walked in.

"Mr. Spellman," she said, approaching Charles, "we are so pleased to have you all here. We've done our best to close the whole left side of the restaurant just for you." She smiled when she saw Charles nod his head at this. "Right this way," she gleamed.

The hostess led us to the "left side" of the restaurant, passing several customers who gave us varying looks as we walked by them. We all began to pile in and sit. As Charles pulled out his chair, Sofia instinctively took the only seat beside him. Other performers began to file in near Sofia. Mac and I were standing off to the side, not really realizing how quickly the seats were being filled.

Charles leaned toward Sofia, likely trying to be subtle, but I happened to be standing close enough to hear what he said to her. "Sofie, darling," he said softly. "I need Zade to sit next to me. Can you and Mac find seats somewhere else?"

"What?" Sofia hissed, shooting a look at me that could have killed.

"Don't make a big deal about this," Charles warned, fixing Sofia with a stare that made it clear this was not up for discussion.

Sofia straightened her back, pushed her chair back from the table, and stood up. "Well, Mac, come on," she said, putting on her best impression of a sweet voice. "Let's go find a seat at the kids' table, I guess." She crossed around to where Mac and I were standing, waiting for him to follow her. Mac, who had not overheard the conversation, looked confused.

Mac looked at Charles with a question in his eyes. Charles simply stared back. "Mac," Charles said, "you don't mind, do you? I need Zade to sit next to me."

Mac looked at me, then back to Charles. He shrugged. "Uh," he muttered, "no. I guess not." Sofia, stormed off to the very other end of the room, the only place at this point with open seats. Mac trudged along behind.

Most of the cast and crew were too busy talking and laughing to even notice what had happened. As Mac caught up with Sofia, I heard him remark, "That was kinda weird, right?"

Sofia rolled her eyes. "Guess we know where we rank now." She glared back at me.

I looked at Charles, feeling sheepish. I hadn't expected this at all, and didn't know why I needed to sit next to Charles—or what we needed to go over. I had glanced over to Mac to give him an "I'm sorry look" when Jackson, who happened to be in the seat that had been next to Sofia, nudged me. I glanced his way and smiled. Jackson had just started to say something when Charles cut him off as he also had just noticed that Jackson was there.

"Oh, good!" Charles said. "Jackson, my bandleader, I wanted you to be with us as well. Zade and I want to discuss intro music." I shrugged at Jackson; I wasn't really aware we needed to talk about intro music but, if Charles said so . . . .

Charles had remained standing through all of this, and now lifted his water glass and tapped it with a spoon to get everyone's attention. "I wanted to thank you all for all your hard work these past few months, revamping and—in my humble opinion—revitalizing the show with me," he began. "I'm very excited for the premiere, I hope you enjoy the next two days off before the big night. Your hard work is much appreciated and

I am grateful and honored to have such a wonderful cast and crew. So . . . food and drinks are on me! And cheers to you all!"

He paused, lifting his water glass higher in the air, and the cast and crew cheered loudly. When the noise had died down, he continued. "Most importantly, I would like to thank Zade for coming to join our little family. She has made our show that much better and has elevated us all. She helped kick the dust off and brought in some new and much-needed blood. My little starlet." He winked at me.

Everyone cheered again. I took a sip from the water glass that was directly in front of my seat; I hoped it was actually mine. I then glanced back down to the far end of our group where Mac and Sofia were seated. Sofia was saying something to Mac, and I could see that they were both frowning. Mac looked frustrated and upset. I was pretty sure that he wasn't upset that I wasn't seated next time him—after all, at work, things were still very much on the down low, so we couldn't make a show of wanting to sit together—but I was sure he was less than thrilled to be seated next to Sofia. I scanned the room for Tad to see if Mac could maybe find a seat with him, but Tad was squished into a booth surrounded by people.

On the other hand, I was also sure that Mac wasn't thrilled that I was sitting with Jackson, who had already put his arm around me. I grabbed my cell phone and thought about what I could iMessage to him. Nothing great or clever or helpful was coming to mind. I finally picked a really sad-looking emoji, ☹, and sent it. I waited a few seconds for it to go through to his phone, which I could see was sitting on the table in front of him. I knew he kept it on vibrate and never with an audible ring, but figured he would hear it vibrate on the table and I would see it light up. *There it went.* He looked at the light flash and picked it up. I watched him open my iMessage and read it. I then saw him text something back. I anxiously waited for my phone to go off and opened it to the iMessage. It was a slightly different emoji with no text to help me understand what he was feeling.

Zade: ☹

Mac: 😑

The next two days were a blur for me, full of press, interviews, and no actual time off leading up to the big night. Charles and I had been working on an all-new show and most importantly a brand new and impressive illusion for the last several months. We had finally worked everything out only a few days earlier.

In the midst of it all, I did realize—and I'm not sure why it hadn't dawned on me before, that Zeb might have had an issue with me because usually only he and Charles worked on illusions. Even though more than half the show was still his designs, I was probably stepping on his turf. I would have to find a way soon to make things okay with him. The closing illusion was complicated, to say the least, and actually pretty dangerous for me to do—and I did most of the work.

The cast had just walked the red carpet for the premiere of the revamped show. I had talked to so many reporters on the carpet, and I could feel the anxious excited energy in my blood. I wanted to do cartwheels down the hall but I refrained somehow, partially because it would have hardly been appropriate considering the dress I was wearing.

I made my way to Charles's office and pushed the heavy door open while I squealed with delight and walked into the room. I pushed the door closed but I didn't notice whether it had closed all the way because my attention quickly turned to Charles. He was leaning over the desk in his backstage office looking over sketches of our new stunt. He was intensely looking over everything so I think I scared him and he jumped a little when I came in, but he smiled when he looked up. I could see he was slightly tired and he removed his glasses for a moment to rub under his eyes. I could see worry on his face, as well.

"It's going to be fine," I stated matter-of-factly. "Nothing should go wrong, and Mac will be running the board; I'll be perfectly safe. You're forgetting what I can do. We've practiced it enough that I could do it blindfolded. Stop worrying." I smiled and nodded confidently.

"I can't help but worry. You know that. It's my job." Charles put his hand on my face and rubbed the side of my check before slowly moving his hand to my shoulder. We were standing very close together and I realized that I loved the close attention. Charles gave me a tight hug, and it was warm and comforting.

*Mac walked up to the door to Charles's office and watched Zade and Charles through a slight gap in the open door. He was about to knock when he noticed their long and loving hug. He wasn't sure that he had ever seen Charles hug anyone and it struck him as being very odd. Instead of knocking, he decided to take a moment to see what was going on with them, since he had been noticing something a bit strange between them ever since he'd found those David Copperfield tickets and thought he might be able to answer his questions this way.*

*"It's going to be the most amazing illusion the world has ever seen," Zade exclaimed happily.*

*Charles pulled back and looked her right in the eye, his arms still around her.*

*"I'm just being an old man, I guess. I love you more than life itself. It would kill me if something happened to you."*

*Zade was smiling as she put her hands on his face. "I love you, too." She leaned in to kiss him, her face beaming.*

*Mac was disgusted and devastated. How could Zade betray him like that? After everything they had together? Hadn't he put up with enough with the whole Jackson situation? Angry and frustrated, he couldn't bare to watch her kiss him.*

*Had he only watched just a moment or two longer he would have seen Zade kiss Charles—innocently on the cheek. Mac didn't see that, though, because he looked away before he saw the truth and therefore in his head he had turned around right before he saw them make out with tongue. Furious and upset, he stormed down the hall. He needed to think before he did anything that he would regret.*

My excited energy had turned to nervous energy and I could feel the knots in my stomach as I walked down the grid to take my place for start of show. The harness made a clunking noise as I walked and the straps rubbed against my skin just a little but I didn't mind it too much. Even so, I pulled at the straps of my harness to adjust it some.

I stopped in front of Riley, who seemed really nervous as well. He muttered something about the pressure the night seemed to have, above and beyond all the other normal nights. He smiled at me and played nervously with the clips he would use to hook me into the wire. Riley might have been younger than all the other riggers but he was also not as grouchy as some of the other guys. He was always sweet and fun to hang out with when we were waiting on cues. Somehow, he was able to make me feel very comfortable, which was pretty important.

I pushed my hips out to make it easier for him to put the clips on me but, just as he started to grab the ring on the harness, his hand dropped and he started to back away. Without seeing him move away, I instantly could feel something was wrong. I looked up at his face and he looked like someone was going to shoot him in the head. I turned around to see what had struck the fear of God into him to see Mac walking up with anger radiating from his core. He was furious. On his face he had the look guys get when they are somewhere between crying and punching someone.

I could tell Riley thought Mac was pissed off at him, but I knew Riley wasn't his target. I knew he was mad at me but I didn't know why. Mac slowed down as he came to where we were standing and Riley instantly started to stammer, practically shaking.

"Hey, M–Mac . . .What's wrong? D–Did I do somethi—"

"Nope," Mac said gruffly, but you could tell he was trying to be nice to Riley, who was clearly not who he was upset with. "I just need to talk to Zade. Do me a favor and go down to low grid and watch the fly-rail for now."

I could tell that Riley was unsure if Mac was telling the truth, so he looked again at Mac, who was staring at me with the most intense glare. Mac was breathing hard and his nostrils were flaring, but he was not looking at Riley, who finally concluded it really must not have been about him and started to leave.

"Copy. I guess . . . um . . . let me know when you want me back up here," Riley called out to Mac as he backed away.

Mac grabbed the clips and held them out to clip me in, but I instantly felt nervous.

"Hey. What's wrong?" I smiled as best as I could at him and tried to soften his glare but it wasn't working.

He gritted his teeth at me for a few moments as if he was thinking about what he was going to actually say to me. He grabbed my harness and pulled hard, jerking me along with it.

"Have you got anything you want to tell me?" he finally said in the coldest monotone voice he'd ever used with me. I looked into his face for a moment trying to see if I could pick up on what was wrong. My emotions were running too high for me to see anything, though. I couldn't sense what this was about at all.

"No. Why?" I asked, confused and worried. I ran through in my head any scenarios that might tell me what the hell he was talking about but came up with little to nothing that seemed to make any sense.

He locked his jaw and angry tears welled in his eyes. I had never seen Mac cry, or even come close to crying. I didn't know what to do. What was going on? He grabbed my arms with both his hands and was almost shaking me. He was too angry for us to be safe so high off the ground. I had to get a grip on the situation. I collected myself a little before calmly speaking.

"Well, why don't you stop playing silly games with me, then. You're obviously talking about something specific; so just ask me!" Even I had begun huffing. I tried to clear my head again to see what was in his thoughts, but I just couldn't do it.

His palms were sweating onto my arms where he still was gripping me tightly.

"I know we aren't in high school and I didn't give you my class ring or anything, but I'm pretty sure that I have the right to know if you're in love with someone else." Mac scowled at me.

I was really confused. *In love with someone else? What on God's green earth does that mean? Where did that idea even come from?* I started to answer him without really thinking about what had even happened earlier in the day, or who I had had conversations with for that matter. My mind had jumped to

Jackson and I going to the movies, and I wondered if he had somehow gotten upset at that.

"I don't think going to a movie or a guitar shop qualifies as love, and I—"

Mac cut me off and interjected, "So you haven't told anyone today that you're in love with him?"

I started to answer without really thinking about it. "That sounds like a pretty ridicu— Oh." I sighed. Everything had finally clicked and I knew exactly what he was talking about. I shook my head. I wasn't sure how, but he must have heard me talking to Charles. I dropped my head slightly. What could I tell him about what was going on? I didn't know if I should tell him everything or not. I knew I needed to say *something*, because I had just acknowledged that something had been said and that I knew what he had been referring to. As I rolled it all around in my head, Mac was intensely waiting for an answer from me. I thought about my next words carefully. "Yes. I told someone I loved him. Not that I was *in love with* him. It's two totally different things."

"Looked pretty similar. I heard him say he loved you more than life itself. Pretty intense words, don't ya think? And what *about* movies and a guitar shop?" He narrowed his eyes as he waited for my response. I guess if you didn't understand the situation, those words would have sounded pretty intense. He was right about that.

"Forget the movies and guitar shop. This isn't about that, anyway. I promise you it's not what you think it is," I said as calmly as I could.

Pete's voice sounded over the radio. "*Top of show, everyone. We go in two minutes.*"

"Well, what is it, Zade?" He gritted his teeth again and I could see his jaw clenching. I wasn't sure how to respond. The cause of his anger—and how I should respond—became even clearer as he continued, "You're just like Clara. Maybe worse. At least she had the decency to come clean when I confronted her."

My anger boiled to the top. My jaw dropped and my eyes widened. I couldn't believe he had actually said that to me. I shot back at him, "I'm not anything like Clara."

Mac scoffed, "How would you know? You never knew her."

I tried to calm the situation—and him—down as I spoke in a more subdued tone, "Sometimes relationships aren't black and white, Mac. And sometimes what you see isn't what's really there. How about you let me do the show, then we can talk about this?" Hopefully he would hear reason. We both had a job to do and we both needed to concentrate on that and do it.

Mac wasn't hearing any of it, though, and snapped back, "So I can give you a chance to construct your story about why you needed to sleep your way to the top? I'm such an idiot. We haven't even slept together, yet." I was shocked and horrified that he actually thought I would ever do that. I don't even know why that's where his mind went to, and it cut to the core that he would say that to me.

I didn't have it in me to fight when the show was just about to start, and I had just become more hurt than angry. I proclaimed softly, "If you think I'm that kind of a person, then you obviously don't know me at all."

Mac shook his head, "I'm beginning to think you're right. Maybe I *don't* know you at all."

I realized, as I tried to get us both to re-focus, that he still had not actually clipped me in and the show was about to start. I shut down my feelings as much as I could. "You need to clip me in. We can talk about this after the show. We both have a job to do right now." I said it as assertively as I could.

Mac didn't say anything but he grabbed the harness and clipped me in quickly, not doing a safety check like Riley normally would have. He jerked me around some more while holding the harness; it hurt a bit but I refused to show him it caused even an ounce of pain. As much as I was trying to shut off my feelings I wasn't doing a very good job and started to add, "I can't believe you would even think—" but Mac cut me off, glaring directly into my eyes.

He was as close to my face as he could get. His words were stark and cold. "Can't believe I would think you were like everyone else? I believed you *weren't* until you showed me that you are." He turned and stormed down the catwalk away from me.

I couldn't help myself and called after him before he was out of earshot: "Clara's gone, Mac. She's been gone a long time. But clearly you still need to let her go." With that, he was gone and a whole sea of emotions washed over me. The pain of everything he had said ripped at me and I could feel tears welling up in my eyes. I had to pull myself back together as best as I could and try to shake it off. *Just breathe, Zade,* I told myself.

*Just breathe.*

*Mac had radioed Riley and sent him back to his spot with Zade. He had almost made it to the main automation board when he barreled past Tad, who saw Mac approaching and could tell by the look on his face that something was terribly wrong. Mac was so upset and focused he didn't even see Tad and wouldn't have noticed him if Tad hadn't grabbed his arm urgently.*

*"Mac, are you o—," he began.*

272

"Not now, Tad!" Mac snarled as he shook his arm away without even slowing down. Instead, he kept walking and stormed up to the main board. Mac paced around the board for a minute, but realized he was not emotionally together enough to run it for the show. And why should he? He was only doing it because Zade wanted him to for reasons he wasn't actually sure about. She had asked and he had just said okay, but he wasn't even in automation—he was the technical director. Screw that, he thought. Running the main board meant many performers' lives would be in his hands—one wrong move and someone could get seriously hurt, or worse. He had no idea why he had agreed to do a job that wasn't his—and other people actually got paid to do. He turned around and put his head down, running his hands over his face. He pulled his radio mic up to his mouth.

"Mac to Cam."

"Go for Cam."

"I need you to come to the main board ASAP."

"Copy. On the move."

Mac stared down at the ground, agony in his very bones. His eyes welled up with angry tears, his fists beginning to clench. His breathing grew heavy. When it looked like he was finally going to explode, Cam showed up.

"Holy Hell! What's wrong?" Cam could also see right away how upset Mac looked and was startled by it. He'd never seen Mac so upset.

Mac looked up and glared at him, hard. "You're runnin' main tonight."

"I don't know the cues for the new illusion. Heck, I haven't worked in automation in over a year. I can't—" Cam tried to argue.

"Run it on the fly," Mac yelled as he stomped off, wrapped up in a flurry of emotion.

Cam wanted to argue that the better choice was Tad, who was head of automation, but he knew without asking why Mac had radioed him instead. He knew that Tad would have refused since Mac was supposed to be running main—and Tad was the only one who could say no to Mac in a situation like that and get away with it. Cam knew Mac wasn't going to listen to him in any regard, so he let him go, focusing on the task at hand. He began to sweat under the pressure of being handed a job he barely knew how to pull off and buried his face in his hands. Trying to calm himself, he took a deep breath, and slid his fingers down across his face. He raised his head up and started pushing buttons on the board.

"Heaven help me," Cam muttered to himself.

# CHAPTER 15

# THE TOWER

THE SHOW STARTED AND I PUSHED ALL MY FEELINGS out of the way for the time being. Everything was going surprisingly smoothly, despite how upset I was. We had made it through the entire show and had finally come to the finale. I took a deep breath and tried to focus and clear my head. I needed to; I had to have a clear, focused mind to pull it off.

Charles came on stage, looking calm and collected. He stood directly in the middle of the platform, pausing before the main spotlight hit him.

"This is perhaps the hardest illusion anyone has ever attempted to do. I ask that everyone stay completely quiet while my gifted performer makes her very first attempt at this." I had heard his speech hundreds of times (and even helped to write it) so needless to say I knew it well. Regardless, I concentrated on the words he was saying so I would keep my mind off of Mac.

The water around the stage below me began to bubble, and the lights changed color with dramatic precision on cue. In simplistic terms, the illusion used complex deep chaos-based magick; not the simple kind that I typically used. It was dangerous because, if not done correctly, it could backfire. I had actually never done an illusion that was so hard or complex, and—outside of work—I rarely did them at all. I was nervous, to say the least.

I took one more long deep breath to clear my head as I listened to Charles continue entrancing the audience. I waited for the music to start and for Sofia's voice, which I knew was my cue. Once she started to sing, I pulled myself over the bar of the catwalk and maneuvered my body into position as I was lifted by the harness and pulled upwards. I positioned myself in the air before locking my body while I slowly floated down to the stage. My hair and clothes rippled as the wind caught them, making a familiar popping noise. My red velvet cloak fluttered as well, but since it was made of heavy velvet it only softly fluttered.

Once my feet hit the platform on the stage, I, as gracefully as I could, sat down with my legs crossed and I quickly unhooked the clips on my harness. The cloak was hooded and I pulled the hood back, allowing it to drop around my neck before briefly smiling at the audience. My stomach ached, tying itself in knots. Even as I sat in front of a packed audience, my mind kept drifting to my conversation with Mac, and I had to keep telling myself that I couldn't think about it. I couldn't let myself get distracted or the whole illusion could completely go sideways. My mind had to be clear and I had to focus on the spell. I closed my eyes and shook my head a little as I tried to push aside the thoughts of my argument—and what I should tell Mac about who Charles really was to me—aside.

I began to make a waving motion with my hands and, as I did, the water around the stage began to go from bubbling to lapping back and forth with the same motion as my hands. The lapping got stronger and stronger like the ocean in a storm, and the music that had been playing softly through the venue from the band became more aggressive to match what was happening on stage. The room got even darker as gray clouds formed above the audience.

Just as we had rehearsed, Charles continued to narrate the scene, setting the tone for the audience, and gesturing toward me for effect. "This has never been performed in front of anyone, including the crew. It's a very dangerous illusion for the lovely Zade. If anything goes wrong while we are doing the illusion, she could be lost forever, never to be seen again! So, please, to help her we ask you hold your applause to the end of the illusion."

The audience gasped, and Charles grinned mischievously. Though, as I've said, there was real truth in what he was saying: it really was a very dangerous illusion, even if his words were mostly scripted to get a specific reaction from the audience. I was messing with a particular kind of magick—a kind of magick that was both strong and volatile.

I was messing with a particular kind of magick, which I hadn't quite yet mastered. Chaos magick, is both strong and volatile, as it's name implies and is by nature very unpredictable. It involves pulling power from sources that are, to a certain extent, uncontrollable—kind of like trying to ride a wild horse. In either case, you can do it—and if you really know what you are doing and you do everything right it may go off without a hitch, but one wrong move and it can all go to H-E-double-hockey-sticks real quick. I wouldn't be "lost forever" as Charles put it (that was there for dramatic flare) but lots of things could go very wrong—and even I really didn't know just how wrong they could go.

It was like the old saying "trying to catch lighting in a bottle"—it sounds great, until you're the one who has to hold the bottle.

The tension in the audience had become palpable, causing a ripple in my concentration.

Even though I had Charles's speech memorized, I still listened to each and every word he uttered intently while concentrating on my breathing. I was hoping it would help me only think about what we were doing and not other distracting things.

He spoke calmly and, as with most magicians, was a skilled storyteller—no listener could resist being drawn into his words. Everyone was completely vested in what he was saying and hanging on to each and every word. He could have been reading the phonebook, I think, and he could have made it just as intriguing.

"We call this illusion 'Creation,' because that is what we are doing," Charles continued, drawing the audience further into the mystery of the illusion. "To create, we start with a storm."

The noise of thunder boomed through the theater and the audience shivered in their seats. The water around the platform I was sitting on began to lap even harder and began to soak into my clothes. I knew that this was supposed to happen but, even though I knew, the water still shocked me a little and I shivered. *Here we go*, I thought, as a huge wave washed over me. From the audience perspective, I had just disappeared, leaving only my cloak, which looked like something that had washed up on a beach.

The audience's attention shifted as they began to notice rain beginning to fall, very lightly, from the ceiling to a spot in the middle of the stage. As the water hit the ground and splashed up, it turned to sand and started to pile on the stage. The pile grew larger and larger, and I heard someone in the audience scream as lightning rippled from nowhere and one bolt struck the sand.

Out of the sand rolled a glass sculpture: a life-size statue of me. (I wasn't too fond of the statue part, to be honest—I though it was weird and creepy—but Charles thought it would be a good effect.)

At about this point in the illusion, I just barely began to notice that I was starting to feel not-so-great. I thought it was because I was allowing the thoughts of what had gone on with Mac to enter my head, and I started to get mad at myself for letting it happen. I told myself that I just needed to work through it and finish the illusion—and then I could go think about whatever I wanted. In my head I was yelling at myself: *Concentrate, Zade!* I pushed past my nausea and ignored the feeling that something might actually be wrong.

Another bolt of lightning struck the stage, and then an apple tree began to grow quickly and high out of the sand, with apples already heavy on its branches. I heard the audience gasp again. (The apple tree was my idea and I thought it was a great part of the illusion, so their gasp gave me a good boost.) The tree branches began to rustle and move before a crack sounded as one of the limbs at the top fell and a handsome young man suddenly tumbled out of the tree and landed at Charles's feet.

The young man landed on his butt, with his legs stretched out in front of him and his dark hair disheveled, looking like he had just been awoken from a long nap. He looked up momentarily at Charles. Not many people realized it, but the boy looked just like what Charles had looked like when he was a teenager.

I could actually feel the wonder in the audience. The whole audience was poised on the edge of their seats. The illusion had them hanging on every movement the performers made. I could tell that everyone was afraid to take their eyes off the stage for even a moment for fear they might miss something.

The boy stood up; he was tall and lanky, but handsome, with strong cheekbones and smooth skin. The boy first pulled some of the apples off the tree and, with a mischievous smile, tossed some into the audience. Charles continued his narration, letting the audience know that the people who were lucky enough to catch the apples should feel free to eat them and see that they were real. He made sure that they knew that they would be the best apples they'd ever eat.

After throwing out several of the apples, the boy looked around for a moment before reaching down and pulling an ax out of the sand; he then started to chop the apple tree down.

His swings were swift and cut through the tree quickly. The heavy chopping sound of the ax hitting the wood hard echoed throughout the theater as chips of wood flew from the tree. If anyone had doubted it was a real tree they would have had to believe it at this point. The tree fell straight onto the stage and, as it hits the ground, sparks and fire blew through the wood of the tree. The tree began to burn while the sand swirled in an invisible wind. It blew high and hard, blocking the tree and the fire from the audience's sight.

When the sand had settled, the fire was gone and in its place there was a beautifully carved wooden wardrobe—he kind that looked like it should have been in the book *The Lion, the Witch and the Wardrobe*. That had always been one of my most favorite books, and I had added that touch as an homage to that story. The young man pulled the doors all the way open to show that the wardrobe was empty, he then shut the doors and reopened them to reveal a guitar. He removed the guitar from the wardrobe and then put the glass sculpture that was sitting next to the wardrobe inside it and closed the doors.

He picked the guitar back up and sat on the ground and began to play a haunting melody that complemented what the band in the theater had been playing. Sofia had actually been singing throughout the entire illusion, but her voice got louder at this point and I actually focused on it for the first time. It sounded beautiful and perfect, and I would have enjoyed it a lot more if I hadn't been in so much pain.

I realized I was feeling really sick at that point, and that maybe my illness wasn't just because of Mac. I knew I had to hold it together, though; I was so close to being done. What was going on with me? I knew it would take all my strength to push the last bit of energy needed to finish the illusion and spell. I was also in a dangerous limbo state and had to bring myself back. I forced down the overwhelming desire to let myself just fall apart.

I struggled to bring it all back together and bring the energy and focus back to what I had to do. My head was pounding; I finally knew that whatever was going on was bad—*really* bad— but I also knew that I had to struggle to make it through somehow.

The wardrobe was struck by lightning and split in two, and the crack of the wood echoed through the theater, giving chills to the audience and momentarily breaking their concentration. I was now visible again, standing in the middle of the two broken pieces of the wardrobe. This is why Charles wanted the glass sculpture of me. He loved the idea of a glass sculpture of me going into the chest and living Zade or you know me, comes out.

I prayed that no one could see the pain on my face as I pulled an apple out of my pocket. I saw all of the audience's stunned faces filled with real amazement. The apple in my pocket was a clever touch, I thought, and clearly they did too. I smiled and everyone jumped to their feet, bursting into thunderous applause. The excitement from the crowd gave me a much-needed temporary burst of energy and I told myself I could finish the illusion. I put my finger to my lips, showing that I still needed them to be quiet and, with a devilish grin, I winked at them.

I then playfully took a bite of the apple, and "fainted." The crowd gasped in horror, not knowing that it was part of the illusion. They thought something was really wrong—just like they were supposed to. The boy caught me as I fell and kissed me, waking me from my "slumber." I gave the boy my apple, and he took a bite. Suddenly, with a flash of light, he disappeared and the apple fell to the ground.

Charles, who had been standing off to the side, went to pick my now-dry cloak up off of the ground and helped me put it on. I kept going with the routine, although inside it felt like I was dying. I raised the hood and then lifted my arms.

Lightning struck where I had been standing, and—at least to the audience—I disappeared again. The cloak fell. From the audience's point of view, this was going exactly as it should. But I had taken the impact of the lightning and I could feel my body burning—which was *not* supposed to happen. I'd never felt the lightning, before, and the pain was excruciating.

As the lightning strike faded, another apple rolled out on the stage from the arm of the cloak. Charles walked over and picked it up. He took a bite, and then he, too, disappeared with a spark of light as the apple fell to the ground.

The music began to play, at that point, signifying the end of the illusion and show. The audience erupted into applause once again. It was another standing ovation, and the noise was deafening. They were enthralled.

There were spotlights shining on the two entrances to the stage. Charles had walked out of one to take his bow. The second entrance to the stage remained lit, signifying that someone else should have been there to take their own bow—that person was me, but I couldn't do it.

I was trying to summon my last bit of strength to do it, but I couldn't. I was in so much pain that it felt like my insides were being ripped out. I stood backstage swaying, still unsure what had gone wrong. Charles was too engulfed in his bowing and applause to notice I hadn't appeared on the other side. Mr. and Mrs. Wynn were in the front row blowing kisses to him and he was taking in their admiration. When he held his arm out to acknowledge me, as we had rehearsed, he finally noticed that I wasn't there.

The spotlight, which had stayed focused on the second stage entrance, finally went out. Charles took one more quick bow before all of the stage lights went out. A few seconds later, the house lights came on and he had vanished from the stage.

The show was over and no one from the audience was the wiser that something had gone wrong—at least in that I had succeeded. I could hear the crowd begin to leave, murmuring excitedly.

I knew I wasn't going to be able to hold on much longer, the pain had become overwhelming and my whole body was burning like I was on fire from the inside. It was burning all the way through me to my fingertips and it felt like I had swallowed gasoline and then lit a match inside my throat. Somehow I managed to walk—or more like drag—my body the five feet or so over to Zeb—the only person I was in arm's length of reaching.

I was on the verge of passing out when I was able to grab Zeb's shoulder with the last ounce of strength that remained in me. He turned around just in time for me to collapse into his arms. Zeb was definitely not my first choice for the person whose arms I would want to collapse into—after all, I'd had some practice with Jackson—but surprisingly there was something about his arms that made me feel safe. I hadn't expected that at all. Zeb mumbled a bunch of things that I'm positive were *not* English— though I couldn't tell you what they were— quietly in my ear.

Then much more loudly he said, "Zade, can you tell me what's happening?"

Tad was the next one to get over to me. As I'd always suspected, Tad turned out to be the best kind of person to have with you under pressure. He started to deal with the situation, instead of just freaking out. He reached out and helped Zeb hold me up, since half-unconscious people get heavy quickly.

"Zeb, let's set her down gently. What in the hell happened? Someone—" he looked up and saw Riley, who had just made his way down from the grid and walked up to see what was going on. Tad pointed at Riley, "Riley, call 911! *Now!*"

I heard Riley's name and struggled to see him. I heard him shout in sheer terror, "*Zade?* What's wrong with her?" I thought I heard him fumble to pull out his cell phone and call 911.

I wanted to tell him it would be okay and that he should calm down, but I couldn't say a word as I found myself going in and out of consciousness.

I started to cough and I was struggling trying to breathe, as Tad pulled me up slightly. I got my eyes to open and there was Charles standing in front of me, panic stricken. I heard him say, "Oh, God, what do we do?"

"Call my mother," I muttered right before my eyes rolled back in my head and I passed out completely. Even though Charles had asked what to do. I mostly was saying that to Tad who was probably the only person who could have actually heard me, since he was so close to my face right then. Maybe Zeb heard, too.

That's when it all went black for me.

That's the last thing I personally remembered from that day. Later, after I'd had some time to rest, I pulled out the memories of what everyone else saw and what happened. When you "pull out" memories using magick, they pretty much feel like they are your memories—but you're also seeing yourself from that other point of view. This means that you're only seeing what the other person saw, though—so you might not get a full picture of the information you're looking for. In this case, because people were scattered around at the end of the show, it took pulling several different people's memories to get the full picture of what had happened that day.

Mac was apparently the next major presence on the scene. After completely leaving the theater during the show, he had finally come back into the venue just as the commotion was at its peak, and heard that someone had gotten hurt. His own intuition must have kicked in, because he instantly knew it was me. Hoping he was wrong, he pushed his way through the crowd, panicking.

"What the hell happened?" Mac asked everyone, frantically trying to get some answers. He finally saw me and pushed in toward where Tad and Zeb were holding me and keeping me from choking on my own blood.

Mac instantly grabbed me and pulled me towards himself. Zeb let Mac take over holding me, but stayed in the same spot, protective and close. Mac looked up to Tad for the answer to his question.

"I don't know. I looked over. She just collapsed and started bleeding," Tad said, at a complete loss. He was distraught, shattered. Mac was waiting for more answers but Tad didn't have any so he just shrugged.

"I turned around, and she . . . she . . . uh . . . she just collapsed in my arms," Zeb offered, still stunned, with glazed eyes. He seemed somewhat upset that I was hurt—which surprised me. *Maybe he didn't hate me after all.*

Poor Riley couldn't talk as tears began to well in his eyes and he began to hyperventilate. He didn't have anything to add as far as information went. Zeb grabbed him and let him lean on him as he started to collapse on the floor.

The paramedics arrived and rushed over with their bags and equipment and started working on me. Little did they know that what was happening to me wasn't anything they had ever seen before. There would be no answers to my sudden collapse from anyone from this world. The first guy made sure my airway was clear and put an oxygen mask over my nose and mouth while his partner was checking my vitals.

"Tell me what happened!" shouted the first paramedic to no one in particular.

Tad, the calmest person with the most answers in the immediate vicinity, was the first to respond. "We don't know. We had just finished the show. Something must have happened right at the end because she finished the final illusion but didn't make it out to take her bow. She reached Zeb right before she passed out and started bleeding."

"No signs of external trauma. Must be something internal," the first paramedic said to his partner. "Let's get her to the hospital."

In the compiled memories of the day, I saw Mac and Tad let go of me so the paramedics could pick me up and get me on their gurney. Blood was still oozing out of my mouth and trickling onto the floor. Mac leaned down and kissed me on the forehead.

"What hospital are you taking her to? I'll meet you there," Mac asked as he slowly backed away.

"Sunrise. They have a trauma unit." The second paramedic advised.

"I'm going with you," Charles quickly asserted, speaking for the first time since I'd passed out.

Mac glared at Charles for a moment, but realized it wasn't the time or place to argue about anything at all. Mac relented, "Well, let's go then."

He had turned to leave, but Tad called out, "Hey, Mac, before you go—"

Mac turned back around quickly and looked directly at Tad. "Yeah, Tad?"

Tad quickly told him what I had said. "Not sure if this is important, but right before she passed out she mumbled to call her mom. Just thought you should know. I'll check on you all in a bit."

Mac nodded, knowing he didn't even have my mother's number, had never spoken to her, and wasn't sure my mom even knew about him. "Uh . . . Okay. I'll deal with that later," Mac responded before giving Tad a weak smile and turning again to walk out. Mac remembered that Charles was coming with him and the annoyed look on his face returned, but he allowed Charles to follow him to his car.

Zeb and Tad both had blood all over their clothes and there was even blood pooled on the floor. Riley stood there just staring at the floor, pretty shaken and distraught. As everyone started to disperse, Riley couldn't take his eyes away from the red pool of blood.

"Come on, Riley, why don't you come help me and Zeb get cleaned up. She's going to be okay. It's going to be okay," Tad assured him as best he could. Tad didn't really need help to get cleaned up but knew he shouldn't just leave Riley standing there. He didn't quite sound like the usual confident Tad and worry had crept over his face. "Yeah. It'll be okay," he added, sounding like he was telling himself as much as Riley. Zeb finally looked down, noticing he was covered in blood, and in an almost daze, followed after the others.

The memories I pulled from everyone were hard for me to sift through, which is not to say they were hard to see because they were memories of me being sick—and not because I have no memory of any of the situation or where I was—but because of how upset the people I loved were at that moment. Feeling the pain they felt as I combed through their deepest thoughts was incredibly hard for me, but I needed to know what happened during the time I was "gone." So I kept sifting.

I was trying to find out what happened between the theater and the hospital, but since no one I was close to was with me in the ambulance, I had to admit that it would be a bit harder to find those memories. I had to assume that not much happened that was important (to me, at least), so I skipped trying to pull those moments, which seemed to be more work than they were worth. Instead I focused on the memories of the people I knew.

The next collection of thoughts I could pull were from Mac and Charles on the ride to the hospital—basically at the same time that I was in the ambulance. Aside from watching Mac drive, there wasn't much to learn. They mostly sat in silence on the way to the hospital. Luckily, Sunrise Hospital was only a mile or two from the casino. From what I could tell, Charles was too upset and nervous to notice how cold Mac was acting. If Charles noticed any weird emotions at all, he seemed to chalk them up to Mac being upset about me.

They got to the hospital right after the ambulance but had to wait to be brought back to the intensive care waiting area. As I compared their memories, two things were consistent: you could cut the tension with a knife; and the pain they both felt for me was so strong it was pretty unbearable. Finally they were brought to the waiting room and both were anxious to get some kind of update from a doctor. Mac was sitting, but not very still; he fidgeted every couple of seconds and shifted in his chair constantly. Charles was pacing back and forth and kept hoping to see someone head their way to tell them something—anything.

After what, to them, felt like an eternity, an older-looking man with deep lines around his eyes and a look of someone who never got enough sleep walked into the waiting room. He looked at them as if to ask if they were waiting on him. By his white coat you could tell he was a doctor and obviously well experienced—most likely the head doctor of the hospital. Mac stood up and got directly in front of him. Charles also moved in to stand as close to the doctor as possible. The doctor looked uneasy—nervous even—but began to talk anyway.

"Hello, I am Dr. Schmidt. I'm treating—"

Mac interjected before Dr. Schmidt could even finish his sentence. "How is she? Is Zade going to be alright?"

"Are either of you family?" Dr. Schmidt asked, cutting into Mac's panic.

"I'm her friend . . . um . . . I'm her boy. I'm her . . . boy . . . friend," Mac stammered. He knew enough to know the doctor would want to speak to family. He immediately regretted not lying and say something like fiancé—or even husband.

Dr. Schmidt pressed his lips together, contemplating whether a friend—who might be a boyfriend (he wasn't really sure based on Mac's answer)—really qualified enough to get the medical updates. He scratched his head before responding.

"I really need to be talking to someone in her family since she is unconscious and can't give the okay for me to discuss her condition with you."

"Her mother lives in Tennessee," Mac answered realizing he wasn't even sure exactly *where* in Tennessee; the best he knew it was near Nashville, but he knew Nashville wasn't it. Actually he vaguely remembered Zade saying something about the fact that Nashville was at least an hour away from her mom.

"Perhaps I can be of assistance?" Charles said hesitantly.

"Are you related to her?"

"I am her employer—"

"Sorry, that doesn't qualify," Dr. Schmidt said dismissively.

"Could I speak to you in private?" Charles asked, resulting in a death glare from Mac.

"Whatever you want to tell the doctor, you can say in front of me," Mac insisted, crossing his arms and putting himself between the two of them. Charles looked back at the confused doctor and sighed deeply.

"I am also her . . . ," he paused, glancing at Mac. "I'm her father."

Mac started to protest, but then his eyes went wide as he processed the words that Charles had said. Mac turned the words over in his head to make sure he had heard what he thought he heard.

"Wait. What?" Mac asked in disbelief of the news, eyeing Charles up and down.

Charles looked away and then stared at the floor before looking back up at Mac. Charles looked directly into Mac's eyes while he spoke slowly and purposely: "Zade is my daughter."

I realized that this may have been the first time Charles had ever said those words out loud—and I wasn't even there to hear them in person.

"I saw you kiss her!" Mac protested.

"What are you trying to imply?" Charles said, flabbergasted.

Mac began to breathe heavily before holding up his left hand, extending his pointer finger, and shaking his head. He pressed his lips together and looked directly at the floor. Mac pulled his gaze off of Charles and turned to the doctor, who seemed to be more confused than ever. "Sorry, Dr. Schmidt, can you give us a moment, just one moment? I'm sorry to ask."

Dr. Schmidt glanced at his watch, then, gave them both an odd look but decided that maybe it was best to give them what Mac had asked. "Uh, sure, I'll come back in just a minute. There are some test results I need to check on, anyway." The doctor turned away from the two men. "And this sounds like it could turn into a *Jerry Springer* episode at any moment," he mumbled to himself more than to them, as he walked away.

Mac glared at the ground, going back over what he remembered seeing, playing it over in his head.

"Was that nonsense true, or did you say that for the doctor's sake—to get him to give us answers?" Mac questioned.

Charles shook his head and very seriously responded, "It's 100% completely true."

"Does she know?" Mac queried

"Yes," Charles said, nodding slowly and in a flat tone. "Why do you think she came to our show?"

"Does anyone else know?" Mac held Charles in an intense, unblinking glare.

"I am not aware of anyone else knowing. Besides her mother, of course."

"Why?" Mac asked, still very confused, his stomach in knots.

"'Why,' what?" Charles asked; he was also becoming confused.

"Why make it such a big secret?"

"I cannot explain most of it to you, but I can say that . . . well, it was her mother's wish, and I had no choice but to respect it. 'Wish' is a polite way of putting it, honestly. It was only recently that Zade found out that I was her father; and that's when she came to work with us," Charles responded in a very matter-of-fact tone.

"Funny that she grew up to do magic, just like you." Mac relaxed a little as he spoke.

"Well, her mother does do something similar to what she does. That is how we met."

"I thought you guys were having an affair," Mac confessed. "She has been spending so much time with you, lately. I guess she did want to get to know you well, but not for the reasons I thought." Mac seemed to be lost in thought as he uttered the last part of the sentence. He was thinking over all the things that in the past few days hadn't sat well with him but now made total sense.

"Hardly, from what it sounds like," Charles concluded.

Mac was still mulling over all the details of recent events and his mind had stopped on the one detail that couldn't be explained so easily if Zade was Charles's daughter. "I saw you kiss her, though."

Charles cocked his head to the side before asking, "You did? Are you sure?" Charles looked directly at Mac with his eyebrow raised. He was trying to figure out for himself what Mac could have seen that looked like they had made out, because he positively had not made out with his daughter. Of that he was certain.

"Well . . . ." Mac thought through what he had actually seen, sort of thinking out loud. "Well, no. I saw you lean in to . . . what I *thought* was to . . . make-out with her, and then I couldn't bear to watch, so, I turned away. It was when you were in the office earlier, and you both were saying how you loved each other."

Charles nodded and smiled; he knew exactly the time frame Mac was speaking about.

"If you would have spied on us just a moment longer you would have seen her kiss me *on the cheek*. I am sorry you misunderstood, and that it caused you pain." Charles's explanation was short, to the point, and polite.

Mac, feeling pretty foolish, ran his fingers through his hair as he thought through all the things he had misread. "That conversation you had with me that one day makes much more sense now, too," Mac said thoughtfully, then his whole attitude sank. "I yelled at her tonight. We got into a big fight right before the illusion. Now everything she said makes sense. She wasn't lying, and I wouldn't listen. I just walked away. I was so upset, I couldn't even run main during the show—I had Cam do it."

"You weren't on the board when we did the creation illusion?" A panicked look crept across Charles's face when he echoed what Mac had said. He stepped even closer toward Mac.

"No. Why?" Mac asked, wondering what not being on the board had to do with anything.

Charles swallowed and paused for a moment before responding, "I think I may have an idea of what's causing Zade's health issues."

Mac looked confused again. Dr. Schmidt returned to the room looking about first to make sure that things had calmed down. Mac and Charles both looked over at him, ready to hear what was going on.

Something else really important and alarming happened at that exact moment. Of course, I was the only one who knew it was important, and so it wasn't till I was pulling memories—long after the fact—that I saw it.

The girl who had stopped me that day in the parking garage of the mall, the one who pinned me to the wall using magick, arrived at the hospital. Not only did I find out that she was there but she seemed to make a point of being seen when she didn't have to—which led me to believe she knew I would look later (or at least that *someone* would) and would see her. I still have no idea why she was there—or why she purposely wanted to be seen.

What I do know is that, when Dr. Schmidt came back into the room and had made his way over to where Charles and Mac were standing close together, the mystery girl made a point of pushing her way between them and past the doctor. She could have easily walked around them in the almost-empty waiting room and not been seen at all.

She had made sure to burn a spot in Mac's memories, and that was only because she actually pushed him out of her way. As I looked through Mac's thoughts and tried to process them, her presence sent a shiver down my back. It was really bizarre and had me very worried but there obviously wasn't anything I could do after the fact. And she was gone as quickly as she'd arrived—Mac didn't even see where she had gone to as he had already turned his attention back to the Dr. Schmidt.

"So, *father*, correct?" Dr. Schmidt asked, awaiting confirmation from both Mac and Charles. They looked at each other first, and then back to the doctor, and nodded. Charles smiled slightly. "Yes, and you can speak in front of Mac."

Dr. Schmidt began talking to them using his hands to describe what was going on. "She's stable for the moment, but I can't guarantee that to be a permanent situation unless I can figure out what's causing this—and right now I really haven't a clue. There is internal trauma and bleeding that I can't even figure out—we can't seem to place where it's coming from, or why. I just have no idea. There is nothing broken, and—frankly— it doesn't look like she even bumped into anything hard. It's the most bizarre thing I've ever seen."

"So what are the options?" Mac asked anxiously. The panic and stress in his voice were evident and almost overwhelmed me.

Dr. Schmidt swallowed hard and flattened his lips in frustration "I never thought I would say this, but I am currently wishing Dr. House was a real person. It's definitely the kind of case he would solve."

"That's not very reassuring." Mac sighed, glaring at the doctor and looking rather upset with that comment.

"Who is Dr. House?" Charles asked, showing his lack of pop culture knowledge. Charles never watches TV and lives in his own world to a certain extent in that regard.

"He was a fictional doctor on a TV show," Mac explained. He knew that Charles was pretty out of the loop on subjects of this nature no matter how popular or well known they were to most people. When Charles goes to big events with famous people he frequently must be told by his assistant who someone is—and why they are considered famous. He's good at pretending he knows in those cases.

Mac knew he would need to explain why that answer was far from reassuring. "He solved impossible cases no other doctor could—the ones that were crazy, unusually rare, and unfathomable."

"Look, I'm not trying to make light of the matter," Dr. Schmidt assured them. "I'm simply not usually stumped like this. We're doing everything we can. She's a healthy young woman. There seems to be no explanation for this condition. We are running all kinds of tests. As soon as I know anything more I'll let you know."

"Can we see her?" Mac pleaded, concerned the doctor would say no.

"Yeah, I think that would be okay. Right this way," Dr. Schmidt motioned for them to follow him out of the waiting room. They all walked down a long hall and into a hospital room in the ICU unit.

The image of me lying on the bed unconscious, with IV lines and tubes sticking out of me was hard enough for me to bear, but the scene was far worse for Mac and Charles. Mac stopped in the middle of the room and for a few moments couldn't move; he had never seen anyone he cared about like that—and it was pretty shocking for him. Charles came closer and ran his hand over my hair.

It was right then that his phone started to ring. Startled, he pulled his phone out of his pocket, apologizing to Mac and the doctor for the disturbance. However, when he saw the name on the caller ID, his expression turned to shock as he quickly answered.

"Hello? Dela? Hang on." Charles looked directly at Mac, still looking pretty startled by the phone call itself. "It's her mom. I'm going to step out in the hall. Come get me if anything happens."

"Yeah, of course." Mac nodded, overwhelmed by the entire situation as it seemed to get stranger and stranger.

Charles quietly shut the door behind him and began to pace up and down the long corridor, but never moving too far from my door.

"Dela, I was just getting ready to call you."

"*How bad is she?*" Dela asked, the pain and anguish in her voice palpable through the phone.

"How do you even know?" Charles questioned.

"*You seriously didn't just ask me that,*" Dela snapped back harshly.

"Right. Sorry. It was a silly question. I'm just stressed and somewhat beside myself. I am not used to feeling this helpless. Dela, the doctors don't know what's wrong, and they don't know what to do."

"*Of course they don't. You didn't really expect them to, did you?*" She scoffed, though her voice did soften a little.

"I never know what to expect. Maybe you should come up here?" Charles suggested out of desperation.

"*No. You need to bring her here as fast as you can. Tell them whatever you want. Just get her down here, and bring that boy, Mac, with you. I may need him, too.*" Dela's voice had shifted to sounding sure and strong, drawing on a talent she had to always sound confident, no matter the situation.

"Why can't you come up to us? That would be safer for her," Charles pleaded.

"*Charlie, I need my tools and my altar—all that is here. Do you understand? I can't do what I need to in a hospital room with people everywhere. The best thing for her—and her best chance—is for you to bring her to me as soon as possible."*

Charles was silent for a moment, breathing into the phone.

*"Trust me, Charles. I looked. This is what has to be done."* I could tell that my mother was trying to sound kind, even though she was being forceful.

"She could die. Couldn't she?" Charles asked. He hated the question. He hated the words and they tasted like vomit coming out of his mouth. It hurt every inch of him and his ears began to burn waiting on the answer. The only thing worse than asking the question was the anxiety of waiting on the answer. He hated to ask, but he had to know what the odds were.

There was a long pause of silence. What Charles couldn't see was that Dela was sitting at a table with her cards out. I had to assume that she had a lit candle on the table as well, and some cards already laid out.

Dela closed her eyes and breathed in deeply, shuffling the remainder of the cards in her hands. She laid out three cards and placed them on top of another card that's already lying on the table. She examined the cards carefully as if she were deciphering a code. That's kind of how reading cards goes.

For everyone it's different, but there is a mixture of reading the cards and what they mean individually—but also how they relate to each other. How they come up and in what order and what situation—and even how the question was asked—all make a difference in what they mean and say. Your guides are sending messages and it even depends on what all they want to tell you versus the lessons you may need to learn on your own. Beyond that when you are someone like my mom, and to a lesser extent me, who can actually see the future—or at least that is mixed in with what you can see and hear. Sometimes you can get very clear and direct answers and other times they can be much more vague. We all have Destiny to deal with. We all have some of that, some things we are just born to do. It's not all Destiny, though—some things are open and subject to freewill. Only sometimes can you change your destiny but *that is hard* and is a subject for another time and a later book. It is possible to change it for the better or mess it up. When you learn your lessons you move to new ones, kind of like levels in a video game. There are simply so many variables, which is why sometimes some readings are crystal clear, and others are almost like educated guesses.

The silence became deafening and Charles got impatient.

"Dela?" Charles bemoaned, wondering if he had lost the connection on the phone.

*"They won't give me a clear answer. The only thing they will say is that you do need to bring her down here. The faster you get her down here to me, the better her chances are of making it. It's a waning moon tonight and tomorrow night, at least. That will help."*

Charles knew enough about Dela's arts to know what she meant when she mentioned the moon. With some kinds of spells and the whatnot, if the moon is waxing then it will affect what you are doing in certain ways and when it is waning things will be effected in the opposite way. Waxing means it's "getting bigger" on its way to becoming a full moon, and waning means it was already a full moon and it's "going away." If you are trying to start something with a love interest for instance, waxing moons are best. Though, for getting rid of, say, a broken heart that's "taking away," a waning moon is good.

"Okay. I'll get her out of here; we will take my private jet. We can be there by midday tomorrow, I think."

"*I don't even want to know why you have a private jet, but I'll start getting things ready.*"

"Thanks, Dela. I'll see you soon." Charles puts his cell phone back into his pocket. Looking around for only a couple of moments, he spotted Dr. Schmidt in front of my room with a chart. Charles figured it was as good a time as any to make his move.

"Dr. Schmidt, we have found a specialist I'd like to take Zade to. I'd like to have her discharged."

"What hospital?"

"He has a private practice . . . in Tennessee. He came highly recommended from my personal physician."

"Your daughter is dying and you want me to discharge her so you can take her to a private practice in Tennessee?" Dr. Schmidt was obviously appalled that Charles was even suggesting such a thing. I'm sure he was thinking that Charles must have been a lunatic or at the very least a little insane to want to remove me from the hospital.

"Yes," Charles affirmed. He was doing his best to be polite, but there was strong conviction in his voice.

"What kind of specialist?" Dr. Schmidt questioned him. He thought the whole thing sounded a little fishy, and it did. Charles hadn't spent enough time constructing a convincing story, but it was too late now. He just had to go with what came to mind.

"Internal specialist," Charles asserted, expecting Dr. Schmidt to respond. The doctor just stared at him as if he had said pigs could fly. Charles decided to push a little more.

"I know you are a great doctor, but you've already admitted you're not sure what to do at this point. You're not even sure what's wrong. Our specialist thinks he does." Charles realized he might need to make up a name for this supposed specialist and hoped Dr. Schmidt didn't ask him for any more specifics. He realized he really should have googled a few things and thought this through a little more before he approached him. He usually planned things out with precision, but he was trying to get me out of the hospital and to my mom as fast as he could, the words "Get her here as soon as you can or she can die" kept echoing in his head. Even though my mother never said those exact words Charles knew that was what she meant. He also thought about the idea of losing his daughter so soon after she had come back into his life and that thought crippled him.

Dr. Schmidt looked at Charles dubiously. He didn't think this was a smart idea in any regard. He stared directly at Charles and deeply into his eyes and, after a long, hard look, responded: "You have to sign a release that you understand this may very well kill your daughter." He muttered something about how he didn't need a lawsuit from the whole situation. He also admitted that he knew that Charles was famous and, though very calm at the moment, he didn't know what would happen later—especially if I died. Who knew what he or my mom might do at that point. He sure didn't want my death to be his responsibility.

"Not a problem."

"What about her mother? You don't think her mom will have an issue with this?"

"We are doing this at her mother's request, I can get you on the phone with her if you need."

"Against my better judgment and professional opinion, I'll go get you the AMA form. I will need her mother to sign it as well; we can send her the form and she can fax it back." Dr. Schmidt gave Charles another very long look before nodding slightly and walking away to begin the paperwork.

"Thank you," said Charles, sounding equal parts relieved and grateful. The conversation had gone smoother than he had expected. He was relieved that Dr. Schmidt hadn't asked any more questions. *I'm pretty sure Dr. Schmidt could tell he wasn't going to talk Charles out of it, which is why he didn't put up a bigger fight.* Charles looked out the window, leaning near the glass, looking very heart heavy. He took a deep breath and was thinking about what he should tell Mac when Mac stepped out into the hallway. Mac could instantly tell something more was wrong, or at least bothering Charles, and that decisions were weighing heavy on him.

"What's wrong?" Mac inquired.

"Nothing more than what is already wrong, but we are making a change," Charles said, trying to sound positive.

"Change?" Mac queried, unsure what Charles meant.

"Per her mother's request, we are to take Zade to Tennessee. Her mother feels that only in Centertown will she stand a real chance of survival and recovery." Charles knew that what he was saying was vague and would sound very strange. He hoped Mac would trust him enough to just go along with the new plan.

"Why? What or who is in Centertown, Tennessee, of all places?"

"Her mother. I thought you knew that."

"Uh . . . What's her mother able to do? This isn't exactly the kind of issue that Mom's homemade chicken soup fixes!"

"Zade's mother can do quite a bit, son. Far beyond chicken soup. You have much to learn about this family. For starters, as you will soon see, I am actually the one with the *least* amount of ability."

"Well, I'm not sure if I understand what you're saying, but if you're taking her somewhere I'm going with you."

"Of course. You definitely should come. You're needed, anyway." Charles nodded and was thrilled that Mac had come to this conclusion on his own. Charles realized that convincing Mac to tag along was far easier than he thought it would be. Charles was about as pleased with himself as he could be considering the circumstances. He took credit for spinning the whole thing to Mac in a way where Mac wanted to come with them even though, in reality, Mac would have probably wanted to come regardless. Dela had told him to get Zade out of the hospital and make sure that Mac would also be heading to Tennessee with them and, in short order, he had succeeded in both of those tasks and fairly quickly—and for that he was grateful.

"*Needed?*" Mac asked. He was beginning to feel like he had walked into something bigger than he expected. His eyes narrowed as he waited for an answer.

Charles nodded confidently. "Needed."

# CHAPTER 16

# JUSTICE

Mac was more than puzzled about what he could do or why Charles had chosen the word "needed" but considering he was determined to go regardless there didn't seem to be a need to argue. After some paperwork and arranging for medical supplies, an ambulance from the hospital to the airport, and then a ride on a private jet around dawn, the three of us (though I was still unconscious) arrived in Woodbury.

Woodbury is a slightly larger town next to Centertown and it has its own very tiny airport. My mom had brought her SUV to meet us at the airport, which is actually just one runway and a tiny office, She decided that the fewer people involved in getting me to her house, in the state I was in, the better. After all, people already talked enough about us and what went on with our family. I've always made fun of how little my mom fit the "soccer mom" profile and her SUV was probably the only thing about her that was normal.

Once they got to the house, my mom got me settled in my old room before dealing with anything else, making sure that I was as comfortable as possible under the circumstances. Charles and Mac stood in the living room feeling like they were only observers, not saying much to each other. Mac looked around at the photos, which were mainly of my mom and me. She looked almost the same in every photo, she barely aged; it was how old I was in each framed picture that gave you any real insight as to how long ago the photo had been taken.

After Mom had taken as much care of me as possible, she returned to the guys and wasted no time getting to what she wanted to know. After all, there was no time really for preliminaries, anyway.

"So he knows?" she asked, pointing at Mac and talking about him as if he wasn't able to hear her, even though he was standing three feet from her.

"That I'm her father? He does." Amid the memories I dug out, I got the feeling that Charles always had a knack for knowing what Dela meant, even though she was the one who could actually read minds. He was pretty sure he knew what she was referring to when she asked that "he knows?" question, even though there were several other things she could have been talking about. On the other hand, he was a tad rusty interrupting Dela, though he tried. "But only as of recently,"

Charles continued. Dela just stood there in the center of the room taking in what he was telling her.

Charles was actually very nervous standing in front of my mom for several reasons; there probably isn't a soul on the planet that made him nervous other than my mother. The thoughts I found in his memories were jumbled, but that anxiety seemed to stem from *everything*: from how magical and powerful she was, to how madly in love with her he still was, to my condition, and even to just the bold presence my mother possesses. He looked panicked waiting for her to say something... anything, and the longer her silence became the more he thought he was supposed to keep talking. "Very recently," he finally added.

"At least, you've admitted it to someone," my mother said, frowning and casting a glare that got under Charles's skin enough to cause a bolder response from him.

"You are mostly at fault for that, my dear."

Normally that would have caused anger or rage from my mother. *You know that expression "hell hath no fury," well I'm pretty sure they were talking about my mother.* Instead of a brash reaction, though, she balked. I guess she knew he was right. In her thoughts I sensed guilt in her feelings about it. Maybe she realized, as he was standing there—and just seeing how upset he was and how much he cared about me—all the things she robbed us both of by not letting us spend time together. She was aware how hard it was for me to go through childhood without a father and now maybe she was finally seeing that it hadn't been easy on him either.

She smiled weakly, and he smiled back. For one small moment, they gazed into each other's eyes before quickly turning away. They both might have broken down on each other right then, but Mac was also standing in the room and finally reminded them of his actual presence.

Mac cleared his throat. "Can I go and sit with her? Would that be okay?" Mac still had no idea why they were in Tennessee—or why it was the best idea for me—but he was going along with it for the time being. After all, he had his own guilt to deal with in regards to the situation.

"I think that would be okay," Dela said, smiling at him as she turned away from Charles. "It should be fine, go ahead."

Mac nodded and walked into the other room. Dela watched him leave, contemplating what she might say and gathering her thoughts before looking up at Charles.

"Thank you for getting her here." She said the words slowly and sincerely. As she gazed at him, she couldn't help but notice how handsome he still was regardless of the fact that he was almost twenty years older than he had been the last time she had seen him in person. He had some gray hairs now and a few wrinkles on his face but underneath that was the handsome boy she had met so long ago. His eyes still twinkled despite his current pain and sadness.

"I know that Dr. Schmidt wasn't going to be able to save her. Only you can do that now," Charles responded confidently. He knew the only hope I had was with my mom.

"Hopefully I can. She's pretty far gone right now, but she seems to be hanging on. That's a good sign." My mother tried to sound as hopeful as she possible. It had been a long almost-twenty-four hours for everyone.

"Dely, I'm sorry. I'm sorry I let her do the show. It's my fault." Mom softened as he called her "Dely," the name he had called her when they were both younger. It sounds like "Deli," as in sandwiches, which I guess Charles would claim was a joke about his two favorite things: my mother and submarine sandwiches. *I had to admit that it was cute the way he said it, even if it reminded me instantly of corn beef and Dr. Brown's cherry soda.*

She looked deep into his eyes, and when she saw he was being very sincere her face softened.

"It's not your fault, and you couldn't have told her no. God knows, I've tried to tell her no before, and it certainly hasn't ever worked. She's as stubborn-headed as—"

"Her mother." Charles was smiling as he finished her sentence and I'm pretty sure it was an attempt at flirting with her.

"Not what I was going to say; I was thinking more 'mule,'" Dela said with a twinkle in her eye as she smirked, "but that's probably correct, too."

"She's as beautiful as her mother, as well." Charles couldn't help but say things like that to my mother.

"No, Charlie." It was a soft no, cushioned by a past filled with affection.

Charles responded quickly. "But, Dely, our daughter has become a beautiful young woman." Not understanding what the no was meant to imply, his words were quick and defensive.

"That's not what I was saying 'no' to." She paused for a moment before continuing. "Yes, she is very beautiful. I was saying 'no' to you. You are quite the charmer, and I have always been unable to resist you. It's not going to work this time, Charlie. We are all only here for her sake." My mother is very strong willed and when she says no to something it takes quite a lot to get her to change her mind, if she will change her mind at all.

"I still love you, Dela." He had been in the same room with my mom for no more than an hour and Charles was already confessing that he was still in love with her. *I had seen it when I was growing up, too. She had always been a head turner for sure and beyond that you couldn't deny she was just one of those woman that men just can't resist falling for. Beyond the physical she turns their souls too, I guess.*

"Charlie, we aren't even going to discuss this right now. Our daughter is dying." Dela stood up and looked around the room. She was holding back her emotions as best she could, and it was obvious. "I have some other things I need to prepare." She walked away quickly into the kitchen through a swinging door.

The moment the swinging door had completely stopped swishing back and forth, my mom became completely overwhelmed and melted into the floor. She stood leaning against the wall for a moment before sliding down to the floor and beginning to cry. So many emotions in such a short amount of time, between what was going on with me and being in front of the only man she's ever loved for the first time in years—it was a lot for anyone to handle. The wave of feelings rushed over her like the wave of an ocean would: strong, fierce, and completely engulfing.

A couple of minutes later, Charles joined her in the kitchen hoping to help her with whatever needed to be done. Seeing Dela sitting on the floor in tears, he quickly leaned down to hold her. Time means nothing to those who share such a strong bond, it was remarkable to me to see—even if through the window of memories—how they actually were in person, and the love that instantly flowed between the two of them despite how long they had been apart.

With his arms wrapped snuggly around her, he comforted her, "Shhh. It will be okay, my love. It will. I have faith in you."

Amongst the tears, in almost a whisper, she returned his hug and softly stated, "I love you, too."

Charles had his own irresistible charm and they both had an undeniable draw to each other.

After a few moments she let go of her grip on him, shook herself, stood up, and wiped her eyes. She breathed in deeply and knew that it was time to get serious. She turned to Charles and quoted a favorite saying of hers: "It's okay to fall apart for a moment but then dust yourself off and get back on your feet and get back in the game." She sounded better already; Charles's soft hug must have helped. "It's eleven already. I need to start preparing. Pretty soon I'll have to explain to Mac what he has to do."

Too caught up in each other, neither had noticed that Mac had walked into the kitchen in time to hear that he had something he had to do.

"How about you just explain to me now, exactly what is going on. I think I've been in suspense long enough at this point. What can you do, Dela, that her doctor at the hospital couldn't?" Mac leaned against the wall with his arms crossed. His forceful tone brought Dela completely back around. The upset, tearful women who had folded on the floor was a far cry from her normal self. She instantly perked up and quickly wiped the tears from her face.

"More than you're capable of imagining, young man." Her eyes glimmered and a small smile crept out upon her lips. She tilted her head to the side thinking about how exactly to explain everything to Mac without causing him to completely flip out. "Perhaps I should start by explaining to you exactly how Charles and I met. It will have to be the quick version for now as we have a lot to do here." She nodded and clasped her hands together as she spoke. "Maybe you should sit down?" Dela smiled and offered Mac one of the chairs at the dining set in the kitchen.

Mac looked around for a second and then cautiously sat down, trying to fathom what Dela could do that could help Zade. It had to be something a doctor couldn't do—was she some kind of herbalist? He couldn't believe he was in my old house, just going along with what was happening. Then again, what choice did he have? He wasn't sure what any of this had to do with the way my parents had met or why that mattered—unless, perhaps, I had some rare disease that ran in our family. But, even so, why were they being so weird around each other? He had so many questions to be answered, maybe he would get some answers by listening to what Dela wanted to tell him. He was beginning to feel like he was in some dream world where nothing seemed real. He instantly felt uneasy and curious all at the same time.

He pulled out a chair from the table in the kitchen and slid slowly into the seat before scooting the chair really close to the table, his eyes focused only on Dela. Dela and Charles sat at two of the other chairs at the table, leaving only one of the mismatched chairs open. *That would have been where I would have sat had I been conscious, which somehow made me sad.* The chairs don't match the table—or each other—and yet somehow they all go together and work as a set. My mother's taste was much like her life, and mine too. It looked like it shouldn't work but it did, and it was beautiful and unique.

Dela took another deep breath and began: "Charles and I were both a part of a touring show in the '70s. I was barely eighteen, and Charlie was almost twenty-one. He was working as a magician, and he was so arrogant; I couldn't stand him." Mac looked to Charles, who just shrugged as Dela continued. "He had attracted some fame and was the main attraction at the circus; he thought he had hung the moon." My mother babbled a little, thinking about when Charles was young. The thought of how handsome he had been back then made her crack a smile, until he interrupted.

"And she was just a silly card reader," Charles interjected. He grinned devilishly, knowing how much Dela would bristle at those words. They apparently still knew how to get under each other's skin.

Mac raised an eyebrow as Dela shook her head at Charles and cracked her knuckles.

"Anyway . . . as I was saying . . ."

# CHAPTER 17

# THE LOVERS

DELA BEGAN TO TELL MAC THE STORY OF HOW MY parents met and how I came into existence. As I scanned through Mac's recollection of her telling him the story, I was reminded that my mother can be a magical storyteller, weaving the words of any story into a beautiful tapestry so vivid you'd swear you were watching a motion picture directed by Steven Spielberg. Mac had been hesitant, but then her voice changed, becoming majestic as her eyes lit up like fire. A smile spread across her face and both Mac (who had no idea where the story would go) and Charles (who had lived it with her) both leaned forward to hang on to her every word.

It was 1977. There was a large field full of small festival tents, gypsy wagons, circus animals, and fair rides and games. In one of the smallest of tents sat a gorgeous, young girl who was wearing a beautiful long skirt of vibrant colors that rippled

323

as it fell toward the ground, her brown sandals peeking through past the hem of her skirt. One leg crossed over the other, she was swinging her foot slowly. Her off-white cotton top had slipped off her left shoulder and the front was open just enough to show a little bit of cleavage. She was laying cards down and examining each of them carefully before laying the next one down. Her long hair fell in front of her face and blew slightly when the tent flap opened and in walked a young and very handsome man. Dela, just eighteen at the time, didn't even bother to look up.

"What are you doing here?"

Twenty-year-old Charles replied sarcastically, "Didn't you see me coming in your little cards? Didn't they tell you why I'm here?" He smirked as he talked.

Dela still hadn't looked up, while the boy who was known as Charles meandered around the tent nosily analyzing everything he could see. Though she hadn't looked up, Dela knew that he was tall and handsome, with thick and wavy dark brown hair, his piercing blue eyes glancing around the room.

"I don't see something if I'm not looking into it," she stated in a very matter-of-fact tone, still not looking up. She continued laying cards down and reading each of them.

Charles was perplexed by the answer and finally asked, "What does that mean?"

Dela finally looked up and made a huffing noise, exasperated; she shot him a look while scrunching her nose. He found the annoyed Dela to be very cute somehow and thought she looked utterly adorable when she scrunched her nose. He had noticed how stunningly beautiful she was the first time he had met her but they hadn't exactly hit it off then.

For her part, Dela had thought he was terribly pretentious when she met him and was not the least bit impressed at the— in her own words—"so-called celebrity." Charles—even at that young age—was not used to girls who didn't immediately fall all over themselves in front of him. He didn't know how to deal with a girl who didn't care. He also didn't believe in what she did and he didn't understand how she could take herself seriously. So, needless to say, they did not hang out—and weren't friends.

Charles was so busy thinking about how he might charm her that he almost didn't pay attention to her response—which would have annoyed her more (which he would have found also cute and therefore might have been a win-win for him either way). He did, however, catch the gist of her answer.

He might as well have asked her why she ate food or breathed air. "It's like being in a house," she explained. "If you want to know what's going on outside you have to look out the window and see what's actually there. How crazy would it get if I just 'saw' everything all the time? That kind of overload would drive a person insane." She rolled her eyes and returned to shuffling her cards.

"So, now that you can focus on me, tell me why I am here." Charles was cocky and being rude, because he felt like he could get away with it. Underneath it all, he was very curious how this beautiful young woman managed to swindle people into believing her lies. Even deeper than that, if he were being truthful, there was just a slight chance that he believed that she had abilities. He truly wanted to know if card reading was real.

"Oh. I'm being tested now?" Dela clenched her teeth and tapped her fingers. She eyed him up and down and breathed heavily in irritation. With an angry look she picked up all of her cards and started to shuffle them, nodding her head in his direction. Under the table, her foot began to swing faster. "Sit down then," she said swiftly and firmly.

He hesitated just long enough for her to notice.

"Charlie, if you want me to actually read for you then sit down, otherwise leave and stop wasting my time," she growled.

Suddenly nervous, he finally sat down. Dela couldn't help but notice that, when he sat, he looked exhausted. He almost melted into the chair. Across the table from him, Dela also noticed the deep, almost black-looking circles that were under his pretty blue eyes, and she could see that his skin looked dehydrated and showed some redness—all signs of a lack of sleep. Closing her own eyes, she breathed deeply and shuffled the cards a bit more. She then began to lay them down on the table, stacking them in sets of three.

Examining them, she tilted her head to the side. She tapped her nail against the table. "Are you sick?" she asked without looking up.

"I don't think so."

With a puzzled look on her face she put down three more cards.

"Having trouble sleeping?" she asked again, still not looking up.

"Yes, quite a bit, actually." *That could be a good guess*, he thought. *I have deep circles under my eyes and I look sleepy. Not impressed yet.*

Dela nodded and pressed her lips together before laying down more cards. A grin spread across her face. "You're having nightmares." This time she didn't ask but told him; she was pleased that she could get some information about him so clearly and quickly. She knew that each time she read for someone new the person could turn out to be an "easy read" or a hard one. She was surprised they were so attuned to each other, since she usually got along instantly with people who were this close to her, psychically. They clearly had a strong connection considering that it didn't take her long to tune in to him.

"Yes." Charles had answered her with just the one word but in his head he was thinking, *Well, that's a very logical reason for not being able to sleep, so I'm still not impressed.*

Dela placed more cards between them. Her smile faded, and she began to look far more serious. She bit her bottom lip. All of a sudden she clenched her fists together and closed her eyes. After a few moments, with her eyes still tightly shut, she reached out and grabbed Charles's hand. She gripped it hard and both of them felt the jolt of energy. She opened her eyes slowly. Charles couldn't help but notice how pretty her eyes were—or how calm he felt looking into them. Solemnly, she went on to explain his nightmare, staring into Charles's eyes with a soft, firm gaze.

"You die in the nightmare, every time. You get shot. You feel the pain in the nightmare. That's what wakes you up; your chest hurts. That's why it scares you so much . . . and it feels so real to you that you can't go back to sleep."

Charles's eyes got big, and he shook his head a little in disbelief. He ran his fingers through his soft and silky hair and his eyes shifted away from hers. He was more than a little freaked out that she had hit the nail right on the head. Her response hadn't been an educated guess—it was exactly what he'd been dreaming every night. He hadn't told anyone about his nightmare. He was freaking out and just stared at her, his heart racing, his breathing heavy, and mouth wide open.

"I'll take that as a 'yes,'" she gloated just a little bit—but it was also a somewhat solemn response.

"Jesus, Dely. That's my nightmare exactly. I haven't told anyone. How did you see that in the cards?" He looked completely freaked out. He fidgeted in his seat before he pushed back his chair, causing it to rock on the back two legs. His heart pounded harder as many thoughts ran through his head.

"Don't call me, Dely. You know I hate that. I don't serve sandwiches," she snapped at him.

Her quip bought Charles back quickly from his shock. A broad smile spread across his face. He thought of a quick retort to cover his near-panic. "You *could* serve sandwiches, I believe it would help a lot with sales. *Free sandwich with every reading!* Great for business." He shrugged and winked at her. He put his hands up and above his head as if he was reading a sign that said "FREE SANDWICHES."

For the first time, Dela realized that he was flirting with her. She couldn't help but notice how amazing his smile was and how handsome he was—not handsome, actually, but stunningly gorgeous as she watched his amazing beautiful blue eyes light up. *He's funny, too, apparently*, she realized. He had always just annoyed her so much that, whenever he was around, her guard would instantly go up. She had never allowed herself to notice the positive things about him before. She briefly cracked a smile and laughed lightly as he prompted her back to their more serious issue.

"You got all that from pictures on the cards?" he asked curiously as he leaned over to look at which cards were on the table and what pictures were showing. They were colorful and at first looked like simple drawings but the more he looked at each one the more he noticed that there were subtle details that seem to point to hidden meanings within each card.

"I don't *just* look at cards," she explained. This was the first legitimate question he had asked since he had entered her tent, so she was willing to explain her process to him—and even be nice about it. "I'm both clairvoyant and clairaudient. 'Clairvoyant' you may have heard of. It means you can see things like they're happening on a TV show. 'Clairaudient' means you can hear it just like when you listen to he radio. The cards are tools, but I can see and hear things too. I saw your nightmare just like you do."

"Oh." He paused to process what she had explained, considering it all seriously for the first time. He swallowed slowly as he sank deep into his chair and stared off into the distance mostly because he—for once—didn't have a witty comeback.

"You believe yet?" she asked him with her eyebrow raised and a smile that had crept across her face; she knew she had pretty much won him over already. "I can keep telling you things you already know, or I can find out why you're having that nightmare. Your choice." She collected the cards off the table, stacked them back into her hand, and started to shuffle them. She made a point to give him the impression she didn't care one way or the other, but she may have actually started to care—a little bit.

"I'll do anything to make them stop," he emphatically stated. He was close to pleading; she could see that his eyes were begging for help.

"Shuffle the cards then," she said as she leaned forward. In her hand she was holding a well-worn deck; he could tell she had been using it for a quite a while. Her long fingers wrapped around them, with her perfectly painted sharp red nails.

"Huh? Me? Why?" Charles seemed to be frightened to shuffle them, as if they might burn him. He was truly afraid to admit that he was fascinated by tarot cards—yet still scared of them at the same time. His palms began to sweat, and he started to fidget again restlessly in his chair.

Dela tried to calm him by explaining her process. "I was just looking at the present. That's the easy part. I need to look at the past and future now. If you put your energy into the cards it will

be much easier. They don't bite, I promise. I may, but they don't."
She knew how to be witty as well.

Charles laughed a little at her joke and, being a twenty-one-year-old guy, he was instantly intrigued to find out if she really did bite. He then shrugged and looked down at the cards in her hand again. He took them from her and began to shuffle them. Dela could tell he was nervous, but she didn't know that it was both because he was not completely convinced the cards wouldn't bite—and he was also still wondering if she might.

"Clear your mind and do your best to keep it clear for the next few minutes. Try not to focus on any one thing or let your mind wander if you can," Dela instructed him. She spoke calmly and with concentration; he noticed for the first time that her voice had a sultry tone to it that he liked. "Shuffle them until your hands feel warm and tingly and . . . well . . . you feel like they're ready to be read. It will feel almost as if they might jump out of your hands if you don't start reading them. Then cut them into three piles and place them in a row on the table." He was careful to listen to every word so that he could do as she asked.

Charles began to shuffle the cards faster than anyone Dela had ever seen. The magician in him kicked in and he even did some quite spectacular sleight of hand speed tricks with them without really thinking about it before cutting them. The cards flew fast and quickly, as if they were dancing. She couldn't help but be impressed by his skills and, for the first time, she realized how entrancing he could be, and how his eyes glistened. He could tell she was impressed and smirked in spite of himself before leaning forward so they were almost face-to-face, staring at each other.

"Impressed?" he queried, with a cocky attitude but grinning from ear to ear with the nicest smile she had even seen from a man—well, *almost* man. *He's still a little more boy than man*, she thought, *but he could become a great man.*

"By card tricks? Hardly." She scoffed at him, even though she secretly was becoming impressed and a little giddy from his flirting—though she hid it well. She knew enough to know that she needed to be coy; he was someone who only liked the chase. She paused for a moment before beginning her speech, which she told everyone who came for a reading. She'd said it so many times she instantly sounded like a record.

"The three piles represent your past, present, and future. What I see in the past cannot be changed and the present is happening now, but the future is yet to be. Some things are meant to be and they will be, but most of what happens in our life is not set in stone so, therefore, our decisions cause our course. Even by just knowing how it looks currently and by getting this reading about it, you can affect it. Do you understand?"

"I guess so." Charles shrugged. He was too busy looking at her to really let the words she said sink in or to try to understand them fully.

"Then let's begin." Dela smiled and nodded at him.

She picked up the "past" pile and began to lay out cards in sets of three again. As she laid out each set of three she studied them for a few moments before laying out the next set of three cards. She had set out four rows of the three-card sets before closing her eyes and breathing deep. She fanned the cards but kept them in order while she did this. After a few seconds she did the same thing with the "present" pile, putting the "past" pile back where it had been and then repeated this with the "future" pile. Finally, she set the "future" pile down and asked to hold Charles's hands. With her arms stretched to him, she closed her eyes one last time, breathing deeply.

Charles closed his eyes with her at first but found himself opening them and staring at Dela's face. He was beginning to truly realize how beautiful her face was, her smooth complexion, rosy cheeks, and even her bright, plump, and kissable lips. Though, like most guys, his eyes did eventually wander slightly south of her face. She was wearing an off-white cotton top over her frilly colorful skirt, and the top framed her chest in all the right places. He couldn't help but stare.

When Dela opened her eyes, it was obvious what he was staring at—especially when he didn't even notice she had opened her eyes and was staring back at him. She waited for a moment to see if he would look up. Finally, she loudly cleared her throat to get his attention.

"I said try not to focus on any one thing and keep your mind clear," she reminded him while she shook her head as if she was slightly disgusted. In reality, she was flattered that he clearly liked her. She tried to look mad for a moment, but ended up only looking annoyed and so he shrugged and threw up his hands.

"You said *if I could*." His impish grin showed off his dimples and she couldn't even pretend to be upset anymore.

Dela laughed and smiled back at him.

"So I did," she agreed as she raised her eyebrow at him and nodded.

"Well, you got any answers for me?"

Dela nodded before a huge grin spread across her face. "It's that wandering eye that's got you in trouble, actually."

"What's that suppose to mean?" His eyes narrowed and he looked puzzled.

"Where should I begin?" Dela's response was almost too cheery. "You slept with your assistant Betty, and while to you it was nothing, to her it was everything. She's been in love—and slightly obsessed—with you for over a year. And even though you were both drunk, she thought it was the start of a life together." Dela made a face of disapproval. Charles wasn't sure if it was disapproval of Betty or of him.

"You've got to be kidding me," Charles burst out. He cocked his head sideways and a puzzled look flashed across his face. "I knew she always liked me. I didn't think she was *in love with* me." He placed his hand over his face in disbelief. Not that he didn't think what Dela said was true, but he couldn't believe that Betty would have fallen in love with him when he never really made any indication to her that he would even date her. "Anyway, I avoided it for a while because I knew it was a bad idea and then, you know, one night it just happened. I was drunk. It wasn't that big of a deal." He paused for a moment, doing mental math. "Wait . . . you said it's been over a year? It hasn't been a year. It's only been like a month since we've slept together."

"She's been *in love with* you for over a year. It's actually been six weeks since you slept together. As you've stated, it wasn't a big deal to you but, to her, it became a big deal the moment you slept together." Dela was very sure about the details as she had seen them all very clearly.

"Like I said, you've gotta be kidding me," Charles repeated himself with more emphasis on each word.

"No, and it gets worse." Dela nodded her head. Her smile, which had faded, was replaced with a concerned look. "Since you slept with her that one night, you've been brushing her off, and she's been getting more and more upset with you. She sneaks through camp at night and watches you sleep." She glared at Charles as if to say "how stupid could you have been to sleep with her in the first place?"

Charles made a perplexed face and, replied sarcastically, "That's not creepy at all."

"Well, she saw you two weeks ago with some girl who came to the show. She lost it when she saw you with that other girl." Dela looked Charles dead in the eye. He returned a blank stare. It was obvious that he didn't even remember the girl he had slept with only two weeks earlier. Dela, however, wasn't surprised, considering his reputation. He looked down and his eyes got bigger. She could see he was racking his brain for what girl she was referring to, and hoping that if he thought long enough he could remember.

"Oh? Oh! Right. I remember her!" He snapped his fingers together and nodded. "Yeah," he said. "Pretty blonde. Nice to look at, turns out not even really that much fun. Betty was better than her. Not that Betty was amazing." He shrugged. It sounded harsh but truthful..

Dela shook her head. "Well I'm glad you recalled her finally; thank you for the play-by-play. Not that I really needed a run-down of their rank and ratings. Anyhoo, Betty is a woman scorned, and she's finally realized that it meant nothing to you, and that *she* means nothing to you, and she can't handle that. She's decided if she can't have you then no one will. When you do your bullet trick on Sunday, she's going to switch out the shells for real ones, and when she shoots you in the chest, she's going to kill you." Dela clasped her hands together and rested her chin on them. Charles could tell she was pretty certain about what she had seen.

"That's insanity," he protested. "So, what do I even do about this?"

"I figured that would be your next question. That's what the next piles are for. Each one stands for a possibility of what could happen, based on what you do." She pointed to each pile, showing a different grouping of cards. "I've run through all of your possibilities. This is the only one that works out okay." She pointed to the third of the four piles.

Based on the pictures he could see, Charles thought that the pile she indicated seemed to have the somewhat happier cards, but he really didn't know what any of them meant. He would have to trust her judgment on that grouping being the best. He looked them over, trying to give the impression that he knew their meaning, then nodded in agreement about them being the best group.

"The only way for this to work out even sorta okay for you, is for you to pretend that everything is fine until Sunday. Then, on Sunday, you will need to wear a bulletproof vest. When she shoots you, you'll need to fall to the ground as if you were dead. She'll convict herself through her actions when she thinks you are dead. Just make sure that you call the cops *right before the show* and tell them that you have an idea of what's going to happen. Tell them you overheard her talking to someone, but that you don't know who it was, so they can't try to confirm the story. *Do not* tell them that I told you, or they won't believe you. If you do this right, they will take her away. Your problem will be solved and your nightmares will go away. If you try to do something beforehand, no one will believe it, and you will have no proof. In that case, the problem will simply get worse, and she will become more obsessed. I can't even run all the scenarios of what could happen if you try to do something before Sunday but I am certain that none will work out very well."

"So . . . wait . . . Are you trying to tell me *I'm* psychic now, and I saw the future in my dreams?"

Dela sighed. His question was full of arrogance, but she somehow felt the need to explain. She shook her head and rolled her eyes at him.

"Energy is the most powerful thing in the world; it can literally move mountains. We all have the ability to use it. Yes, some of us have greater abilities than others, but we all have it. It's like strength; some people are naturally stronger than others. Energy is like a muscle; if you work it out it grows stronger." She hoped she had explained it in terms that made sense to him. "Your assistant's energy is so intense on this subject that it's manifesting as nightmares in you. You are seeing what she imagines; the problem is that she's going to actually do it. That's why you never see the shooter: because you're seeing it from her point of view. Make sense? The fact that you can see it also probably means that fate is trying to step in as well. It means you aren't supposed to die in that way—or at that time."

"Yeah. Okay. What else do you see on this subject?" Charles asked, trying to get more concrete answers before deciding whether to put all of his faith in Dela's story.

"Nothing," she said very matter of fact and point blank.

"What the hell do you mean, 'nothing'?" he snarled. He didn't understand how she could not see anything else.

Dela shot him a look before warning him: "Don't get mad at me. You haven't made the decision to believe me about this issue, therefore you haven't decided to wear the vest. If you don't wear the vest, you *will* die. So there isn't anything more for me to see. Your fate relies upon whether or not you decide to believe me about this." As she spoke she leaned forward and got almost directly in his face. She pointed at him to make sure he understood that she was very serious about the whole situation. As far as she was concerned, the ball was in his court.

"I don't know how you knew all this stuff, but what you're saying she wants to do sounds pretty crazy, don't you think?" His eyes were wide and he definitely didn't sound angry anymore, the question sounded a bit rude but it wasn't meant in that way, and she could hear by his tone he was asking it as a question. Charles was still mostly digesting the overwhelming information Dela had laid on him.

"People do crazy things sometimes—especially women and especially for love. I'm not really sure what she sees in you, but love is deaf, dumb, and blind as they say." She threw in a jab, though to be honest, she was starting to see what Betty had seen in him. He was charming, magnetic and extremely good-looking. She was sure that when he was trying to woo a girl he was probably pretty irresistible.

"You sure seem to have all the answers for someone so young," he remarked.

"I was born old, and I have an even older soul. Look into my eyes." Dela wiggled her nose and smiled. She grabbed Charles's hand and pulled him close, staring into his eyes as much as he did into hers. A breeze seemed to come from nowhere, and the smile that had been across her face turned into a strained look. Her eyes got big as if she'd seen something she didn't want to. She quickly pulled away.

"What did you just see?" Charles asked excitedly, speculating it was something to do with his nightmare.

"Nothing. It was nothing." Dela had obviously seen something, though, and Charles could tell she had been shaken by it. She was breathing heavily and her heart was racing. She looked away, trying to hide her reaction, and stared at the floor.

"You're lying."

Dela glared at Charles and informed him, coldly, "I have an appointment coming. If you want to live, wear the vest. If you don't, well, either way you won't have any more nightmares after Sunday."

"It's part of the act to show I'm not wearing one." Charles was starting to believe her, but he wasn't sure how to fake not wearing the vest while actually wearing the vest.

Dela shrugged and then reiterated, "Then don't wear it . . . and it'll be your last act." Charles just sat across from her, unsure of what to say. One moment became several, and it could have probably been that way for the rest of the afternoon. Thankfully, for her, Dela wasn't lying and she really did have another appointment.

The tent flaps got pushed open and an older woman walked in cautiously and looked at both of them. The tension was high in the room, and you could cut it with a knife. The woman was obviously already apprehensive about coming to see Dela and the feeling in the room wasn't helping her at all.

"Ex–Excuse me? I think I have an appointment?" the old woman made it sound more like a question than a comment, as she nervously scanned the interior of the tent.

"Of course. I was just leaving," Charles said politely as he stood up. He reached out a hand to help the woman to the table, then pulled the chair out for her and, in a gentleman's fashion, allowed her to sit before sliding the chair back in for her. The woman, though pleased, was still anxiously clutching her bag in her lap as Charles turned towards Dela. "Thank you for your time." He reached for her hand and kissed it, looking directly in her eyes.

Dela simply nodded, though the kiss sent shivers up her arm and her eyes fluttered. Charles stayed for just a moment longer to see if she had anything else to say. When she didn't, he nodded at both women and left.

Dela, composing herself through a deep breath or two, smiled at the woman in front of her and once again began to shuffle the cards.

# CHAPTER 18

# THE CHARIOT

It was the noise of the last of tea being sipped out of Mac's mason jar and straw and then the ice hitting the bottom of his empty glass that temporarily stopped the story.

"Do you want some more, hon?" Dela said, looking directly at Mac.

The beautiful way Dela weaved her words and her prowess as a storyteller had Mac listening so intently the whole time that the sudden pause in the story brought him jarringly back to reality. It took him a moment to process her question—and to also realize she was waiting on him to answer.

"Uh . . . ." He looked down at his empty mason jar and shook it a little, causing the ice to rattle around the bottom. He listened to the popping and the snap and hiss of one of the cubes cracking as if they might tell him the answer. He finally looked up once the ice settled and nodded. "Yeah, sure. Thanks."

You could tell by the look on his face that he was starting to see Charles in a different light. Mac had seen Charles only one way for so long. Mac vaguely knew that Charles had toured as a traveling magician when he was young but had never known that he was basically really a carnie and a gypsy in a traveling circus. He knew others who had experienced that life. Often, people who started off that way did so because they had nothing and no one. That life was a collector of the odd and the misfits. Charles must have also started out with nothing and really had no one to end up there. Mac knew that kind of life was really hard, as well, especially back when Dela and Charles would have met—and it was far from glamorous. Mac had just always thought of Charles as a man who always had everything and got anything he wanted. His eyes darted towards Charles, who was off in thought, thinking about the past and the woman sitting next to him. Mac's opinion was rapidly changing and he really was starting to see why Charles had achieved all of his fame and greatness.

As Dela got up to get more tea for Mac, Charles decided to chime in on part of the story; he figured he could tell the next part in better detail than Dela, anyway.

"I wasn't going to wear it," he asserted to Mac who, at first, looked rather confused, as he wasn't sure what Charles was talking about.

"Oh . . . the vest," Mac said aloud as it finally dawned on him what Charles meant.

Charles nodded and then continued, "I was convinced that what Dela had done that first day was some sort of really good parlor trick. I was a magician who pulled off these impossible feats everyday; if folks knew how they were done they would know how easy it is to fool people. I had always believed we were both tricksters, deceiving people in our own ways. The difference—I always thought—was people came to me to be fooled; they wanted me to deceive them, but they came to her for the truth. I finally realized that she didn't have 'sleeves' to hide her kind of cards, though, so I tried to have conversations with Betty to see if I could tell what she was thinking or if she acted odd. It didn't take long for me to see that Betty was incredibly hard to read—and reading people was usually something I did easily. Even if I had upset her, Dela insisted that Betty still loved me, and she seemed to go back and forth between wanting to please me and seeming like she might actually want to kill me. I had convinced myself that, while Dela was probably wrong, it couldn't hurt to do what she said. If she was wrong, then nothing would happen; but if she was right, well, then I was stupid to take the chance."

Charles paused. Dela was a good storyteller but Charles was a master. Half of his success as a magician was based in how well he told a story. It wasn't just the words or the way he spun them but it was the inflection of each word as it rolled off his tongue and the speed and volume of each and every sentence. Charles's eyes lit up at the right moments and his lip would curl right on cue, because of course the most important element in theater and performance is timing. He knew how to pause at just the right moment so that the audience (in this case, Mac) was so on the edge of his seat that he almost fell onto the floor. Charles glanced at Dela from the corner of his eye and she smiled back. He looked to Mac and grinned only slightly from the corner of his mouth. His eyes sparkled, making Charles look mischievous and full of secrets, and Mac took the bait.

"So?" Mac asked, eager to hear the rest of the story—though he knew that Charles had obviously not died—and he also guessed that Dela must have been right. As I scanned through Mac's memories, I could tell that he still wanted to hear how it all played out from Charles and what happened afterwards to get them to this point. He wanted to know what had made his two hosts—who were obviously still madly in love with one another—break up, and then to not even allow their daughter to see her own father. Mac had been drawn completely into the story between the two of them. He was more hooked than a housewife watching, *Days of Our Lives.*

"Well, figuring out how to hide the fact I was wearing a bulletproof vest from not only the audience but from my own assistant was quite a feat in itself. That Sunday I wasn't even sure whether I was hoping for Dela to be right—or whether I should hope that Betty wasn't really that crazy. I decided to just hope I lived either way. Betty had worked with me for well over a year and it was terrible to think that someone I knew and had traveled and worked with would be capable of something like murder. But, well, when Betty pulled the trigger, I knew Dela was right. The bullet knocked me to the ground, even with the vest—and the shock and surprise on my face was real."

"So, she totally shot you?" Mac, wide-eyed, queried. Even though he was expecting that answer it was still insane in his mind that it happened. "That's completely crazy. I can't even fathom . . . she really shot you!"

"Yes." Charles nodded before adding one final part of the story.

"So, Betty went to a mental hospital where, I believe, she received help—and I lived to see another day."

Charles added the last bit in for dramatic effect; obviously he had lived to see many more days. Mac was puzzled. He looked into Dela's eyes and, after contemplating whether or not he should ask a question, he finally took a breath and asked. "What did you see at the end, when he was still in the tent?"

"Oh." Dela nodded. It was clear that the question didn't bother her, nor it did seem to be a big deal for her to answer it. She began to respond but stopped for a moment and contemplated exactly what she wanted to say. A slow smile crept across her face as she thought about herself and Charles back when they had first met. She figured that telling Mac just the simple facts was the easiest way to answer, so she explained: "Well, I saw that if he listened to me about the vest, and survived, we would be together—and we would have Zade. The vision was fuzzy, though, because it depended on him living, and—as you know—he hadn't decided at that point that he was going to wear the vest; he was only thinking about it." She looked over at Mac and could tell that, to him, her answer wasn't clear. She realized she might need to go into more of an explanation.

Before Mac said anything, she continued: "It's actually very hard to see your own future, even if you look. This is because it's easy for you to put your own thoughts into your interpretation and not allow the vision to be seen accurately. So the whole vision I had of Zade shocked me for two reasons: because I wasn't looking, and because I wasn't sure it was completely real. It also was odd because I had despised Charles so much before that day and would have never thought I would like him—or love him—like that, *not ever*. I knew I wouldn't have put the thought of having a child with him into the reading. If anything, I would have wanted to see it differently, if it were up to me."

"What do you mean he hadn't decided yet?" Mac asked, having apparently hung on to one of the first things that Dela had said and she realized that must have been the perplexed look.

Dela appreciated the question and replied thoughtfully: "We all have free will. Now, when you get a reading, you are opening up the possibility of changing what happens based on the information you get and, therefore, you are making a decision at that time. It's kind of like when you get in a car to go somewhere. The people you ask about in a reading are the people riding in the passenger's seat of your car. You, the one getting the reading, are the driver of the car. Your decisions based on the reading determine where everyone who is riding with you goes. If someone else gets a reading they then become the driver of their own car." She paused, waiting to see if her explanation had sunk in. "I can explain further, but are you starting to understand?" Dela asked while smiling softly at Mac.

"Uh . . . yeah it's a little hard to follow, but I think I get it. But . . . then . . . what happened?" Mac asked, realizing that while he was interested in the story—and even more intrigued by the gift that Dela possessed—he was pretty sure that he missed the point as to why this was all relevant in regards to what was wrong with Zade.

"Dela actually became my assistant, which is kind of ironic," Charles had answered the actual question, which was what Mac had asked, "Then what happened?" but what he really meant was what happens now? Or why was it necessary to tell me all this now?

"No. Sorry. I mean . . . Well, that was a great story, but I'm confused, and I think I must have missed something. Why did I need to know this now? What does this have to do with Zade dying? What happened . . . *to Zade*?"

Dela looked happy that Mac had gotten himself to this conclusion. "That's a great question, Mac. I was just about to get to that part, actually, the most important part." Dela pursed her lips together and, for a moment, looked deep into Mac's eyes. She hoped she was doing the right thing. She hoped that he could handle the truth about what their family was—and she hoped Zade would be okay with him knowing. She thought about looking into it for a moment with her cards, but the reality was that she knew he was going to have to understand it all to save my life. Beyond that, if Mac and I were to have a future he would need to be okay with who I was, so he might as well find out.

At the same time, Dela regretted that I wasn't able to tell Mac myself—and she was sure that it might have been easier on Mac if he heard the truth from my own mouth, but, alas, it was what it was. *I also would have preferred to tell Mac myself and I still wish he didn't have to find out so soon after we met, but there wasn't an another option and I wasn't in the capacity to voice any opinions. I knew she had no other choice.* Dela took a deep breath before explaining to Mac what was even "crazier" than being able to tell the future. She opened her arms wide and began to use them to talk more than she had before.

"I, and therefore Zade, come from a very long line of tarot readers, but we are more than just that. The one skill actually has nothing to do with the other. They are separate trades. Kind of like welding and carpentry: they are two totally different things, but it can be very helpful if you can do both. There are many that do only one or the other."

"I think you lost me, even more than earlier," Mac responded, the perplexed look back on his face and with a confused tinge in his voice.

"Mac, my daughter and I are tarot readers—but that's only the side thing we do. Tarot will help to guide you and give you answers to your life's questions and it points you down your life path to the lessons you need to learn. We all come into the human form to learn lessons and to grow. Tarot helps you to correct the mistakes you've made in your life. Tarot, if we go far enough back, actually comes from an ancient form of Judaism, which we can trace back to the kings of old—soothsayers are in the bible, and kings would not make moves without consulting one. But Zade and I also come from an even longer line of practicing witches, and even beyond that, magical beings. We do magick of all kinds, spells and things. The real kind—spelled with a 'k' at the end—not what Charlie usually does. Not mortal but not immortal either, clearly."

Dela paused for a moment and let Mac digest what she just had explained to him. You could see Mac hadn't truly taken in all the words she had just pushed through his mind. He just sat there for a few moments before wondering out loud.

"Like the TV show *Charmed*, witches?" Mac asked warily.

"Oh, no. That show got to be pretty silly. They did get some things right, like the power of three. We do a lot in threes. Ever seen a movie called *Practical Magic* with Sandra Bullock?"

"Yeah, I think so." Mac nodded.

"Much more like that. Actually, I am almost sure a real practicing witch either wrote that or helped write that, though a real witch probably wrote *Charmed*, too."

Charles chimed in to help explain what Mac was stumbling over. "What I do—what every magician does—is the art of deception, we are very good at being con artists. What Zade and Dela do is real magick—yes, with a 'k'—not grand parlor tricks."

"Real magick?" Mac said the words slowly, and as if he was being taught how to say them. He felt like he was in way over his head, and he wasn't sure what to do about it. You know the expression, "mind blown"? That is how Mac felt at that very moment. Then another thought ran through his head, something that bothered him greatly.

"So, do you worship the devil?" he speculated. He wasn't a "go to church on Sunday" kind of guy, but he did believe in God.

Dela scoffed at his question while shaking her head. "Hardly. No, just like everything beautiful, magick comes from God. Prayer is a form of magick. He gives us all the ability. Some are just afraid of it. Of course, just like any other skill some are better at it than others. You may play basketball well. I do magick well." She raised her eyebrow and smirked slightly.

"I grew up going to church. I don't remember anything about prayer being magic," Mac retorted.

It came off sounding rude, but Dela knew he hadn't meant it to. She smiled kindly and tried to explain further without being mean or judging. She knew Mac had been through quite a lot in the past twenty-four hours, and having to try to understand all of this now was a lot to ask anyone.

"You don't think Jesus turning water into wine sounds like a magick trick? Or Moses's rod turning into a snake, or parting the Red Sea? What about the kings of old, like David? They had priests that practiced magick and told the future. Once upon a time, people were fine with magick. But people get afraid of what they don't understand and start telling people that it's bad. People who wanted power but couldn't do magick wanted to stop those who could. This gift, like all others, comes from God."

Dela looked at Mac, waiting for a response. She was satisfied that she had given him enough to begin to question what he had been taught growing up—or at least enough information to doubt what he had believed all along.

He sat quietly for a moment before finally saying, "Guess I never thought of it that way. Zade said something to me one day about people hating things they just didn't understand. I don't know that I agreed with her then. I think I get it now."

Charles chimed back in. "When Dela became my assistant, all of a sudden my illusions got better, and then Dela started having me work on bigger illusions. I would do them, even though I didn't even know completely how they worked. She would tell me they were family secrets." Charles used his fingers to make air quotes when he said the final two words. "Sound familiar?"

"Sounds very familiar," Mac said, nodding knowingly.

"Yeah, well, I didn't ever want him be with me just for my skills, but I loved him so I much that I wanted to help him. I explained that we had magicians in our family, too. I just conveniently left out the fact that they could do *real* magick."

"It was great—and we were happy for a long time," Charles added.

"So, when did you tell him?" Mac wondered.

"After we had Zade and I knew she had powers. He had to know at that point," Dela replied as she looked fondly at Charles. It was evident by looking at the two of them that true love never dies—nor does it know time and distance. When you love someone it's a force that exists despite what walls you put up to hide how you feel. Their eyes couldn't lie about how much they loved each other.

"Why do I feel like I am in some bad episode of *Bewitched*?" Are you both being serious right now?" Mac was struggling to swallow the story he was being given. He felt his whole world turning upside down—whether because these people were crazy, or because what they were talking about was actually real, he wasn't sure. Either way, he felt like he couldn't win. He couldn't be certain which option he preferred at the moment: did he hope everything they had said was true or did he hope they were crazy? He figured it was probably better for him if they were telling the truth, but he wasn't sure how much more he preferred that. "Come on. Tell me straight. Are you both being serious right now?"

"Yes. Dead serious," Dela confirmed. "I know it's a lot to take in, and I'm sure you are anxious about Zade right now, but I need you to understand these things so that you can do your part in helping her." Dela fidgeted with the necklace that she was wearing; the thick, heavy chain sparkled and the round object that dangled from the chain glittered as it moved.

For the first time, Mac noticed the metal pieces wrapped around into a ball with an unusual-looking stone dangling in the middle. The metal looked like it was either silver or platinum and it seemed to have odd writing on it. Mac became fixated on Dela as she pulled at the pendant and ran it back and forth over the chain it hung on. *He fixated on it because it was a nervous habit that I also had—and knew I had almost the exact same necklace, too, though mine was slightly smaller and the writing was less noticeable. He had never seen me without it and knew it was important and something to do with my family.*

"That's why all of Zade's illusions at the theater were a secret and weren't being explained. Because they *can't be* explained," Charles clarified; he felt that the more Mac could line up the things he knew were true the easier he could accept all of the rest of it.

"So, I'm still not getting it. What does all this have to do with her being inexplicably sick?"

"When she did the Creation illusion, she built you into it. She was using you as a . . . how do I explain this? You were a *conductor* of sorts. Some magick needs to be grounded, basically, like electricity needs a grounding wire. She needed really strong energy to ground that magick and keep it stable. The magick she was doing was dark and old magick that . . . well . . . that isn't always very stable on it's own. It's referred to as chaos magick for obvious reasons. That's why she wanted you to be on the board for the illusion."

"In the old days she would have wanted to hold your hand, but, as I said earlier, it's all about energy. She realized that if she had you running the automation board that that would be enough," Dela elaborated.

"When did you walk off the board?" Charles asked.

"You mean during the show? Never. Like I told you, after we got into our fight I was so upset that I knew I couldn't run it, so I had Cam do it." Mac was sure he had told Charles this already, so he felt like he was repeating himself to a certain extent.

"So you weren't on the board *at all*?" Charles was stunned; if Mac had told him before, he obviously hadn't caught it the first time.

"Not during any of the performance, no. I was in the theater for most of the show though, but not running the board—or even near it, really," Mac said solemnly, reiterating what he had already told them.

"Did you leave the theater at any time?" Dela asked, hoping he'd be clear about remembering the details.

"Yeah, in the middle of the illusion. I was still pretty upset, and everything seemed okay, so I went outside to the dock to smoke and clear my head. I figured we would need to talk after the show. I hadn't decided what I was going to say." He was feeling a little queasy about the fact that he hadn't been there for me during such a critical moment—even though he'd had no idea I was relying on him in such a way.

"So as long as you were in the theater, she could draw from you. It was when you walked out that the energy backfired through her, and that's why she's hurt." Dela surmised from what Mac had just told her. He thought her comment held a tinge of blame—or at least it sounded to Mac like he was being blamed—but Dela wasn't blaming him at all, just talking out loud.

There was a long pause, during which the wheels inside Mac's head began to turn. The slow realization that everything had happened because he stepped out of the theater suddenly clicked. I was on my deathbed because of him. A pain in his stomach started to churn and he instantly felt ill. He turned white as a ghost and his heart began to pound.

"So . . . I–I caused this?" Mac asked horrified.

"Well, I wouldn't put it that way," Dela clarified, calming him as much as she could while being realistic about it. "You didn't know, so it's not your fault. It's not like she told you so you were aware. She's a lot stronger than I knew, though. I don't know how she made it through to finish the illusion, considering that you left halfway through. It's amazing that she could pull from you as long as you were in the theater."

"Why would she do that without telling me?" Mac asked, sorrow in his voice and pain reflected across his face.

"Well, I did it with Charles for years without him knowing, and she knew that. Of course, Charles was in the show, so he couldn't have left. It's really dangerous to use someone who is unaware without a surefire way of knowing they won't leave." Dela was trying to reassure Mac it wasn't really his fault, but it was only partially working.

"Well, I wasn't supposed to leave. I was just livid at the time. I let my emotions get the best of me. That's something I don't usually do. If only I could make it right." Mac said the last words as he drifted off in thought. He felt more regret than he ever had about anything in his life.

As I pored through Mac's mind, I could feel his stomach churn as the realizations came to him in waves of nausea.

"Well, it's funny you should ask. . . . How do I explain this? Um . . . This isn't exactly the best explanation, but, basically, because you caused the energy surge, you have to fix it as well." Dela explained, she figured she might as well get to the whole point of why they had told him everything they had up until now. Mac could tell from her face that she didn't like the explanation she had just given but that she couldn't think of a better way to describe the issue.

"What do I have to do?" Mac asked, ready to help fix the situation—even though he wasn't sure what it meant he had to do. He didn't really sound confident at all in his question and, frankly, he was nervous as to what her answer might be.

"Normally I would sugarcoat this, but we don't really have that kind of time. I'm just going to get down and dirty and to the point. Please try not to freak out. I have to forge a . . . umm . . . well, it doesn't matter what it really is. It's going to *look like* a dagger—though it won't actually be a dagger at all. It's not worth explaining to you what it really is, other than it's magick. At three o'clock sharp tonight, you're going to have to plunge it into her heart on my altar outside." Dela had said all of this without any dramatics. Her face was stone cold and her gaze was completely focused on Mac's face and eyes.

Mac sat still for a moment, processing what she has said. Had he heard it wrong? Was she really serious? His head started swimming even more than it had been, and he felt even more like he was ready to vomit. When he snapped out of his reverie, Mac was shocked and horrified—and the feeling that the people around him might be totally insane was creeping back to him. His eyes were wide and he tugged at his hair. He looked at Charles and Dela as if they each had three heads and the tail of a dragon. There were no extra heads or tails, though. Charles—whom he had known for eleven years—looked exactly as serious as Dela. "Are you screwing with me?"

"I wish I were," Dela said sorrowfully and in a very serious monotone voice.

"How in the hell could stabbing her through the heart help her? Do you know how crazy you both sound right now?" Mac snapped and snarled back. His eyes narrowed and he gritted his teeth while he waited for the answer.

"It's extremely difficult to actually explain but, in a way, it will release the energy that she's battling with, plus—remember—it's not a real dagger it's a just going to *look* like one. It's magick, with healing properties—think of it like an EpiPen. And, once the overload of energy is released, then I will be able to heal her. Right now, the energy is bouncing around her body and ripping her apart inside." Dela ran her hand over her hair as she waited on a reaction from Mac. She could only hope that he would be willing to believe their story—as crazy as it probably sounded to him.

Mac stood up and began to pace the room, beads of sweat starting to drip down his face. He stopped in front of the window over the sink and stared out into the large backyard. Dela couldn't see his face from where she was sitting and she had to wonder what he was thinking. Would he be willing to trust them? Without him, the whole procedure was near to impossible. Dela's hands traced over the table out of nervousness, the tips of her fingers tracing the grooves of the tabletop in alternating slow and swift movements as the clock ticked by.

Mac couldn't believe everything that had happened in the past forty-eight hours and everything he had heard—and what he had just been asked to do. He was experiencing emotions he had never felt, mixed with what seemed like a sheer nightmare; to say he was overwhelmed would be a gross understatement. There were no words to describe how he felt and even he wasn't sure himself. His nerves were raw. He hadn't slept. He was scared—and then there was this whole story of magick that he was supposed to just believe. Mac shifted his weight but didn't turn around and only continued to stare out the window into the moonlit night. "Is this really the only way to save her?" he asked solemnly as he placed his right hand on the glass of the window.

"That I know of, yes," Dela responded softly.

"She'll die otherwise?" he asked quietly, still facing the darkness of the night, his breathing shallow and coarse.

"Yes." Dela nodded as she said it. She glanced at Charles and her eyes seemed to say that he needed to add something to the conversation.

"Dela's not sure that at this point that even this will save her. Zade is pretty far gone already." Charles's voice resounded with pain and urgency.

Mac finally turned around and faced the table. He leaned against the sink and looked directly at my mother. "Dela, is that true? She still may not make it?"

"There is no guarantee right now, but her chance is zero if you won't do this," Dela concluded with desperation and a hopeful pleading in her voice. She didn't beg, but she asked him for his help with all the love a mother has for her only child.

There was a long silence and the sound of Mac grinding his teeth before he finally spoke. His voice was louder and more forceful than he expected, though every emotion had drained from his face and he looked completely stone cold.

"You don't know how insane what you're asking me to do sounds . . . ." He shook his head in disbelief of the next set of words he was going to utter. Dela thought he was going to say no and so she started to stand up to beg him when he continued. "Okay, I'll do it." From the look on his face you could tell that it was about the last thing he wanted to agree to. He sighed loudly, then softly said, "I can't believe I'm agreeing to this."

Dela looked at him tearfully. "I *do* know how insane it sounds, Mac. But thank you." Relief crept over her face and the tension she'd been carrying fell away from her. "I need to get to work. I'll be back in a bit. Thank you. You don't even know; I . . . thank you." Dela didn't know what else to say. She put her hand on Mac's shoulder for a moment, squeezing it in appreciation before walking out of the room.

Charles sat silently, studying Mac's face carefully. He had only ever known Mac in a work environment, and "work Mac" was always a confident and really sure of himself kind of guy, arrogant even—someone who never for a moment showed a side that was vulnerable, weak or scared. The Mac who stood in front of him was anything but those things. He looked nervous, on edge, and beyond scared. Terrified might even be more like it. Instead of a man in control of his world, Charles saw a boy in front of him—and realized that he saw a lot of himself in Mac. Charles also finally saw how much Mac really cared for Zade.

Mac, for his part, had been trying to hold his emotions in but couldn't anymore and, at that moment, broke down allowing a few tears to stream down his face. It was something Mac had never done in front of anyone, at least not since he was a little kid. "What if I lose her? And it's all my fault." It wasn't a question. Charles could tell that the reality that Zade could die had hit Mac and he was feeling the full force of that truth.

"You won't. *We* won't. You can save her," Charles assured him, hoping fervently that it was true.

Mac, trying to get the attention off of himself, figured he might as well get some answers while they were waiting on Dela to return. His voice was week and crackled a bit as he spoke. "Can I ask you something?"

"Anything," Charles agreed, smiling softly.

"Why did you and Dela break up, and—even more importantly—why did you walk out of Zade's life?" Mac's eyes narrowed and his brow furrowed. He couldn't understand why this man could have possibly left the only woman he ever truly loved—or a daughter he adored.

Charles understood the question instantly. He thought for just a moment about how much of the real answer he should give at the moment. After some quick contemplation, Charles decided it was best to be completely honest.

"In regards to Dela, well, the biggest reason is that I was a very stupid, ignorant man—and it's a very long story." He paused for another moment before he carefully chose his next set of words. "Also, I'd like you to understand that I never left them. Dela left *me* and took Zade away. Though, yes, it was because I did her wrong and deserved it—at least for the most part." Pain and sorrow filled Charles's voice and his eyes looked heavy and pierced with regret.

"I think that's the first time I've ever heard you admit you were wrong," Mac teased him softly.

"Yes, I know it doesn't happen very often." Charles chuckled at himself a little. Mac cracked a slight smile before asking another question.

"You said it's a long story. What's the short version?" Mac had quickly gotten serious again. It dawned on Mac that, in their eleven years working together, he and Charles had never really shared much of their personal lives. In fact, he was pretty sure that they had shared more in one night than they had in all the years they'd worked together.

Charles nodded before continuing. "Let's just say you handled all of the information about Dela and Zade remarkably well compared to how I handled it when Dela told me. I lost it when she told me what she was. It was right after we had Zade. I thought maybe she had made me love her—which, by the way, even they can't really do. Lust yes; love, no. Magick can help open your eyes and heart and even change circumstances to make it optimal, but it can't force anyone to love you." Charles gave Mac a long hard look while he stated the last part of what he said. He wanted it to sink in so Mac wouldn't worry about the same thing at some point and make a similar mistake. "Because I wasn't sure if I could believe her, I cheated on Dela to see if I could. When I was able to cheat, I realized that if she had put a spell on me she wouldn't have 'let' me be able to do that. I felt so guilty about what I had done that I started drinking heavily and even started doing drugs. Dela said she understood and forgave me, but I got to a real low point.

"To make matters worse, I also started talking about putting Zade in the show. I guess Dela saw that guy I used to be—the jerk that slept around and was power- and money-hungry. When she asked her cards, she saw that going back to my old life was one path I could take. There was another path where we would all be happy together, but she couldn't see which of the two I would choose in the long run. So she chose her own path. She just up and left. I came home one day . . . to a letter." Charles paused again, waiting until he felt Mac understood the gravity of what he had said before continuing with the story.

"In the letter, she said she would come back when—and if—I had decided to take the right path, and when she saw it clearly. Her leaving made me so much worse, because when she left it made me depressed. It caused even more havoc on my thoughts; on top of everything else, I was embarrassed. I never talked about my failure. I found out later, though, that she did put a spell on me to not talk about Zade—or to admit to a connection to either of them. That never made any sense to me, but I think it was because our break-up was just too hard on her. I broke her heart, so she thought it was best to push me out of her life altogether. She just didn't want to have to deal with our past at all. That's the short version, anyway. Someday I'll tell you the full one."

From what I learned when going through his memories of that night, Charles had not opened up to anyone about his past like that ever. Even he was rather surprised how honestly he had told Mac his story. It apparently felt good to tell it all to someone—especially someone who could relate to the situation at least on some level.

"You might want to start writing, then," Mac said cryptically.

"What?" Charles asked, confused by the statement.

"You might want to start writing the book. After all, the long version has to be a book if that was the short version." Mac looked very serious for a moment and then broke out in a large smile. It was a quick injection of levity they both needed.

"Maybe I'll just send you the CliffsNotes?" Charles joked back.

Mac nodded and laughed lightly. "Sounds good."

The weight of keeping so much of his life hidden for so long had been so hard on Charles that he felt a sort of instant peace after telling Mac—he was amazed how nice it felt. He breathed in and out fully and felt lighter than he had felt in a long time.

## CHAPTER 19

# DEATH

IT WAS LATER THAT NIGHT THAT CHARLES AND MAC
found themselves sitting on pins and needles in my room. The
seconds felt like hours, the minutes felt like days, and the hours
felt like years while they waited for Dela to be ready. Charles sat
solemnly in a large blue velvet and wood plush chair next to the
bed where I lay unconscious.

My body, if you missed the shallow breaths I was still taking,
looked cold and lifeless. I couldn't tell you where "I" was (as far
as my spirit was concerned) because I have no memories of this
except theirs. I've been told that sometimes people remember
being around in situations like this, but wherever I was I remembered nothing, maybe I was there and just not awake.

Based on the memories I pulled from him, I know that Mac
sat on the bed almost hovering over me like a worried puppy,
while gripping my hand. His fingers wrapped so tightly around
mine that it looked as if he was strangling them and his eyes

were fixed on my chest, practically willing the continuation of my breathing. His gaze was somber, hoping this would not be the last of his memories with me. If I could have at the time, I would have hoped for the same thing.

While Mac looked hollow, like his soul had been drained of any life, Charles knows how to maintain the appearance of looking like things were okay even when they aren't. It's something he picked up during years of being a performer.

When Dela finally walked in, she looked around the room and assessed the energy of them both. She *felt* how empty and drained they were, and it matched her own feelings. She looked weary—and probably felt worse than she actually looked. She breathed in and out deeply before beginning to speak to them. "Everything is ready."

As she sighed, she turned directly to Mac. She tried to smile softly. "Mac, do you remember what I told you? You understand what you have to do?" He stood up from the bed and, for a moment, simply stared at her. Thinking through what she had said, he worked to convince himself that he could do what he had been told he would have to do. He slowly nodded his head in agreement. "Uh, yeah, I think so." He didn't sound very convincing. He was also feeling the pressure of what he was responsible for. He wanted me to get better. He needed me to get better and he shuddered to think about the alternative.

"Okay. Well, it's time now. We need to go, but there is one last thing, Mac. You have to *believe* this will work. The mind is a powerful thing—the most powerful thing on earth even— and it can will magick into existence . . . or extinguish it." Mac swallowed and nodded; he understood that my life was most certainly in his hands and it terrified him. Dela said slowly as she motioned toward the door. "Mac, can you carry her outside please?" Dela looked forlorn. It didn't look like she had much faith that what they were going to do was going to work—or maybe she was just completely exhausted. Mac leaned over me and examined me closely. Looking through his eyes, it shocked me that my body looked so lifeless and the only thing that contradicted that was just small breaths that you could barely see. It was odd to see how I looked through everyone's eyes—but even more so through Mac's. My skin was pale and when he touched my hand it felt cold and clammy.

He slowly slid his hands underneath my back and under my knees and gripped me tightly before lifting me up and starting to walk toward the doorway. He was pretty strong for a guy who wasn't really big and muscular. I'd always thought he was just more tall and slender, but he was tough.

Dela touched my face lovingly and tenderly once more and sprinkled something on my chest that was oily and warm, she seemed to say a quick prayer under her breath before leading us out of my room. Charles finally stood up and followed behind, and they walked through the house and out the back door into the yard. Solemnly, they marched to the back part of the grounds behind the house and stopped under several large ancient oak trees near a couple of weeping willows. In that moment, the trees truly looked like they were weeping. Mac's grip seemed to tighten as he walked, clutching me against his chest and kissing my forehead softly, in a way that was both caring and protective. If I had been awake, I would have felt very loved—and very safe.

A few evenly placed fountains had been cleverly built by my mother so that they could be converted into an altar whenever needed. The moonlight was shining through the trees and beaming directly on the spot where Mac was going to lay me down. It was almost perfect—and also very strange—the way the eerie silvery light hit exactly on top of the altar as if it were part of a lighting plot from the theater. The sinking feeling Mac had been having—as if he had just stepped into a bad dream or an equally bad B-movie—hadn't gone away and, if anything, had gotten worse. He was still trying to grasp the situation and accept that it was really happening.

Dela led the walk wearing a cloak and carrying a large lit candle, which made her look practically regal. She was also carrying something oddly shaped and wrapped in velvet, which she held close and protectively. They walked to the long, stone table in the middle of the backyard. Mac laid me on my back on the cold, unforgiving stone. He was very gentle and slow as he put me down and then carefully straightened out my arms and then my legs.

Charles took the ropes that Dela also had in her hands and bound my legs and arms to the table. From my vantage point inside their minds, I sort of knew what she was attempting, but I didn't even know exactly what kind of magick it was; my mom knew things I didn't.

Watching everything happen, Mac was being pushed just a bit closer to coming apart at the seams, even though he could tell that they were treating me as gently as possible and he understood that this was part of the process. Dela had explained everything that was about to happen to him as best as she could and—though it sounded crazy when he heard it—he thought that perhaps when he saw it, it would seem better and not as insane. He realized it was ridiculous to think that, in person, it would seem even slightly less deranged. In fact, it was actually more upsetting to him than he imagined it would be. A big part of him wanted to run as far away from all of it as possible. He had to keep telling himself that it was too late to change his mind—and that going through with the ceremony could help me somehow.

The winds were blowing hard and thunder could be heard off in the distance. Lightning danced across the sky and ripped through the clouds coming closer as the storm blew in; suddenly it was bellowing and intense. I had to admit that the storm made for a dramatic type of evening and was very fitting considering the situation—though it was a bit too Vegas for my taste. Mac wisely wondered if they were causing the storm or if it was just happening on its own.

Dela ripped my shirt just enough to expose the middle of my chest, then took out a vial and rubbed something red on me. It reminded Mac of something he had seen in a movie once where it was called dragon's blood. It crossed his mind that maybe the folks in Hollywood had gotten the idea from something that was actually real. That began to make him wonder: if magick was actually real, what else did people go around thinking was made up that really existed as well? What about werewolves, vampires, fairies, genies, or Never-Never Land? Was everything made up really based off of reality? He thought of all the wonderful *and terrible* things that might actually be out in the world, and silently laughed at the irony, not really knowing if he was actually correct.

Dela walked around and stood on the other side of the stone and me, her beloved daughter. She paused for a moment to stare at my face. Her words echoed in my head as she gazed at my face and thought about how hauntingly beautiful it was. *Though I wasn't sure if I liked the "hauntingly" part of her description.* She lightly grazed my face with her fingertips while making one last silent prayer. She held back tears as she opened the dark velvet sheath and unwrapped the item she had been carrying, which resembled a very odd and strange-looking dagger, as she had said it would.

Dela grabbed Charles's hand and held out the dagger. She nodded towards Mac to let him know it was almost time, and he gripped the dagger with Dela. Mac and my mom stood like that for a few moments as the electric pulse coming from the dagger made it hard to grip and Mac fought the urge to just drop it right there.

Once Dela let go of the dagger and only Mac was holding it, he had to grip it with both hands as the pulsating energy grew stronger. Mac could feel it coursing throughout his entire body. The moonlight hit the dagger and it almost began to glow.

As the winds picked up and rain started to fall, the sky seemed to open right above the altar. Bells from a church, off in the distance, started to chime, and the sound pealed loudly through the woods, despite competing with the thunder and wind.

Dela had to yell to be heard over the storm. "That's the church bells! It's 3am. *Now!*"

376

Mac had been taught the chant that he needed to say, but for a moment panic spread over his face. He had forgotten the chant. How had he forgotten the simple words that Dela had taught him just moments earlier in the house? His heart, which was already pounding, went into overdrive and he started to sweat even though it was cold, windy, and raining.

Dela instantly recognized the frantic look in Mac's face and knew she needed to feed him the first words. "Mac!" she screamed. "*Sa ovim.*" She hoped that was all he needed because if she said much more of the chant it would be her saying it and not him, which would affect the spell and casting in a bad way. His head snapped up. That was all the reminder that he needed to remember the rest of the sacred words.

He started to recite the ancient text he had been taught as he held himself steady directly over where I lay. The words were odd and Mac didn't know what they really meant, because when Dela offered to explain them to him, he said he didn't want to know. His exact words had been: "As long as I'm not conjuring demons, I don't want to know."

Mac yelled into the wind and the rain: "*Sa ovim bodežom, prožet magije starih, i moje vere, neka ljubav preokrene kletvu Ja vaskrsne duh, dušu i telo Via Gardrich Verdicy!*"

Then, he did the unthinkable.

Though his hand quivered, he plunged the dagger into my chest. Something I had a hard time watching, even through his eyes, and even though I wasn't experiencing it at the time.

The moment the dagger went all the way in, my body lifted from the altar everywhere but from my chest. Lightning struck the dagger, and Mac flew backwards, falling to the ground; in his hand he found that he was holding an oddly shaped glass sculpture, similar to what sand looks like when lightning hits it. In the flashing of the lightning, the weird contortions of the glass were twisted and yet beautiful.

My parents watched as my body fell back to the table and I began to cough up blood, something else I don't remember. The sky seemed to scream as more lightning, brighter than ever, lit up the night. The booming sound of thunder shook the trees, as the rain fell even harder from the dark mystic sky. The ropes that had bound my hands and legs seemed to slide off as if they had never been tied.

As he watched, the sight of blood pouring from my mouth terrified Mac. He realized that he had no idea whether that meant things had gone right—or horribly wrong. He hadn't actually been told what to expect once he did his part. He had been so wrapped up in what he had to do that he hadn't bothered to find out what happened afterwards. Mac began to wonder if maybe Dela didn't know herself, or she didn't want him to worry if it didn't work. It was also possible that what he was seeing was supposed to happen—and Dela knew but didn't want to scare him too much with the details. All Mac knew for sure was that it didn't look right to him.

"Let's get her out of this nasty weather!" Dela shouted over the storm, rain droplets dripping down her face, as she visibly shivered in the flashing light.

Charles picked me up this time and started to carry me up through the yard. His steps were fast and direct as he clutched me tightly to his chest and hunched over me as much as he could to shield me from the piercing wind and rain. *I never really got to ride around on my dad's shoulders as a kid. And though I didn't get the real chance of experiencing him holding me then, either, at least I got his view of it.* Mac and Dela walked quickly and closely behind Charles as they followed us back into the house.

Charles laid me back down on my bed before kissing me softly on my forehead and pushing back the wet hair that had been stuck to my face. Dela then pulled my rain-soaked clothes off and wrapped me tightly in blankets that had been waiting on the edge of the bed. I still lay basically lifeless with the same slow and shallow breathing as the only evidence that showed I was alive somewhere in there. I had no personal recollection of this either, but just more of the memories I pulled from them, which were very clear—because everyone was in the same room.

The three of them stood and watched me, hoping for some sign that something was working—or that I was getting better or improving in some way. Finally, Mac couldn't stand the silence and lack of any info. He looked directly at Dela and in an exasperated tone asked, "So, is that what was supposed to happen? Is she okay now? She doesn't look okay." I knew he was trying not to sound mean and so did Dela, but he was almost beside himself with worry. He did not have the patience my parents seemed to be exhibiting, probably because he expected all magick to just go "poof" and be completed. He was confused by how calm they were and how they seemed to not be the least bit anxious.

"Yes, that was all supposed to happen. So now we wait. We'll see if she gets better. It's up to God and the spirits." Dela spoke evenly, tamping down all of her own anxiety.

"How long till we know?" Mac demanded.

"It could be hours, but it could be days. She'll either start to get better or she won't. We'll see," Dela spoke softly; she knew getting worked up wouldn't help anything.

"How can you be so calm about this?" Mac snapped at Dela and at Charles, who hadn't spoken since putting me back in my bed. He hated Dela's answer. It was too blasé and noncommittal for someone used to action and split-second decisions. He was learning what it was like to have anxiety—something he didn't really deal with normally.

Dela reached out and put a motherly hand on his arm. "Honey, what else can we do? We have to be patient. One thing I've learned in my all my years is that getting worked up over something when you can't do anything more than what you are already doing—or have already done—is pointless. We've given her the best chance of survival and we just need to have faith that it will work. The best thing you can do right now is relax. This could be a long night—or maybe even several long nights," she proclaimed, assuring him as best as she could.

"I suppose so," Mac muttered. He realized, though, that Dela had a point and tried to calm himself down. He sighed before sitting down next to me on the bed and grabbing my hand. He once again entwined his fingers with mine and traced the lines that ran across my palm with the fingertips of his other hand.

In the meantime, Charles had stepped out of the room and called the theater to relay a message to what he knew would be a frantic cast and crew so that he could tell them that I had been stabilized, and that he and Mac were waiting for further news. When he came back in, Mac questioned Charles about why he would call them and tell them anything. The questions flooded the room: Wasn't he afraid they would find out things that he didn't want them to know? Wasn't it risky to tell them things? The air was filled with "What ifs?"

Charles had a very logical reason, though, which didn't surprise Mac. After all, if Charles was anything, he was logical. Charles explained that when you don't want people to ask too many questions you try to make sure they feel like they are in the loop with information so they don't start poking around. It made complete sense, and Mac saw how good Charles and Dela both were at making sure people only learned what they wanted them to—even though they made everyone feel like they knew everything.

Charles told Mac that he had made a special call directly to Jackson, ensuring him that they would also keep him in the loop. Charles knew that Jackson hadn't been thrilled that Mac went to the hospital when he wasn't able to since he was still on the floor with the band, unaware what had really been going on backstage. By the time Jackson learned anything, Mac had already been on the way to the hospital. On the other hand, Jackson did *not* know that Mac had made the trip to Tennessee.

Mac sat up with me for hours, just holding my hand and watching over me sorta like a guardian angel would. Eventually, though, he fell asleep crammed into the loveseat in my room just as the morning sun crept through my window. He had been up for almost two days straight and, combined with all the excitement and stress he had been through, he was more than drained and exhausted. It wasn't surprising that the moment anything seemed the slightest bit calm he passed out of sheer exhaustion.

As Mac slept, Dela took over keeping a close watch of me and my vitals, since any little variation could mean something, and someone needed to be paying attention at all times. On the surface she seemed to be patiently waiting—but that was because she'd been through quite a lot during her life and had learned to not show weakness. If she showed a great deal of emotion, it would cause everyone else around her to get worked up—and what good would that do? So she calmly kept one eye on me while she kept busy with the other. Since there was a table in front of her, and she decided to lay down some cards. When Charles walked up and put his hand on Dela's shoulder he couldn't tell if she was asking the cards questions or just playing with them to keep herself occupied.

She didn't even seem to be really looking at them once she laid them down. She seemed to glance at them and then a frustrated expression would spread across her face briefly before she reshuffled the cards and threw them down again almost haphazardly, which was very different from the slower, more precise way he was used to seeing her read them. Then again, he couldn't remember when the last time was that he had even seen her read cards. It must have been a lifetime earlier, though she still looked the same as she had the day he had walked into her tent asking for help. In fact, the scene felt just the same, with her looking at their future through cards. This time, however, it seemed that the cards were too haphazard and that there was no way that she was trying to read them. "Dela, what are you looking into?" he asked, curious about what was actually happening.

At first, Dela didn't hear Charles ask his question—or at least she didn't process what he said—but she finally noticed the weight of his hand on her shoulder as he waited for some kind of response. She snapped out of her almost-trancelike state and gave him a slight smile as she shook her head in disapproval of herself. She sighed deeply before responding to him. "Nothing, really. I think I am laying down cards out of habit. I can't pick up anything anyway. They won't cooperate and read on the situation at all."

Dela realized that if Charles had noticed her mood then she wasn't hiding her stress nearly as well as she usually did. She leaned back against the chair as she slammed the cards against the table. It was a difficult situation for her to be in. She was so used to being able to help everyone. She was used to having power and yet she was suddenly unable to help the one person in the world she loved more than anything—the one person she had been trusted to save, the one she would give her own life for. Instead, all she could do was sit, powerless and unable to do anything but wait.

"This must be what it's like to be a mortal," she joked. "It's a terrible experience." Slowly she looked up at Charles, who was studying her carefully. She could see care and love in his eyes and she could feel her own barriers breaking down. She knew he still had the power to make her swoon even after all this time.

"I'm not sure this is a proper example of what us common folk go through, but perhaps it's as close as you will ever get," Charles assured her, moving his hand from her shoulder to hold her hand in his.

"Remind me that I don't ever want to do this again, will you?" Dela was trying to lighten the mood, as she knew it wasn't helping either of them to feel so deeply depressed. He nodded, and seemed to look like he had also lightened up—if only a bit. He could see how everything was taking its toll on Dela.

"You should take a break, maybe. Normal, average, and everyday mortal people would probably want some caffeine—and maybe even some food—by now," Charles suggested, smiling even a little bit bigger.

"Yeah, I think I'll go make some tea. You want something to eat?"

"Sure." He wasn't really hungry, but he thought it would help Dela to stay occupied doing something mundane for a few minutes.

"I'll make something for Mac too. He'll wake up soon, I'd imagine," Dela commented as she glanced over to where Mac still lay sleeping in the corner of the room. He was out cold; I'm pretty sure a jetliner could have landed next to him and it wouldn't have woken him. Dela and Charles also were sure that a freight train crashing into the room with the jetliner wouldn't wake him either, so, they felt pretty safe to talk about him as if he wasn't there.

"What do you think about him?" Charles asked, drifting to a subject other than whether or not I would ever actually wake up.

"He seems like a wonderful guy. We certainly have put him through quite the test—and he seems to be dealing with it far better than most men would. I'll give him that," Dela said, looking thoughtfully at Mac's face.

"You see this being something that becomes serious?" Charles asked, pointing to Zade and Mac in one swift finger swoop.

"I mean . . . her future is unclear. I see a path that could lead to them being together, but over the past few days so many other paths have popped up. This incident has set into motion something bigger than I know . . . bigger than I have ever seen. And, based on my readings, I also think she has been hanging out with another guy, who has potential. At this point, though, I'd root for Sleeping Beauty."

"They seem good together. I feel like it has promise," Charles commented.

"Well, don't go buying them a wedding present yet. You know how few things are set in stone or meant to be. No matter how promising they seem." Her last sentence seemed to drift off and Charles couldn't help but wonder if she was speaking about the two of them when she spoke of promise.

"Yeah, I do . . . and there is the issue of him being mortal—but we can worry about that later," Charles acknowledged as the light from his eyes dimmed and a look of sadness washed over him.

Dela smiled weakly, in her own way acknowledging his feelings and the comment about him being mortal, and walked out of the room.

Charles moved over to sit down in the chair that Dela had been occupying, his knee making a popping sound as he did so—one of the effects of being older. He glanced over at the cards sitting on the table and, after a few moments of contemplation, picked up a few of the cards on the top of the pile and turned them over. He turned over three or four of them and then looked at them, first as individual cards and then as a group of cards together. During his years with Dela he had learned what most of their general meanings were and even understood how some of them related to the other ones. He also had learned that it was much more complex than what showed on face value, and that, regardless of the amount of information he had, he still probably wouldn't know what they could be saying.

He laughed ever so slightly at himself for even trying to read the cards before leaning back in the chair. He couldn't help but feel that almost everything that was wrong was his fault—from the failure of his relationship with Dela to their daughter being in this life-and-death situation, both were completely his fault. He also felt as if he should have tried harder to be a part of my life even though he knew Dela had cast a spell to keep him away. He decided that he should have found some way to fight her on that—he didn't really blame Dela for why she'd done it, though.

As I riffled through his memories, I realized that while Charles was sitting next to me as I fought my way back to life, he just felt like he had made all the wrong things priorities in life, and that his life had been mostly wasted. Charles sat with me for quite a while in the silence studying my face and holding my hand tightly. He kept hoping for a sign that showed I was slowly recovering—any sign of hope at all that I was getting even just a tiny bit better. Nothing seemed to change and with every moment the growing dread that I might not be getting better at all began to take a toll on him. It had once again grown dark outside and the fireflies and stars that I loved so much were out dancing together. Charles looked out the window for a moment, staring at their beauty before looking back at me.

"Oh, Zade, I am so incredibly sorry, will you ever forgive me?" he said as he buried his face in his hands and collapsed on the table. Tears streamed down his cheeks and his emotions started to bubble up as he felt the weight of everything that was happening crashing down upon him. His overpowering amount of guilt washed over him and it caused every part of him to ache inside. Out of all of his accomplishments he still believed I was by far the greatest and most wonderful thing he had done, despite his failures surrounding being a dad. The thought of this being the end of my short life was unbearable to him. He felt like his heart was shattering on the inside when a small sound broke the silence.

A cracking soft voice startled him right out of his chair. "Forgive you for what?"

Charles raised his head and his eyes met my weary eyes as they struggled to adjust to the dimly lit room and the dizziness that had hit me almost immediately. *This was the first thing I remembered on my own since I had collapsed in the theater.* Everything that had happened between then and waking up in my old room I wouldn't know until later. For the moment, I didn't know where I was and I was unaware of everything the three of them had been through.

Charles leaned in and caressed my cheek as a huge burst of happiness spread across his face, he responded to me very softly, "Hey, you. You're awake." The relief flooded his body so quickly that he practically felt like he was floating and his eyes welled up this time with happy tears.

"So it seems. What happened? Where are we?" I asked, half-realizing that I sounded dazed and confused. My head was pounding and I kept blinking my eyes trying to get them to focus enough so that I could see where I was. I felt like I had been asleep for years and that I had awoken from a terrible dream. My entire body ached everywhere. My joints felt swollen and painful. My chest felt as if I had been stabbed. My head felt like someone had ripped all my hair out by the roots. My veins felt as if ice and needles were coursing through them and my stomach felt like someone had punched me as hard as they could. I was pretty sure I couldn't have felt worse. More pain washed over me and even my throat was burning—though I couldn't really tell if that was also pain or just extreme thirst from the lack of water I had been experiencing. I couldn't help but lock one of my legs and grit my teeth in hopes of powering through as a wave of pain crashed over me.

Charles seemed sad, though I wasn't sure why. "Are you in pain, my dear?"

I bit my lip and shook my head. "Yeah, it's pretty bad. What happened though?" As much as I was in pain, I was also deeply confused and wanted to know what was going on. The last thing I remembered was finishing our new illusion in the theater. And . . . something had gone wrong. Maybe having him tell me the story would help take my mind off the incredible amount of agony ripping through my body.

"Well—short version—things didn't go exactly as planned, and we almost lost you. You almost died. We had to bring you to your mother's," Charles began explaining. The moment he said the words "we," the thought of who that could be flashed into my head. No one else at the show knew anything about who I was. Maybe he meant my mom when he said "we," but that would be an odd way to word it if my mother was also part of the "we." I decided to stop the story for a moment to clarify whom he meant.

"We? Who is 'we'?" I asked, almost afraid to hear the answer.

"Myself. And Mac."

"Mac?" The last thing I remembered about Mac was that he had been furious with me and had stormed off in a fit of rage. As I was lying there, I hadn't yet pulled their memories to understand what had happened; so how he, of all people, ended up at my mother's didn't make much sense. Charles nodded his head, assuring me that I had heard him correctly. "Oh boy. How did that happen. What does he know?" Another wave of pain rippled through my body and I gritted my teeth again and arched my back as I gripped the sheets waiting for it to pass. I held my breath until the feeling subsided again before turning back to conversation.

"Well, I think the story of how will take a bit and perhaps we should save that for when you are feeling a tad bit better but as far as what he knows . . . well, at this point, he knows pretty much everything," Charles replied solemnly. "Everything" could have meant a few different things but I was pretty sure that when he said "everything" I knew what he meant. My heart sank. After all, I was pretty sure that Mac knowing "everything" would be the end of whatever he and I had between us.

"How quick did he run outta here?" I asked, trying to sit up in the bed just a bit. It was taking all the energy I had to move, but I still felt the need to try. Even as a kid I never liked being sick and always tried to do things sooner than my body could handle. I pulled myself up only a couple of inches before my burst of energy gave out and my arms collapsed.

"Well, if that was him running, he's not a fast runner." Charles chuckled as he pointed across the room. I was able to raise myself up just barely enough to get the slightest glimpse of someone curled up asleep on the loveseat in the corner. Honestly, I don't think I would have known it was Mac if Charles hadn't been talking about him. I could mainly just make out a body kind of piled in the corner. I took his word it was actually Mac.

"Wow," I said softly, shocked to find that after finding out about me, Mac was still here. I forced myself to consider that Mac being there because I was on the brink of death and him being there because he wanted us to work on our relationship were two very different things. I figured that I would find out what his thoughts were soon enough, probably about the same time I found out what he actually knew. As I rested back onto the bed, I mainly wanted to hear about what had happened from the last thing I remembered in Las Vegas till I had woken up in my old bed, but the burning in my throat was getting worse. I realized that maybe I should focus on things like getting some water, first, and then everything else . . . maybe some painkillers, too.

"Um . . . I'm pretty parched and could use something for all the pain. Got any morphine lying around?" I asked, trying to be lighthearted, but realizing that if I waited much longer I wasn't going to be able to swallow at all.

"Oh yes, of course. I should've thought about that. I'll go right now. Are you okay if I wake Mac up before I go? He'll be so relieved you are okay." He patted my arm briefly before turning around and walking over to Mac to shake him. "Son? Son." My dad's voice, which had been just a whisper as we talked, boomed into the corner of the room, as he shook Mac.

Mac awoke, completely startled. Though I was still having problems seeing across the room, I could tell that he literally jumped off of the loveseat, almost knocking Charles over. "What happened? Is something wrong?" he asked with panic in his voice. I couldn't help but notice how concerned he looked and how worried he was.

"On the contrary. She's awake," Charles said calmly, pointing at me as if Mac didn't know where I was. "I'm getting her some water and letting her mom know she's awake. She's still very weak and in a lot of pain, so try to keep things calm."

Mac's eyes met mine as he saw for himself that I was awake. I smiled faintly as another streak of pain ripped through my body, trying to temper my expression so he didn't think my grimace was because of him. Mac quickly sat down by my side as Charles left the room, grabbing my hand, twining his fingers with mine, and kissed me softly on the forehead. There was something in his smile that made me think he hadn't seen me in years—but maybe it was because he thought he would never see me awake again.

"Hi," he said softly as he breathed a heavy sigh of relief. "You awake is a sight for sore eyes."

"I've heard." It was the best response I could come up with considering the circumstances.

"I am *so* sorry," he said with regret and guilt riddled all through his face. The look he gave me was that of a begging dog when you walk into the room and they've knocked over something priceless and important.

"Why is everyone apologizing?" I asked still unsure as to what everyone was so sorry about. Based on what I knew, no one had purposely tried to do anything to me—except for trying to do anything they could to save me.

"'Cause, your dad and I screwed up—and you were the one that paid the price."

I wanted to ask how they had screwed up—and why they thought it was their fault—but my head that had already been throbbing began to hurt worse and I just couldn't even think straight. The shooting pain in my temples took over and I couldn't help but grab my head and start to moan. "My head hurts."

"Should I get you something for it?" Mac asked as he intuitively rubbed my head.

"I think Charles went to get me something for pain from my mom. A cold towel might be helpful though."

"On it!" Mac responded quickly and bolted out the door as if he had been sent on a mission from God.

"Thanks," I said, closing my eyes as the light in the room was starting to really bother them even though the room had very little light as it was. I summoned enough energy to call out just as he reached the door. "Oh!" I shrieked, which caused Mac to grab the doorframe and pivot back around to me. I opened my eyes just part of the way to make sure he was listening. "And, when I'm feeling better, someone is going to have to explain exactly what all I've been through and what all happened." I took a breath before I could finish with as much force as my weak body could muster. "And I mean *everything*."

"Of course. I'll leave no detail out. I promise." Mac smiled, then headed toward the kitchen.

I smiled weakly and started to close my eyes again as Mac walked out the door and headed toward the kitchen. I had begun to drift off when I heard the rustling of the door again. I didn't reopen my eyes but somehow I knew by the sound that it was Mac. I could hear him shift from one foot to the other and fidget while clearing his throat. I could tell he wanted to tell me something and was almost about to ask him if the cat had gotten his tongue when he stumbled over his first set of words.

"Zade, I really need to talk to you . . . err . . . to tell you . . . something. I'm . . . uh . . . I'm uh . . . umm . . . I'm really sorry I didn't trust you with your Charles . . . err, your dad . . . I mean

*Charles*. It was wrong of me, and I'll . . . I'll never question your motives again."

Since my eyes were still shut I waited a few moments before responding to see if he had more to say, or if he was waiting for me to say something. After a few moments of silence—kinda awkward silence at that—I realized he was waiting on me. I wanted to open my eyes and look at him when I spoke, but the pain was too much. *I guess this is how blind people feel*, I thought.

"Mac, I appreciate that a lot. I know that was hard for you to say." My words were starting to leave me, and I could feel myself starting to pass out. I realized I couldn't fight it. Your body does, sometimes, make you sleep when you are in severe amounts of pain. It's an automatic response designed to help you survive the discomfort. If Mac said anything after that I have no idea what it was. My brain was shutting down. I am pretty sure I was asleep before he even had time to respond.

# Chapter 20

# Judgement

Over the next couple of weeks I slept much more than I was awake, and the times I was awake I was pretty much in a haze. Looking back on it, I think my mother may have had a hand in that. After all, she'd have known that sleeping through most of the pain would make it much easier for my body to heal from the ordeal it had gone through.

Every day I got just a little bit better until I was finally feeling well enough to hear the story of what happened and at first they all took turns explaining it to me. All three of them wanted to tell me the story on their own, but I found that there were so many gaps, and I really wanted to know everything that happened in detail, so once most of my strength had returned I asked if I could pull their memories. They all gave me permission, which is really the only way to do that easily. You can force memories out of someone but it's a difficult process and some people can even block you so you can't do it.

I started with Mac, though he made me promise I would only pull memories from the time when I passed out until the moment I woke up. My mom and Charles didn't make me promise, so I decided to peek into a little more than just the accident—just a few other things I had always wanted to know.

Memory pulling is not a quick process, mind you, and it's extremely draining—even though it's much easier if the person does it willingly. The best way when you have willing participants is to sit with each of them and put them into an almost catatonic state while you comb through their thoughts. That is what I did.

Compiling all of their memories took a few days—and a few sittings with each of them—until I was sure I had gotten them all. I was glad I had done it, but by the time I was done I could see why it's not something anyone does very often. I wondered if I could find a way to do it easier, and better, without asking for permission. Having spent so much time on it, I decided that I was definitely going to try to look into it later; someone in the magick world might already have perfected the process in a way I didn't know.

Charles and Mac stayed with me at my mom's house while I recovered and, back in Las Vegas, the show went on hiatus. The official announcement stated that this was happening so that the theater could have some new set designs put in, but, really, Charles just didn't want to leave me while I was healing—and neither did Mac.

I don't think I was the only reason Charles didn't want to leave though. I noticed that he and my mom got cozier as they days went by. If I was paying close attention I could catch stolen glances from both of them. I wasn't sure what to make of it or if it was even a good idea, but then again, who was I to really judge?

When I was a kid, I had had odd fantasies about my parents getting back together. It was something I had always only slightly hoped for as I really never thought it could happen. As I watched them during my recovery, it looked more and more like a real possibility. It was too bad it hadn't happened years earlier.

Mac kept everyone at the show updated, and even though some people from the cast and crew offered to come visit me at the "hospital," Mac was good at finding different reasons why it didn't make sense for them to, mostly by keeping the crew pretty busy. He made sure to put the crew to work actually building some new sets, as that's what the press had been told. They would be expecting to see them when the show returned. Mac also made sure all the yearly maintenance was being done while the show was dark. A lot of the cast said they wanted to come but I think it was more something to say. They were, for the most part, easily talked out of it. Some didn't care about visiting me at all, though they enjoyed the paid vacation they had been given. Jackson was the only one who put up a fight about it and was going to come, but then a quick tour opening for Imagine Dragons came up that timed perfectly with our break and his band had to take that.

As my recovery stretched on, we realized that we had to make up an explanation for what had happened that we could tell everyone. It took some googling, some illness-researching on WebMD, and a couple of conversations with a doctor my mom knew before we came up with a story that sounded like it made sense. We told everyone I had a combination of ailments, including double pneumonia—which supposedly was why I couldn't breathe and what caused me to pass out—and something called "Osler-Weber-Rendu syndrome." Osler-Weber-Rendu syndrome, we found, is a really rare disorder of the blood vessels that can cause excessive bleeding and shortness of breath. That was how we explained why I had been bleeding everywhere, including out of my ears, nose, and mouth. The possibility of having both illnesses together was almost an impossible feat, which is how we explained why the doctors in Las Vegas had been so confused. Once we had our story created, we tried to be vague when we told people about it and not go into details. Charles and Mac explained to everyone I didn't want to talk about it because I was embarrassed and upset that I had collapsed in front of so many of my friends and co-workers. Luckily, no one in the show pushed for too many answers and they seemed satisfied with the little we told them.

As I worked on my recovery, I counted down the days until I was able to get back to work. I knew I had been very lucky that everything had worked out the way it did.

When the big day finally came, Mac and I were walking towards the front of the doors of the theater. Right before we got to the doors, Mac stopped right where the carpet changes patterns. We were holding hands and he had his fingers wrapped around mine so tightly that when he stopped walking his hand pulled tightly on mine and soon I had stopped walking, too. I turned around to face him and took a step forward, closing the gap between the two of us.

"Are you sure you're ready to go back to work?" he worriedly asked.

I squared off my body to his and looked him straight into his eyes. I nodded confidently. "Yeah, I feel great. It's been a month, Mac. I'm more than ready." I breathed in deeply and the flow of extra oxygen gave me a jolt of energy. I truly felt vibrant and strong. I realized, though, that there was something

I should do before we went into the theater so I relaxed a bit and leaned into him. "Can I say something though?"

"Sure," he said, though he sounded like he thought I might tell him something was actually wrong.

"Thanks for not running for the hills when you found out everything. You handled it better than Charles did back in the day. That's impressive; he can handle anything." As I finished my sentence he wrapped his arms around me and spoke softly in my ear.

"Well, I've grown pretty fond of you, Magi Girl. I would go to Hell for you if it needed to happen." I think he suddenly realized what he was saying and that, in my world, that could be a real possibility. He put his face directly in front of mine while giving me a worried look. "I won't *actually* have to do that, will I?"

I couldn't help but start laughing. "Not this year, anyway, Superman." I raised my right eyebrow. "Guess you've come over to the dark side?" I poked, teasingly.

"I heard you had cookies," he replied with a grin plastered on his face. He pulled me even closer to his body and pressed his lips passionately to mine. I melted into him and my heart began to race as I let my mind go and became so lost in his arms, and his kiss, that I forgot where we were.

It wasn't long before someone cleared his throat, loudly, to interrupt us. "AHEM." It came from close enough that we both jumped apart. Mac and I looked over to see Tad standing next to us with a shit-eating grin. We couldn't help but laugh. I blushed an almost peach color, bit my lip, and clutched Mac's arms tightly.

"You're gonna be late for rehearsal; that looks pretty bad on your first day back," Tad insisted, a smile creeping across his face as he glanced at his watch.

I hadn't seen Tad since the accident. I excitedly let go of Mac and quickly wrapped my arms around Tad hugging him tightly. He returned the hug with an even-tighter squeeze.

"Tad! I'm so glad to see you!" I kissed him lightly on the check.

"*You're* glad? I'm ecstatic. The last time I saw you in the flesh you drooled blood all over me." He said it very matter-of-factly and used his hands to mimic the motion of goo dripping all down his body, while making a disgusted face.

"Sorry about that," I said, only mildly apologetic.

"It's cool, kiddo. I'll send you the dry cleaning bill later." He grinned again and winked at me while he shoved his elbow into me playfully. "I'm just glad you're back and you're okay. I really thought we were going to lose you there for a minute.

Did you guys just get back last night?" Tad inquired, looking at both of us.

"No, we got back day before yesterday, but we were running around with all the wedding plans," Mac said, almost rolling his eyes. Guys never seem to understand the importance of all the details for a wedding. I'm pretty sure Mac would have worn his show blacks if he thought I would have let him get away with that.

"The hardest thing was this one, finding a dress," Mac said, pointing at me. "It's *one day* for heaven's sake."

"It is one day—but a rather important day for me," I said firmly.

"So . . . Did you find a dress?" Tad asked, looking directly at me this time.

"Finally," I answered in exasperation. "I think we went to every store from Tennessee to here." I laughed a little at the exaggeration.

"Exciting stuff," Tad commented, though I could hear the sarcasm in his voice.

"It is." I smiled and agreed, though it was with some hesitation that was probably noticeable in my voice. I had looked into the future and it did look promising—but things had looked promising before and gone wrong. I did think that it was possible that things might go wrong again. I just wanted to have things be okay with everyone—at least for a while.

Tad walked over to the large doors of the theater and my mind flashed back to my first audition and that moment where I had pushed the same doors open from the inside and peeked my head out for the first time. That moment had become such a big turning point in my life. Tad pulled the handle of the left side door and I once again I walked through the oversized doorframe. Just inside, I noticed that it was oddly dark inside the theater. *It's never completely dark in here*, I thought, fumbling a little as my eyes adjusted to the blackness. Tad and Mac had followed quickly behind me and the small amount of light that had been in the room faded once the door shut.

"Guys, why are there no lights on in here?" I finally asked, my eyes still trying to adjust to the dark as I put my hands out to feel around and see if could find my bearings.

All of a sudden the main stage lights started flashing, and then the house lights turned on. For a moment, instead of being able to see, I felt completely blinded.

My eyes were burning from the light, but when I could finally open them I looked around and saw the whole cast and crew standing in front of me. The area right inside the doors in the theater had obviously been decorated for a party. Several balloons were floating around me and they all said "Welcome

Home." Everyone was staring directly at me, smiling and yelling, "Surprise!"

Riley came running up to me, smiling bigger than I'd ever seen him smile. He picked me up and hugged me so tightly I was gasping for air.

"Hi . . . can't breathe," I said, the wind knocked out of me completely.

"I've missed you. It's so great to have you back," Riley said ecstatically.

"Hey, kiddo," I said as he set me back down. "It's great to be back!"

Jackson came running up to me next and hugged me and kissed me lightly on the lips. "Aren't you are a sight for sore eyes. It's so nice to see you, beautiful!"

I was happy to see him too. "It's nice to be seen, let me tell you!" He laughed but, before he could say anything else, Cam came around and picked me up and spun me around till I felt dizzy and then Pete came and hugged me, and I was swept away from Jackson. Even Zeb made a point to come over and let me know he was happy that I was back, which was the nicest thing he had said to me up till this point, making me think that maybe Jackson had been right—it just takes time with Zeb. The biggest surprise may have been when Sofia came over, gave me a hug, and told me she was glad I wasn't dead. *Hey, I'll take that as progress.*

As everyone surrounded me, I could hear "welcome back" and other nice things from the crowd as they pressed forward to show me they cared. I hugged every single one of them. It felt like my first day again, meeting and talking to them, except this time they weren't strangers; they were friends—but, more than friends, they were my family now.

Later that night, I found myself lying in bed in Mac's apartment. "Was the coming home party your idea?" I asked sleepily.

"Actually, it was Jackson's, to be honest."

"Really? You seem pretty okay with him?" I questioned. I kinda thought that after everything we had just been through Mac would have been pushing for commitment.

"I'm just glad you're okay. I think this has taught me that whatever's supposed to work out, will. I think Jackson and I have an 'All's fair in love and war' approach to this." Mac paused for a moment and then continued as if he had needed to think about his next words, "Actually, I *know* we do, because he literally said it a while back. I know he's kinda there waiting to sweep you off your feet, and he's more than welcome to hold that broom for as long as he wants. If I have my way, he'll be holding it for a very long time."

"Interesting. I wonder if he'd still feel that way if he knew everything." I thought for a moment about the possibility of Jackson knowing everything that Mac knew.

"You could ask your cards," Mac said, obviously trying to play the conversation very cool. I smiled.

"I could," I said, waiting a couple of moments before adding, "Maybe later. I'm kinda busy at the moment."

"Busy?" he asked.

I nodded and grinned. "Very busy."

I grabbed and kissed him passionately as a feeling washed over me. I think that feeling was the happiest I've ever been.

# CHAPTER 21

# THE WORLD

"YOU MAY NOW KISS THE BRIDE!"

The Nevada sun shone down on the bride and groom, and the breeze blew her hair as their lips met. It was like a perfect sight out of a magazine, and I was pretty sure I had never seen anything more magical—and I knew magick. After a few moments, the bride pulled back and Charles looked at Dela with tears in his eyes.

At the party after the ceremony, Dela and Charles sat at the high table while they watched the crowd of friends and family around them dancing and talking. They felt relaxed and happy. So much had happened, and they had come so far.

I had been dancing and mingling with several people and finally decided to sit for just a bit and rest. It was a fun sight to watch, everyone having such a great time. After a couple of minutes I felt a hand on my shoulder and looked up to see my mom. I rose up to hug her tightly—my first real moment semi-alone with my mother since she had officially become Mrs. Charles Spellman. I already knew she was keeping her own name, though.

"I can't believe you and Charlie got married. You've always said you didn't believe in marriage," I commented to my mother.

"I never told you this, but I always saw your dad and I getting married. But I also saw that it was only going to happen if he truly changed, which is something I never had faith in. I guess I should have believed in him more; maybe if I had things could have happened sooner. I never wanted to get your hopes up."

"Well, it was an amazing surprise!" I said happily.

"Everything can change in an instant, can't it?" Dela laughed and smiled at me before getting serious again, "You should learn a lesson from this: always have faith and remember sometimes the darkest moments really do come just before the dawn."

"Yeah, everything can change in an instant, though I hope from now on it's just mainly good changes. And I will keep all that in mind".

Tom from Jackson's band got on the mic. "Can I get everyone's attention please? It's time for the bouquet and garter toss. Can I get everyone up to the front of the stage? All you single ladies line up, please!"

Dela and I walked over to the dance area, which was clearing out. I stopped at the front of the floor, while Dela continued to walk over to the stage to stand next to the band. She got into position to throw her colorful bouquet.

"Aren't you going to join the single girls?" Mac asked gingerly as he walked up behind me.

"I don't believe in those silly superstitions," I remarked, smiling.

"Oh, really?" He laughed. "Either way you should go." He tried to shove me to the area where all the girls were standing and trying to vie for the bouquet, as Dela turned her back to the crowd.

Tom gave the cue: "Alright, ladies. One . . . two . . . three . . ."

Dela tossed the mass of beautiful flowers and then, as it flew, turned back around to face everyone. She saw Mac and I talking, facing each other and paying no attention to the festivities, my arms were out and animated as usual.

As Mom watched, the bouquet, miraculously, flew past all the women who were desperate to catch it. At the last second I turned to see what was going on, just in time to see it flying at me. I was completely startled as it landed right in my arms.

"How in the world . . . ? I wasn't even trying to catch it!" I was stunned, trying to explain to all the women who were looking at me in disbelief. Then I looked over at Dela, who was grinning like the Cheshire Cat, and I knew *exactly* how it had happened. I sighed and shook my head at her.

"Can't fight Destiny, sweetheart. Some things are just meant to be. I learned that the hard way," Mac said as he smiled and nudged me.

"So it seems," I said thoughtfully, laughing to myself.

"Think there's a book or something out there?" Mac asked.

"Book?" I turned to clarify whether I had heard the right word. I wasn't sure what he needed a book for, because I had already caught the *bouquet*.

"Yeah, you know, like a handbook for mortals, just so I can keep up!" He grinned and winked at me. I smiled back.

"I'll try to find you one."

*And they lived happily ever after...OR DO THEY?*

**Can't wait to find out what happens next?**
**Enjoy this teaser from the second book**
**in the saga due out in 2018!**

Mac had walked away to go talk to someone, and, at the same time, my mom walked over to join me and congratulate me on catching the bouquet. I was shaking my head at her and she was laughing, when all of a sudden the laughter was gone and a surprised look spread across her face. I could tell Dela was reacting to someone or something behind me, so I turned around and directly in front of me was a handsome older man with beautiful eyes. The suit he wore was perfectly tailored—he was a magician if I have ever seen one. He looked familiar, but it wasn't until my mom said his name that I remembered who he was.

"Namaste, Aunt Aldyth," Dela said in happy surprise. "I didn't realize you actually came. I feel blessed. It's so good to see you. I am honored you made the trip all the way from England." After a quick kiss and hug, Dela turned to me and asked, "Zade, you do remember your Great Aunt Aldyth?"

"Hello, my dear. It's been quite a long time," Aunt Aldyth said, looking me over. My "aunt" . . . yes, now I finally remembered. I had never quite understood why we called him my aunt. I once asked my mom and she made it clear that he had always been a male. I guess as a child he wore make-up and female clothing and so his nickname was a joke that stuck. I had always been deeply fascinated by him, although I was never around him much as a child—or as an adult.

"I do remember visiting with you at Solstice events when I was younger." I nodded, not even realizing that my mom had invited him to her wedding.

Aunt Aldyth gave me a hug and a light kiss on the cheek before he turned back to Dela. "I am glad I could make it, Dela. I hate to ruin your bliss, which is why I gave you the blessing of ignorance for most of your wedding day. But, now that the festivities are drawing to a close, I must come directly to the point. I am here because of Zade."

"What about Zade?" Dela wondered, worry creeping into her voice.

Aunt Aldyth scoffed. "Don't act so naïve. I know you have seen the cards. You are just as concerned as I am."

Dela's tone turned more serious, "Do you have additional knowledge? I don't know what to think."

I frowned and folded my arms. I hated it more than anything when people talked about me as if I wasn't there. "Would someone please explain what you're referring to?" I raised my eyebrows and glared at them both in disapproval.

Aunt Aldyth's eyes snapped to me and narrowed. He took a moment to collect himself before explaining. "There is a strange and powerful force of magick in you. What happened in the theater that day is proof of it. The fact that you survived is further proof." I was confused. Proof I could do magick? We knew that already. I must have been missing some piece of the information. "There were prophecies foretold about magick as strong as yours," Aunt Aldyth continued. "There will be many white, black, and grey magick entities vying for you and your power."

"Why was I not able to see this occurring?" Dela asked. "I knew about the prophecies."

"It was cloaked in the deepest of secrets. It was not to be known by anyone until the proper time." He looked me up and down. "I always knew the child was special. I did not know it was this."

Dela swallowed. "Did the—"

"Did the boy have anything to do with this?" Aunt Aldyth finished. "I believe so, but there are others who are near and know for sure, and could have affected things even more."

I understood their words, but was very confused by what they were saying. "Does this mean that Mac and I are destined?" I interjected, just to feel like I could say something more than anything else.

Aunt Aldyth shook his head. "No. It means the opposite, actually. Both you and this Mac person have several paths that will present themselves in due time. There is a path that will lead you two together, but not before each of you have gone on your own journey. Nothing is certain. It is not known if the two of you will be together. There are others—magical ones even— nearby for both of you."

"What should we do?" Dela asked, trying to hide the panic in her voice. She inhaled deeply, and seemed glad her aunt was there to consult with.

"I feel like I just stepped into an episode of *The Twilight Zone*," I whispered, overwhelmed. It hadn't been long since the incident that had nearly left me dead. Now it sounded like my world was about to be thrown into even greater turmoil. I completely brushed off the comment about someone magical being out there for me, all together. I didn't even want to get into that topic, yet. I had been hoping to get back to a more normal life instead of what this sounded like.

Great Aunt Aldyth looked at me and said, "Hopefully, no one else knows everything about you, yet."

For some reason I instantly recalled the strange girl I had run into at the mall a few months earlier, "Uh . . . I had a girl come up to me at the mall a bit before the accident. She had powers and she . . . well . . . she basically attacked me and forced me to fight back. The minute I showed her some magick, she left." I wasn't sure if this was what he meant but it seemed relevant to mention at the moment.

Great Aunt Aldyth took in my revelation with a look of concern and unhappiness. "Troubling. We will need to look into that further."

Mac approached, grinning. "Zade!" he called. "You gotta come here and see . . . ," he trailed off, frowning.

"Mac, this is my Great Aunt Aldyth," I said softly and matter of fact, my voice slightly flat and cold.

"Hello, young man." Aunt Aldyth smiled at him.

"Hello." Mac paused, turning to me for confirmation. "Uh . . . *aunt*?"

Mac looked extremely perplexed. I whispered under my breath, "Magick. I'll explain later." He gave me an odd look but nodded.

"Yes. *Aunt*. Anyway, we were just discussing family business," Aldyth stated perfunctorily, but then brightened a bit as an idea grew behind his eyes. "Zade, will you be a dear and hold Mac's hand? Then hold mine as well."

Aunt Aldyth gently took Dela's hand in his own. I looked cautiously from my great aunt to Mac before I grabbed their hands tightly. I was about to say that it probably wasn't the proper time or place to do whatever it was he was about to do—or have me do—but before I could say anything he was already doing it, whatever it was.

"Powers that be, show thy strength," Aldyth began.

I shook a little and began to breathe hard. I wanted to let go but both of them were holding my hands hard. Clouds that had moments ago been miles in the distance were suddenly above us, and the biggest bolts of lightning shot from the sky, striking every tree in the garden and setting them all ablaze. The flames were the bright blue of extremely hot fire. The crackling of the wood of each tree could be heard along with the lightning and thunder that accompanied the storm.

In an instant, Mac pulled his hand away.

"Zade! Did you just do that?" he asked, stunned.

I looked up at Mac and then at all the trees, which were still burning, though the fires seemed to be dying quickly. "I think that's what they're about to tell us." I gestured toward my mother and Aunt Aldyth who were already murmuring to each other. I swallowed hard before I finished my thought, "But that's probably the least of our worries . . ."

# ACKNOWLEDGMENTS

The thank-yous were, by far, the hardest part of writing this book. I literally edited and rewrote and added to this section the whole time I was writing. I have so many people I want to thank and I am so very grateful to so many who helped make this happen.

First and foremost this book is dedicated to anyone and everyone whom I have ever loved and anyone who has ever loved me. While I know that's a very vague and blanket statement, the person I have become was shaped by each and every one of you and you all affected me in your own way. A piece of each of you is somewhere in this story in some form. If I tried to list each and every name of the people who mean something to me I'd need to add a lot more pages (I fear that list would be more pages than the actual story), but I hope you all know who you are. My friends and family are the most important things in the world to me and I feel extremely lucky to have had your presence in my life.

I would also like to thank anyone who put me down or tried to cause me to fail along the way. I am grateful for your presence in my life as well. You helped me to be strong and gave me the push I needed to be successful. Every time one of you told me I couldn't—or wouldn't—make it, it just made me want that much more to show you I could. Motivation might just be the most important thing in achieving any goal, so thank you for giving me that.

Thank you to my muses for giving me the story that exists here; you'll all forever stay in my heart. The people in this story are all bits of each of you.

This is also dedicated to my family; some blood and some adopted but loved equally all the same.

While I can't personally thank everyone who helped make this happen—and while I am also sure the minute this comes out I will hate myself for forgetting someone that should be listed, because that's how it always works for me—I'm going to try anyway. The good news is I'll be able to include you in the next book! :)


My biggest thank you goes to Thomas Ian Nicholas, who has proved to be the best business partner and friend any girl can ask for. It is so very rare to find someone you can work so well with and have them be the yin to your yang for such a huge project, and to take it on as his own and ran with it till it became just as much yours as it was mine. You have put just as much effort into it as I have put into it and I will never be able to truly convey what that means to me. This is even truer when that project is the thing you've been working towards your whole life. I may never be able to express in words my gratitude for everything you have done to help make my dream come true—and for making my dream your dream—but hopefully some day I can come up with a way to repay you. A big thanks also goes to Colette, Nolan, and Zoe, who have been super supportive of the project in many ways and by sacrificing time away from Tom so we could make this all happen. And also to Tom's mother Marla, for being such a strong role model for Tom to make him into the incredible man he is today; thank you for that—and for everything you've also done to help us along the way.

To David Copperfield, Chris Kenner, Homer Liwag, Rene Nadeau, the Mondells, Aruba, Matt Bloom, Kazper Willams, Ben Butner, Paul Tobey, and the rest of MODC family (past and present), and the crew of the Hollywood Theater: You were always my family and my most favorite group of people. The crew in this book is partially each and every one of you.

Chris Kenner, you are so awesome I had to put you in here twice. I want to thank you for being one of the most amazing people I've ever met and for doing so much and for truly making real magic happen. I can't put into words my gratitude for you, but hopefully one day I can find a way to show it . . . either that or I will give you my first born. To Nicole and Zoe for being the wonderful women in his life and for loving the idea—and to Pauline Hawkins for more than I can ever put into words.

To John Matta, Peter Katz, Jerry Milani. Katherine Johnson, Ryan Ball, Catrina Dennis, Annie Esposito, Joe Avino Sr., Joe Avino Jr., Tyler Newman, and the rest of our Wizard World family (so many more of you—including all the wonderful celebrity guests that we've had the pleasure of meeting): thank you for your amazing support—without you, no one would even be reading these words.

A HUGE thank you to Brian Keathley and everyone at GeekNation! You all are our Hero!

To everyone at Sally Beauty Supply for well making us all beautiful and for the support, but especially Kim Johnson, Laura Voracek and Christian Brinkman.

To Mat Black for getting on board, and for helping in all the ways I needed it when I needed it; for caring, for being a true friend, and for making sure I didn't give up. You also turned my project into yours and believing in it and me when I needed it the most. You were our knight in shining armor and I will never be able to thank you enough. You and Sabrina will always be family to me.

To my dad, Richard Chasez; my brothers, Alex and Greg; their wives, Kristen and Melissa; my cousin Heather and her husband and son; and my cousin Kara (the sister I never had) and her husband Ruslan—who has taken me shopping more than any man I know.

To my cousin JC Chasez, who has constantly reinforced for me that I could take on the world and conquer it—and showed me you can still stay grounded while doing it. Thank you for being always supporting me and for having the same taste in movies as me.

To my Uncle Roy and Aunt Karen, and my other cousins Heather, Tyler, Sarah, Eliana, and Delilah Chasez for being the rest of my amazing family I can't ever be grateful enough for.

To my Grandpa Dean, who has put up with me despite how crazy I can be.

To Will for always believing in me and loving me when I'm not loveable. To Niece for being my rock, and to Bonni McCliss and Alice Primm for showing me the future. To Darius Rucker for being one of the most amazing people I know who taught me that half of life is surrounding yourself with the best people, thank you for always treating me like family and a welcome part of the group and to my favorite band Jeff Marino (who is also my favorite band leader), Lee Turner, Quinton Gibson, Garry

Murry, Sasha Ostrovsky and of course my favorite John Mason; the best BFF any girl could ask for. For Robyn Butner, who always listened and never judged; and for Chrissy Reter, who makes me feel like all stars are in reach—and to her awesome husband, Paul, for just being awesome. To Jerry Harvey, Andy and Sue Regan, and Thomas Reid and JH Audio for helping me hear. To John Eaton who taught me everything important in the entertainment business. To Del Breckenfeld, who supported me from the moment we met, and to Bob Lundeblud, who did the same. To Craig Comstock and Eric Freeman for seeing me for what I could be, not what I was. To Shawn Mullin for being a truly amazing friend, and to his wife, Chelsea Welch, for being awesome from the moment we met. To Alex Edelman for making me laugh and giving me the right push at the right time. To Ryan Adams for making sure I knew magick is real, and for making sure I did this instead of Tv's.

To Dimitrije Curcic for more things I can't even count and for also loving me when wasn't very lovable. To Gordan Vuchovich and Nada and Alex Curcic for always treating me like family. To Robert Dolan and everyone at Cashman photo for making sure I knew how much a picture was really worth.

Thanks to Debbie Richman for showing me a woman could be a strong, successful businesswoman, and to Laura Rheal—and everyone at my Dalton Steak n' Shake—for teaching me values I still hold close to my heart today.

To Micky, Elaina, and Sarah "Epic" Sheppeck: this book would not exist without you. To my roommates at Mansfield: Alisa, Jeannie, Gregg, and Rick for being far more than roommates. To every band I've ever worked with but especially to all bands that like bananas: the Monkees and 100 Monkeys, and even more to Ben Graupner (who always makes sure I have a place to stay in LA), Blues Traveler, the Plain White T's and their manager Deb Klein—but especially Tom Higgenson and the T's family (Dan Monahan, Darren and Eric Vorel, Cindy and Ott Chris Mason and, of course, Lennon Higgenson). To my original *Life is Beautiful* fam Craig, Lauren, Natasha, Ashley, the Twins, etc., for reminding me Life is Beautiful. To Michael Lawyer for always protecting me and being the voice of reason. To Jeff Beacher and Adam Meyers and my whole Beacher family for things that can't be written about. To Brian B., Howie, and Brian H. for always living with—and putting up with—me. To John and Alex May Mason for always making me feel at home and making sure I have a roof in Nashville, (yes John somehow you made it in here twice). To John Hebert for fixing up my home. To Leila Gerstein and the town of BlueBell for helping me find my Mac. To Skye Turner for giving me hope and lots of great advice.

To Braden Kulman, Jordan Zur, Scott Parker, Tyler Kaufman Don Forman, Karl Forman, Marissa, Cerullo, Dallas Fueston, Evan Ferrante, Adrian Grenier, Gabe Sunday, Susan Murphy, Eddie Izzard, Arnold Engleman, Robert Reynolds, Natalie Kilgore, Susan Ruth, Niki Tyree, Jordan Mitchell, Noah Brown, Amanda Avila, Sameer Gupta, and Karen Fritz for your friendship and help along the way.

To the Wynn Hotel and Casino—and Steve Wynn—for giving me inspiration and a place for the show to call home, and to Kim Spurgeon and Danette Tull and the whole Nevada Film Office and the Tennessee Entertainment Commission for ensuring we can still make films.

To Scott Thompson for always making me laugh and for making sure I had the right amount of balance in my book; and to Jeff Molitz just for being Jeff!

To Kim Estlund for being the best PR woman a girl could ask for; and to Theresea Fortier for help and support in many areas.

To Preston and Steve at *Preston & Steve* on WMMR—and everyone at the show—for being the first to let us talk about our project!

To Phil Wagner and everyone at Bang Printing and To Jared Walton, Christopher Gonzalez, Sasha Scott, Jose Medina, Chad Nykamp,Cindy Engalla, Donald Newman and to everyone over at Salem Author Services.

To Emmanuel Withers for being the very first person to buy this book!

To Jim Lonrando, Ken Pulsin, Carrie Certa, Mat Miller, Krista Tetreault and Denise Lieberknecht for help in other major areas that we needed.

To Sterling, Bailee, and everyone at Teen Made for the webs and the graphics.

To Bonnie Brown and Alex Westmorland for always making me feel pretty.

To Aimee Mann and Susan Gibson for allowing me to use your amazing lyrics to convey things I couldn't, and to Jana Pochop and Michael Hausman.

To Robert Schmidt, my editor, for making me look like I paid attention in English class and actually know where commas go.

To Ryan Kincaid for the amazing artwork on the cover of this book: you gave life to an image that Thomas and I made up in our heads; and to Milen Parvanov for giving our artwork the color it needed, otherwise our world would be black and white.

To Lisa Hendricks for being my second mom, and for more things than I could ever write into words. Some girls need more than one mom, and lots of guidance, and I would probably be curled up on the side of the road somewhere if it weren't for you. Thank you for letting me make your home mine, for being the voice of reason, for just being awesome, and for showing me who I should always strive to become. And to Kali for all your love, and for helping me stay young.

Most importantly, this is also dedicated to my mom, Martha Sarem, the most incredible woman I know. She taught me that I could do anything; therefore, I keep doing the impossible because she never taught me the meaning of that word (for good or bad, she also never taught me the word no . . .). I love you more than anything and thank you for all the huge sacrifices you have made for me.

This book was written in loving memory of my grand-mothers Jetta, Hilda, and Rose, who were incredible, strong magical women and did things at a time when woman were not supposed to do them. Thank you for helping create a world where I could be the woman I wanted to be. In loving memory also of Aunt Marie Vinson, Joshua (Lex Phillips), Jeff Pollack, Joey Marshall, Uncle Larry, Frye, Jim Johst, Morton Judd, Brandy Rae Bonney, Joan Koplan, and Donald Sarem. You will forever be missed. Also to John Scarne, I never knew you but you had a hand in all of this and you inspired so many people that I had to include you here and thank you.

To Charles Bukoski, Beau Taplin, Christopher Poindexter, and Tyler Knott Grayson: I have never met any of you, but you've given my feelings words and meaning. To C.S. Lewis, Neil Gaiman, J.K. Rowling, Terry Pratchett, and Stephanie Meyer: thank you for showing me how to create worlds and characters we all love and want to be.

My biggest thank you, of course, goes to God, who gave me my gifts and abilities—and even the ideas. There are days when I have felt completely alone except for His love, which I could not live without:

"For with God nothing is impossible." (Luke 1:37)

"God is within her, she will not fail." (Psalms 46:5)

As you are reading this I'm sure I've already thought of someone else that I forgot . . . so for you here's what I have:

I always said if I won an Oscar my speech would be something like this: For all those who helped me along the way—and in any way at all—thank you. You all know who you are. And for those who didn't: you can eat dirt ☺

And, lastly, I know so many strong women who are in my life and I want to thank you for being people I can look up to, so many of you are friends I know well, while some are just woman I admire—trailblazers and fire starters.

To all the little girls (and boys) out there with big dreams . . . this is proof you can get there if you keep trying and keep believing. Never let anyone tell you that you are not good enough. It just means *they* are not good enough. You have magic in you if only you believe it—and you can make anything happen. The word "IMPOSSIBLE" literally says "I'm possible." Go be great, find your purpose, and show the world who you really are. Some people will reject you simply because you shine too brightly for them. That's okay. Keep shining, and when they complain tell them to wear sunglasses. And remember that magic is real but you have to believe in it. Your mind is a powerful thing—the most powerful thing on Earth even—and it can will magick into existence...or extinguish it." .

Go make magic happen. I'll be waiting to see what you do!

With all my love,
Lani
P.S. Go Cubs!